THE GIRL WHO FOUND THE SUN

MATTHEW S. COX

DIVISION ZERO PRESS

The Girl Who Found the Sun
© 2019 Matthew S. Cox
All Rights Reserved
This novel is a work of fiction. Any similarities to persons living or dead, actual
environmental catastrophes, or mutant life forms are coincidental. No portion of this
book may be reproduced without written permission from the author except for quotes
posted in reviews or blogs.
Cover and interior art by: Ricky Gunawan

ISBN (ebook): 978-1-950738-14-4

ISBN (paperback): 978-1-950738-15-1

CONTENTS

NINETY FEET DOWN

It started with the insects. Whole species died off one after the next. No one cared. Maybe if they had, we'd remember what the sun looked like. – Ellis Wilder.

Confining walls closed in around Raven, shrinking more and more the deeper she crawled into the wiring conduit. Already stale air thickened, leaving the taste of dust and melting plastic on her tongue. Other maintenance tunnels had enough room to let her walk hunched over, but this one barely allowed her up on all fours. The feeble crank light hanging from her shoulder tossed a wobbly nimbus of yellowish light around ancient concrete walls, long ago stained various shades of green and rust.

Thirty-six fat wires ran along the passage, spanning the 268 meters from the northernmost end of the Arc to a field of eighteen wind turbines. Technically, the conduit led to a spot directly below it, not the field itself. Half the wires had been originally installed as redundant backups, but they'd all been swapped into use decades ago, the original wires cannibalized to repair them when they failed again.

The same held true for all the pipes, tubes, PVC lines, and everything else running around the Arc. One would be hard pressed to find a stretch of any wire, pipe, or hose more than three feet long that didn't have a patch or six.

Raven grumbled under her breath as she dragged herself forward. Every wake cycle, she hoped for a lull to shorten her work period so she could read or spend time with her daughter, Tinsley. However, the Arc had other plans. Of the seven people in the engineering group, she had the dubious distinction of being the smallest—hence whenever one of the power lines crapped out or something looked wonky with the voltage levels, Ben, her boss, sent her to do the repair. Shaw would probably do more damage to the wires trying to squeeze himself down here. If not for Trenton, she'd also be the youngest, even if she only had him by one year. Neither of them had any real seniority despite her having done the job since age seventeen.

You'd think five years' experience would give me some say, but oh no. Power main problem and it's 'Oh, Raven, need you to check the wiring.'

Every few feet, she stopped to trace her fingers over the suspect wire, 14B. Unlike the others, it had become cold. The chemical air scrubbers and hydroponic farm lights drew so much electricity these wires routinely heated up. In her experience, they'd always been hot to the touch. The others only thought it a problem if they burned fingers on contact. Raven disagreed. Wires an inch thick shouldn't be heating up so much.

Fortunately, two things worked in her favor. One: the indicator lights at the inside end still worked, so the team knew exactly which wire failed. Two: the main wires ran in mostly straight lines along the conduit walls—even on her right, odd on her left—which made them far easier to check. Ordinary power cables all over the Arc connecting the capacitor system to power outlets hadn't been installed so thoughtfully. Tracking down breaks there could sometimes take several days merely to *find* the offending wire in the spaghetti. But at least those passages had room to breathe in.

The failure had probably occurred close to the L-bend where the conduit went vertical. On her last slog down here, she'd noticed multiple iffy patch repairs likely to fail within months. In all honesty, she should have preemptively replaced them, but the big boss, Noah, hated shutting down power lines for repairs. It made sense though, since without power, everyone in the Arc would die in short order. The hydroponic farm couldn't process CO2 fast enough for the current population. Electricity kept the air scrubbers going.

No electricity meant no oxygen... and everyone dying quietly in their sleep without ever noticing a problem. Thoughts like that had been keeping Raven up at night for months ever since she noticed her normally energetic six-year-old acting as sedate as a middle-aged adult.

She stopped dragging herself forward, gave the crank on her flashlight a few rapid turns, then held it up to examine the wire before the battery drained again. Rapidly dimming light illuminated green spray-painted '14B' on the wall above the dusty black wire. Even winding the little handle for ten minutes straight would only yield about forty seconds of usable light, so she didn't bother overworking the coil. Given the thing's age—measurable in centuries—the flashlight working at all surprised her.

Not seeing any obvious breaks, she hooked the light on her poncho and continued crawling, sniffing at the air. With power remaining in the line ahead of the break, the failure point would probably be smoldering. Ages ago, a console in the engineering room could shut off power in each line selectively. The wire linking the control box there to the switching unit at the L-bend failed some years back and no one bothered fixing it. Why waste materials when operational switches existed at the far end?

Easy for him to say. Ben's not the one who's gotta drag his ass down this tunnel.

Even if the break occurred twenty feet in from the access hatch, she'd still have to crawl the whole way to the L-bend to turn off the wire before she could repair it. The energy level of the turbines might be well below optimal, but each cable still carried enough punch to cause serious injury.

Upon reaching the midpoint of the passage, she caught a suspicious whiff in the air: dampness.

"Oh, no..."

She froze, shining her weak light into the murky passage ahead of her, momentarily gripped by fear. Eighteen pairs of wires continued ahead into the void, surrounded by dusty concrete. This conduit didn't have any water pipes. She could think of only one reason to smell moisture here—the seal at the top of the vertical shaft protecting the Arc from the toxins outside failed. A moment later, another theory came to mind, allowing her to relax. Moisture here could also have come from a crack in the concrete, allowing groundwater to seep in.

Get a grip. Dad's been outside. He didn't melt instantly like everyone says will happen.

Still, hearing stories of what he did couldn't compare to the idea of being face to face with outside air in person. Growing up, she'd been taught the world outside was so toxic a person would literally melt into a puddle of slime-covered bones within minutes. Somehow, despite her father having been outside and back multiple times, everyone still believed it. Other than his word, he'd never brought back any proof... so maybe they all thought he made up stories for attention.

She grabbed the flashlight, cranked it up, and shone the beam at the walls, examining numerous stains on the concrete. Some of the brackets holding the cables up bore visible signs of moisture corrosion. *Damn! The red-brown is rust. Water's been getting in for years.* She angled the light at the thick gunk coating the floor. The loose, dry uppermost layer reminded her of the snow described in some of the books she'd read, though not the right color and certainly not cold. Beneath it, the sediment had hardened into a cement of sorts, another sign moisture routinely crept into the tunnel, dried out, and re-wet.

The side walls didn't have marks suggesting a significant quantity of water flooded it, but rust trails streaked down from most of the brackets holding the cables in front of her.

"Uh oh. This isn't good."

Raven cringed, thinking of numerous splices all up and down the conduit lacking insulation. Damp air would definitely lead to corrosion. If she couldn't find the source of the water and plug it, they'd have to find a way to insulate any exposed wiring.

She hurriedly crawled onward, still sniffing for a burning fault in the line while continually cranking the flashlight to better see her surroundings. Seventeen active power cables throwing off heat in the tight confines made the passageway uncomfortably warm. Sweat got into her eyes and dripped off her nose, but it didn't deter her. The lives of all 183 people in the Arc depended on her keeping things running.

The faltering flashlight reflected back at her from a neon-orange paint line indicating the three-quarter mark of the conduit, closer to the L-bend. She traced the beam along the wire, searching for damage until the charge died and it went out, leaving her again in darkness.

While she felt around to find the crank, an unexpected flash and a sizzle went off a short distance ahead, startling a yelp out of her. She winced, closing her eyes. After a few dozen blinks, the spark pattern glow faded from her retinas.

Well... found the fault.

As soon as she could see again, she cranked the flashlight and scooted up to the spot the spark came from. The thick cable had indeed broken, a six-inch chunk sitting on the floor, detached from both sides. Silvery splatter marked the concrete around it. From the look of things, an old splice had fallen out. Likely because the wire had overheated to the point the solder liquefied.

Damn. That's a bad sign. Are the scrubbers malfunctioning?

Considering the obviousness of the break, she didn't need to leave a yellow rag so she could find it again. Cursing the idiot who installed such a half-assed repair job, she continued on toward the glowing green lights in the chamber at the bottom of the L-bend.

Roughly thirty feet from the end, her hand squished into wet muck rather than dry dust. She stopped short, tensed with worry. She angled the flashlight down, examining the dark grey mud on her fingers.

"Crap. Crap. Crap."

She shifted her weight onto her knees and cranked the flashlight hard, trying to eke a little more brightness out of it to survey the walls. They appeared dry and devoid of cracks, suggesting the water flowed along the floor rather than seeped in from the sides. However, water down here didn't *prove* the seals at the top failed. The crack could be anywhere along the vertical portion. Also, despite what everyone 'knew' about the deadliness of the outside world, she didn't fully believe it. If topside was as dangerous as everyone claimed, how could her father have gone off for days at a time and returned? It would've taken more than a filter mask to keep him alive. The stories he told her made her want to see something more than a world of drab concrete.

Raven dreaded spending her entire life underground in the Arc.

Perhaps she could see a scrap of sky if the seal had failed? Shaking from nervous excitement, she crawled forward. Eerie green light filled the chamber at the end, cast by the status lamps on the control box. No visible puddle of water remained, but discoloration on the walls indicated about an inch of it had collected at the end of the conduit not long ago.

She ducked into the chamber at the L-bend, a place she could stand up in but didn't bother to since she intended to crawl right back out after cutting the power to line 14B. Thirty-six cables, half of them scavenged to dangling bits of scrap, entered the chamber along each side, curving upward to follow the vertical shaft to the surface. Somewhere outside, far above her, eighteen wind turbines converted moving air into electricity.

Schematic diagrams of the turbines usually occupied her time during breaks or if she had a few minutes to herself or ended up waiting on someone else to do something before she could work. She'd studied them for hundreds of hours, but never once laid eyes on the actual machinery. Often, she'd daydream about going out there, wondering what color each part would be. How tall were the towers they sat on? What had exposure to the toxic atmosphere for centuries done to the metal? How in the hell did they keep functioning after so long? It didn't seem possible for any machine to go centuries and continue working, an unexplainable reality that only served to add to their mythic nature. The lives of everyone in the Arc depended on those turbines.

Squinting, Raven stared up along the wirepaths to the limit of her weak flashlight. This passage couldn't be opened to the outside world, but if the seal really had failed, it might be possible to force the cap plate up and peek outside. Temptation to see the turbines got her reaching for the narrow ladder bolted to the wall. She hesitated, gazing toward the top—until a single droplet splattered on her forehead.

"Ack!"

She recoiled, wiping at her face, then glared up into the darkness, unable to tell if the droplet had fallen all the way from the top or from an old scrap of damaged wire only a few feet above her. However, touching water from outside the enclosed system of the Arc set off a minor case of the jitters. Any manner of disease or toxic chemicals could be in it. Still pawing at her face, she whirled around and knelt again, faced the switch box, and flicked the toggle marked 14.

The green light next to the switch went out.

Supposed to turn red. Guess it broke, too.

Part of her wanted to shut down everything before touching any wire, but Noah would lose his mind if she did. Also, a complete loss of power to the Arc for as long as it would take to repair the broken wire could cause serious problems with air toxicity. Those CO_2 scrubbers had to keep operating. Besides, turning everything off and back on again would probably blow out a third of the ventilation fans and any number of other important machines.

After crawling back to the damaged section, she picked up the detached piece to examine. Whoever fixed it years ago had cut the wire exactly to the length of the gap, relying on solder alone to fuse it in place, as opposed to doing a correct splice.

"Ugh. No wonder. Idiot."

She stowed the hunk of wire in her satchel, since she'd need a longer piece—by at least two inches—to repair the break properly.

For the better part of the next hour, she crept around the conduit, checking the decommissioned A-set wires (the original ones) for a usable length. According to Ben, the A-set wires had been active from the date the Arc went live and lasted anywhere from eighty to 150 years before the last of them had been cut over to the B-set. By then, the A wires had become so damaged their usefulness amounted to little more than providing spare materials. And... the more she looked around, the more it seemed the B set verged on complete failure as well. The makers hadn't installed a C-set, nor did Ben and the rest of the engineering team have enough materials on hand to manufacture a C-set. At some point in Raven's lifetime, they'd need to start coming up with alternatives to use in place of wire.

17A finally offered a scrap of usable length to mend the break in 14B. Raven held up the former patch wire as a measuring gauge, added three inches, then cut a new length of old wire to use as a splice.

After crawling back to the break, she set to the task of meshing the wire frays together, mulling over the power demands on the system. The two biggest draws came from the air scrubbers and the hydroponic equipment. Considering all the artificial sun lamps in that room plus the pumps for the growth fluid, maybe the garden consumed more energy than the ventilation system. The farm did help contribute to re-oxygenation, but the doc—Preston—said the plants couldn't keep up if the scrubbers ever shut down. Some claimed the Arc had been designed to support 2,000 people, and may have even had as many as 3,000 citizens at one point. Raven found it difficult to imagine so many people crammed into the underground warren she called home. The 183 who lived there now stressed the ventilation system's ability to keep everyone alive.

How could there ever have been thousands here? If it's true, why did we lose so many?

She carefully wrapped the exposed copper with insulating tape, likely a pointless gesture considering the voltage that would flow down the line as soon as she hit the button. The thin black material might last a few days before melting off. Still, it made her feel better to do the job 'right,' the way Dad taught her, the way people did it however long ago before the Great Death.

Her father's voice spoke from her memory, bedtime stories he'd told her long ago about vast flooding, high temperatures, and Plutions killing off everything except the people who'd taken shelter in the Arc.

"Hmm. Stories." She squeezed the tape in place and leaned back, examining her work under the feeble glow of her crank light. The repair appeared solid. "Not all stories are true."

Raven sighed out her nose, then made her way back to the control panel. She put her finger on the switch for wire fourteen, made a wish that her father had been right about topside, and flicked it. The green lights all flickered as the system adjusted to the power flow. Hopefully, repairing the wire would ease the stress on the other wires and let them cool off a bit.

Eager to escape the narrow confines of the conduit, Raven secured the flap on her satchel and crawled into the dark.

She didn't need a flashlight to go in a straight line.

2

LESSER EVILS

Vast fires ate the jungles, choking the sky with smoke. Whole cities drowned when all the world's oceans swelled past coastlines. The people who survived that didn't last too long either. – Ellis Wilder.

Strong light in the engineering room hurt Raven's eyes.

Squinting, she crawled out of the conduit, kicked the hatch closed behind her, then stood, brushing dust from her poncho and pants. Eighteen wires—and eighteen dark trails where backup cables had been—ran along the wall to the right, connecting to the massive power transformer unit in the corner, a giant steel cabinet as tall as the ceiling and a quarter the size of her bedroom. It combined the incoming power lines into a single electrical source feeding the Arc's active usage and diverted any excess power into the capacitors. The system tried to store any excess power generated to compensate for periods of little to no wind, but the charge meters always showed the batteries at twenty percent, plus or minus a little in either direction.

Ben said it meant demand more or less equaled generation. Raven suspected the capacitors lost their ability to hold much. If they hit a lull devoid of wind for too long, the batteries would drain in hours, requiring the Arc go into emergency power management, shutting down everything except the ventilation system and the garden. That happened once already when she'd been fourteen. Using a crank light in the wire tunnel sucked, but she had little choice. Using them everywhere while the entire Arc sat in pitch darkness felt like living in a nightmare. She kept waiting for monsters or zombies to jump out at her.

Lark, the other woman on the engineering team, sat in front of her workstation, tinkering at a small water pump. She, too, wore a poncho, but an older one, made from multiple swaths of material scavenged from old shirts and pants all stitched together. Raven got hers soon after turning twelve. The brownish-green fabric came from a fibrous plant the hydroponics team occasionally grew for use in making clothes or blankets. Apparently, the plant—which they called cotton-plus—had been a genetic creation from before the Great Death. It also sucked up a rather high concentration of nutrients, so the farmers didn't raise a crop of it often due to the strain it put on food production.

To conserve materials, most everyone in the Arc wore poncho-like garments in place of shirts and loose-fitting pants. Children received smaller ponchos, swaths of fabric wrapped around them like togas, or threadbare leftovers until they hit their tweens—at which point they got an adult-sized poncho. With resources so limited, no one made child-sized garments only to have them sit idle after the owner grew out of them.

It didn't bode well that an Arc of 183 people only contained five children under sixteen. Noah wanted people to have more babies, but they needed to be careful to avoid inbreeding. Also, their population had only about twenty-five women of an age suitable for motherhood, Lark being one of them at thirty-five. She and the man they'd matched her with—Gerald from the kitchen staff—had been trying, but no luck thus far.

She eyed the other woman's tread socks, also made of cotton-plus, and debated going back to her quarters to get hers. Since she already expected the trip into the wire conduit, she'd worn her boots instead. The old things had been patched and re-patched to the point they'd become about half duct tape. Supposedly, the Arc once had a storeroom filled with clothes and shoes for a population of 2,000 people, but she'd never seen anyone wearing a garment that didn't have dozens of patches. Level six, the lowest floor, held manufacturing facilities capable, in theory, of producing everything from nice clothes to computer circuitry... but no one knew how to operate them or make the materials required.

Smooth concrete corridors didn't require hard soles, so most people wore tread socks. Raven loved hers, much more comfortable than the old boots. Being so far underground kept the corridors and rooms perpetually chilly. According to books she'd read, topside had different periods called seasons where the temperatures varied. No one ever went there, so no one had any need of clothes suitable for cold temperatures or shoes thicker than socks. Some of the hallways in the Arc had been worn smooth in visible trails, the concrete eroded in a manner reminiscent of paths in the forest from her novels.

"Hey," said Lark, finally noticing her. "How'd it go?"

"Fixed." Raven pulled the satchel strap off her shoulder, setting the bag on the table as she sat in her chair. The cushion disintegrated before her birth, but a too-worn-to-wear poncho worked as a replacement. "Old patch failed. What an idiot."

"Idiot?" asked Lark.

Raven fished the short length of cable out of her bag and held it up. "They cut the old splice to the exact length of the break and welded it in place with solder."

Lark whistled in disbelief. "What a dumbass."

"Yeah. I guess." Raven tilted the scrap back and forth. "It's possible the wires didn't overheat back then. I don't think they're supposed to be so hot all the time."

"I kinda thought the same, but Ben says it's nothing to worry about." Lark cursed under her breath as her screwdriver slipped for the sixth time. "I hate working on these damn fan motors. Every single screw is in a hard to reach place and full of crud."

"Yeah, seriously. And that's BS about the wires." Raven rolled her eyes and grabbed the nearest object on the table in front of her, an electric hot plate someone had dropped off for repairs. "Ben's only worried about keeping Noah from yelling at us."

"That, too. But a little heat on the lines is normal."

"Hot enough to melt solder?" Raven glanced left at her. "It makes me think there's a short somewhere."

"Maybe." Lark fidgeted. "But nothing blew up when you turned it back on. It's an old repair. Maybe it partially separated, caused an arc, and melted loose."

"Didn't look like enough charring, but I guess. Or a spike in draw superheated the line." Raven shrugged one shoulder and proceeded to test the hot plate. When it didn't turn on, she unplugged it and grabbed a screwdriver.

Even though she performed a vital function and helped to keep things operating here, long hours sitting at her worktable repairing everything from clocks to lamps to hot plates made her miss being younger. Not so long ago, she could spend most of a wake sitting in the library reading… at least when they could spare the electricity for a light. Used to be, people could take books out of there, read them in their quarters, and return them when done. No one who lived in the Arc now could even remember the point at which policy changed, but they didn't let anyone remove the books anymore. If she wanted to read, she had to stay there, wearing special gloves to touch the pages. Even the best-preserved novels had swaths of faded text where she had to guess her way through a paragraph. Too-rough handling would destroy the precious paper.

Eventually, she disassembled the hot plate enough to discover the brush contact on the rheostat had broken. Raven searched among her various drawers of scrap wire for a length suitable enough to repurpose into a brush contact. After repairing the hot plate and putting it back together, she lost focus and ended up staring at the plain grey ceiling, trying to imagine what topside really looked like.

Dad told her stories about what he'd seen, but they all sounded so fantastical she had trouble believing him. Maybe the others were right and he'd simply found a spot on level five or six to hide, pretending to go outside. Topside should be full of swirling mists of corrosive vapors that could eat a person's flesh off their bones in seconds. But her father wouldn't make up wild stories about seeing topside, would he? He'd seemed so genuine in his unstoppable need to explore the outside world.

She didn't like to think he might have simply gone nuts and imagined it all.

His description of the sky sounded a lot like what she'd read in novels. Many of the books spoke of the sun, a fiery spot far overhead giving off light and heat. Could standing in sunlight feel like sitting near the now-working hot plate? How much warmth did it give off? It couldn't be too much if frozen water could exist on the ground sometimes. Alas, her father probably read the same novels, so he could've gotten the description from there.

How does the sun work? In summer it's so hot people sweat, but in winter there's ice.

As a child in school, she learned a little bit about planets and orbits. She didn't remember it too much, though. Back then, her head had always been in the clouds, or more accurately, on topside. She'd been nine the first time her father admitted to going outside. He might have been making up stories to amuse his daughter. The tales of how her mother used to get mad at him for being 'reckless' could also have been made up.

Maybe Sienna would know how the sun changes temperature.

She laughed in her mind. Sienna, eight months older than her, grew up alongside her. They'd lived a few rooms away in the same hall, sat next to each other at school, and spent most of their free time together. They still did, even if 'free time' had become an artifact of the past. Raven considered Sienna her sister, the only person in the entire Arc she trusted enough to confide anything to. For all she knew, they might have been cousins considering the small population.

Patricia Reed, the former teacher, died somewhat unexpectedly two years ago. Sienna took over. With only five kids in the Arc, she served as the only teacher—as well as the caretaker/parent for four of them. Only Josh was a legitimate orphan. The other four ended up in her care as their biological parents had no interest in raising them. Being mom to four kids between the ages of nine and twelve consumed most of Sienna's time.

Thinking about topside got her fidgeting, distracting her from rebuilding a doorknob mechanism. Ben, for the most part, never seemed to care how many small items any of them repaired in a given work period. He'd prod them for sitting around doing nothing, but as long as she appeared to be engaged in productive activity, he kept quiet. Unless, of course, something major broke and needed to be fixed. The queue of appliances and other small components on their workstations never seemed to end, but it always came second to critical repairs of the Arc's systems. Basically, the stack of junk on her station table amounted to busy work.

What is it like up there? She flicked a gear back and forth in the housing, alternating between curious and frightened. Everyone believed topside held only death, a barren, empty wasteland of grey dust, windblown sand, and poison. Some even said the Plutions had taken over and would kill humans who ventured outside. No one knew where the aliens came from or why they decided to flood the Earth with toxin, but most people in the Arc knew about them. Mrs. Reed never taught the class about the alien invasion, which Dad blamed on people in charge still wanting to hide the existence of life on other planets. It bothered her how all the citizens knew about the aliens but still the official teacher didn't mention them once. She wouldn't even answer questions one way or the other about the Plutions, usually saying it didn't matter anymore.

Of course, Raven would never get permission to leave the Arc. She still had no idea how her father managed to get approval. He claimed to have gone out multiple times, though. If he'd broken the rules, they'd have put him in jail and not let him go out again. So, Noah had to be okay with it—assuming of course her father hadn't been nuts.

He'll never let me go out there. She squirmed. *Not sure I want to. Don't wanna die.*

"Raven…"

She twisted around in her seat, the ancient office chair giving off a labored creak.

Benjamin Ruiz, his drab brown poncho bedecked with dozens of small tools and pouches, walked up to her. As long as she'd known him, he always wore his hair mostly shaved. The man claimed to be a few years away from turning forty, but didn't look anywhere near that old.

"Hey." She set the knob down. "14B is good."

"Great. Exactly what I wanted to ask… saw you out here, figured you either finished or couldn't fix it. What happened?"

She rested her elbows on the table behind her and explained the failed patch. "We could have another problem. The whole end of the conduit is damp. Water's getting in from somewhere. A drip landed on my head in the L-bend, but I couldn't see where it came from."

"Damn." Ben kicked his toes at the floor, his tread-sock making a soft scuffing noise. Tools in the giant cargo pockets of his pants rattled. "Let's hope it's a crack allowing groundwater in."

"Hope." She twirled a screwdriver over her fingers, shaking her head. "A groundwater seep wouldn't stop. Water had been an inch or two deep not too long ago. That had to be from rain. The seal could be damaged. Or maybe it's a crack near the top letting rain in."

Lark gasped. "That's bad! We have to check it. Outside poison could get in and kill us."

"It's not *that* bad out there." *If Dad wasn't schizo.* Raven stared at the tool in her hand, weaving it around her fingers. "Dad went topside all the time. Once, he stayed out there for three days. His skin didn't melt off."

"Girl, your father got some incredible luck." Lark's eyes widened. "Ain't no way I'd risk it out there."

Yeah… he's got such great luck, he disappeared. Raven caught the screwdriver in an icepick grip, but stopped herself from jabbing it into her table. She'd searched everywhere in the Arc except for the forbidden uppermost floor. If her father *had* made up stories and only hid himself in an empty area, he wouldn't still be missing. A pile of junk blocked off the stairwell to level one. It hadn't appeared disturbed when she'd run around trying to find him in case he'd been making it all up… so he couldn't have snuck past it to hide there.

"It's definitely something we should check." Ben looked at her. "You up for going back down there?"

"Yeah sure." Raven plucked her crank light from her chest and lobbed it to him. "Got a better one? That one's too weak to do a wall inspection."

He tossed it up and caught it. "Yeah, think so. I'll go check—right after I turn the scrubbers back on."

Both Raven and Lark gasped simultaneously.

"You turned them off?" Raven blinked.

"Not all of them. Only three. Had to mitigate power consumption with line fourteen down." He jogged to a control panel on the other end of the room.

Raven followed, stopping beside him in the modest downdraft from a ventilation duct on the ceiling. The breeze had an unusually stale quality and a metallic taste. "Is it true or is it not true the Arc was designed for a population of over a thousand?"

"You know as well as I do that according to the documentation, our systems were designed to support approximately 2,000 people." He pressed his thumb into a big, rubberized button on a panel with eight such buttons—and corresponding plastic 'off' buttons.

"Yeah, just putting it out there so you know where my reasoning is coming from. Okay, so, if eight CO_2 scrubbers are supposed to be able to process enough air for thousands of people to breathe, don't you think it's kind of a problem they're struggling to keep the air good for less than 200?"

He gave her a sideways look she read as 'don't say that too loud.' "It's something to keep in mind, but there's no reason to start worrying people." Ben sighed and pushed the button again when the light failed to go green. Mechanical whining came from the adjacent room, pumps straining to move. "Come on, you bastards. Start up."

"Don't call them names if you want them to behave." She folded her arms. "Those machines are as old as this place. At least 300 years. Maybe older. The reason it's taking eight of them to do the work one should be able to handle is that they're all close to breaking down. We can fix and patch and modify only so much."

"Yeah, yeah… I know. But there's nothing else we can do. Not like we can head down to the quartermaster and requisition a new CO_2 scrubber or a new batch of substrate." Ben wiped a hand down his face, rearranging some grime. "I get what you're implying. It's on my mind, too. But… what else can we do?"

"Please tell me you're not just hoping they last until you're old and it's the next guy's problem?"

His fidgeting replied to the affirmative.

"That attitude is exactly why we're down here." Annoyed, Raven huffed at the vent overhead.

"What?" He raised an eyebrow.

She thrust her arm out at the console. "People seeing an obvious problem and not doing anything about it because it looks too hard to fix. Leaving it to the next guy. My dad always told me the people who lived before the Great Death knew it was coming and didn't care because they'd get old and die before it mattered. No one did anything in time. Maybe if they did, we wouldn't be stuck underground."

Ben faced her, hands on his hips. "You got a spare CO_2 scrubber hidden somewhere? What do you think we're going to do other than keep patching the ones we've got?"

"Maybe cannibalize one to bring the rest back up to full power?" called Lark from her workstation.

"I was thinking of something more long term." Raven tilted her head. "What if my dad's right? Why don't we pull in outside air and filter it?"

"You're gonna kill us all," muttered Lark.

Ben cringed.

Raven glanced at Lark. "The outside air can't be *that* bad. My father—"

"You keep saying that." Lark bit her lip. "Sorry, but if it's not poisonous out there, where is he?"

"Out there… somewhere." Raven's stomach clenched into a tight knot. Even if the stories of topside's danger were overstated, no one could last for four years out there. She'd accepted he'd died a while ago.

"Exactly." Lark gestured at the ceiling. "You want to risk the same thing happening to everyone?"

"No." Raven squeezed her fists, trying not to glare at the woman. "But, if the scrubbers completely crap out and can't be fixed, we're going to suffocate."

"At that point," said Ben, "it would make sense to risk outside air. A choice between definite death and possible death is not difficult. But, the outside air is dangerous. Even if we filtered it, we wouldn't be able to clean the filters fast enough. We have to maintain a closed system and trust the combination of natural oxygenation from the hydro farm and the scrubbers."

Raven eyed the panel in front of him. The weak green glow in the status lights for the three offline scrubbers gradually intensified to the same brightness as the others. The labored whine of fluid pumps struggling to move finally quieted to the normal vibration. Air falling on her from the overhead vent sweetened a little in flavor, losing some of its metallic essence. They'd successfully restarted, but it shouldn't take six minutes for them to kick in.

She stared at the panel and let a long sigh slide out her nostrils.

The next time he turns them off, they're not gonna come back on.

3

SICK

People aren't supposed to live in burrows. We're not damned rabbits. –
Ellis Wilder.

Repetitive dinging too close to Raven's left ear hammered at her consciousness, an almost physical attack on her brain. A dream of listening to her father telling stories ended with her playfully frustrated at him for making her go find out what a rabbit was on her own. The librarian didn't trust letting an eight-year-old anywhere near the books at first, but she refused to give up. It had taken him three months to finally cave in and let her read under supervision.

"Mommy, I hate the alarm," said a half-awake Tinsley, cuddled up to her side.

"Yeah. Same here." Raven reached an arm out without opening her eyes, resting her hand on the vibrating metal framework, her finger muting the bell by getting in the way of the striker. She flicked the lever to disengage the cog, silencing it. "Actually, I don't hate the clock. I hate having to wake up."

Tinsley let off a contented sigh, thanking her for stopping the noise.

A few minutes more rest threatened to become a lot longer. As soon as Raven caught herself about to drift off to sleep again, she forced herself to open her eyes. The dingy grey ceiling of her quarters greeted her, mostly drab except for where her daughter had hung up colorful shapes she'd cut out from various scrap materials. Stars, crescent moons, a few blobs she intended as animal faces, and a couple 'flowers.' The hydroponic garden didn't have any decorative flowers, only edible plants, but she'd learned about them in school.

Somehow, Raven doubted flowers looked like the fingers of a crumpled medical glove. But, her daughter made it, so she loved all of them.

She squeezed Tinsley a little closer, the child's body warm at her side. Thin nightgowns that had once been bed sheets didn't offer much warmth, though the blankets made up for it. Every time Raven looked at her clothes, or the rags her daughter—and the other kids— had to wear, she questioned if the designers of the Arc made an error. Or maybe the people living in it had screwed up. Perpetual sustainability shouldn't mean a gradual decline and loss of technology.

The place should've held many more people than it did. It *should* have provided ample resources for growing cotton-plus, food, purifying air, and so on. Everyone ought to have decent clothes and shoes. The Arc had the necessary machines to produce all of it... but not the resources. They'd stopped making anything close to rubber or plastic years ago, like for boot soles or sneakers. Some rumors blamed lack of materials while other people thought the air filtration system couldn't handle the toxic fumes the process threw off.

Of course, tread socks worked just fine. Most people didn't have to deal with terrain more dangerous than smooth concrete floors and the occasional frayed rug. Those who worked in the water station on level six with all its metal gridded floors and walkways, as well as the technical team, got first dibs on hard-soled boots. The chill of being so far underground made going barefoot uncomfortable, but some people still did it. Tread socks tended to wear out relatively fast and replacing them would require a new crop of cotton-plus, which hadn't been high on the priority list.

Raven fussed at her daughter's hair, black like hers but frizzier. No one would accuse her of being a big woman, but Chase, the girl's father, counted as a human toothpick. Tinsley inherited his build, having arms like mop handles and legs slimmer than her mother's arms. Granted, the girl was only six, and the youngest resident of the Arc at the moment. She didn't have any other six-year-olds to compare her to size wise, but still worried her daughter might be *too* skinny, too small for her age.

The kid had no qualms eating, and appeared to be getting enough food. At least, no less than anyone else here ate. Could be everyone lacked nourishment. Meals didn't seem to be noticeably different from what she remembered growing up. Probably only her being overprotective and prone to worry. Still, she couldn't help but accept that her feelings toward the Arc changed. It no longer felt like a place of shelter and safety from the Plutions and the dangers of topside. Lately, it had taken on a more sinister presence, as though it had become a living, breathing thing that wanted to gradually kill everyone.

Maybe it had been evil all along. How else could a population of 2,000 people dwindle down to 183? No wonder so few children existed. It had to be difficult to find matches between people who had no genetic relationship. At sixteen, Raven wanted to do everything she could to help, even if it meant saying okay when they asked her to have a baby with Chase. She still hadn't made up her mind if it had been foolish to agree, but Tinsley let her cope with her father's disappearance in a way nothing else—not even Sienna—could.

In another six years or so when her daughter grew too big—or too independent—to share a bed, she'd move across the hall to one of the empty quarters or maybe they'd both move to a larger room with more than one bunk. The Arc had many empty residence halls, further proof the designers made it for a large population. Everyone clustered as close as possible to the central core so they didn't have a long walk to the cafeteria, the doc, or their job stations.

Grumbling, Raven rolled her head to the left and sighed at the mechanical clock, a boxy frame of exposed gears and clockwork guts. Four white plastic dials on the front face each bore numbers from zero through nine, tiny metal hands indicating the time in four digits: presently 0-9-5-1.

Dad said topside has light and dark times. I wonder what it is now. She daydreamed about the sun, fascinated by the concept of light that didn't require electricity. A sharp *click* from the clock indicated the furthest right minute dial advanced one spot.

Her wake started at 1-0-0-0, which meant she needed to be at the engineering room around then, and she had to do the job until 1-8-0-0. Reading often kept her awake until after 0-1-0-0, but the only books she could read in her room had belonged to Dad, and she'd already read them all multiple times.

That the clock still worked made her proud. She'd built it herself some years ago, before she had Tinsley, her effort to copy the electric one her father used to have, a LED display showing the time in red glowing numbers. Almost all of those electric clocks had broken beyond repair now. She'd hoped a wind-up mechanical clock would outlast them. Much easier to replace a worn gear or cog than figure out what went wrong on a circuit board. Even the people who lived before the Great Death didn't fix circuit boards—they replaced them. While the Arc did have some machinery capable of producing circuit boards, it hadn't been touched in a while. Ben once mentioned the engineers who used to know how to design and print circuits and chips suffered unexpected health problems and died before they could fully train their replacements.

As generations went on, highly-advanced technical knowledge faded.

Same with the doc. From what she'd read in her novels, doctors once had to go through a vast amount of school, testing, exams, certification, and so on. The Arc's current—and only—doctor, Preston

Baxter, learned only from the teaching of his predecessor and a room full of books.

It doesn't sound right. How could all the experts die off so fast they couldn't teach anyone else?

"It's almost wake, Mommy," said Tinsley past a yawn. "When the clock is one-zero-zero-zero we gotta be up."

Raven sat up and stretched. "We really ought to be up at 0-9-4-5. You need to be in school by 1-0-0-0."

Laughing, the girl climbed over her and ran to the toilet room, her dingy sheet-nightgown trailing after her like the wrappings of a haunting spirit. Raven cast the blanket aside, got to her feet, and pulled her nightgown off over her head before tossing it on the pillow for later. She yawned, scratched a few random itches, then put on a sleeveless inside shirt and a clean pair of inside pants. Since her father taught her to sew, she and Tinsley each had enough of those not to have to wear the same pair more than once a week. She'd made them extra sets out of bed linens she'd 'borrowed' from unused quarters on the fifth level. Maybe she'd get in trouble for it, but she didn't care. A reprimand would totally be worth not having to wear the same inside pants three or four days in a row. Not like they didn't have hundreds of other bedrooms no one needed. Who cared if one lacked sheets?

She put on her outer pants, then poncho.

Tinsley darted out of the bathroom carrying her nightgown, ran over to her clothing shelf, and scrambled to get dressed. Her inside clothes were smaller versions of Raven's, though instead of baggy pants, she pulled on a tattered red skirt, then her poncho. On her, the garment dragged on the floor, but she'd be able to wear it until twelve or so before needing an adult-sized one. The girl started for the door barefoot.

"Socks," said Raven. "You don't want your toes to fall off."

"They're not gonna fall off!" Tinsley's shout made her cough. "Don't lie. It's not nice."

"The floors are cold. You can get frostbite."

Tinsley smirked. "Floors don't have teeth. They're not gonna bite me."

"Come on." Raven picked two small tread socks up off the rug and tossed them at her daughter.

"Oh, okay. Fine." Tinsley rolled her eyes in an overly dramatic manner, sat on the floor, and put the thick socks on. "You too."

Raven glanced at her feet. She'd probably end up being sent down the wire conduit again to check the seal, so she stepped into her boots despite preferring the more comfortable socks. Tinsley remained seated on the floor.

"C'mon. Time to go to school."

"Can I skip today? I don't feel good."

Raven crouched nearby, brushing the girl's hair off her face so she could see into her eyes. Her daughter appeared tired more than anything. No crust at her nose, no unusual crud leaking from her eyes. "Open your mouth."

Tinsley did so, emitting a long 'Ahhhh.'

Nothing looked strange in her throat. Raven put a hand on her daughter's forehead, finding her skin normal temperature. The girl coughed again.

"You don't look sick. What's bothering you?"

Tinsley rubbed a hand across her chest. "My head hurts an' feels like I spin around a lot."

"Okay. Let's go see the doc."

"I'm not that sick."

Raven sighed in her head. *Is she fighting with another kid? Gotta talk to Sienna.* "Well if you're not sick enough to see the doc, you're not sick enough to skip school."

"No." Tinsley flopped flat on her back. "I don't wanna go anywhere."

Chuckling, Raven brushed a hand over her daughter's head. "You have to learn. Don't wanna grow up to be dumb, do you?"

Tinsley rolled on her side. "No. But I really feel bad."

Not seeing any childish deceit in the girl's eyes, Raven's suspicion gave way to genuine concern. She scooped her up and carried her out into the hall.

"C'mon, kiddo. You need to see the doc."

"Aww. I don' like when he puts the cold spot on me."

Raven patted her on the back. "No one likes that thing. But if you're sick, he should check on you."

She headed to the four-way intersection at the end of the hall. Straight went deeper into the Arc, toward the engineering area and manufacturing rooms. Left led to the cafeteria and common areas. She turned right, following the corridor into the section full of offices intended for administrative workers and managers. Most of them sat empty except for the infirmary, Noah's office, and the security station all the way down on the left. A plain metal door at the end looked like a storage closet, though she'd never been in there or seen it open. No other hallway in the Arc had a door right in the endcap, which struck her as odd, but not so strange she did anything more than wonder.

The second door on the right, close to the central core, led to the infirmary.

Preston didn't look old enough to be a doctor, barely into his thirties, but he'd been apprenticed to the former doctor since the age of twelve. Perhaps the old doc knew he didn't have much time left, found a genius, and got him started early. Raven considered herself smart, but compared to him, she felt average. His intelligence made him a good choice for learning medicine. He would have been perfect if not for his personality. The man became highly uncomfortable when interacting with other people, especially if he had to dumb down his language to explain things to them.

If not for being ten years younger than him, she might have tried to get to know him more personally. Despite his social aversion, he forced himself past it to help others. She respected him for it. He never acted overly awkward around her. Perhaps because he didn't need to explain things four times; she could mostly keep up with him.

"Hey, Doc," said Raven. "Busy?"

The man looked up from a book that had to weigh more than a small child. "Oh. I didn't hear you come in. What's wrong?"

She approached the exam table and set Tinsley seated on the edge. "She's complaining of feeling sick and dizzy."

"All right." He stood, grabbed a stethoscope from the desk, and approached. "Hello, Tinsley."

"Hi," muttered the girl. "Do you have to use the cold thing?"

"Sorry… yes, it helps. But…" He rubbed the stethoscope back and forth on his sleeve for a moment. "I can try to warm it up for you."

Tinsley swung her feet back and forth, waiting.

"What hurts?" asked the doc, while lifting the girl's poncho to place the listening end on her back. "Take a deep breath for me, please."

"My head." Tinsley puffed up her chest, held the air a second, then huffed it out. "And my breathing."

"It hurts when you breathe?" asked Preston.

"A little. My head feels funny. Like I spun around."

He listened to her breathe from several different spots on her back and chest, then looked in her mouth, at her eyes, and spent a few minutes poking and prodding at her sides, neck, and throat. Except for squirming under the stethoscope, the child sat there and patiently tolerated the examination. Whenever she coughed, Preston appeared concerned.

"Is she sick?" asked Raven.

"It's possible she's in the early stages of a cold. But her temperature isn't elevated. She has some light sinus congestion, irritation of the eyes and throat." He glanced at Raven. "Has she been unusually tired?"

"She hasn't exactly been yawning or passing out, but yes. She's not her usual hyperactive self. Hasn't been for a couple weeks."

"Hmm. Any unusual giddiness, nausea or fainting?"

Tinsley shook her head. "No. I got sleepy at school last wake, but I didn't fall."

The struggling green light from the CO2 scrubber appeared in Raven's mind. "Doc… you think she's suffering the effects of low oxygen?"

He folded his arms. "Hypercapnia is one of the things that might fit. Early, early stages though. And we shouldn't jump to conclusions. I understand they shut down half the ventilation system yesterday. That could've led to a drop in oxygen ratio. One of the labs down on five has equipment capable of testing the composition of our air. I should really go check. Normal saturation is about twenty percent. If O2 levels in the air dip below ten percent, onset of disorientation and unconsciousness can come on so rapidly a person would be unable to escape or seek help. And body mass does play a part as well."

Damn. Raven squeezed Tinsley's hand. She'd felt a little lightheaded herself yesterday, but dismissed it as a side effect of being stuck in the narrow tunnel. "Thanks. So she's okay?"

"I think due to her age and small size, she's particularly vulnerable to fluctuations in air quality. I'd like her to use a mask for a few days and see if it helps at all. Not going to do much about O2 levels, but if the issue is due to elevated levels of dust or other contaminants, it should help."

"Okay."

Tinsley stuck out her tongue. Everyone had to have a filter mask handy in case of emergency, but no one liked wearing them, especially the kids. Raven smiled at her daughter's reaction. That had been her at the same age.

"Doc, will you please let me know what the air's like after you test it?" asked Raven.

"I... suppose. Normally, I'd take the results to Noah or Ben."

"I'm on Ben's team, keeping things running, ya know." She smiled. "If we need to do something about the air quality, I'm going to be involved."

"Fair enough. Sure. I'll let you know."

"Thanks."

Preston faced Tinsley. "How bad is your headache? Is it annoying or do you want to go to sleep so it stops hurting?"

Tinsley made a face of contemplation. "Umm. It's annoying, but not as annoying as Josh."

"All right, then I don't think it's too much of a concern. If it worsens, or if she has a bout of nausea or any other unusual symptoms, please bring her back." Preston patted Tinsley on the head.

"Thanks, Doc."

Raven plucked her daughter off the exam table, set her on her feet, and led her back to their quarters. She plucked Tinsley's little filter mask from the top of the dresser and put it on the girl. Sand-colored material covered the child's mouth and nose, a shade or two lighter than her skin. Tinsley flattened her eyebrows, her amber eyes radiating strong discontent.

"I know you don't like having to wear this, but you need to for a few days, okay? I don't want you to get sick."

"I'm already sick," said Tinsley, her voice muted.

"Well, *really* sick." Raven ruffled her daughter's hair. "C'mon. Time for school."

Tinsley grumbled, the mask reducing whatever she said to an indecipherable murmur.

It's not like her to want to avoid school. She momentarily considered letting her skip, but a six-year-old couldn't be left alone in their quarters, nor could she take her down the wire conduit. Better to have Sienna watch her.

"I know you're not feeling well. I'll ask Sienna to give you a break today, all right?"

"'Kay," mumbled Tinsley.

4

SHORT STRAW

There are three kinds of people. Reckless fools who don't care how dangerous something is, those who understand the risk and stare death in the eye, and those who spend their whole life hiding under their beds.
– Ellis Wilder.

Raven led Tinsley down the hall to the cafeteria where they both had a quick breakfast of muffins, more or less the same thing she ate at the start of every wake. It might have been bran or molasses or pumpkin flavored. After so many, the brown, vaguely sweet, vaguely spicy pastry simply tasted like the start of another long period of work. Every so often when the people in hydroponics gave some tank space to berries, the cafeteria offered berry muffins as an alternative for a while.

It relieved her Tinsley didn't hesitate to eat, a sign she took to mean her daughter didn't feel *too* bad. They ate fast, then headed into the south corridor. Sienna's voice drifted out from the classroom door up ahead, in the midst of a lesson on English vocabulary.

At their arrival, Sienna paused. Four other children, two boys and two girls, sat along the front row of desks in a room set up for thirty students. The kids, all in the same basic outfits—oversized ponchos and tread-socks—turned to look back at her.

"You're late," said Ariana, the next closest in age to Tinsley at nine. Her tone held no mockery or amusement, merely a statement of fact. The girl's parents, Donnie Chen and Elena Vasquez, didn't really know—or even like—each other, and handed her off at birth.

Ariana considered Sienna her mother.

"Why's she got a mask on?" Josh, the eldest at twelve, cocked his head at her, then at Raven. "Someone fart?"

The other kids laughed.

Raven stopped herself from making a snide comment. The pale boy with mouse brown hair reminded her of a younger Chase, minus the attitude. He didn't deserve nastiness because of how Tinsley's father was. They really only had the color of their hair and their whiteness in common. Where Chase acted like the king of his own little world, Josh tended to be a bit shy and overly friendly. Also, their faces looked nothing alike, clearly no familial connection at all. Unlike the other kids, Josh's parents both loved and wanted him, even if they'd only conceived him upon a request from the boss. Sadly, his father died two years ago when a pipe in the waterworks explosively burst too close to his face. His mother had passed away to a mysterious illness a couple years before that.

Xan, a scrawny eleven-year-old with unusually dark skin, laughed himself to coughing at the fart comment. Like Ariana, his biological parents didn't have the patience or interest to raise a kid. The boy had an unusually mature personality, being thoughtful and perhaps too brave for his age. He'd been caught exploring the mostly abandoned level six several times.

The second girl, another eleven-year-old named Cheyenne, had to be the sweetest, most adorable person in the entire Arc, if somewhat shy and timid. Her mother Savannah had been the same way, adored by everyone for her kindness. Sadly, she died during childbirth. The girl's father, a loner everyone merely called Sanchez, had never been particularly friendly and became even worse after she died. He, too, worked in the water system, and rarely talked to anyone else unless forced to. Sienna once mentioned that despite his grumpy exterior, he had truly loved Savannah and blamed Cheyenne for her death to the point he didn't even want to look at the baby, thinking she'd curse him.

It's amazing that girl is so nice considering how much of a jackass her father is. Even worse than Chase.

"What's up?" Sienna moved out from behind the teacher's desk and walked up to them. "Everything okay?"

"Think so. She's feeling a little off today. Think you could let her rest a bit?"

"Sure. What's with the mask?" Sienna patted Tinsley on the head.

"Doc thinks it might help her feel better. Dust in the air getting to her." Raven hugged her daughter. "Sorry about the lateness, was at the clinic."

"Oh, it's fine." Sienna nudged the girl toward the desks.

The other kids exchanged looks. Cheyenne appeared worried, Xan blasé. Ariana gasped, which made her cough. She covered her mouth with both hands, eyes fearful. Tinsley sat in the desk beside Ariana and the two girls promptly began talking.

"Great. I need to head down the hall before Ben loses his mind." Raven jogged to the door.

"Anything to worry about?" asked Sienna.

"Dunno yet." Raven bit her lip. "Talk later?"

"Okay. All right, back to where we were." Sienna waved and headed to the front of the room. "Xan, please read the fifth word and tell us what it means."

Raven went out into the hall, oddly aware of every discoloration, crack, or rust smudge on the walls. Dozens of lighter spots dotted the corridor, wherever the concrete had been patched throughout the years. She stared into the square lights on the ceiling, spaced every twenty feet. One in three worked. The others could be fixed, but they decided not to, saving parts. Better to have dim light for a longer time than burn all the LED bricks out and end up in complete darkness.

Thoughts of bulbs haunted her on the way to the engineering

room. Her father believed the people who made the Arc intended it to be fully self-sustaining. Running out of vital parts, clothes, medicines, and such shouldn't have happened. They had everything they needed to keep going… but something went wrong. How no one else appeared worried about this baffled her. Surely, the doc had to be smart enough to see reality. Ben, too. Maybe even Noah… but why would they all act as though things were just peachy? Could she be freaking out too much, or did the others truly remain oblivious to the situation? Or worse, had they resigned themselves to extinction?

She stopped short in the doorway, whirled around, and jogged back to the doc's office. Elena Vasquez sat on the exam table while the doc wrapped her left arm in bandages. The stink of chemicals and feces hung in the air. Considering how the woman treated her daughter, the stench felt appropriate, but it came from the hydroponic room in which she worked. Elena, being something like twelve years older, didn't have much contact with Raven and probably had no idea how she felt about her. Even if a pregnancy happened as a result of the big boss asking a woman to sustain the population, Raven felt a mother shouldn't abandon their child.

She waited near the doorway for the doc to finish treating Elena's injury. Eventually, the woman made her way out, offering a brief nod of acknowledgement as she passed. Raven resisted the urge to scowl at her, returning a neutral nod, then walked inside.

"Back so soon?" asked Doc. "Did something else happen?"

"No. I just wanted to ask you about the filter mask. If oxygen is too low, what's the point of asking her to wear it? Do you really think it's dust?"

He gestured at the door. "Couple wakes ago, Brian from hydro came in with a busted elbow. He'd slipped in a puddle of growth medium. Told me he'd accidentally discovered a sizable leak in one of the wheat tanks. The chemicals in that fluid can make people sick if aspirated. As I'm sure you know, the farm is a vital part of our ventilation system. Air is forced through the hydroponics chamber constantly, so it would pick up any vapors. My concern is our ventilation system may be spreading these chemicals around the Arc."

Our hydroponic tanks should be sealed, the plants embedded in clear plastic beds with only small holes for the roots to dangle in the fluid. The syrupy muck shouldn't be free to evaporate into the air. "Wouldn't we smell crap everywhere, then?"

"If the concentration was high enough, yes. Everyone down here is used to the smell, though. Constant exposure to a stimulus desensitizes the nose to it. A long enough period absent that stimulus would be required before we'd notice it again. You can't run a hydroponic farm in a closed system without the odor being everywhere already. People probably wouldn't notice a slight intensification of the stench."

Raven wiped at her nose. "Oh. There's another problem, and Ben isn't taking it seriously."

Doc raised an eyebrow.

She explained the air scrubber shutdown and how they almost didn't come back online. "The Arc was made to support like 2,000 people. Eight CO_2 scrubbers should not have any difficulty handling 183 people. I think they've been running so long the gas exchangers are pretty much shot. My estimate, they're running at less than ten percent efficiency. It's unlikely we're going to be able to do anything about that, so we've got two choices. Either we test the possibility of drawing in outside air or—"

"You're serious?" He stared at her as though she'd suggested culling half the population to save oxygen. "Outside?"

"Doc, you know my father went out there. He—"

"Was incredibly lucky."

Raven sighed, then hesitated. *He didn't accuse him of lying. Doc's acting like it's true.*

"It's not so simple." Preston waved dismissively. "I'm not equipped to treat people for exposure to all the toxins circulating out there. Besides, he'd likely gone out during winter when the temperature was only 109 degrees or thereabouts. What's your other suggestion?"

"The only other option would be for the hydroponics team to grow a significant amount of plants with high CO_2 absorption. They're only using about eleven percent of the available tank space,

I assume to make the growth medium last longer. We'd need to bump that up to at least thirty percent. Plants won't wear out and break like machines. We have to wean off the scrubbers or we're going to asphyxiate. I get that 2,000 people living underground would be too much for the farm alone to support, but it's not a problem anymore."

"Hmm. The combination of hydroponic chemicals getting into the vents, dust, and the CO_2 situation together are worrisome." He tapped his foot, fidgeting… but still didn't seem as worried about it as he'd been at her suggestion regarding outside air. "I'll talk it over with Noah, see what he thinks."

"Okay. Thanks." She exhaled. *Maybe we should all be wearing the masks inside.* "I gotta go. Already late enough."

Preston managed a smile, clearly looking forward to being alone again. "All right. Stay safe."

Her mind swimming with dread, Raven hurried to the engineering room, six doors down from the classroom in the south hall. She lived and worked in the heart of the Arc, on the third level. The second floor contained mostly living quarters and storage rooms, all largely abandoned. Something bad happened on level one years ago that caused several deaths. At least ten different versions of the story floated around as rumor, from chemical leak to radiation to disease to someone going psycho. Whatever the cause, it had been serious enough to make the boss of the time declare the entire level off limits. As far as Raven knew, no one had been up to the topmost level in at least fifty years, maybe even longer.

At least, no one who admitted to it.

She suspected Chase and his friends might have gone up there as kids. Nothing particularly made her think they did. It came mostly from his reckless attitude. Defying a lockdown just sounded like the sort of thing a thirteen-year-old version of him would do.

As soon as she entered the engineering room, Ben—who'd been waiting at her workstation—shot her a look filled with guilt and dread. He couldn't quite make eye contact, kept his hands in his pockets, and continuously shifted his weight from leg to leg. She half expected him to ask her if she'd be willing to let the Plutions take Tinsley in exchange for new air scrubbers.

Of course, she didn't seriously think he'd ask anything of the sort, but the level of hesitation in his demeanor worried her. Most likely, he tried to summon the nerve to ask her to do something with a good chance of killing her.

She slowed from a jog to a creeping walk, narrowing her eyes at him as she rounded the end of the work table to stop beside him. "Yeah, I know. You want me to check the seal. Sorry I'm late. Tins got a little sick. Had to take her to the doc."

"She okay?"

"Think so. Whatever she has is pretty mild. I think it's due to the scrubber shutdown yesterday. Doc said she had symptoms of mild oxygen deprivation."

Lark looked up from her work soldering inside a water pump motor. "That's not good."

"Don't worry about the late thing. Gotta take care of your kid." Ben smiled at her, still unable to make eye contact. "She's lucky to have a mom who wants her."

"Yeah, well... maybe they should stop forcing people to have babies." Lark smirked.

On some level, Raven agreed with that sentiment. But, intellectually, she knew they had no choice. Between genetic diversity and a rapidly dwindling population, the continued existence of humanity depended on them. If the Arc survivors all died out, the Plutions would win. No humans would remain on Earth. Besides, they didn't really 'force' anyone to have babies, more guilted them into it.

"It's not ideal, but it's better than going extinct," muttered Raven while grabbing her tool satchel. "I'll go check the seal now."

"Wait." Ben lightly grasped her arm. "There's another issue."

"Why do you look like you're about to ask me to do something stupid?"

He exhaled.

"Because he's probably about to ask you to do something stupid." Lark laughed.

"Look, Raven…" Ben exhaled. "I realize you've got a daughter and you're only twenty-two. But… I've already run it by the others and they've all said no."

Lark swiveled her chair around to face him. "You didn't ask me."

"Because I know exactly how you'd react." Ben scratched at his head. "I didn't fancy having a wrench flying at my face."

"Out with it," said Raven. "And what happens if I say no?"

"Everyone dies."

Lark started to laugh, but the humor drained out of her in seconds. "Wait. You're serious?"

"Mostly." He stuffed his hand back in his pocket.

"Shall I assume this something is so dangerous you're not interested in doing it, either?" Raven flashed an impish grin.

Ben chuckled. "I'd rather not. Still have too much to teach all of you guys before I die."

"How valiant of you." Lark poked him. "Send the little girl to do something you're afraid to."

"I'm not a little girl." Raven playfully swatted at her.

"Compared to me, you are. Little don't necessarily mean a child." Lark winked.

Raven gazed at the grimy ceiling. "I am not unusually short. I'm normal."

"You're a little shorter than average, but I wouldn't call you *short*." Lark stood taller, her chin about at Raven's nose level.

"Okay, so what's the thing everyone's scared shitless of?" Raven folded her arms.

"Remember how you fixed 14B yesterday?" asked Ben.

"My memory's not *that* bad. Only did it like twenty hours ago."

"Right, well… it's dead again. But, this time, the problem isn't a fault in the wire." He cringed as if about to tell her someone she loved died. "The turbine failed. I need someone with the balls to go topside and check it out."

"Oh, F that." Lark shook her head and spun her chair back to face the desk. "No effing way. *Nooope.* I'm no Saint."

Ben gestured at her. "This is why I didn't ask her."

Fear and excitement burst deep in Raven's gut. She clenched her hands into fists and looked again at the ceiling. The Arc was home to 183 people. 182 of them believed a person would die within ten seconds of exposure to topside air, even after her father made multiple trips out and back. Most of the people also believed Plutions roamed the surface and would attack any humans they saw. The toxicity didn't bother them. They brought it here. Raven didn't fear the air as much as everyone else. Doc's completely straight response to her mentioning Dad going outside had to mean he knew it to be true. The air couldn't be as deadly as everyone claimed, but those aliens might be a problem.

However… turbines. She'd wanted to see them in person for years.

Going to topside might kill me, but… staying down here could kill me, too. Dad survived. If no one fixes that windmill, we're all going to die anyway.

"But… it's forbidden," said Raven, amazingly not sounding worried.

"That's true. I've already explained the situation to Noah. He's given permission for someone to go check on the turbines and come right back." Ben rested both hands on her shoulders. "We're not asking you to take crazy risks. If your mask isn't enough, if anything feels wrong, turn around and come right back inside. This isn't an emergency… yet."

She looked down. *People before the Great Death didn't think it was an emergency when the insects started dying off.*

"Okay, sure. No problem." said Raven. "I'll do it."

Lark coughed. "What? Are you serious?"

Ben's hesitant air gave way to relief. "I wouldn't have asked if it wasn't important. Again, don't do anything risky."

"Going outside is already risky," said Lark, almost shouting. "Are you serious? We haven't had hazard suits since the Saints. And she's basically a baby."

Raven winced internally. Over a century ago—no one remembered exactly when—a group of eight techs suited up and went topside to fix a major failure of the power turbines. Exactly what happened up there remained a mystery beyond two known facts: the team got the turbines working again, and they never came back inside. Legend grew over the years, and the eight men and women who gave their lives to keep the power on had become known as the Saints. The more superstitious among the residents sometimes claimed their ghosts watched over the Arc to this day.

"Did you ask me because of my father, or did everyone else really refuse to go?"

Ben laughed. "Yeah... they think they'll disintegrate as soon as fresh air hits them."

"There's no such thing as fresh air." Lark grabbed Raven like she tried to hold her back from getting into a brawl. "Don't do it!"

She squirmed around to look at the woman. "My dad went out and back multiple times and never melted. Noah wouldn't give permission if he didn't think it reasonable to do. And... I'm pretty sure we're already getting some exposure to outside air in here."

"What?" Lark gawked at her.

"How do you figure that?" Ben furrowed his brow.

Raven pointed at the access panel leading to the wire conduit. "Water at the L-bend. It had to be from rain since it's not building up, which indicates to me the break is near the surface. If rainwater got in, outside air is getting in."

"Oh, shit." Lark shivered. "If she's right, we have to fix that!"

Ben held a hand up at her. "Hang on. This is just her theory. When you're out there, if it's not too crazy, check on the seal, too?"

She shivered, dread and excitement in equal measure thrumming along her veins. "Will do. When do you want me to do this?"

"Was hoping for as soon as possible."

"Like, now?" She blinked.

"Basically." He cringe-smiled. "If you're up for it."

This could be incredibly stupid, but I'll never get this chance again. "All right. Let me go grab my mask."

Lark sank back into her seat, tears gathering in her eyes. "Don't go. She's still just a baby."

"I'll be back in a little while. Please, trust me. I wouldn't go if I didn't think it was safe or possible." Raven slung her satchel over her shoulder then patted herself down, checking she'd remembered all her tools. "Isn't the security team going to freak out if I try to go outside? And, level one's locked down. How am I supposed to get out there?"

"They know we need to send a tech out and, I, uhh, already told them it would probably be you." Ben chuckled. "Noah thought so, too. There's another way out via an old elevator shaft. It's not widely known. By the main security station down the hall from Noah's office."

"The silver door." She blinked. "It's not a closet, is it?"

"No..." Ben couldn't hold eye contact with her. "Your father went out that way, too."

They think I'm just like Dad. Maybe I am. It could be stupid, but... She gazed up at the filthy concrete ceiling again. *The Arc isn't a shelter anymore. It's a tomb.*

5

OBLIGATIONS

Big problems always start off as small ones people think can wait until later. – Ellis Wilder.

Raven walked to her room, forces in her mind pushing and pulling at her the whole way there. Eagerness to fulfill her longstanding wish to see topside, to touch the actual turbines, tried to make her run while worry held her back to a deliberate stride. Even though her father survived several visits to the surface, she couldn't help but wonder if *everyone* else in the Arc being terrified of the outside world had merit. Their fears had to be founded in some truth. How could so many people all firmly believe something —and be wrong?

Except for the kids, everyone knew her father. They had to be aware he'd been outside and didn't drop dead right away, if they didn't brush him off as delusional. Admittedly, she'd worried he might have been crazy, too, before her conversation with the doc. Preston absolutely would not have hesitated to suggest her father had imagined it if that's what he truly thought of the situation. The man didn't have any sort of social filter. It baffled her to consider her father's apparent proof didn't change any of their minds. Hell, Lark practically fainted at the idea of being asked to go outside.

Grr. It doesn't make sense for them all *to be wrong, but I think they are.*

She hurried into her quarters, plucked her filter mask from a shelf, and put it on. The masks didn't see a lot of use, which hopefully meant the membranes would protect her despite everything being centuries old. Stuff didn't last forever, even if it sat on shelves most of the time. Her rational side warned that the filter masks all had to be useless, but wearing it reassured her like talking to the ghosts of the Saints reassured some people.

Raven prepared herself the same way her father used to before his expeditions. After securing the mask, she put on protective goggles, then wrapped a long strip of cloth around her head and face for extra protection. Finally, gloves. Before she went outside, she'd pull the hood up, so only a little bit of skin between her eyes where the goggles didn't cover would be exposed to the world.

Her father spoke of traveling for several days sometimes, and he'd come back. The turbine field wasn't too far away. She'd technically been there multiple times, but underground. Despite the danger of the toxic atmosphere, the idea of walking upright to the turbines instead of dragging herself down a narrow tunnel sounded far more appealing.

Should I tell Tins before I go out? She snugged the gloves tighter purely to keep her hands occupied. Her daughter had been two the last time her father went outside and didn't remember him at all. The girl's reaction to her mother going outside could be anything from a complete terrified freak-out to a blasé 'oh, okay.' She chuckled to herself at the faces Tinsley made whenever someone told a scary story. For such a small kid, her daughter was fearless. Raven worried her reaction would be begging to go outside, too.

Nah. Better to tell her after. She faced the door. *I'm not really scared. If I was, I'd definitely talk to her before going out there.*

The primary entrance up on level one hadn't been opened in centuries. As far as anyone knew, the giant door closed a long time ago behind the initial group of people to take shelter here and remained shut ever since. It didn't help that the top level had been declared a forbidden zone. Permission to go outside didn't include permission to go up there. Even if she did reach the primary entrance, it probably wouldn't even work. According to the engineering plans, the giant door consisted of two armored slabs, each roughly ten tons. The electric motors responsible for moving them apart would surely be dead after sitting idle so long. It *did* have a backup mechanical system involving counterweights, but using it would open the giant door permanently. If she was wrong about the outside world, activating the mechanical failsafe would doom everyone in the Arc.

Not knowing how her father could've possibly opened that door or gotten into level one had been one of the reasons she suspected he might have been delusional. But... Ben mentioned a secondary exit. Though surprising, hearing about an alternate way out made her father's adventures sound more plausible. The schematics she'd spent years studying didn't show any other ways out of the Arc. What did he mean by 'old elevator shaft'?

Years ago, a few elevators in the central core ran between the six levels. None went to the surface, however. If some other elevator existed off the plans, it, too, probably no longer worked. That meant she'd end up dealing with a 110-foot climb up a metal ladder, similar to going up inside the vertical portion of the wire conduit. Perhaps the Saints, long ago, had taken this way out. The stories weren't too clear on the timing, but she had a fair degree of certainty the Saints had gone topside before level one became off limits.

Noah's not going to let me go to the big door, and I can't even open it.

She exited her room and turned left, crossed the middle of the Arc, and walked all the way to the end of the administrative hall. The last door on the left before the one she mistook as a closet contained the headquarters of the security team, and the jail cells. They reminded her of the police she'd read about in several novels, except they didn't have guns. Mostly, they broke up fights or investigated if someone accused another person of stealing. Supposedly, they'd even dealt with a murder or two or crimes like rape… though nothing so serious had happened in years.

While that should have reassured her, it had the opposite effect. It suggested everyone knew, or at least suspected, the Arc was on its last legs. Humans tended to help each other when facing mutual danger. People had been nervous enough for at least the past ten years not to commit any serious crimes. Also, given the entire population of the arc numbered 183 people, five of them under thirteen, everyone more or less knew everyone. It would be impossible to get away with anything. Maybe some people *did* have the inclination to cause trouble, but held back for fear they'd certainly get caught.

As soon as she walked past their office heading for the door at the end, a handful of security officers rushed out into the hallway.

"Hey," called Jose, a fortyish guy who had a little premature grey in his otherwise black hair. "What do you think you're doing?"

She turned to face him, lifting her goggles off her eyes. "I've been sent to check on a turbine."

Tyrone, perhaps the beefiest, tallest man in the entire Arc, winced. Ann, a soft-spoken redhead, stared at her the way one might regard a little girl about to be thrown into a volcano as a sacrifice when powerless to save her.

"Oh, Raven." Jose grimaced, giving her a 'better you than me' look. "You sure, hon?"

"Someone's gotta do it and I don't see anyone else lining up for the job." She grinned, not that they could see it under her mask. "Seriously, though. It's cool. It's not as bad out there as everyone thinks."

The officers chuckled nervously.

"How do you know that?" asked Ann.

Hope, mostly. And I'm sure the wire conduit is full of outside air. No way the seals are intact after this long. And Dad. "Educated calculation."

"Don't go making yourself into a saint," said Jose.

"Not planning on staying out there forever. Just long enough to fix the power. Turbine fourteen stopped generating. If it stays down too long, the others will overload and probably burn out. Someone needs to get it running again so we don't run out of air."

The security team exchanged nods and murmurs of worry for her safety. Tyrone and another, older, guy everyone called French didn't sound happy she had permission to go outside, but couldn't overrule Noah. Leaving them to their discussion, Raven re-seated her goggles and walked to the 'closet' at the end of the hallway. It didn't look like the sort of door that belonged on an elevator, being a fairly standard steel one with a single knob. It confused her since Ben mentioned elevator, and the schematics showed nothing existing beyond the end of any of the primary hallways.

She tried to open it, but found it locked.

Jose walked up to her. "Key might help."

"You guys lock the elevator?"

He smiled. "Elevator?"

"This is supposed to be an elevator shaft."

"Oh. Yeah, umm. The elevator shaft is at the far end. This door leads to an emergency evacuation passage. We started keeping it secure after an incident."

Raven furrowed her brows. The Arc schematics did not show an emergency escape passage anywhere. Wouldn't something like that be taught to every resident, so they knew what to do in the event of a disaster? Who in their right mind would want to keep it secret, much less locked?

"Gonna close the door behind you, but not lock it."

"What incident?" asked Raven.

"Ehh… about five years ago, some fool ran down there and went topside. Left the hatch open." Jose bowed his head, shaking it as well. "Better ways to end it all than running out there, especially leaving the damn door open as a screw you to everyone else."

What if he got out there and didn't die? She took a deep breath, fidgety with anticipation. *It would feel like escaping a cage. The only reason he'd come back is for food... if there's none out there.*

Breathable air sounded great, but it didn't seem likely there would be anything to eat topside. Vegetables humans used for nutrition wouldn't grow spontaneously. Disappointment that the man had most likely been nuts and ended up dead sent a sigh out her nostrils. She didn't let the thought stop her, and stepped into the doorway.

Light from the outer hall reached a short distance past her, illuminating a few yards of plain concrete hallway like every other corridor in the Arc. Jose leaned in the doorway and flipped a switch on the left, activating a series of LED bricks down the middle of the ceiling. Plain walls stretched so far into the distance she couldn't see the end. The total lack of any branching passages or doors made this hallway stand out as beyond weird. One thin pipe running along the left ceiling corner probably carried electrical cabling.

"Wow... it's so long." She looked back and forth from the hallway to Jose.

He laughed. "Not the first time a girl's said that to me."

Tyrone's deep laughter resonated in the corridor behind him.

Ann rolled her eyes.

Raven ignored the remark. "This isn't on the schematic. Why would an escape passage be kept secret?"

"No idea. I don't make those decisions," replied Jose, his voice echoing into the empty corridor. "Go on then. I need to close this door to keep the bad stuff out. It shouldn't be locked when you come back, but if whoever's stuck watching this door has to run to the can, might be. Just wait a few minutes."

"Right... okay." She waved at him and started the long walk.

The none-too-soft *thud* of the door closing behind her didn't really feel like she'd been kicked out. It didn't exactly reassure her either. Anxiety prickled at the underside of her stomach, worsening with each step. Her father must have taken this corridor to the exit the last day he'd been in the Arc. Being here, alone, the only one brave enough to attempt going topside, made her feel as though she'd become her father.

What was he thinking about when he left for the last time?

Not far from the door, a steel plate on the left covered what appeared to be the opening of a maintenance crawlspace. She glanced back at the door, which Jose had already closed. Not being watched heightened her curiosity. Quiet as she could be, Raven tugged the plate back enough to peer past it. Sure enough, a four-foot-square crawlway led about fifteen feet in before cornering to the left, heading back toward the Arc. She moved the plate aside, rested it against the wall, and scurried into the passage. Its primary purpose appeared to be a pathway for the power wires feeding the hallway lights, though dry standpipes for water and sewage also hung on the side wall.

'Escape tunnel?' More like incomplete expansion. No wonder it's not on the schematics.

Did that mean at some point in the past, the population of the Arc exceeded its capacity? They would have started off building the long corridor, then branched sideways to make rooms. But... what made them stop with only the hallway finished? Some long-ago disaster? Her throat dried out at the thought the population dropped drastically from several thousand to several hundred in a short period of time rather than the gradual loss she'd assumed occurred.

Or, maybe an ambitious head administrator started building an expansion for predicted population growth that never happened. Whatever the reason for the supposed escape tunnel, it didn't matter. Finding out the truth wouldn't change the situation she and everyone else in the Arc faced now. She did, however, creep back along the maintenance conduit until she realized where she was. In the years since she started working as a tech, she'd crawled right past this opening multiple times but never bothered going down there since it looked empty.

Hmm. Odd that they lock the hallway door but didn't try to block this off.

With a shrug, she turned around and hurried back to the corridor, taking a moment to replace the steel plate as she'd found it. Satisfied no one would notice she'd checked out a 'secret passage,' she continued.

A moment later, she paused to look at a dust-covered metal sign on the wall bearing the words 'Arcology 1409 - United States Federal Emergency Management Service. Authorized Personnel Only.'

Considering how old it had to be, the sign appeared in remarkably good condition. Most likely because it sat in a little-used corridor safe from the elements and any disturbances. Seeing mention of 'United States' gave her a sense of witnessing history up close, even though she still hadn't technically left the Arc. The teacher before Sienna, Mrs. Reed, taught the kids enough for Raven to know 'United States' had been what they called the land outside the Arc before the Great Death. Society had once created hundreds of different regions, all having different names. Some had been so far away the people who lived there didn't even talk in the same words.

And they're all gone now.

A thought hit her in the head hard enough to make her dizzy. The sign proved this corridor had been here from the beginning. It would have *had* to be on the schematics. Either the designers left it off, or someone modified the drawings. Neither scenario made any sense.

Raven turned away from the sign and kept going. She had bigger problems than daydreaming about a world that had been gone for several centuries or wondering who told what kind of lies and why. Red and orange markings on the walls up ahead confused her until she got close enough to realize someone spray painted graffiti. The paint reminded her of the distance markings in the wire conduit, reflective bright orange. This hallway hadn't been kept locked prior to the crazy man running topside and leaving the hatch open. Whoever had come down here before decorated the concrete with crude drawings of dead beetles as well as scrawled warnings like 'Danger! Poison ahead!' and 'Turn back or die.'

The dire predictions and dead insects further unsettled her already unstable stomach.

If I die out there, what's going to happen to Tins?

When they'd asked her to help out by having a baby, she'd been happy to do her part even if it had been awkward, messy, and not terribly pleasant the first time. Her mother died when she'd been small, so she had no one to talk to about sex type stuff. Actually doing it with Chase ended up being nothing at all like what she'd read in romance books. She had intercourse several times over a week, but as soon as Doc confirmed her pregnant, Chase barely even looked at her again. Perhaps the worst part had been trying to get through the sex with a guy she barely knew and didn't even like. She liked him much less now due to his indifference to Tinsley.

More than any other factor, his attitude kept her from agreeing to get pregnant a second time by him. Thus far, they hadn't matched her with anyone else 'safe' enough from a genetic standpoint.

Chase Oakley... stupid, selfish white boy.

She couldn't even remember the last time she spoke to him exactly, but it had to be before Tinsley turned two. Naturally, they had an argument over his lack of interest in their daughter. He said something about a third of babies don't survive past age three, and theirs had been born a little premature and underweight. Maybe he expected her to die within months.

No way, asshole. Tinsley's a fighter. Damn, I hope she throws it in your face if you try to involve yourself after she's twelve. Somehow, Raven had kept her mouth shut. No one in the Arc except for her 'sister' knew how much she hated the man. Between him and watching those other people dump their kids off on Sienna, she'd made up her mind not to have any more babies no matter how desperately Noah asked her to. *If ever she had another one, it would be with a guy who wanted to be with her, not someone who'd been ordered to.* She couldn't saddle another kid with a disinterested father.

Before long, the end of the corridor came into view. Plain steel elevator doors hung halfway open, slightly bent.

"Huh... so there really is an elevator."

Someone had spray painted 'express elevator to doom' on the doors and 'this way to hell' on the wall below an upward pointing arrow. The vacant shaft behind the relatively flimsy doors indicated the elevator cab had either gone up already or been cannibalized for spare parts like every other elevator in the Arc. People didn't *need* elevators to go from one floor to the next, so a prior boss ordered them disassembled and used as materials to repair other more essential systems. In fact, her alarm clock's frame had once been part of an elevator.

Raven gripped the left door and stuck her head in, peering up. The shaft didn't have any LED bulbs, so she unhooked her crank light—

the replacement one Ben gave her that worked better—gave it a few turns, and shone it straight up on a steel ladder surrounded by nearly-black concrete. Total darkness beyond the reach of the beam set off a momentary sense of vertigo.

The air smelled stale and dry, untouched by the Arc's ventilation system. Obviously, *some* air moved in and out of this corridor via the door at the end, but she didn't want to spend a lot of time in a dead hallway. Like Doc said, if the air didn't have enough oxygen, she could fall unconscious so fast she'd not be able to save herself.

Question being, would it be better or worse than what awaited her topside?

I could die if I go out there. Everyone could die if I don't.

She clenched her jaw, not sure if relying on external wind power had been smarter or dumber than building a nuclear reactor in the Arc. A reactor wouldn't have been vulnerable to damage from the conditions outside... but it also would have introduced the possibility of a nuclear accident, not to mention storage of spent fuel. Also, after two, three, or maybe even four hundred years—no one remembered exactly how long ago the Great Death happened—they'd certainly have run out of fresh fuel rods. If the wind ever 'ran out,' humanity would have far bigger problems than lack of electricity.

She reattached her flashlight to her poncho and gripped the ladder in both hands. According to every other adult in the Arc, going outside would be about as dangerous as walking into the core room of a nuclear reactor. Did Noah expect her to go out there, fix the turbine, and drop dead? She couldn't believe topside remained as dangerous as everyone else believed. Not after hearing about her father exploring so many times. Topside clearly had its dangers, but instant death by melting into a puddle of goo wasn't one of them.

A downed turbine will most likely cause another one to fail within a few days or a week at most. That will set off a cascade, and everyone suffocates in the dark. She closed her eyes, shaking from dread at the thought she might never see Tinsley again. But... if she didn't do this, her daughter would certainly die, along with everyone else. The last humans on Earth.

Maybe I should *have more babies.*

Grumbling, she used her anger at Chase for motivation, and began the climb.

The wire conduit had a slight uphill angle that put the L-bend at the same elevation as the first—uppermost—level of the Arc, ninety feet under the surface. The emergency escape on the third level hadn't angled up or down. Another two stories of ladder didn't make much difference. Climbing a long ladder in a wide elevator shaft definitely beat crawling 200 feet down a cramped conduit.

She neither rushed nor dawdled on the way up into the dark. Once it felt like she should be nearing the top, every three rungs, she stretched an arm up overhead in search of the ceiling. At least climbing in a complete lack of light prevented looking down from being scary. Eventually, her hand made contact with a solid surface. She hooked an arm on the ladder for a better grip and used her free hand to crank the light. In a few seconds, a weak, yellowish glow appeared on the dry concrete wall in front of her.

Angling the beam upward revealed a square metal hatch she assumed to be quite thick. A dinner-plate sized metal wheel stuck out on a post from the center, connected to a series of gears that extended or retracted four locking bars securing it shut. She clipped the crank light to the side of her filter mask so it pointed wherever she looked, and grabbed the wheel.

One-handing it didn't work. No matter how hard she tried to twist it in either direction, the wheel refused to turn.

Dangling by her hands 110 feet over a solid concrete floor did *not* sound fun. It took her a moment to find the courage to release her left hand from the ladder, relying on leg strength alone to keep her in place. Jaw clenched, she strained to turn the wheel counterclockwise, expecting a sudden unstick to practically throw her off the ladder.

The wheel still didn't move, so she paused to study the twist on the threads circling the shaft. *Yeah. Definitely counterclockwise. I'm just not strong enough. Or I'm hesitating. Screw it. I don't weigh much... if I slip I can hold myself up.*

After taking a few preparatory breaths, she braced her feet on the ladder, tightened her grip on the wheel, and wrenched it counterclockwise using her entire body. Seconds later, the mechanism broke free from crud, a loud metallic *pank* echoing into the depths. Surprisingly, she didn't lose her footing.

As soon as the spike of dread from risking a fatal fall faded, she faced only the fear of being one steel hatch cover away from to the outside world, a world everyone regarded with absolute dread.

"Well, Dad. You kept coming back home... until you didn't." Raven closed her eyes, holding back a tear. "The air didn't kill you, did it? Something else did. I'm gonna be fine. It has to be okay out there. I believe you. You weren't nuts."

She patted around her filter mask to check the seal against her face, steeled herself, and spun the wheel until the four metal prongs retracted fully out from the rim. Only the hatch's weight kept it closed.

Moment of truth. Last chance to chicken out. Raven grinned to herself. *No way. Here I come, Dad.*

6

THE ENDLESS MARCH

Going topside is like sex. First time's painful and confusing. Second time, you're a little more used to it. Then you end up loving it. – Ellis Wilder.

Raven scooted up one more rung and gave the hatch a hard upward shove.

Unexpected blinding light filled the passage, stabbing her in the eyes like hot knives and startling a scream out of her. Some dry, crumbly material fell all over her, but she couldn't see it... or much of anything. Too worried about falling to care about anything else, she grabbed the edge of the opening and hauled herself up and out onto the ground. *Now* it made sense why her father had the tinted goggles. As a kid, she'd gotten into his kit and found them, but had no idea why he'd have something that made it impossible to see.

"Ow. Shit." She cradled her face, waiting for the burning sensation in her eyes to lessen.

It stung more than if someone snuck up on her with a sunlamp from the hydroponic farm, shoved it in her face, and turned it on.

After a moment, Raven shielded her eyes with both arms,

tentatively opening them to a narrow squint, but flinching closed at the painful brightness. Soft rustling came from everywhere around her, shifting in time with gusts and ebbs in a fairly strong breeze. She knelt in place, trying to stay low in case the Plutions might be close by. Hopefully, she'd hear them coming and be able to scurry back into the hatch without slipping and killing herself.

Over the course of several minutes, she acclimated—somewhat— to the intense light. At first, she had to squint, then little by little, she forced herself to open her eyes more as the discomfort lessened. Tears streamed down her face, flowing involuntarily in response to such bright light. Never before in her life had she seen anything like it. Not even the farm came close to this level of illumination.

The blurry mess around her resolved into shades of green, brown, and grey—mostly green. She knelt in a swath of grey dirt, not far from a square hole in the ground and a thick metal hatch door. It hurt to peer straight up, but she did anyway, wanting to see the sky. It didn't look like she'd pictured it from the books she'd read, being all grey and smoky.

It's supposed to be blue. With white stuff. Wait... is this bad weather? Like, a rainy day? Oh, crap! The sun gets brighter *than this?*

The crumbling remains of structures surrounded her on three sides beyond the edge of the bare dirt field, all thickly engulfed by vegetation gone wild. Here and there, she spotted rusting metal amid the foliage, but couldn't tell what it had been aside from some manner of machinery. The density of the forest prevented her from seeing too far in, but she suspected the debris mounds might have once been houses. Still squinting at the oppressive brightness, she wobbled to her feet. Steady wind pelted her with sand, making her thankful for the goggles and the filter mask.

But... plants.

They're everywhere! The Earth isn't a dead planet!

Overcome with giddiness, Raven almost pulled the filter mask down to sniff the air, but didn't quite have the nerve to go that far. She clearly hadn't disintegrated upon exposure to the outside world. And, with *so many* plants growing everywhere, it didn't seem possible for the atmosphere to be poisonous anymore.

Still, out of a sense of obligation, she closed the hatch. The top didn't have a wheel, only a small staple-shaped handle. No one from the outside could open this passage unless it had been unbarred from below. Probably a good idea.

Raven surveyed her immediate surroundings. The dirt around where she stood had a few depressions that might have been footprints made years ago, or simply wishful thinking on her part. Considering the wind, it didn't seem possible for her father's prints to still be visible. Of course, the people in the Arc were the only humans left on Earth, so it couldn't have been anyone else.

Plutions?

The hatch surface didn't show any signs of damage. If the Plutions had found it, they either didn't try to get in or didn't recognize it as an entrance to a hiding place where vulnerable humans cowered away from the destruction outside.

A few broken posts jutted up from the ground in the forest to her right, one suspiciously similar to an image she'd seen on a book cover —a traffic light. In a slow turn, she gazed out over the ruins of what had to have been a small city or town. Finally, she spotted the reason she'd been allowed out of the Arc—the turbine farm, directly opposite the ruined residential area.

Eighteen metal towers stood in a grid pattern about a hundred yards away over mostly open dirt, only a few scattered weeds sprouting from it. Each tower supported a turbine generator with three ten-foot blades. From here, they reminded her of enormous fans. She hadn't expected them to be white. Granted, they weren't so much white as they had once been. After so many years, they'd become a rust-mottled dark grey. Small patches of still-white paint among the corrosion suggested long ago, they'd been beautiful and pure. Not so much anymore.

Being out here surrounded by all the green growth lessened her sense of urgency. She no longer felt like she had to rush to the busted turbine, fix it as fast as she could move, and run back to the hatch to stay alive. Experiencing topside for herself confirmed what she'd hoped to be true for years of listening to Dad. He never hesitated at the idea of leaving the Arc. No fear at all. He'd known all along what she knew now.

Maybe the air is *safe?*

She looked around as if someone might be watching her to scold her for misbehaving, then tugged the filter mask down enough to get a sip of direct air, lush with the essence of vegetation but also a funny smell she couldn't quite place. Not unpleasant, merely alien.

Is that what it smells like not to be re-breathing the same air over and over? I've gotten so used to scrubbed air, maybe not *smelling those machines has a scent of its own.*

Not quite fully ready to trust the world, she re-seated her mask and strode across the dirt field toward the towers. Based on the distance between the bottom of the blades and the ground, she estimated the turbine cores to be thirty feet up. Not too much of a problem as the towers had ladders. Eight-inch thick metal pipes ran from every turbine to a ten-foot-square metal plate at the approximate center of the windmill farm. Those pipes had to contain wires, shielding, and padding.

Awestruck at seeing the windmills for real as well as trees, grass, and plants she had no name for growing all over the ruins of whatever town the Arc had been built in—rather under—left her standing there, staring for a while.

"There couldn't be this many plants without bugs to pollinate them." She bounced in happiness. "If bugs have come back, maybe there's hope."

Raven hurried in among the windmill farm, mesmerized by the giant machines. Most had holes rusted into their housing. Miraculously, none had lost any blades, though a few had broken partially off, shorter than they ought to be. Turbine fourteen rather obviously had a problem—its blades didn't spin at all.

At a sudden crunch under her right foot, she stopped, finally peeling her stare away from the graceful windmills to look down—and gasped at the sight of a mostly disintegrated environmental protection suit. A naked skull peered back at her, shrouded in the remains of a melted helmet. The suit had suffered so much damage, it entirely exposed the skeletal remains of the person who'd been wearing it. Not far off on the right lay another body. Two more slumped against the base of a turbine tower farther ahead on her left. A bony arm stuck up from a dirt dune she'd walked past. All the suits looked as though they'd been doused in strong acid, enough to eat into the person. It called to mind the stories of how people would melt into slime puddles.

"The Saints," she whispered. "It's true... they really did die out here."

It took a moment for the shock of her discovery to wear off enough for her to do more than stare at the remains in horrified reverence. Collecting herself, she crouched to examine the corpse she'd stepped on. No trace of flesh remained on the bones, and nothing offered any clue if they had been a man or woman. Perhaps someone with medical training could've figured out how long ago they died, but she assumed it had to be quite a while. Most stories about the Saints claimed they'd gone out to repair turbines over a hundred years ago.

"Gotta be longer than people say... plants couldn't live in air that melted these suits... unless the Plutions shot them with some alien gun."

A hard plastic case roughly a foot square lay mostly buried beside the corpse, the disintegrated remnants of a shoulder strap jutting up from the corner. Curiosity got the better of her. Raven brushed her gloved hand over it to clear away dirt. No writing or icons identified what the object might be, so she pulled it up out of the ground, rested it flat, and flicked the latch.

The case opened like a clamshell. Inside, amid crumbling foam, lay an olive-drab device with the approximate shape of a thick book. Two narrow tubes protruded from one side, the opposite face had two lenses each three inches wide. Both tubes had rubberized cups on the ends that crumbled at her touch, however the lenses appeared intact.

This is some kind of seeing device.

She held it up to examine. Two rubbery buttons on the top right didn't seem to do anything. A plastic curve in the middle turned out to be a small wheel embedded in the device she could rotate by pushing. Eventually, she tried holding it up to her eyes and looking through it. The device made far-away things appear closer.

Oh... binoculars. She lowered them and made a face. *I thought they'd look different.*

Whatever the buttons once did, she had no idea, but felt pretty sure it had run out of battery power already. Still, the manual focus wheel worked, which made them useful. The Saints had likely used them to survey the turbines from the ground. Again, she glanced down at the bones inside a rotting suit.

Proof the world *had* been deadly brought back some of her prior nervousness. However, she couldn't ignore the vast amounts of greenery everywhere. More than a hundred years had to have passed since the Saints died... unless something other than a toxic environment killed them. She looked around for signs of a hazardous tank that might have exploded, but no obvious sources of doom caught her eye. The position of the bodies also didn't suggest they'd been killed violently or died while attempting to run away from anything. It looked as though they'd simply been trudging around and collapsed.

"Strange."

Raven stood, muttered an apology for stepping on him, and wandered deeper into the windmill farm. Looking at schematic diagrams hadn't fully prepared her for the scale of the actual turbine, or the severity of the disrepair. Even the towers, simple steel lattices, suffered pockmarks as if exposed to acid, corrosion, and rust. Two even warped under the turbines they supported, appearing like a toy made from plastic straws left too close to a heat lamp. It seemed the weight of the generators had begun to exceed the ability of the disintegrating towers to hold them up.

She stopped at the approximate center of the turbine field, using the binoculars to survey each generator. The world hung in near silence, save for the constant *whuff-whuff-whuff* from giant fan blades underscored by the nigh imperceptible whine of gears. Every so often, a *clank* announced a piece of metal falling somewhere. Three fan blades had broken off a little past the midway point, still operational. She questioned how fans with two long and one short blade didn't shake themselves apart. For some reason, they appeared stable, and most of the turbines appeared to be working despite their decrepit condition. The only way she could think to explain the sight is if the Saints had installed ballast weights on the broken blades. Turbine eight spun much slower than the rest, while turbine fourteen had come to a complete stop, its fan blades bending backward at the tips from wind pressure.

Either the brake has somehow been turned on or it jammed.

A narrow ladder, as rusty and pitted as the rest of the structure, ran up inside the center of each tower to a maintenance deck around the turbine. Raven didn't think her weight would be significant enough to cause the ladders to fail completely, but still approached the climb cautiously.

"Well, might as well start there. That's why I'm out here."

She approached tower fourteen, gazing up at the tip of the fan blade twenty feet overhead. The scale of the machine astounded her. Nothing inside the Arc came close to it in terms of size, the closest being the CO_2 scrubber units. Seeing a machine so large, so far beyond the capacity of the Arc to manufacture, hit her like witnessing a feat of magic.

Another *clank* somewhere off to the left made her jump. That time, she caught a glimpse of a metal fragment falling, bouncing off Tower 3, and hitting the ground. It had to be a chunk of the turbine's outer housing, and didn't bode well for survivability. Even in a normal atmosphere, ordinary rain getting inside the generators could cause problems. The coils and magnets inside were enclosed at least, so damage to the outer housing would not mean immediate failure. However, she thought it a good idea to come back out here with plastic sheeting and cover as many holes as possible.

With any luck, once she returned, seeing her come back alive would convince the others to help. Tarping eighteen turbines herself would take days.

Raven paused under Tower 14 and stared up the length of the ladder to the hole in the platform thirty feet up. The metal lattice around her made unsettling noises in response to the wind, shifting and settling. Alarmingly, she spotted a few missing rivets where frame beams crossed. The remaining ones all had rust rings, clearly loose. Turbine tower fourteen had become a bunch of metal sticks kinda-sorta held together by failing rivets.

This is bad… if a serious storm hits, half of the towers are going to collapse.

Her mind raced. It might be possible to replace rivets with bolts. One thing the Arc had in vast numbers was spare bolts. That, too, would be one hell of a project involving climbing and working while hanging off the side of the towers. Again, nothing she looked forward to doing alone. However, the generators kept people alive. Seeing them in this condition, so close to a catastrophic failure, took her off her feet. She sank into a squat, holding onto the ladder for balance until the dizziness of adrenaline faded. The lives of everyone in the Arc depended on electricity. One storm with strong winds at some point over the past few years could have flattened multiple towers. The stress on the power system would have burned out the rest, causing the last remnants of humanity to die in the dark, suffocating without ever knowing why. No electricity meant no oxygen. No light. No heat. Raven had been restless as of late, and this realization cemented her opinion the Arc had become a grave waiting for the people in it to die.

What would Noah have done if everything shut down all at once? Would he have risked opening the door or just had everyone huddle in the hydroponic room hoping the plants let us breathe? At least until they died. No light.

"Not time to give up yet. I have a job to do."

Despite wearing gloves, she took care to avoid grabbing rust spots on the way up the ladder. Having been outside for a while and suffering no ill effects from it took away the panic of having to rush back inside before death. She made her way to the steel mesh platform encircling the gimbal upon which the turbine housing rotated, and pulled herself up to stand. If looking at plans hadn't prepared her for seeing the generators in person, checking them out with binoculars didn't prepare her for the sheer massiveness while standing three feet away. Sleek and aerodynamic, the mostly cylindrical device tapered to a relatively thin point on her left, eighteen feet long from the tip of the nose cone to the back end. The thickest part had a diameter of seven feet, filled with gears, wire coils, magnets, and circuitry.

Once the initial awe of being this close to the turbines while *outside* waned, she experienced a disorienting sense of wrongness. A machine with so many moving parts like this left to its own devices for hundreds of years should not still be operational. Someone had to have come out here before her, probably many times, to maintain them. Could it be the Saints hadn't really been sent out as a team of eight, but rather pairs or even individuals spaced out over years? None of the remains appeared at all recent, which meant either the people in the Arc had the most incredible luck imaginable—or someone's been routinely going outside in secret.

Why wouldn't Noah tell everyone the air outside is breathable? She frowned. *Says the girl still wearing a filter mask.*

Turbine fourteen continued to shift, keeping itself oriented into the wind, but its blades didn't spin. Creaking came from inside whenever the breeze picked up speed, sounding as if the entire mechanism might collapse to pieces at any moment under a strong enough gust. She moved to the edge of the platform and looked down the length of the bowing fan blade.

It's lucky the wind isn't too strong or these would have snapped off.

Many hours staring at schematics had familiarized her with the turbines enough that she had little difficulty finding the primary hatch cover, opening the machine up like she'd worked on them her entire adult life. Some of the internal components didn't quite look the same as the drawing—more disorienting as she didn't have the plans in front of her to compare. However, after a few minutes of poking around, the layout made sense. At the front end, she discovered the problem in short order: a large fragment of the outer housing had fallen into the primary transmission gears responsible for transferring rotational energy from the enormous fan to the driveshaft, wedging them to a halt.

No amount of pulling freed it, as the force of the wind attempting to turn the fan kept it pinned. Even the strongest guy in the Arc couldn't overpower the force generated by the wind on the giant fan. She'd either have to wait for the breeze to drop off to nothing or feather the blades.

Since the wind appeared in no mood to take a break, she headed to the front end of the massive turbine, opened a much smaller hatch, and extended a crank connected to the gear system that altered the blade's pitch. In normal conditions, an electric motor did the work, operated from a control board back in the engineering room. Unfortunately, the wiring responsible for the command signals failed before she'd been born. No one inside the Arc received any information on the status of the turbines other than the amount of power each one sent down the main wire.

Getting her wish to see them in person had been both a thrill and terrifying due to their condition.

It will be amazing if we can keep them limping on for another five years.

Raven pulled the large handle down from the collapsed position, grabbed it in both hands, and cranked it around. Deep metallic creaks rang out as gears that hadn't moved in at least a century struggled. Rusty spots and small bits of debris made for tough going. Grunting, cursing, and gasping, Raven strained at the hand crank in between short rest periods. Gradually, the three huge wing-like blades rotated so their leading edges faced directly into the wind, relieving the pressure and eliminating rotational force on the turbine shaft. Once finished, she pulled on another lever to activate the brake—but it came off in her hand.

"Okay... so much for that."

She sighed at the cracked rod, tempted to toss it aside out of spite. But she could possibly reuse the metal. The furnace in the Arc had already run out of fuel, but if the outside world truly had become habitable, maybe she could come up with some sort of kiln to amplify an ordinary wood fire to the point it could melt or soften metal. She gave a noncommittal shrug and stuffed the broken lever into her satchel. The fan jostled about in the breeze, which could make it dangerous for her to put her fingers anywhere close to the gears. Her only option for applying the brake involved stealing one from another turbine, which would create a new problem if that turbine had a similar issue.

I shouldn't have to disassemble the gearbox to clear the jam. Hope not. Then, I'll definitely have to fix the brake first.

The fragment of outer shell appeared to have broken away from the top and fallen into the gear system connecting the relatively slow-moving primary shaft to a faster-spinning secondary drive shaft going into the generator. She leaned inside for a closer look, but kept her hands a safe distance from harm. A main gear four inches thick and as big around as her torso had chowed down on the hunk of steel cladding, drawing it in a ways and perforating it. The sheet of one-eighth-inch steel bent around at least four other smaller gears as well. Extracting it would require enough strength to make the primary gear rotate a span of at least fifteen teeth.

"Damn. I'm not going to be able to pull that out without it breaking off in my hands."

An idea hit her.

She hurried back to the large crank, turning it until the blades angled into the wind the other way, effectively reversing the direction of the windmill. As soon as the fan responded to the wind, she ceased cranking and ran back to the main access hatch.

The giant gear crept around, spitting out the mangled hunk of metal at an excruciatingly slow pace. *Better slow than having pieces break off.* She grabbed the hunk in both hands, holding it steady as it disengaged from multiple intermediate gears. Some of the smaller gears suffered minor damage, but the big one laughed it off. Fortunately, nothing looked too smashed up to make her worry about serious problems.

Raven took a step back, examining the chunk of debris, a generally rectangular section about the size of a cafeteria tray, one end chewed up and crimpled where gears pressed the pattern of their teeth in. Rust ran around the edges except for a foot-long spot where the metal snapped. She leaned into the turbine housing and peered up at a matching hole in the top of the housing, cringing again at the brightness of the cloudy sky. Rain would fall directly on the transmission gears. She had to do something to cover the hole before the weather became worse. If her novels were accurate, a sky this grey and overcast meant rain would come soon.

Oddly, the gears didn't lack in lubrication. That further confirmed her suspicion someone had been maintaining them, especially considering the grease looked exactly like the plant-derived stuff they used inside the Arc and not petroleum-based like the people who built the turbines would have used. She narrowed her eyes, turning her head to stare at the distant hatch down to the Arc.

Why the hell are they lying?

7

GLINT

Breaking down is the only thing you can ever be absolutely certain a machine will do. – Ellis Wilder.

Having cleared the jam in the gear system, Raven cranked the fan blade pitch back to thirty-five-point-five degrees, or at least as close to it as the indicator dial was accurate. That offered the most efficient angle of attack based on the lift characteristics of these blades. It took almost four minutes of cranking to get there, but soon, turbine fourteen spun up to match speed with the rest—except number eight, which remained sluggish.

A slow fan could mean anything from gunked-up insides to a stripped gear, both problems she likely hadn't brought—or didn't have access to—the necessary parts to repair. At least number eight still rotated.

"Since I'm already out here and not melting, I should check on it."

A final look around inside turbine fourteen failed to reveal anything out of the ordinary. Confident she'd done as much as she could to bring it back online, she reached up to grab the huge access hatch, and swung it down to close. As she turned toward the ladder hole in the platform, a bright glinting flash in the corner of her eye made her pause.

Raven spun toward it, but couldn't tell exactly where it had come from—only that it appeared quite far away. Miles of former suburban ruins stretched out into the distance, vanishing amid a hazy fog blended with the overcast sky. Weeds and other plants enshrouded pretty much everything except for the wind farm.

Is the dirt here poisonous or are the mysterious people maintaining the generators clearing the area?

"Ooh!" Remembering she found binoculars, she fished them out of her satchel and held them up to her eyes, searching around for what flashed.

Three dark shapes in the haze somewhat resembled the turbine towers except for not having windmill generators on top of them. Another flash came from beyond the left limit of her vision. She twisted toward it at the nearest of those towers. The glint reminded her of the way light could reflect off the surface of a shiny object, only many times more intense. Then again, the sun—even on such an overcast day—had to be thousands of times stronger than the sad light bulbs down in the Arc.

That meant something shiny had to be moving.

Bleh. Maybe a hunk of metal dangling on a wire.

She homed in on the spot and gasped when a shadowy form moved, almost as if reacting to her looking at it. Given the distance and haze, she had no idea what it might be, but it definitely hadn't been a bug. Part of her wanted to say she'd seen a man in a blotchy green-and-brown poncho scrambling to climb down, but it couldn't be possible. All the humans except for the population of the Arc had died long ago. An animal, perhaps? But, they, too, had died off—supposedly. Of the animals she'd learned about in school, only apes or gorillas walked on two legs, and those creatures didn't live in this region before the Great Death. Not to mention, like everything else above ground, they'd all died.

The shape looked so much like a person she shivered with

excitement. Her mind filled in details her eyes couldn't reach: a figure pointing a single lens in her general direction, the sunlight gleaming on the surface. Could she have seen another living human being who didn't come from the Arc? Too thrilled to contain herself, she waved and called out in greeting... then lowered her arm, overcome by a sense of foolishness.

If the moving shadow had been another human, they would've been so far away they couldn't hear her, or even see her without binoculars. Everything she'd learned growing up made the Earth sound like a dead ball of grey dust with nothing left but poison, wind, and aliens who may or may not still be out there hunting for living things to kill.

Maybe I saw a Plution?

None of the stories ever went into detail about what the invaders looked like, only that the Plutions killed everything. They could be human-shaped as easily as flying serpents, jelly blobs, or even insectoid. One downside to reading all those books: her imagination had no shortage of ways to envision monsters.

Raven continued watching the distant tower for a few minutes, hoping to get a better look at 'the thing that moved.' Alas, whatever it was, it either didn't really exist or had run off. The longer she searched, the more she wondered if her mind played tricks on her. A flash so far away could have come from metal scraps falling. It didn't prove another person looked in her direction. It *couldn't* mean another person.

Could it?

Even the poncho, so many little blotches of green in different shades, might have been a branch of leaves wobbling in a strong gust. Reluctantly, she lowered the binoculars from her eyes and sighed.

"They tell us it's deadly out here just like they tell us we're the only people left."

Raven finally understood what kept her father going back out here. He'd known the air wouldn't kill him even though everyone firmly believed it would. Curiosity burned in her to find out what else might not be true.

From the vantage point of Tower 14, she looked out over the land in all directions. Opposite where the glint came from, larger shadows darkened the haze, riddled with rectangular holes. Her binoculars revealed the remains of great structures many dozens of stories tall miles away. They'd crumbled into tattered skeletons of steel and concrete wrapped in green plants.

She knew people before the Great Death lived in such places, cities above ground. Some of those cities had been so large it could take a person hours to walk from one edge to another. One book she'd read made reference to a single city being home to over a million people. Raven couldn't even fathom such a number. The 2,000 who initially lived in the Arc sounded outlandish enough, but a million?

Temptation to go explore the ruins almost won out. But... she couldn't simply charge off into topside with no plan and no provisions. She also couldn't disappear on Tinsley no matter how much she trusted Sienna to take care of her. Despite the allure of exploring ancient ruins, reality had to come first. People in the Arc depended on her essentially to keep them alive, even if they didn't know how perilous their situation had become. Raven long suspected problems, but now she couldn't figure out what would fail first: the CO_2 scrubbers or the power system.

Scowling at nothing in particular, she climbed down the ladder and headed across the dirt field to Tower 8.

There's no way Noah wouldn't know about people going outside to work on the turbines. He's definitely been lying. Ben... He'd appeared genuinely guilty when asking her to check on number fourteen. *No, he believes it's really bad out here.* The possibility remained she'd walked out into a lucky patch of good air. Nothing guaranteed the conditions would remain safe. However, all the plant growth tended to suggest it would. Intermittent toxicity would not have allowed anything to live here. Trees did not reach such size in months. Shifting areas of poison and not-poison couldn't be cycling around based on weather.

Tower 8 appeared relatively solid. A cursory examination didn't find any missing rivets nor did the structure sway and creak as much as Tower 14. Raven set aside her growing urge to explore, and committed to the task at hand. She climbed to the maintenance deck and approached the primary hatch. The latch didn't want to move at first, but a little jimmying at it with a mini pry bar from her tool satchel unstuck it. She gripped the underside of the huge door and pushed it upward, grateful for the shade it threw over the interior.

The massive primary gear rotated at the same speed as the fan assembly, however the subordinate gear it drove slipped as much as it spun, having suffered damage from wear as well as environmental exposure. Multiple teeth on several gears had worn down to smooth metal. Someone also set the fan blades at a shallower angle to slow them down... most likely to prevent the gearbox from being totally stripped.

Crap. We're going to have to rebuild this entire transmission to save this turbine.

A cursory check of the generator unit confirmed it in passable shape. Fixing this generator would require replacing at least three of the transmission gears, but to do it, someone would have to completely disassemble it—a multi-day project for a small team. Hopefully, the brake on this one wouldn't fail. She pulled out a small notepad and pencil, using it to make a basic sketch of the gears and note the damaged ones.

Nothing I can do here now. Ben should be able to machine new gears for it, but it's going to take a while.

She lifted the hatch cover off the post that held it open and let it swing down to close with a *whump.*

After one last look around at the landscape from an elevated position, Raven descended the ladder. Another *clank* came from the vicinity of Tower 17, a hunk of metal bouncing off the steel lattice.

"They're falling apart in real time."

Again, she considered trying to breathe without the filter mask but chickened out due to too many years of hearing scary stories. Not all poison had obvious smells. Excessive carbon monoxide, lack of oxygen, and even some lethal gases could build up without smell or taste.

Upon reaching the hatch back to the Arc, she crouched to open it.

Spending over an hour outside had allowed her eyes to acclimate. The sunlight only hurt a little. Since she could see normally again, she studied the hatch, curious about the crud that fell on her earlier. Small hunks of grey material littered the dirt around the opening. Nervously, she picked up a larger chunk, a piece about the size of her thumb. It crumbled when she squeezed it, breaking apart into dust.

Dried out rubber.

Raven opened the hatch, releasing another burst of the same material. The gasket seal in a recessed groove around the lid as well as around the base had completely failed. Bare metal sat on bare metal. The emergency exit looked about as airtight as an ordinary interior door, if even that. Outside air had been leaking into the Arc for some time, probably years. If the story Jose told her about the locked door was true, someone left this hatch wide open for however long it took people to notice. Hours? Days? Yet, she couldn't remember anyone falling ill.

There are no vents in that long hallway. Whatever leaked in could have stayed there. It wouldn't have gotten into the whole Arc.

She twisted to peer over her shoulder at the direction the glint came from. The longer she stared into the haze, the more she wanted to trust her instincts.

So many plants.

One minute slipped into another. She crouched there listening to the faint howl of the wind and the creaking turbines. Finally, she got up the nerve to reach up and pull the scarf off her face, tucking it under her chin. Cradling the filter mask in both hands, she tugged it away from her cheeks, allowing a rush of cool air to wash over her skin. Her mask imparted a rubbery flavor to each breath she only noticed by its sudden absence.

The unidentifiable scent in the air somewhat reminded her of the hydroponics room if the chemical-poop stink of the growth fluid didn't exist. Some plant nearby must have flowers giving off a fragrance. Grass had a distinct aroma as well. Beneath it all, she picked up an oily-metallic essence, perhaps contamination in the dirt.

That might explain why the rampant growth hadn't invaded the windmill farm.

Raven filled her lungs again and again with outside air, making herself dizzy. An instant of worry dissipated; light-headedness came from breathing too fast, not poison.

The air's okay... We're not gonna die if the scrubbers fail.

Giddy, she pulled the filter mask off entirely and stuffed it in her satchel before hurrying down the ladder.

8

HALLUCINATIONS

If we've learned nothing from the old government, remember that whenever someone tries to hide something, they're up to no good. – Ellis Wilder.

Going underground plunged Raven into darkness. The LED brick lights on the ceiling gave off such a feeble glow she could barely see the walls. It seemed impossible for the electrical system in the Arc to have failed during the two-ish hours she'd been outside. For a brief moment, she worried something in the air outside might have damaged her eyes… but she hadn't taken her goggles off.

Ugh. Stop freaking out at everything. It is my eyes, not the lights. I've been out in daylight.

She stood still for a little while waiting for her eyes to compensate for the drastic change in light level. A few minutes later, the passage had brightened somewhat, though still felt dimmer than she remembered from before. That, she blamed on her want to be outside.

Even though she knew it would take hours for Ben to consider, discuss, and implement a plan to go out and tarp the turbines, Raven jogged along the evacuation tunnel. Already, the staleness of the air down here grated on her. The unusual fragrance she didn't recognize outside might simply be the way air *should* smell. For all twenty-two years of her life, she'd breathed continuously recycled air, artificially oxygenated by machines. More than ever, her idea of using outside air sounded like the only way to save the Arc.

However, such an idea faced one great challenge. The primary purpose behind the Arc had been to isolate the residents from the surface, protecting them from all the toxins. As such, it did not have many conduits leading topside, and certainly lacked a dormant exterior ventilation system. The designers intended for the Arc to be self-contained, isolated from the world. To draw in outside air would be a massive undertaking.

However, a crapton of back breaking work appealed far more than suffocating to death.

The alarmist graffiti on the walls took on a comical irony. Maybe at the time people wrote those words, they had been true. After all, something killed the Saints. Her father used to say everything healed after a long enough time period; perhaps that included the planet.

She rushed to the door at the far end, hoping Jose—or whoever got stuck with sentry duty—hadn't gone off to the toilet and locked it.

Jose screamed in surprise when she shoved it open, nearly falling on his ass.

"Sorry!" She gasped, out of breath from running.

"Good to see you back in one piece." He patted her on the arm. "Don't know what they're thinking sending a young woman out there."

She folded her arms. "I'm quite capable of fixing things."

"Not that..." Jose patted his belly. "You're too important to our survival to risk."

Being thought of as a baby factory annoyed her, but she couldn't argue the necessity. People had to reproduce or there wouldn't be any people left. Then again, the population had already dwindled down under 200 souls. They'd probably already passed a point of no return.

Eventually, everyone would be related to everyone if it hadn't happened already. The notion Chase Oakley might be the only person in the entire Arc she could have kids with safely made her skin crawl.

"Yeah, yeah. I know. But..." She pointed down the hall. "There's nothing to worry about. It's fine out there."

Jose shook his head, sighing. "If it was, we wouldn't be living down here."

"That's because people believe the stories and won't look for themselves. Go climb the ladder and peek outside."

"No, thanks. I like my face un-melted."

She lifted the goggles off her eyes, setting them atop her head and struck a pose. "My face isn't melted... is it?"

"Doesn't look like it, but could be you got lucky. Found a good shift in the wind before a killer cloud rolled by."

"My father went out and came back over and over again. We're scared of stories, not reality. There are plants growing *everywhere* outside. Seriously. Go look."

He waved her off as if declining an extra helping of potatoes.

Sighing, Raven gave up on arguing with him. It would be difficult enough to convince Noah, but she couldn't wait to try. She hurried down the hall and went straight to the big man's office.

Noah Hayes had been the chief administrator of the Arc for about twenty years, being voted in after the previous admin—an elder named Owen—died. Previously, Noah managed the water processing group. Only section administrators were eligible to become the big boss. All admins from the woman in charge of managing trash to the big boss remained in their position until more than half the people in that group wanted them gone, at which point, a vote happened. For the big boss, more than half the people in the Arc needed to call for a vote. As far as anyone knew, he'd been the youngest ever head admin, assuming office at age twenty-one.

Raven largely ignored politics and didn't much care who ran what. As far as she knew, all the admins did a reasonable enough job. If someone turned into a power-mad fool or displayed a severe lack of competence, she'd want them gone, but as long as they could do the job, it didn't matter to her who sat in what chair.

Her feelings toward Noah remained mostly neutral. She neither admired nor disliked him, though could count on one hand the number of times she'd been in the same room with him. The only one she remembered with any clarity had been the time he'd approached her about having a child. However, if he'd been hiding people going to the surface routinely to check on the turbines, she'd question everything he said.

That he resembled a pale, somewhat younger, version of her father made it more difficult to challenge him. Both men had short salt and pepper hair and approximately the same build. Her father turned fifty-nine a few weeks before he disappeared four years ago. Noah's forty-first birthday 'party' happened months ago. Everyone in the Arc received a cupcake decorated with the number 41.

Noah occupied a large office at the end of a side corridor out of the administration section. It had once been quite fancy, having a big sofa, table, and even artwork on the walls. The years had not been kind to the furnishings. Most of the space in the huge room held darkness, as the only working light sat on his desk. It exemplified the mindset with which he ran the Arc. No point lighting empty space. She had a feeling he'd have made his office smaller if he could have.

"Raven..." Noah looked up from his old terminal screen, one of perhaps six working computers in the whole Arc. "How did it go?"

"Good and bad." She approached the desk.

He leaned back in the chair, giving a faint chuckle. "I had a feeling it would be significantly bad news if you came to me rather than Ben."

"Yeah. The turbines are all in rough shape. I got number fourteen working again, but there's a problem. They've become so deteriorated that the housing is rusting and falling off in pieces." She explained the jam, the holes, her fear about rain getting into the mechanism, and the need to cover them with tarps. "Another problem is some of the towers are starting to buckle under the weight of the windmills. Rivets are falling out. I don't think we have much time left before they collapse."

Noah mulled her words, pursing his lips.

She didn't like his complete lack of shock at seeing her return alive. That implied he already knew the outside world didn't have the instantly deadly mix of poisons everyone believed it to. It baffled her how everyone could know how her father had been out and back so many times, yet still somehow fear they'd melt on contact with topside.

"There's something else... I think I saw someone out there."

"What?" He flinched, then blinked at her. "Saw someone?"

"I think so. Something flashed far off. I found these"—she pulled the binoculars out of her satchel—"and used them to look in that direction. Pretty sure I saw someone run off."

Noah leaned forward. "What did they look like?"

"Umm." She fidgeted. "Just a shadowy figure. The air was hazy so far away and they moved real fast. I only saw them for a second or two. Might've been wearing a poncho, but it looked weird."

"Ahh." He sighed. "There are toxic chemicals in the air out there. Our filter masks are, as you know, quite old. There's only so much they can do to protect us. Most likely, you hallucinated seeing something move."

Even though she'd questioned her eyes at the time, hearing him say she hallucinated annoyed her. But... she didn't trust her memory enough to take a stand that would end up having everyone in the Arc thinking she'd gone insane. She wouldn't abandon the notion she might have seen something move, but it didn't mean she had to make a big deal out of it and try to tell everyone. Before he pushed too far in down that path, she'd throw him off balance.

"Actually, I feel fine. The air's better outside than in here. You know, something seemed odd about the turbines. They'd recently been lubricated with vegetable-based grease. The same stuff we make. It doesn't seem possible those machines have been out there on their own working fine for centuries and are *still* going."

Noah shifted his weight to the left, folded his arms, and propped his chin up on one hand. "Even if you really did see someone out there, we have no idea what they could possibly do. They could be dangerous."

"Yes. That's true." The novels she'd read often had different rival groups prone to violence against each other. Strange people not from the Arc could very well be violent and hostile. "No idea what they'd be like if I really saw someone."

"All the more reason… for the safety of everyone here, we cannot be discovered." He fidgeted at the log book in front of him. "The Great Death filled the Earth with poison of every type imaginable. It made mutants and other things. Your father returned with some wild stories."

She raised an eyebrow. "You think I might be hallucinating for seeing another person, but not him for seeing monsters?"

"Uhh." Noah opened and closed his mouth a few times, seeming at a loss for words. After a moment, he shrugged. "I'm only trying to keep everyone safe. We don't know what anyone's motives could be. If there *is* someone out there, they'd have to be primitives. Who knows how they'd react to people like us with technology. Probably attack us to take it. Hopefully, you imagined it… but if someone was there, let's keep our fingers crossed they didn't see you."

It might have been coincidence they ran away as soon as I spotted them. Could the other person have seen me from so far away? I had binoculars. She pictured the flash that first caught her attention. *Maybe they did, too.*

"Okay. For now. We have serious problems with the turbines. First, they're full of holes. We need to cover them. Second, the CO_2 scrubbers aren't going to last much longer. You know the air outside isn't as bad as everyone says it is. When I walked in here, you didn't act at all surprised I hadn't melted into a puddle. Someone's been going out to work on the turbines. I don't know why it has to be kept secret, and I can't say for sure what's going to die first between the turbines or the scrubbers—but something's going to fail, and fail big, soon."

"I'll take your findings under advisement. For now, please don't go starting a panic. By all means, inform Benjamin of your observations about the condition of the turbines. I'd ask you not to mention seeing another person out there unless you are absolutely certain of it."

She half turned away, gaze downcast. *He knows I'm not sure. Some fights are pointless.* "Okay. We should really come up with a plan for when the ventilation system fails. The top of the escape passage isn't too thick. If we knocked out the ceiling to make the opening as big as the shaft, it could serve as an air intake. We'd need to make big fans though... and find another opening to the surface to serve as an exhaust."

His grimace gave away honesty in his opinion the outside world remained poisonous to an extent. "As I said, I'll take it under advisement. Thank you."

The excitement she'd experienced at the possibility of there being more humans out there crashed into a pit of dejection. She felt like a kid proud to show off something she made to her father, only to have him laugh and destroy it in front of her. Not that her actual father ever did anything so cruel. Head down, she walked out of his office, no longer certain she had seen anything but a big flap of metal or plastic fluttering in the wind. Maybe her mind did fill in the details too much. She hated the pressure of believing the Arc contained the last of humanity, the desperation and sorrow of it. Less than 200 people left didn't bode well for humanity lasting much longer.

People would likely go extinct soon, even if she had twenty kids.

9

PLAN B

All wounds heal given enough time. Even the ones you want to hold on to. – Ellis Wilder.

Raven's mood improved from glum to normal by the time she reached the engineering room.

She paused by her workstation to unburden herself of the tool satchel, scarf, and goggles. Lark stared at her with an expression as if she'd seen a ghost, not saying a word as Raven walked past her to Ben who stood in the corner with a mug, observing a control panel of glowing LEDs and gauges. At her approach, he glanced over his shoulder, blinked, then hurriedly set his coffee down so he could grasp both her shoulders.

"How do you feel?"

"Fine." She tolerated him looking her over, not that he could see much more than her face and poncho. "Nothing melted. The air's fine. Forget it. We have a big problem."

He stood there in silence listening to her explain the condition of the windmill turbines and the towers. Her tarp suggestion went over well... the backup plan to consider how to pull in outside air, not so much.

"Wait." Raven held a hand up after he got into a mode of continuously shaking his head.

"There's nothing to discuss here. We need to—"

She shot him the same look she used on Tinsley whenever the girl misbehaved.

Ben set his hands on his hips, but stopped talking.

"It's going to happen during our lifetime. Most likely within a few years. What reality would you rather be in, one where everything craps out and we're standing here with our pants down or one where we've already got a system in place and only need to flip a switch not to die?"

"What you're suggesting is so out there..." He turned away, swiped his mug up in one hand, and took a giant gulp.

She walked around to stand in front of him. "If we do nothing, when the day comes the scrubbers or the generators die, we won't have time to work on a way to pull air in. Assuming it doesn't happen when most people are asleep and we all die not knowing it failed, we'll be lucky to have enough breathable air for everyone to survive long enough to make it outside."

Lark gasped.

"What are you more afraid of?" Raven looked at her. "Staying down here knowing you will suffocate, or believing me that the air is better outside than we have right now?"

"It's dangerous out there," said Lark in a hesitant voice.

"It's dangerous down here."

Ben cleared his throat. "There's a small problem with your idea. If the windmills suffer a catastrophic failure, there won't be any power to run whatever system we come up with to move air. Besides, we don't have the resources to fabricate anything of that scale."

"The power issue is certainly a problem, but a bunch of fans don't draw anywhere near the kind of juice the CO_2 scrubbers need. There are nine fans involved in pushing air up to level one and no one is ever there. We reposition them, pull in some fans from the empty outer residence halls, and we're set."

"What about tunneling?" He smirked. "Moving dead air around inside isn't going to help."

"Easy. Open the front door."

Ben laughed.

"Why are you laughing?" She folded her arms. "If the plan is already to draw in outside air, it's not like we need to keep it sealed. Use the escape passage as an exhaust. Air comes in through level one, and we pump it out from level three."

"What about four to six?" Ben tapped a finger against his mug.

"Simple enough to create an airflow to four. Five is already empty, so is most of six. It's all manufacturing facilities we can't even use anymore. Okay, the water processing is on level six, but that's a relatively small subsection. We already move air to it. The only thing we really need to change is primary intake and exhaust."

"How long have you spent thinking about this? Sounds like you've worked everything out."

"About twenty minutes. It's not exactly rocket science."

He tilted his head. "What?"

"Oh, umm. Something a character said in a book. Means it's not difficult. Rocket science is supposed to be really hard."

"What's a rocket?" asked Lark.

"Something with space." Raven bit her lip. "I think."

Ben exhaled. "Let's see how things go over the next couple weeks."

"You should really go out there yourself and look at the turbines."

"Umm. Yeah..." Ben chuckled and raised his mug to his lips, but paused before drinking. "Maybe if you last a week without growing a third arm, I'll consider it."

"Grr." She almost yelled at him for being superstitious, but the Saints *had* died out there. The people's fear of topside did have a basis in fact. Perhaps fact from decades ago, but still fact. "Fine. What about the tarps? Am I doing that myself?"

"You're really willing to go right back outside?" asked Lark.

"Yes, dammit. It's fine." Raven raked her hands through her hair.

"Turbine fourteen has a huge hole in the top of the housing. Rain can get right into the transmission gears. It's going to be a giant pain in the ass to tarp that thing alone, but I'll try."

Lark stood. "I'll go."

Both Ben and Raven stared at her in shock.

"Seriously?" asked Ben. "Two hours ago, you almost fainted from us talking about going outside."

"She's right. We can't let rain get inside the turbines or they'll short out. If the power dies, we're doomed. And, here she is after going outside. Just fine. She obviously went outside because we're getting power from number fourteen again."

"Go for it." Ben waved in a 'be my guest' manner. "Plenty of tarps in storage."

Raven started for the door. "We're only going to cover number fourteen right now. Surveying the rest and getting them protected from the weather is a big project." She paused, looking back. "Oh, do you have any idea who's been greasing them? Number fourteen has relatively fresh lubrication."

"Uhh." He froze, making a face like a fish out of water. "That shouldn't be possible."

"I know what I saw. Lark will back me up after she sees it." Raven lowered her voice to keep it in the room. "Noah knows who it is. Someone's going out there to maintain them, and it's not from our group."

"If true," said Lark, "why would they have you go out there to fix number fourteen instead of having this secret person do it?"

Raven stared at the glowing control panel on the far end of the room, unable to come up with a good explanation.

"They're dead," said Ben barely over a whisper.

"You knew?" Raven whirled on him.

"Nah." He stared into his mug, swirling the contents. "I'm guessing. You're right. If people have been going out there regularly, they would have fixed it already. The only reason I can think of for Noah to let us handle it is that the mysterious tech is dead."

Lark shifted her weight side to side. "What would've killed them if the air's okay?"

A fleeting image of the figure behind the glint came to mind. Could someone have been observing the windmill farm on the lookout for people? Possible, but she'd been out there for a good while after seeing someone—maybe someone—move. Anything could have happened to this theoretical secret tech that didn't involve violence, including a fatal fall from a windmill.

"When you reported the failure to Noah, it's not like he could've told you not to worry about it without you figuring out he had someone out there." Lark rummaged a filter mask out of her satchel and put it on, then exhaled hard. "I can't believe I agreed to do this. Come on. Let's go before I change my mind."

Ben raised his mug in toast.

"Welcome to come with us." Raven grinned.

"Thanks, but, someone's gotta stay behind to fill out the log sheets." He winked. "It's rough work, but I'm willing to do it."

10

UNDER WRAPS

I wonder if the guy who invented plastic realized he'd created the engine of humanity's destruction. – Ellis Wilder.

R aven led the way down a hall on level four to the storage rooms. The Arc had many storage rooms, though these days, they held mostly empty space. Pallets of raw materials for various manufacturing processes once filled them. Those pallets had almost all been wrapped in tarps or other protective packaging. Her father always used to say plastic represented the closest humanity would ever get to creating immortality. The stuff lasted forever. It used to be recycled, but they stopped doing it decades ago, likely due to the toxic byproducts being too much for the air system to handle anymore.

In addition to spare bolts, another thing they had no shortage of in the Arc was tarps or plastic sheets. Some people even wore clothes made out of them. Not the most comfortable garment material, and it didn't breathe. Plastic ponchos would keep the rain off, but no one had to worry about weather down in the tunnels.

She and Lark hunted down a giant blue tarp adequate to cover a windmill body. The one they ended up choosing had metal eyelets around the edges, perfect for securing it in place using cord.

From there, they headed upstairs and across to the security station at the end of the admin corridor. Raven went there first, assuming the door to the escape tunnel would be locked. Five security officers, including Ann and Jose, looked up at them when they entered.

"Need to run outside again for a little while. Big holes in the turbine we have to cover before it rains."

The security team exchanged looks, probably trying to figure out if this excursion fell under Noah's original permission or not. Lauren, the current administrator of the security group, picked up a desk phone and pushed a button.

"Yes, this is Lauren. That Raven girl wants to go outside again. Something about covering the turbine." Her eyebrows notched up in an expression of surprise. "All right. Thanks." She set the phone down while nodding at Jose. "It's okay. Let 'em go out."

"Whoa, they're *both* going out?" Jose stood, gesturing at them.

"Yeah. Covering a wind turbine with a tarp isn't a one-person job but it's easy," said Raven. "It's going to take us longer to get out there than actually do it. We'll be back soon."

A gurgling noise came from Lark's stomach.

"Wow. Okay." He whistled, grabbed a key, and walked with them out into the corridor.

By the time they reached the door, Lark trembled visibly. Raven tried to act overly confident to reassure her, grinning at Jose on the way past the door. The *whoosh-hiss* of Lark breathing faster and faster in the filter mask echoed off the walls behind her.

"Seriously, you don't have to be this scared. The stuff on the walls lies. Don't believe them. Look at me. I was outside for two hours. You know my father went back and forth many times."

"He died, though," replied a muffled voice. A pause. "Sorry."

"If he fell off a tower and broke his neck, it's not poison in the air that got him."

Lark walked a few steps before saying, "True." A moment later, she added, "You're not wearing a filter."

"I'm not. Doesn't it seem silly to you?"

"Not really. I don't like breathing poison."

Raven hefted the bundled tarp higher onto her shoulder. "Think about it. These filter masks are as old as everything else here. They probably stopped working years ago. Even if they were new, most people believe going outside causes instant melting. Exactly what good would a filter mask do to stop that?"

"Uhh…" Lark stopped walking. "Not much."

"C'mon. We'll be fine." She cringed a little. Most times a character in a novel said 'we'll be fine,' everyone ended up dead.

When they reached the empty elevator shaft, Raven pointed at the ladder and explained the climb. They tied the tarp into a bundle and hung it from Lark's waist. The woman might've been thirteen years older, but she also had Raven by four inches and about fifty pounds, most of it muscle.

Raven climbed first. "Oh, I gotta warn you."

"I knew it."

"No, nothing bad. It's gonna be super bright out there. Hurts the eyes for a while. Don't flip out, okay? It passes."

"Brighter than the hydroponic room?"

"A little, yeah."

"Wow." Lark whistled.

The wheel on the hatch opened easily. Raven squinted in anticipation of daylight and shoved the metal slab up and open. Lark screamed past a clenched jaw when daylight hit them, sounding more like she'd stubbed her toe on something than had the hell scared out of her. Raven, momentarily blinded, climbed out by feel, then turned to reach back for her companion.

"Keep climbing, I got you."

Lark advanced two rungs.

Raven grasped her hand and held on as the woman climbed out onto the surface.

They sprawled there waiting for their eyes to adjust, the tarp still dangling in the shaft on the rope tied around Lark's waist. It seemed less bright than before. As soon as she could do so without flinching, Raven gazed up at the sky.

Is it turning night or is the weather getting worse?

Lark murmured something unintelligible.

"What? It's hard to understand you with the mask on."

"I said holy shit!" half-yelled Lark. "Are those plants? What are they doing out here?"

"Growing." Raven grinned, stood, and pulled Lark to her feet.

Despite having a modestly darker complexion than Raven, somehow, Lark seemed paler. Her long straight hair drifted sideways in the wind. Evidently, the sensation of a breeze on her face that didn't come from a fan so shocked the woman she did nothing but stand there watching her hair for a while.

"You okay?" asked Raven, pulling at the rope to bring the tarp up out of the shaft.

"This is so surreal." Lark turned in place. "Totally not what I expected would be out here." When she faced the windmill farm, she stopped short and gasped. "Wow. They're huge!"

Raven grasped the hatch to close it. "Check this out. The gasket's disintegrated. Outside air has been leaking in already for years."

"Ack!" Lark clutched her filter mask in both hands, pressing it tighter to her face. "Are you serious?"

"Yeah. I mean, that's an isolated hallway with no ventilation system. But look around. Plants. If being outside killed, there wouldn't be plants."

Lark exhaled. "I guess."

"C'mon. You're freaking out already. Let's get this done and go back inside."

"Good plan."

They picked the tarp bundle up together and hurried across the dirt field. As soon as they went far enough to see the skeletons, Lark screamed.

"They're dead. They can't hurt you," said Raven.

Lark dropped to her knees. "The Saints."

"They're only people. Brave people who willingly died to keep the rest of us alive."

"They... melted," whispered Lark.

"Looks that way, yeah." Raven pulled at the tarp bundle. "Come on."

"I don't want to melt."

Raven sighed. "Do you have any idea how long ago they died?"

"Umm." Lark looked between the skeleton and Raven a few times before standing. "No. I've heard everything from eighty years to two hundred."

"Has to be closer to two centuries." Raven gestured around. "Poison capable of melting people in environmental suits would destroy plants. Stay calm. There's nothing out here to worry about, except falling off the tower or getting hit in the head by a chunk of metal."

Lark picked up her end of the tarp and hurried along behind her. "What? Falling metal?"

"Take a good close look at the tower when we get there."

They crossed the field to Tower 14 without another word. Again, they rigged the tarp into a hanging bundle from Lark's waist for the ladder climb. Raven snugged her gloves and scaled the tower, careful not to grab onto anything sharp and rusted. Lark came up behind her, crawling out onto the platform, shivering and stiff, evidently afraid of being high up. They both hauled the tarp up by the rope, then sat there gazing up at the windmill pod.

"Damn. You're right. It's a junk heap," said Lark after a moment.

"A vital junk heap. Here... look at this." Raven stood, opened the big side hatch, and pointed up at the hole. "Check out the size of that hole. The piece fell and tangled up in the gears."

Lark shivered, her entire demeanor once again in 'we're going to die' mode.

"What's wrong now?"

"If you're right about these towers, we really are in big trouble."

"Help me convince Ben to do something then." Raven pointed at a blob of white grease. "See. Someone's been out here. That's recent."

"Whoa. You're right." Lark stared into her eyes. "Why would they keep it secret?"

"Good question." Raven undid the knot bundling the tarp. "We can debate it inside. Let's get this thing covered before the rain starts."

11

A HUNDRED LITTLE FLAWS

Oh, not good. There shouldn't be smoke coming out of that. – Ellis Wilder.

Covering Turbine 14 with a blue plastic tarp had been more challenging than she initially thought. Controlling the tarp in the stiff breeze proved to be a complete pain in the ass. Worse, they couldn't tie it down to the gridding as it would immobilize the windmill and stop it from rotating to face into the direction of airflow—or more likely rip away as soon as a strong enough breeze pushed the massive pod around.

They ended up wrapping the pod and tying the tarp to itself to hold it in place. Anyone trying to work on the generator's insides would need to remove the tarp first, but no rain would be getting in there.

Lark's fear about the outside initially seemed as strong as a legitimate phobia, but by the time they returned to the hatch, she'd calmed down from terror to strong nervousness. Raven hadn't been able to tempt her to smell the air without a filter mask in the way, but she suspected the woman could be talked into going outside again in the future for a necessary repair.

That's how I'll win. One by one, I'll get people to help me work on the turbines. Eventually, no one will be scared of topside.

On the walk down the long escape corridor, she briefly worried about trace amounts of poison in the air. Maybe she'd been breathing stuff in she wouldn't feel right away, toxins the plant life didn't care about. Going out there and not wearing a mask might've taken twenty years off her life.

If we don't do anything, I'm not going to see forty. Dead either way... and I'd rather not die of suffocation in a tomb.

They returned to the engineering room, gave a report to Ben who still appeared stunned at Lark's abrupt turnaround from sheer terror to volunteering to go outside. The doubt in his expression boosted her confidence and set a new goal: convince her boss to visit topside before the end of the next month. Going outside did require the extra complication of getting approval from Noah. She wouldn't be able to simply go out the door. Every trip—at least until she got through to him—would require a valid reason.

Raven grinned to herself. *If he won't let me out there to do maintenance on the windmills, he'll have to admit he knows someone else is already doing that. Hmm. Did they die? Or what...?*

Since her work hours hadn't ended yet, she grabbed her tool satchel and decided to go on an inspection patrol. Her experience going to the surface left her with *way* too much excess energy to spend the next three hours sitting at her desk doing precise repair work on small appliances. She needed to move around, even if the Arc seemed to be shrinking in on her. The air really did smell unpleasant in the tunnels, laced with a mixture of body odor, the chemical twang of the scrubbers, a pervasive poo smell from the hydroponic farm, and the metallic rustiness of dying machinery.

Worse, she missed the sky.

It had been one thing to daydream based on her imagination from reading, but to really see the sky overhead, the vast openness of it, lit a spark deep in her psyche she could neither put out nor wanted to.

I get it, Dad. I really do... why didn't you take me with you?

She spent a while roaming the Arc, checking pipes, air movers, power boxes, and other components. Mostly to avoid Noah coming down on her and making it difficult to venture outside again, she didn't say anything to people she ran into about what she'd seen out there. The faint worry she might have been exposed to contamination eventually grew to the point she visited the doc.

Preston snapped awake from a nap at his desk when she walked in.

"Hi, Doc. Sorry to bug you. Do you have any way to test for... stuff?"

He chuckled. "I'm sorry, but you'll need to be a bit more specific than that."

"I went outside twice to work on the turbines. The first time, I sniffed the air without a mask. Second time, I didn't bother wearing the mask."

She expected him to gawk at her like she admitted to murdering someone, but his demeanor took on a sense of mission as though her situation afforded him an opportunity that he'd been desperate for.

"Yes, there are a few things." He leapt to his feet and gestured at the exam table. "Sit."

Raven climbed up to sit on the exam table, watching him run around the back end of the infirmary collecting an assortment of supplies from drawers. He carried a bundle to a nearby pushcart, dropped everything on it, and approached her, pulling the wheeled table behind him.

"How much of your skin was exposed to the air?"

"First time, just a little bit under the goggles and my forehead. Second time, my whole face."

"Hands?"

"No. Had gloves on."

He picked up a small square cloth patch and wiped at her poncho, dropped the patch in a plastic baggie, then repeated the process again and again, swabbing different spots on her clothing as well as her face. She sat there patiently tolerating it until he went for a syringe.

"Doc?"

"Drawing blood for testing."

"Okay."

He filled one phial with blood, then used a long cotton swab to take a sample from the back of her throat. The nose swab made her sneeze into a coughing fit.

"What are you doing?" She covered her mouth and coughed again. "Wow that tickled."

"Taking samples from your mucosal lining. I can test them for harmful substances you might have inhaled. I'll need to head down to a lab on level five. Hopefully the equipment still works." He dropped the nasal swab into a baggie. "Do you feel anything unusual? What made you come ask about this?"

She half shrugged. "Just worrying. I feel fine. Mostly."

"Mostly?" Preston quirked an eyebrow.

"Slightly dizzy and sluggish, but only after I came back inside."

He looked into her eyes, his expression calm. "Your body is used to the atmosphere down here. After getting a taste of fresh air, it could be upset."

"Do you think it's toxic out there?"

"I don't have enough information to give an opinion." He shot a look at the cart of samples like a child eyeing birthday presents he *really* wanted to open.

"You know something…"

"It is possible I am aware of certain things not considered public knowledge. Nothing I'm permitted to speak of. Patient confidentiality."

Raven tilted her head. "Have you been outside?"

"No."

"But you know someone who has been… the one who's maintaining the windmills."

Preston pursed his lips. "Assuming anyone would be so selfless as to risk the contamination of the outside world for the benefit of the Arc, they would do so knowing it leads to a shortened life and a likely painful death."

"So there is someone. Are you testing them?"

He didn't move.

"You can't. Or at least, if you can, you can't talk about it."

"You're guessing." He half smiled.

"Guessing doesn't prove me wrong." She winked. "So, I was thinking. Why would Noah approve me going out there to check on the windmill if someone already maintained them? At first, I thought maybe this person died. But no one's gone mysteriously missing."

Preston smiled the rest of the way. "The dead cannot die again."

"Huh? That doesn't make any sense."

"It does. If you think. Now, if you'll excuse me, I need to get these samples to the lab."

"Grr." She chuckled. "Okay. Thanks."

He went left; she turned right.

The heck does he mean... can't die again.

The thought rattled around in her brain as she continued inspecting anything along her path that could potentially break down and need repair. Eventually, she ended up on level four and went into the hydroponic farm. Rows and rows of powerful artificial sun lamps hung over massive troughs filled with viscous green liquid. As a kid, she'd have been tempted to bring books in here for easier reading except for the horrible smell, humidity, and heat.

Of the three people tending the plants at the moment, she only really knew one, a woman named Baylee who could've been her mother by age—if she'd gotten pregnant at fourteen. Baylee didn't use a last name, a common habit of those whose births had been a matter of duty to society rather than love. Sometimes, like with Chase, a person made up a last name because they liked it. Raven kept her father's surname Wilder, but didn't often mention it. The only reason she even knew it at all is he'd written it on the storage trunk he kept his 'exploration stuff' in.

Unlike most of the white people in the Arc, Baylee had blonde hair and a serious tan. That tended to happen when one spent most of their wake time bathed in artificial sunlight. Hydroponic workers typically wore only sleeveless inside shirts and shorts due to the heat in here. This room usually stayed at around ninety degrees, making it the warmest spot in the entire Arc.

Being in here also required speaking in a raised voice to be heard over the thrum of ventilation fans. An important part of the atmospheric plan involved running all the Arc's air through this chamber so the plants could process the CO_2. Intakes at one end routed the air back to the HVAC room where it went through the filtration components before being passed to the distribution fans and going around for another cycle.

Having no real interest in spending time in sweltering humidity nor shedding half her clothes, she decided to talk to Baylee and ask about problems rather than inspecting every tank. The woman appeared to be checking the progress of a plant full of hanging pods, peas or beans of some kind, and looked up at her approach.

"Hey, Bayles," said Raven. "How goes?"

"Not bad. What brings you down to the hot box?"

"Couldn't sit still at my desk, so I decided to walk around and inspect stuff, trying to catch problems before they get too big to tackle. Stuff okay in here?"

"Same as usual. Everything is so damn old it's a miracle any of it still works."

Raven almost chuckled, but after seeing the state of the windmills, she couldn't. Breakdowns could be funny when annoying, not when they could kill everyone. "We're doing the best we can."

"It's all any of us *can* do, right?" Baylee resumed checking pods. "I'm happy with these beans. The plants are developing unusually well."

"What's so odd about it?" Raven leaned closer for a better look— and nearly fell on her ass when her foot shot out from under her. She caught herself half on Baylee, half on the tank, causing the fluid inside to slosh. "Gah!"

"Watch where you step." Baylee helped her upright.

Raven looked down at a puddle of hydroponic fluid, apparently coming from a drip somewhere on the bottom of the tank. "It's leaking?"

"Yeah. Been like that a while now. Every time I patch one, a new leak starts somewhere else. It never really ends. Though, past couple weeks, it's starting to feel like I can't keep up with it."

Raven crouched to examine the underside of the tank. The seep appeared to be coming from the join between Plexiglas panels. "It's oozing out the seam."

"Yep. Seams, rivets, screws... these tanks are *way* past their expected lifespan." Baylee gestured at the bean plants. "But hey, the veggies still like them. No idea why this batch is doing so well, but I'm not going to complain."

"Finally, some good news." Raven chuckled, then peered up at the vents. *Is Noah already pulling in outside air?*

"Seriously." Baylee wagged her eyebrows. "Between the tanks, the pumps, seed bins cracking... it's like this place is exploding in super slow motion. Last week, Mel got blasted in the face when a hose ruptured."

Raven cringed. This liquid smelled bad enough. She didn't want to even think what it might taste like. "Ack. Is she okay?"

"Yeah. She's tough. Never saw someone fix a hose while puking before."

"Ugh." Raven shuddered. "I hope she went to see Doc. This stuff can't be healthy to swallow."

Baylee nodded. "Yeah, she saw him. Far as I know, she's good. Didn't swallow any of it."

They chatted for a while more about mechanical failures, leaks, and so on before the heat grew too much and she excused herself. Conversation about continuous failure and problems did little to help her mood, but it cured the restless energy that made sitting at her workstation annoying. More worried than ever a critical number of small problems appeared to be stacking up, she decided to do something more engrossing than walking around.

Once back at her desk, she resumed trying to repair the various devices waiting in a queue for attention. The tedious work successfully distracted her from the fear that at any second the home she'd known her entire life would come metaphorically crashing down around her. Irony in the thought got her laughing. A literal cave-in hadn't even been on the list of possible catastrophes. Having at least one potential disaster seem unlikely felt good in a way.

The toaster she presently worked on bore little resemblance to what it once looked like. Almost nothing remained of its original parts except for the on button. Somewhere, she'd heard the Arc had been activated around the year 2050-something, during the early stages of the Great Death. After generations of living underground with broken computers, no one had a clue what the current year was. Books told her that a 'day' had twenty-four hours with varying durations of light and dark based on the season. People didn't even use the word 'day' anymore, referring to their activity periods as a 'wake.' Time had been disassociated from the sun since well before the last functioning computer in the Arc shut down for the last time.

Based on birth and death records, most people accepted approximately 300 years had passed since the doors first sealed, with some going as far as suggesting 400 or even longer. That *anything* at all continued to function had to be a feat of monumental luck—or sheer determination on humanity's part not to go extinct.

She moved on from the toaster no power on Earth could ever make work again to a medium-sized pump, one of the units responsible for moving drinking water into the gravity tanks that fed faucets and toilets. Forty minutes later, she had it halfway taken apart and discovered the problem: a cracked impellor shaft. Machining a simple steel rod to replace it wouldn't take too long.

All of this stuff is going to break beyond our ability to fix within my lifetime.

Raven got up and crossed the room to one of the three machine presses. They kept a stock of ingots recycled from parts too worn out to repair. Lately, though, they hadn't been able to melt any new scrap down. They'd run out of propane a few years ago, and didn't have a ready source of coal—or even wood. Or so she'd thought. Thick forests outside offered new hope, if she could figure out a way to burn a wood fire hot enough to melt steel. Until that happened, the shelf full of ingots represented the last of their ability to manufacture new parts for various machines. Perhaps using up some of it on a water pump would be a waste. Should she save the metal for fixing something more vital like a CO2 scrubber or the turbines? People could carry water around in buckets. Pumping it to faucets was a convenience.

If the scrubbers fail, it's not going to be due to a small metal part. It'll be the chemicals.

She knew the basics of it. The machines used a monoethanolamine substrate that chemically bound to CO2, extracting it from air bubbled through it. The substrate would eventually saturate and become unable to take on more gas, at which point the reaction could be reversed by heat. This, naturally, released a ton of CO2. As far as she knew, whenever a scrubber got to the point of needing to be cooked off, Ben would run the process and transfer the near pure CO2 into pressurized tanks. What happened to it then, she didn't know. Possibly, some of it went to the hydroponic farm for the plants. Maybe they stored it downstairs. That didn't seem feasible as they'd soon run out of empty canisters.

We're all going to die in here. She sighed out her nose.

The last death occurred a few months ago when one of the Karens succumbed to an illness Doc couldn't identify. She'd been sixty-two. They had a brief funeral for her attended by all. Remembering it got her thinking about other deaths. A younger guy, late thirties she vaguely remembered being named Zac, died suddenly for no obvious reason. They didn't have a funeral for him she could recall.

Oh, shit... Raven gasped, nearly dropping the metal piece she'd been grinding into a rod. *People can't die if they're already dead. No funeral...* She didn't know what happened to the bodies of the dead, but in Karen's case, she'd seen the woman's remains during the funeral. One day, people simply talked about Zac having died the other day. No funeral. No body.

He didn't really die. She peered up at the ceiling. *Outside? Was that him on the other tower? Why would he be so far away?*

"Hey," chirped Tinsley, her voice muted under a filter mask.

Raven about jumped out of her poncho, but managed not to

scream. Her kid adored sneaking up on her while pretending not to have tried to. "Don't do that…"

"Got ya." She giggled, then hugged her.

"You did." Raven kissed her on the head and resumed machining the rod. "Are you feeling better?"

"A little."

"Good. Give me a bit to finish this, then I think I'm gonna call it an early day."

"I'm smiling. You can't see it because I have this stupid thing on my face."

"Hah." She almost said 'take it off, they're too old to be useful,' but didn't. The filter could still protect against dust.

The child watched her work in silent curiosity. Soon, she got the replacement rod to the same size and shape as the broken one from the pump. Tinsley followed her across the room to her desk and sat on a nearby box. She coughed every so often, but not too severely.

"Breathing okay?"

Tinsley nodded. "I think I'm sick."

"Head stuffy?"

"No. Just coughs an' the dizzy."

Raven attached the rod to the impellor and put it back in the flow guide. "Something bothering your throat?"

"Obviously." Tinsley rolled her eyes. "I'm coughing."

"Hah."

"Mommy? What was it like when people didn't have to hide underground?"

"Hmm. It's been a long time, might be hard for me to remember."

Tinsley laughed.

"Well…" Raven smiled as she tightened the screws holding two halves of the flow guide together, thinking of things she'd read about. "Most people lived so far away from their jobs they needed cars to get there and they didn't need clocks to tell them when to wake up because light came from the sky to chase them out of bed. Light they couldn't just turn off."

"You're making that up." Tinsley folded her arms. "There's no such thing as a light you can't turn off."

Raven inserted the reassembled pump unit into the housing. "Didn't you learn about planets in school?"

"A little." Tinsley shrugged. "Sienna's teaching us about words and numbers."

"Okay. See, we live on a planet called Earth. It's basically a giant rock shaped like a ball."

"Yeah. There's a globe in the classroom." Tinsley held her hands up as if holding a big sphere. "The real one's a lot bigger."

Raven ruffled her daughter's hair. "Sure is."

Tinsley coughed into the filter mask. "Did it fall off? Is that why stuff died?"

"Fall off?" Raven blinked. "What do you mean?"

"The metal thing that holds the globe. Did the real one fall off?"

"Oh." Raven poked her in the forehead. "The real one doesn't have a bracket. That's only for the model."

"What holds it up if it's not got a metal thing?"

"It floats in outer space, orbiting the sun. That's the light we can't turn off." Raven plucked a ball bearing from a tray on her desk and a light bulb, holding them up to demonstrate orbiting. "The Earth turns, so when the part we're on is away from the sun, it's dark. When we come around the other side, light."

"Oh." Tinsley watched the ball bearing go around a few times before staring into her eyes—and lapsed into a mild coughing fit.

Raven set the stuff down on the desk and patted the girl's back, her worry increasing. She'd never known anyone to cough in that way without being sick. Yet, Tinsley didn't sound stuffed up. Her nose didn't run. No nausea or fever. She *did* seem unusually sedate. For this kid, that meant tired. Some lethargy seemed appropriate for a cold or flu, but she had no other signs of sickness.

"Mommy..." Tinsley pulled the filter mask down off her face once the coughing stopped, and took a big breath. "I don't wanna wear this. It's hard to breathe."

Despite the doc advising it, Raven found herself doubting his advice. The ancient filters wouldn't be of much use to begin with, plus she didn't really believe contamination had anything to do with the child's discomfort. She suspected the air itself as the problem, and no simple filter mask would help. Perhaps an oxygenating rebreather would, but none of those remained usable.

What happened that three thousand rebreathers all got used up? She glanced up at the filthy concrete overhead. *Level one? Did someone try opening the door and let in a bunch of bad air? Or maybe some kind of accident happened. They used to manufacture plastic and other chemicals downstairs.*

"All right. You can leave it off for a bit and see if helps."

Tinsley flashed a giant grin and let the mask dangle around her neck on its strap. "Did you really go to topside?"

"Where did you hear that?" Raven looked around to see who might be eavesdropping. Lark, at the next workstation, wouldn't care. Ben had gone off somewhere... maybe to talk to Noah about her ideas. Shaw, Trenton, and Ryan weren't at their desks and no one appeared to be hovering by the door. "And yes, I did."

"Ooh!" Tinsley's eyes lit up. "Like grandpa."

Her heart weighed down under a crush of sorrow, which she tried to keep from showing on her face. The girl had been two when Dad disappeared. She didn't remember the hours he'd spent holding her or watching her while Raven had to work. But, she made damn sure her daughter knew all about him.

"Almost. I didn't go very far. Only to the turbine farm. One of them broke and needed to be fixed."

"What was it like?" Tinsley leaned forward and grabbed her arm.

Raven pulled her daughter up to sit in her lap. "Bright. So bright it hurt my eyes."

"Wow. Like the farm?"

"Almost. In a way it was brighter, but also not."

"Huh?" Tinsley's eyebrows formed a flat line. "That doesn't make sense."

Raven swayed side to side. "The whole hydroponic room isn't

bright, only above the tanks. Outside, it wasn't exactly as bright as the grow lamps, but the light covered everything."

"I wanna see it!" Tinsley bounced in her lap.

"Come on, you know it's against the rules to go outside," said Raven with a hint of sarcasm.

Tinsley's 'give me a break' smirk made her look closer to sixteen than six. "You went outside."

"The boss gave me permission because I had to fix the fans."

"Like the Saints?" Tinsley asked in a quiet, reverent voice.

Kind of. Only... I came back.

She exhaled. "They were a lot braver than me. I watched grandpa go outside before and it didn't hurt him. The Saints lived a really long time ago. They knew going out there back then would probably kill them."

"Oh." Tinsley hugged her. "You're not allowed to die."

"I won't. At least, not from just going outside." Again, she looked around to make sure the wrong people wouldn't overhear her. "It's okay out there now. Everything's covered in green plants."

"I wanna see!" whisper-shouted Tinsley, bouncing again.

"I can't just go outside to go outside. We need a reason."

The girl held her chin up. "Wanting to see is a reason."

"It is, but not one Noah's going to like."

"He's a butt."

Chuckling, Raven shifted the girl in her lap so she could finish putting the pump unit back together. "Let me finish this up and we'll get out of here."

"Okay," said Tinsley... before coughing again.

RULES

I never knew your mother. Sure, we shared a room for twelve years, but that doesn't mean I knew her. – Ellis Wilder.

Much like she did every wake after spending enough time working, Raven headed to the cafeteria. With the exception of the primary administrator's quarters, no one's private rooms had food prep stations. It made sense. Less power consumption, less risk of fires, cheaper not to require 2,000 stoves and 2,000 refrigerators. Plus, with all the food being managed and prepared by people who did it as their job, it allowed for better control and management of resources.

That they still put stuff out in a buffet style offered a little bit of reassurance to an otherwise bleak outlook.

We're not running out of food at least. Just air. Small miracles.

Sienna and the other four children already sat in their usual spot at one of the long steel tables, near a concrete column close to the corner up front by the serving area. Josh spotted them and waved. This made the other three kids look up and wave as well.

Raven returned the wave and headed over to the line, collecting a plate of beanloaf, some potatoes, and broccoli for herself and Tinsley. The girl helped out by grabbing two dinner rolls.

The suspiciously rectangular brown slices consisted of a mixture of kidney beans, mushrooms, and flour—or something to that effect—and represented the cooks' best attempt to present a food close to meat. Having never tasted actual meat, only read about it, she had nothing to compare it to for accuracy. They may well have gotten the taste right, but she doubted real meat had the consistency of scrambled eggs left to sit out in the air for hours.

Characters in the novels she read and people who lived before the Great Death had the luxury of liking or disliking food and not eating the stuff they couldn't stand. Arc dwellers, not so much. In truth, she had no strong opinion about the beanloaf beyond them serving a dish primarily made of beans alongside broccoli in a closed atmosphere amounted to a mistake.

The air scrubbers are already dying. We shouldn't taunt them.

They carried their trays to the table, sitting with the others.

Immediate conversation erupted among the kids, who filled Tinsley in on all the games she missed when she ran off to spend time with her mother. Josh, Cheyenne, Xan, and Ariana behaved more like siblings than classmates. Unsurprising since they had essentially become so, living with Sienna and having her as a teacher. It almost seemed pointless for them to bother going to the classroom, but they still did. Since Tinsley lived with her mother, they treated her like a friend more than a sister, or perhaps somewhere in between.

"How'd it go out there?" asked Sienna.

"Hunk of metal fell into the gears. Got the turbine up and running again."

"Say what?" Sienna blinked. "How's a piece of metal end up inside the machine?"

Raven let a silent sigh slide out her nostrils. *I don't want to scare the kids or start a panic.* "A piece of the outer shell rusted off and fell in."

"Oh…" Her 'sister' took a moment to process that, then her eyebrows went up, lips pursing. The implication finally sank in.

"Yeah." Raven looked down at her food. "Exactly."

Sienna leaned forward, lowering her voice. "Just the one, or are they all that bad?"

"None of the others had a hole as big…" Raven sliced off a cube of beanloaf with her fork. "Went back up with a tarp to keep the rain from getting into it. Noah's considering my request for a larger project to do the same for the others."

"He damn well better say yes." Sienna frowned. "Sometimes I don't know what gets into that man's head."

"You know he's only trying to keep everyone safe." Raven ate the hunk of not-meat, continuing to talk around the gelatinous mass as she chewed. "He was pretty young when he got elected."

"What's that have to do with anything?" Sienna stared, her fork— and a bit of broccoli—dangling from her fingers.

Raven waved in a noncommittal gesture. "Just saying. Probably a lot of guessing involved in his decisions."

An abrupt cough launched a piece of broccoli from Tinsley's mouth across the table. It bounced off Xan's face and landed next to his plate. He scrunched up his nose in an 'eww' gesture, cringing. Ariana, seated next to him, grabbed and ate it.

Xan nearly threw up while the other kids all cringed—except for Tinsley who hadn't noticed since she continued coughing into both hands, her eyes watering.

"Tins?" Raven swatted her on the back, worried she might've gotten food into her throat.

"I'm 'kay," rasped Tinsley, gripping the edge of the table. She peered up at her mother, left eye closed, right one squinting, red, and watery. "Not choking."

"Don't be nasty." Xan nudged Ariana.

"It's bad to waste food," said the nine-year-old, blasé as anything.

"Mom!" Cheyenne waved at Sienna. "Ari just ate that after Tins coughed it up."

"I didn't even chew it yet." Tinsley wiped her face.

"Ugh." Xan closed his eyes. "Stop. I'm gonna be sick."

The kids laughed at him. Ariana's giggle broke into a mild cough.

"Uh oh. You made her sick." Josh tossed a napkin at Tinsley.

Josh, Cheyenne, and Xan leaned away from the table.

"I'm not sick." Tinsley resumed eating. "An' people don't get sick so fast."

"Did you take her to the doc?" asked Sienna.

"Yeah. First thing this wake. Remember? The filter mask?"

Sienna rubbed her forehead. "Oh, right. Sorry. It's been nuts today. The kids all have extra energy."

"Maybe she inhaled some dust. Doesn't seem like she's got a cold." Raven eyed Ariana, worry building up in her gut. *The two youngest.*

"I feel better. My head still hurts a little, but not as bad." Tinsley ate another hunk of beanloaf, clearly not suffering a loss of appetite.

Raven twisted to look out over the cafeteria. Roughly eighty other people sat scattered around a room that could seat six hundred. Every so often, someone cleared their throat. Daniel, an older man who'd recently hit eighty, coughed, too. His sounded worse than Tinsley's. He patted himself on the chest, seeming unable to draw a breath inward. Annoyance in his eyes shifted to alarm. For a moment, everything else in the world stopped existing but the old man struggling to breathe. Raven stared at him transfixed at his distorted, fluttering lip, flying spittle, hand swatting at his chest.

Maybe he's got a cold...

Daniel collapsed off the bench, gasping for air.

The man sitting next to him, fortunately, had fast enough reflexes to catch the old guy before his head hit the concrete floor. Raven felt like a ghostly observer apart from this reality, sitting there in mute shock, unable to move. A woman and two other men ran over to Daniel, who'd lost consciousness. They picked him up and hurried him out, heading toward the infirmary.

Once they'd left the cafeteria, she turned back to face her dinner, not sure how to process what she'd witnessed. Daniel had always been nice to her. Despite being no relation, he'd always kind of felt like a grandfather. And... he'd given her the notebook Dad left with him in case he went out and failed to return. Watching Daniel collapse hit her hard, her emotions storming at the reminder of her father.

It wasn't the first time she'd seen an older person have a medical problem, but too many things already stacked up on her mind for her to dismiss it. The leaky hydroponic fluid, struggling CO_2 scrubbers, frequent breakdowns of ventilation fans... not to mention the turbines.

All of a sudden, the idea of *staying* outside didn't feel all too crazy —just mostly nuts.

Raven pressed a hand to the front of her throat at a sensation that could have been a tiny bit of beanloaf she didn't swallow or the beginning of a hole forming in her trachea from whatever horror she'd breathed outside. She swallowed a few times, but the nagging presence didn't go anywhere.

"You okay?" asked Sienna.

"Huh?" Raven looked up, her gaze focusing on her friend.

"Something wrong with your throat? You had this far off look."

Tinsley glanced up at her, worried.

"No, just thinking." Raven picked up her water cup and drained it in a series of rapid gulps. She sat there breathing rapidly for a few seconds afterward, then realized the discomfort in her throat had vanished. Relief almost made her collapse over the table. *Just a bit of food. Dammit, girl. Hold it together.*

"Mr. Daniel's sick," said Josh. "Is he gonna die?"

The kids fell quiet.

"I don't know," said Sienna. "He's pretty old, but he's tough. Not too many people live to eighty."

"Wow. That's *really* old," said Ariana. "More than ten of me."

Sienna frowned. "Come on, Ari. You know math better than that. How old are you?"

"Nine." She swished her feet side to side.

"What's ten times nine?"

Ariana scrunched up her face, thinking. "Nineteen?"

Josh and Cheyenne covered their mouths, snickering.

"She got the word wrong," said Tinsley. "She's got the right number in her head but she said it wrong."

Ariana glanced at her, then Sienna. "Nine... tee?"

"Right. And is eighty more or less than ninety?" Sienna raised an eyebrow.

"Umm. Not as much." Ariana bit her lip.

"School's done for the wake," said Cheyenne. "Can we not math now?"

The kids spent the remainder of dinner time talking about a board game they'd played earlier while Raven forced herself to talk about everything other than her fear about the Arc's systems being so near collapse. Going outside had potentially been a bad thing as it tempted her to think more about ways to survive on the surface than fix the machinery down here.

We've repaired and fixed and rebuilt everything so many times there's nothing else we can do. She squeezed her fist tight, a release of frustration no one noticed. *What would I be thinking if I hadn't gone out there? If topside still scared the hell out of me. If it wasn't an option... would I give up?*

"Be right back."

Raven grabbed her empty cup, climbed out of the bench seat, and went over to the serving station to refill it with water. Tinsley trailed after her. While Raven drank an entire cup of water standing in front of the dispenser, Tinsley took a second—albeit small—helping of broccoli in a bowl and hurried back to the table.

If I had no other option, could I come up with some plan to fix things? Noah will laugh at me if I suggest everyone go outside. She refilled the cup and drank another mouthful. *I still don't know if it really is safe. Looks okay. Smells okay. But, some poisons are invisible.* It occurred to her the tickle in her throat had been about the same spot the doc swabbed earlier. Or maybe she imagined it.

Despite trying to focus on a theoretical situation where topside *was* deadly, her mind kept circling back to futility. All the vital machines had been pushed to the breaking point. The Arc no longer had the capability to manufacture new parts, except for small metal pieces. Her team had pulled off amazing feats of repair work on the CO_2 scrubbers without any of them being a true chemist—but machines that ought to keep the air perfect for 2,000 people allowed 183—possibly 182 now—to gradually suffocate.

If I'm not overreacting, we're in trouble. She desperately needed to talk it out with Sienna, the only one in the entire Arc she trusted enough to bare her deepest insecurities to. But... having time alone with her so they could talk freely away from little ears didn't happen too often lately. She admired her friend's devotion to kids no one else wanted to love, but sometimes, being unable to get her alone proved super frustrating.

She and Tinsley followed the others to Sienna's quarters, one of the large units intended for a full family. Although it made for a longer walk to the central hub, no way could she cram herself and four kids into a single bed. Her place had three bedrooms and a large common area that reminded Raven of the 'living rooms' in houses before the Great Death.

The kids flopped on the floor in front of the C-shaped sofa and proceeded to set up a board game. Raven took the opportunity to pull Sienna off to the little hallway leading to the master bedroom. There, she explained the depths of her worries.

Sienna's eyes widened at the description of the crumbling turbines. They widened more upon hearing her story of how three CO_2 scrubbers almost didn't turn back on. When Raven admitted to taking the filter mask off outside, her as-good-as sister squeaked and clamp-hugged her.

"Calm down. It's fine." Raven squeezed her back.

"No it isn't," muttered Sienna into her ear. "You don't know what you breathed in."

"My gut says it's fine. Dad kept going out there and he never got sick. I actually felt better out there than I do right now."

Sienna leaned back and stared into her eyes. "What?"

"Like I had more energy."

"This is about your father, isn't it? You think you're going to find him."

Raven looked down. "Honestly? No. The idea never even came to mind. He wouldn't have stayed away for four years. Something happened to him out there. But I mean, he spent days topside and didn't get sick."

"That we saw. What if he did get really sick but it's something no one could see until he died?"

"I don't think so. He'd have acted different. Lost weight. You just *know* when something's not right with someone. You should see all the plants…"

Sienna fidgeted. "I think you're kinda panicking. Don't do anything crazy, okay? Take a couple wakes and think."

"Yeah. You're right. I'm not my father."

"Heh. Yeah. The man would get an idea in his head and just throw himself into it without much planning."

"True. He thought greatness never came from carefully formulated plans. People let their fear of failure cause them to fail."

"C'mon." Sienna pulled her into the common room so they could watch the kids having fun. "Your dad loved his sayings, didn't he?"

Raven laughed. "Yeah. Has a whole notebook full of them."

ONCE THE YAWNING STARTED, RAVEN COLLECTED TINSLEY AND MADE the trek down the hall to their home.

Neither spoke as they shed their ponchos and inside clothes, then climbed into the shower chamber. She washed Tinsley's hair using the same vegetable-oil derived soap people in the Arc had been using for generations. It didn't lather much, but it got rid of the dirt. How much longer would it be before that ran out, too? They couldn't have an infinite amount of lye, and they certainly didn't have wood to reduce into ash.

Not tree wood. They burn inedible plant parts.

Tinsley took the soap and washed herself. Raven leaned her face into the spray of warm water. The same water pouring over her had done so hundreds of times. She showered in water that had probably been consumed by everyone in the Arc, gone down the sewer system, and been purified back into circulation over and over again.

The air scrubbers are barely keeping up. What's slipping through the water filtration system?

Sudden, intense nausea—as though she stood under a spray of untreated urine—almost made her throw up. Up until that moment, she'd never thought twice about drinking water or showering. *Everything here is a closed system. Keep out contamination.*

Or at least it used to be. The water crew on level six had tapped an underground water source maybe forty years ago. Drawing from a well so deep beneath the surface had a minimal risk of contamination since they figured the dirt would act like a filter. Of course, they still ran it through the processing system before letting anyone drink it.

Maybe this isn't fully recirculated water anymore.

Regardless of the truth, she convinced herself the water coming out of the shower head came from a subterranean well and had never before gone through anyone's kidneys. That kept her from vomiting. She didn't mind so much the idea of filtering and reusing water. Rather, she didn't trust the filter system to still work properly. Like everything else here, it had been pressed into service well beyond any reasonable expectation of functional lifespan.

What's going to kill us first? The air or disease from bad water?

She grabbed the soap and started washing Tinsley faster, so they could get out from under the potentially dangerous liquid.

"What's wrong?" asked Tinsley.

"Just hurrying up."

"Are we running out of water?"

"I... no. I'm just worrying about everything today." She sighed, handed the soap back to the girl, and waited.

Tinsley didn't rush, though she stopped dawdling or playing in the water. Every minute or so, a weak cough like the girl had walked into a cloud of smoke echoed in the shower chamber. Once she finished, she passed the soap up—and then played with an empty plastic bottle while her mother hurriedly washed. Showering done, she grabbed a toothbrush and scooped some paste out of the jar, then crouched to brush her daughter's teeth. Tinsley stood there making silly faces with her mouth open the whole time, then held her face in the shower stream to rinse the foam away.

Doc tests the water a couple times a week. He'd issue a warning if he found a problem.

Raven brushed her teeth, then they exited the shower, dried off, and got in bed for story time, back in the same nightgowns they'd worn all week. Raven read a few chapters of *James and the Giant Peach* to her, their twentieth or so time going through the book. The mechanical clock dials indicated the time as 0-1-1-4 when Tinsley at last, fell asleep. Raven sat there staring at the contraption she'd made as a teen, the rapid clicking of the mechanism remarkably loud in the otherwise silent room.

That's one of four working clocks. Won't be long before everyone's guessing when their wake starts. Maybe they'll make my clock the official Arc time. The electronic ones are almost gone.

Raven scooted down to lay flat, one arm tucked around her slight daughter, holding the child close. Dread that at any moment they could go to sleep and not wake up, suffocating in their sleep, kept her eyes wide open. She hated not knowing why her kid coughed. She hated the powerlessness of being unable to fix her even more. It didn't matter what Noah said, if she found clear proof the ventilation system was dying, she'd grab Tinsley and go topside.

Random worries kept her staring at the ceiling. When next she looked over at the clock, the dials read 0-1-4-6. Long before she ever took her first breath, time ceased being a measure of planetary rotation and became a simple tracking of passing hours. No one had any idea if their clocks came close to what the old world would have called accurate time.

Just counting hours...

"Mommy? Why aren't you sleeping?" whispered Tinsley.

"Thinking."

"What about?"

Raven pictured the rusting windmill towers collapsing into a twisted tangle of metal and billowing dust, all the lights down here going out. Scrubbers off. The constant whirr from the ventilation fans falling silent. No matter where anyone went in the Arc, they couldn't escape the sound, so pervasive she didn't even notice it anymore unless—like now—she thought specifically about it. When the systems failed, the tunnels would fall truly silent. As silent as it had been outside, far from the rattling thrum of fans.

So many plants.

As much as she wanted to trust topside, as much as she wanted to tell herself she'd felt *better* out there, Raven couldn't simply brush off the scary stories she'd heard constantly as a child about the death lurking outside. If it came down to Noah refusing to listen to her, she'd risk taking Tinsley out there. Her child wouldn't suffocate in a subterranean tomb. Temptation to sneak out there right now and let the girl see the truth gnawed at her, but she also couldn't be reckless with her daughter's health.

She had to know if the doc found anything in those samples.

"Mommy?" asked Tinsley in a dazed half-awake voice.

"Yes?"

"What are you thinking about?" Tinsley pushed herself up to sit.

The girl's voice in Raven's mind. *I wanna see! I wanna see!*

"Just an idea."

"What kind of idea?" Tinsley tilted her head to the left. Her frizzy hair draped off her shoulder, hanging almost to the mattress.

"The kind of idea we need to keep quiet and not tell anyone."

"Ooh!" Tinsley went wide-eyed, but clamped both hands over her mouth as a coughing fit took her. She flopped back down, her head on her mother's shoulder.

Dammit! She's getting worse. Raven sat up and held Tinsley, patting her back until she stopped coughing. A war raged in her mind. Some invisible poison with no smell or taste *might* be outside, but the air here already hurt her child, probably the hydroponic chemicals being sucked into the ventilation system.

The girls' eyes widened. "Are we gonna do something bad?"

"Not bad. A little sneaky. We'll get in trouble if they catch us."

Tinsley grinned, bouncing, an eager gleam in her eyes. "I won't tell anyone. What is it?"

Yeah. The two of us are just like Dad. Anything we can get away with. "Try to sleep now. I have to do some things first."

"Tell me!" Tinsley bounced in her lap.

"If I say any more, you're going to be too excited to sleep."

"Mom..." Tinsley folded her arms. "I'm already too excited to sleep. You've already said too much."

Raven shifted to lie down again. *If she has another choking fit like that, screw what the doc finds.* "Do you want to see topside?"

The child's eyes grew huge and round. She stared for a moment, too stunned to speak, then whispered, "Yeah."

"Okay. End of next wake. Don't say anything to anyone, even Sienna and the other kids... or we won't be able to go see."

"Promise," whispered Tinsley.

Much to Raven's surprise—and worry—the child fell asleep soon after.

13

OUR SECRET

When a person takes risks to serve a greater need, it's heroic. Now, when they take risks for no good reason? That's called having fun. – Ellis Wilder.

Alarm bells rang far too soon.

Raven reluctantly got out of bed, glared at the clock showing 0-9-5-7, and shut off the ringer. Tinsley didn't stir at all. At the edge of panic, she grabbed her daughter by the shoulders and lightly shook her.

"Hey, kiddo. It's wake time."

A few seconds later when Tinsley gave a soft moan, Raven's heart started beating again.

Don't flip out. We both stayed up too late.

She hurriedly changed from her nightgown to her usual clothes, then dressed Tinsley as if changing a life-sized doll. The girl finally woke up at Raven tickling her feet before putting the tread socks on her.

Too close to being late to suffer the dawdling of an overtired six-year-old, Raven picked her up and carried her out into the hall. She stopped by the cafeteria only long enough to grab breakfast muffins, not staying there to eat. Tinsley gnawed on hers while being carried to the school room. Raven set her on her feet at the doorway and waved to Sienna, who'd already started the wake period's lessons. Tinsley gave her a quick hug and trudged to her desk. Mind swimming with anxiety, Raven headed down the hall to the engineering room and her workstation.

She flopped in her chair, eating her muffin while starting on the repair queue lined up along the edge of her table—mostly fan motors used in the vast maze of ventilation ducts. From the look of it, Shaw and Trenton had spent all of last wake swapping dead units out and left the broken ones on her and Lark's workstations.

Fortunately, most of the time the fan motors failed, they only needed a good cleaning. Every so often, she'd run into one that burned out and required replacing the coils, brushes, or in some cases, control board. They had a respectable stock of spare boards and parts from other fan motors too far gone to get back online. A mild sense of security came from not having to worry they'd start losing pusher fans any time soon, but it didn't reassure her much.

Circulating stale air doesn't help anyone.

"What the hell do you expect me to do with it?" shouted Shaw.

Raven jumped, startled at the sudden outburst. She twisted to look at the doorway to Ben's office.

"Fix them," said the boss.

Shaw exhaled hard, then not-quite-yelled, "Have you listened to anything I said in the past ten minutes? Do you know magic? That's the only way we're going to squeeze any more life out of those things."

Ugh. Now what?

"Well… I don't know what you expect me to say here." A loud metallic creak—the spring in Ben's desk chair—drowned out a sigh. "Look, we have what we have. And we've been keeping things flowing here for hundreds of years. We can figure it out. Let me talk to Baylee. Maybe we can convince them to run another crop of cotton-plus."

Shaw stormed out of the office, carrying a forty-inch-square air filter panel. He stopped three steps into the room, spun on his heel, and jabbed the filter square in Ben's direction. "These things are clapped out. They're basically doing nothing but slowing down the airflow."

"Exactly why we'll get them to produce some cotton-plus and we can make new liners." Another creak came from Ben's chair. He appeared in the doorway a moment later.

"That will take months." Shaw banged the filter panel on his leg, releasing an explosion of grey dust. "Months we don't really have. Everyone will end up having to wear filter masks inside until this is taken care of. It's like a damn snowstorm in the ducts, all the dust blowing around."

Ben shooed Shaw toward the adjacent HVAC room. "Understood. Do what you can."

Raven looked away before either of them noticed her listening in. Muttering to himself about 'this is all we need,' Ben hurried out into the hall, most likely on his way to either hydroponics or Noah's office.

As soon as the sound of his footsteps grew too faint to hear, Raven jumped out of her chair and ran out, heading to the infirmary. There, she found the doc checking on Daniel, who lay in one of the recovery beds wearing a breathing mask. Seeing the doctor treat the old man with oxygen further convinced her the air quality in the Arc had reached a point of being dangerous. All the dust that burst from the filter panel... maybe it's what made Tinsley cough so much.

Filter mask...

"Doc?" asked Raven, walking in. "How is he?"

"Hard to say. He never regained consciousness." The doc patted Daniel on the shoulder, then approached Raven, meeting her halfway across the infirmary. "I haven't yet figured out if he suffered brain damage or not."

"Did he have one of those heart things?"

"No. At least if he did it was a very mild one. Best I can tell, he just stopped breathing for a while. CPR worked, though if he was out for too long, he's already gone."

Raven leaned to the side to look past the Doc at the frail old man lying in the bed, too saddened at the thought to come up with anything to say. Making it to eighty had been an impressive accomplishment few people managed. She didn't have much hope he'd wake up again. Witnessing the death of a man who'd been a fixture of the Arc going back to her earliest memories rocked her sense of security.

Her father had given him a notebook with an 'if you're reading this, I'm dead' message, plus a bunch of sappy stories he'd written about stuff she'd done as a toddler. She hadn't been able to read them. Even the apology for disappearing on her left her in tears for days.

A large lump swelled up in her throat. She approached the bed and gently took the elder's hand. He didn't feel dead yet, so she squeezed.

"Daniel, I don't know if you can hear me. Sorry if I didn't really say thank you enough for holding onto Dad's notebook. Guess it's kinda incredible you had eighty birthdays. Maybe you could be stubborn enough to have a couple more, huh?"

Daniel didn't show any signs of reacting.

"Gonna try to fix this place." She bowed her head. "Sorry I'm not working faster."

"Did you come here to check on the light?" asked the doc.

"Light?" stammered Raven, her mind scattered to grief and worry.

"Yeah, one of the tubes is fluttering. Sent in a maintenance request yesterday, haven't heard back."

She let go of Daniel's hand and looked around, easily spotting the flickering LED. "Oh. I can check on that, sure. But... Umm." Raven walked over to the doc, lowering her voice. "Did you find anything in the tests?"

"Ahh, yes. That." He looked around as if to ensure no one listened in. "Surprisingly, no. I tested some of the samples three times thinking the equipment was too old to work properly and had lost calibration."

"No toxins?" Raven felt herself making the same wide-eyed 'ooh' face her daughter did when she mentioned taking her outside.

"In fact, the only test to come back with anything unusual was the swab of your poncho. I found... pollen."

"Seriously?"

Preston leaned in close, studying her face, mostly eyes. "I didn't believe it either until I ran a test on a control sample. It seems you were exposed to the outside atmosphere and did not pick up any detectable traces of toxic metals, harmful organophosphates, or other compounds we know for a fact had once saturated everything."

"How long ago was that?"

"The records are somewhat lacking." He cringed. "Most of them had been on the computer system, which as you know, no longer works. If I had to estimate, I would say likely a century and a half or longer. If you are correct in your description of extensive foliage, perhaps even three hundred years."

She paced. "That's a long time. Maybe enough for the planet to heal? How long ago did the Saints go out? Do you know?"

His eye twitched. "The eight? I'm not exactly sure, but it would have been at least a century ago, more likely two or three."

"That clue you gave me... I figured it out. Dead but not dead. *Publically* dead, but still alive, somewhere."

"We really shouldn't be talking about such things." He hurried to his desk.

She followed. "Why not? What's the secrecy for?"

"Understand he genuinely believes it is deadly out there. One set of tests on you doesn't prove enough. Could be luck, a chance shift in the wind."

"But my father—"

"Disappeared. Noah's convinced he succumbed to the conditions on the surface." The doc rubbed a hand down his face, scraping a week's worth of beard.

"I went out there and breathed without a mask for over two hours and the samples you took from me are clean. We *have* to tell Noah it's not as bad out there as everyone believes."

"It's not so simple. Getting through to him is going to take time."

She resisted the urge to bang on his desk. "Time's what we *don't* have."

"Raven... Look." He lowered his voice. "What I'm about to tell you must stay secret, at least for now."

"If keeping a secret is going to hurt people, I can't promise I will."

Preston shook his head. "No. It's not a dangerous secret. Eighteen years ago, the Arc suffered a failure of multiple wind turbines. Noah was still new at the administrator role back then, but he knew that without those generators—"

"We'd all die."

"Exactly. He conferred with Kathryn, who had Ben's job back then, about what to do. Ultimately, they asked for volunteers to go out there, fully expecting it would kill them as it did the Saints."

"That sounds familiar." Raven smirked. "Did it?"

"The two who initially went out to repair the turbines did both suffer symptoms from toxins they'd been exposed to... or so it seemed. They died relatively young a decade later, but in the absence of conclusive proof that their—most likely cancer—came from topside and not anything down here, Noah assumed. So, under the belief anyone who goes outside would eventually die, he decided to create a volunteer group who'd willingly commit to an early death to keep everyone else alive."

Raven paced, waving her hand about while trying to think of a response. "Why keep it secret? Why fake deaths?"

"I can't give you a clear answer, only he can. However, I suspect it is largely from not wanting the residents to venerate these people as living Saints. There is already enough superstitious nonsense going around. That, and when they agreed to risk the outside world, they essentially agreed to die. Concealing the truth of people venturing to the surface on a somewhat routine basis prevented any problems that could have arisen from it."

"Such as?" She set her hands on her hips.

"Others demanding to go out there when they saw the volunteers coming back alive, unaware they'd been contaminated with toxins that took years to kill. Or the tedium of facing angry people protesting anyone leaving at all. Or perhaps they picked up contagious maladies capable of spreading to others." Preston flicked at a pen sitting on the desk, a pen that likely hadn't worked in decades he kept around only as a fidget device. "Noah was inexperienced back then. And now, it's too late to mention it for fear of backlash."

Raven fumed. "People are already getting sick. If topside air is clean, we need to open the front door." She blinked. "Wait... is *that* why level one is off limits? Are the Saints up there?"

"I don't think so. He hasn't shared with me where they sleep. For all I know, they stay outside. They *do* show up periodically for examinations when most residents are sleeping. I'd been testing them like I tested you. They've been mostly clean, but I am unable to publically discuss those results because the subjects are officially dead."

"But I'm not."

Preston tapped his fingertips together. "Exactly why I was so excited. This is the start of what's needed to begin a debate. Let me talk to Noah about your test results. Give me a wake or two."

She bit her lip, desperate to do something *now* before Tinsley wound up in a bed on oxygen like old Daniel. However, unless the CO2 scrubbers or the turbines catastrophically failed within the next day or two, it probably wouldn't hurt to give the doc a little time. If she did anything drastic, he could call her crazy from toxic exposure. Then, no one would believe her and they'd all die in here.

"Okay. Please hurry."

"I will."

She started to leave, but caught herself, and went over to check the faltering light.

It turned out to be a dirty contact, easily cleaned.

OTHER THAN A GRUMBLY SHAW RANDOMLY KICKING THINGS, THE remainder of her work shift dragged by free of anything out of the ordinary. It bothered her to see the guy so upset since he'd always been the calm one on the tech team. Forty-one, pale as a ghost, and prematurely grey, he'd been a mentor to her as well as Lark, and— except for heavy objects falling on his toes—had never raised his voice before, and it scared her. Mostly because he had a deep, resonant voice not at all fitting his looks: slender and tall, with an angular face and bushy white mustache. Lately, he worked primarily with the new guy, Trenton, who'd been on the team a year, having turned nineteen a few months ago.

He seemed to be a nice guy, if a bit slow to learn things. Shaw trusted Raven to work on her own after four months, but he *still* worked in tandem with the new guy. Of course, Trenton hadn't grown up with Dad teaching him stuff his entire life.

Shaw's gotta know the deal, too. He's shouting because he's as scared as I am.

The doc telling her the samples came back clean made her eager to bring Tinsley to the topside hatch, even if they merely peeked at the world without getting off the ladder. They couldn't stay outside long, but her daughter had been so excited at the idea of going up there, Raven felt like the child who couldn't wait for their birthday present.

At long last, her work shift ended and she hurried to Sienna's room. Upon finding no one there, she headed down to the rec center on level five. Josh and a young guy from the kitchen staff named Vijay played eight ball. Sienna relaxed in a chair by the modest pool while the remainder of the kids swam in the questionable water, tossing a foam toy around. Their tread socks, ponchos, and inside shirts lay scattered around seats nearby.

Sienna appeared to have recently finished using one of the exercise machines. She, too, had removed her poncho. Sweat saturated her inside shirt. If the library caretaker would allow people to take books out of the room, she'd probably have been reading.

Though the kids all appeared in good spirits, she couldn't help but think them acting a bit sluggish. She flopped into the lounge chair beside Sienna, but trying to have a conversation without spilling what she'd learned about the new Saints or her plans to take Tinsley outside later proved impossible. So, after a mere fifteen minutes of inadvertently sounding like an airhead, she lobbed a lame excuse about exercising, flung her poncho and boots off, then hopped on a treadmill. The poncho would make her overheat. Her boots would disintegrate if she punished them on a treadmill. Ancient duct tape could withstand only so much. Besides, normal people didn't go jogging in old combat boots.

She definitely knows I'm hiding something.

While running, she soon came to the conclusion she *had* to tell Sienna everything. The two had been basically sisters for most of their lives. She had no doubt the woman could keep a secret. However, she'd probably try and talk her out of bringing Tinsley topside—or want to go with them. If Sienna went that route, she'd want to bring the other kids... and then the entire Arc would know they broke the rules.

No, to protect her best friend-slash-sister, she had to keep it secret for now. Talking about a secret team of techs who'd faked their deaths to go outside didn't seem as big a deal. That, Sienna wouldn't share with the kids and could definitely keep quiet.

Not since she'd been a little kid on the wake before her birthday had Raven wanted sleep time to hurry up and arrive so badly.

TINSLEY SAT ON THE EDGE OF THE BED, HANDS CLAMPED OVER HER filter mask, trying to muffle her coughing.

Neither she nor Raven had changed into their nightgowns in anticipation of their rule-breaking expedition. The majority of Arc residents followed a wake period from 1-0-0-0 to somewhere between 2-3-0-0 and 0-2-0-0. A much smaller number started their wake at 2-1-0-0 and kept an eye on things while everyone else went to bed. The ideal time to break rules fell after 0-1-0-0 when most people slept, or at least rested in their rooms.

After seeing all the dust fall out of the filter panel, Raven insisted the girl wear her mask. It wouldn't help against high CO_2 levels or low oxygen levels, but since the standard filters had become too saturated with crud to do anything, the air contained excessive particulate dust. Owing to that, Raven also wore her filter mask inside.

When the mechanical dial clock ticked to 0-1-1-0, she decided it good enough to start. She didn't want to stay up *too* late.

"Okay. Time. You ready?"

Tinsley nodded eagerly.

"Remember. Don't make a sound. Don't even whisper."

The girl raised a thumbs-up.

"Not sure what I'm going to say if anyone asks why we're roaming around so late, but I'll think of something."

"You're taking me to see the doc." Tinsley pretend-coughed.

Oh, no. She's as sneaky as me. I'm going to be in trouble when she's a teenager. Raven started to grin, but ended up staring forlornly at the floor. *If she becomes a teenager.*

She took the girl by the hand, crossed the room, and peeked out the door. As expected, no one else ventured outside their quarters. Empty pale grey corridor stretched in two directions. As quiet as she could be, she scurried out and headed to the right, *away* from the Arc's central core. Even with a third of the LED light bricks missing or dead, she had enough light to see.

Tinsley followed in silence, padding along in her tread-socked feet.

If I'd suspected the best way to keep a kid quiet was to break the rules, we would've done some mischief long before this. She chuckled in her head. Chase might've been on the lazy side, but Tinsley took totally after her mother. Ballsy and fearless worked for Raven, but in a six-year-old, those qualities frayed nerves of any adult responsible for her.

This tiny person she helped create had all the seriousness of a spy from a fiction novel, sneaking into—or in this case out of—an enemy base under pain of death if caught. The adorableness of it clashed with her worry both of their lives hung on such a thin thread, one turbine or CO_2 scrubber away from the end.

Raven headed to the nearest maintenance access tunnel and ducked inside. Tinsley had no trouble navigating the passageway, not even having to stoop, though her hair did brush the ceiling. Bent in half at the waist, Raven fast-walked along routes she'd spent years navigating to fix broken wires, water or sewage pipes, fuses, ventilation fans, and just about everything else the designers crammed out of sight.

Barring a sudden emergency, the off-hours tech crew wouldn't be prowling the maintenance tunnels, so being in there offered a near guarantee no one would catch them. It took her a few minutes to make her way across the Arc via the tunnel maze. Fortunately, no part of it narrowed down like the wire conduit out to the turbines, roughly half the size of the standard tunnels.

When she reached the turn into the passage she'd discovered the other wake, she paused to listen. Around the corner at the end, the opening met the forbidden corridor fairly close to the locked door. It didn't seem likely the security team would station someone by the door listening for anyone sneaking around. Locking it probably offered them enough confidence. That, plus everyone in the Arc except for Raven—and apparently Tinsley—was terrified of the outside world. No one would dare try anything like this...

Unless they snapped and went crazy like the kid who left the hatch open.

Holding her breath, Raven snuck to the corner and peered around at darkness. Feeble light in the maintenance corridor didn't reach past the bend. Also, the end had a steel plate blocking it and the 'escape passage' lights would be switched off.

She looked her daughter in the eye and whispered, "It's going to be totally dark for a bit. The hall is empty. Just hold on to me, okay?"

Tinsley nodded.

Raven felt her way along the maintenance passage until she reached the steel plate. Getting a grip on it from the inside proved tricky—until she fumbled across a pair of handles.

Oh, crap. It's supposed to be opened from this side. Are the Saints hiding somewhere in the Arc?

That thought sounded easily possible considering less than 200 people lived in a facility big enough for 2,000. Exactly where they holed up, she had no idea. She never saw anything suspicious when she'd been searching around for where her theoretically crazy father might've been hiding. That pointed back to level one, since she hadn't gone up there. Perhaps they'd simply hid from her in a cabinet or concealed the door to a room behind a shelf. Maintenance requests didn't usually come from areas with no people living in them. Considering these 'saints' started off as techs and had the skills to fix the turbines, they wouldn't need to call her team to do anything.

How are they eating? She shrugged. *Don't need to worry about that now.*

She stifled a grunt and lifted the steel plate, edging out into the corridor while trying not to drag it and make noise. Once out, she estimated a 180-degree turn and set the plate down, leaning it against the wall.

Bracing one hand on the left wall, she led Tinsley along the corridor in the pitch dark. Walking for ten minutes gave her the confidence to break out the crank light, knowing no one in the Arc could possibly see it past a closed door from so far away.

Tinsley looked around at the graffiti, her expression curious, not at all frightened.

Eventually, the silvery glint of the busted elevator doors reflected the flashlight beam. She guided Tinsley into the shaft, pointed at the ladder, then up.

Her daughter nodded once, then traced a smile shape in front of her filter mask.

Raven chuckled at the cuteness, mostly from nervousness. She had no idea what sort of punishment would fall on her if they got caught. The security team had a jail, but only Dad had ever defied the 'no one goes outside without permission' rule. He didn't get in trouble for some reason. Maybe because he agreed to keep his travels quiet? Noah didn't have any reason to fear a sudden rebellion of people all scrambling to go outside. They all believed it toxic. Even if they knew the truth, topside didn't have food or shelter.

She believed Noah truly thought it poisonous out there, but she also disagreed with him.

Tinsley coughed, the sound echoing behind them. Panicking, she pulled her filter mask down so she could clamp her hands over her mouth.

"It's okay," whispered Raven. "Don't hold it in. They can't hear us this far away... but you still shouldn't yell."

Once the coughing subsided, Tinsley grinned, then re-seated her mask.

Raven looked her over. "Do you still want to do this? It's a long climb."

"Yeah," whispered Tinsley.

"If you get tired, tell me right away and I'll carry you up." She gripped the metal ladder, but hesitated. *I'm insane. A six-year-old isn't ready for climbing up a ladder this long. What if she falls?*

Raven rummaged a cord out of her satchel and tied it around her daughter's chest making a harness, then tied the other end around her waist.

"What's that for?" asked Tinsley, holding her arms out to either side.

"In case you slip."

"Okay."

Raven started the climb at a fairly slow pace. Tinsley kept up, scaling the ladder with surprising ease despite her small height. Before she knew it, Raven reached the top. Working by feel, she turned the wheel to unbar the hatch.

"Ready?"

"Yes!" whispered Tinsley. "C'mon. Open it!"

"You're not scared at all?" Raven smiled a little.

"No. Grandpa was okay. And you went out. You wouldn't let me go if it wasn't totally safe."

Raven cringed. Technically, topside couldn't be *totally* safe. It could be free of toxins in this area, but the turbine towers were *far* from safe. They could collapse if the wind blew too strong. She would not let her daughter go anywhere near the windmill field.

"One... two..." Raven pushed the hatch up. She cringed at the squeak of rusty hinges and a brief shower of disintegrating gasket, then stared out in awe at the sight of a dark, starry sky.

Confusion gave way to mild disappointment at the sun not being out, as she'd wanted her daughter to see it. However, seeing the night sky for the first time in her life left her too enthralled to dwell on it. She didn't know how well her mechanical clock synced up with actual day and night, but it couldn't be *too* far off if her scheduled sleep time lined up with darkness.

Tinsley pushed at her backside, trying to get her to move up off the ladder.

Chuckling to herself, Raven climbed out of the shaft and reached back to steady the girl as she, too scrambled up onto solid ground. The child froze on all fours, staring at where her hands mostly vanished in the dirt up to her wrists. After a moment of stillness, she gingerly lifted her right hand, holding a clump of earth, watching as it fell between her fingers. She picked up another handful and sprinkled it back to the ground.

"Scoot forward a bit. I don't like you being so close to the opening."

Tinsley crawled a few feet, then sat, gazing up. "It's not bright. My eyes don't hurt."

"It was bright when I fixed the windmill. Outside, the light comes on by itself and goes off by itself. Remember what I showed you about the planet spinning around?"

"Yeah." Tinsley nodded, still playing by raking her fingers at the dirt between her knees.

"I don't really know what clock times are day and which are night. When I came up here before, the sun was out."

Tinsley leaned back, gazing at the stars. "Who poked all the holes in the sky?"

"Those are stars. They appear at night, unless it's raining."

"What's a star?"

Raven pointed. "One of those light spots."

"How did they get up there?"

"I think they've just always been there."

Tinsley fidgeted at her filter mask. "They're pretty. I hope no one steals them again."

"People can't steal stars. They're far, far away and extremely large. Bigger than our planet, mostly."

"They can, too, steal stars." Tinsley pointed at the hatch. "The Plutions stole them from us a long time ago."

Raven's heart nearly broke. She brushed a hand over her daughter's hair, which refused to be tamed. "Yeah, they sure did."

"Why is the door so small?" asked Tinsley.

"This is a secondary exit. Like for emergencies. The Arc has a great big door on level one." *That might be dead. No one has been up there for years.* "They haven't tried to turn on the machinery to open it in a very long time. It might not even work, but that's okay. We still have this way out."

"Oh. But the old people can't climb ladders. Are we all gonna go outside?"

"I dunno, Tins. This planet we once called home is like an alien world. We don't know what's out there."

"It's gotta be funner than down there." Tinsley pulled her tread socks off and plunged her toes into the dirt, trying to laugh and giggle without making too much noise. After mushing her feet into the ground for a while, she squirmed out of the rope harness, got up, and wandered off to examine the weeds growing here and there.

Did the people who made the Arc expect us to stay in it forever or did they hope we could leave it someday?

Maybe at some point in the past, their society could have been perpetually self-sustaining, able to produce everything from simple clothing to complex components for computers and CO_2 scrubbers. Somewhere during the past few centuries—or however long it had been since the doors sealed—technical knowledge faded as well as supplies and operational fabrication machines. A former administrator must have committed a fatal error in allocating resources that contributed to the complete failure of precision manufacturing of silicon chips and circuit boards. Or maybe her idea of some horrible past event killing off most of the people had some truth to it. All the best and brightest perished, leaving normal people behind.

No matter why it happened, we're still in trouble.

The soft rush of Tinsley taking a deep breath broke the otherwise perfect quiet. A noise that started sounding like a cough ended as more of a throat clearing.

Raven looked away from the weed at her daughter, who'd pulled her filter mask down off her face. An instant of panic hit her, as though she'd accidentally exposed her child to deadly poison. She managed not to scream, clinging to the hope offered by the doc's negative swabs. Tinsley took another deep breath then leaned to put her face right into a bush dotted with small white flowers.

"Tins? Be careful."

"I am." The child backed away from the foliage. "It smells nice out here."

She'd smelled it before, the scent of thousands of plants carried by air that hadn't gone through clogged filter panels and a chemical bath millions of times. Still, Raven pulled her mask down to enjoy it again. It might have been all in her mind, but breathing out here felt as though it took less effort and made her head spin ever so slightly for a while.

"Why's everyone scared of goin' outside?" Tinsley wandered around, evidently enthralled at the feeling of dirt on her toes.

Overcome by a moment of childish abandon, Raven took her tread socks off, leapt to her feet, and spent a little while running around with her daughter. She teased her fingertips at the leaf of a spiky weed as tall as the child. If this could grow on the surface, food crops could as well. Seeing the area surrounding the Arc evidently free of the contamination she'd grown up believing saturated everything topside gave her hope. Unfortunately, it also didn't prove no contamination existed anywhere.

Alas, it didn't take long for the late hour to catch up with her. Tinsley let out a huge yawn, so Raven guided her back to the open hatch.

"C'mon, kiddo. We should get back inside before anyone catches us."

Another yawn later, Tinsley nodded. "Okay."

They sat to put their tread socks back on. Raven secured the rope around the girl for the climb down, then lowered herself onto the ladder, going first so she could catch the girl if she fell in her tired state.

"Mommy?" asked Tinsley while climbing onto the ladder in front of her.

"Hmm?"

"If a rule is stupid, people are s'posed ta break it. I don't think we did anything bad."

Raven gave her a quick hug, then reached up to pull the hatch closed. "All right. Time to be quiet again."

Right before the metal plate cut off the starlight in the shaft, Tinsley raised a thumbs-up.

14

THE GREAT DEATH

The Arc was a good idea. It would've been a whole lot better of an idea if they had the time to plan it properly. But, when your ass is on fire, you don't care what might be in the toilet before jumping in. – Ellis Wilder.

Once back in her quarters, Raven changed into her nightgown. Tinsley hadn't bothered, merely ditching her poncho and skirt before falling face-first onto the bed. Raven sympathized with that level of exhaustion and didn't care if the girl wanted to sleep wearing her inside pants instead of a nightgown.

Raven crawled into bed and pulled the blankets over them.

"I wish the bugs would come back," whispered Tinsley, snuggling close. "Why did they go away?"

"Well..." Raven didn't bother opening her eyes. "A long time ago, there used to be lots and lots of people living topside. So many in fact, they made huge places called cities and needed machines like cars and airplanes to go places. Poison got into the sky and the water and the air. Insects started dying, but the people didn't notice or didn't care. They didn't really like bugs. Even the good ones. When the bugs were gone, the plants disappeared. Then the food. One day, people realized they should have done something about the poison, but it had become too late."

"People died," whispered Tinsley.

"Yes. All the people except for the ones who went into the Arc long ago. We call it the Great Death. Every living thing on the planet from the smallest bug to the biggest creature died in only a few years because of all the poison and heat."

"What was the biggest creature?" Tinsley held her arms out in front of her, sleepily pretending to be a ferocious giant monster.

Raven tried to squeeze memory out of her exhausted brain. It had been a long time ago she'd sat there listening to Ms. Reed teach. "I think elephant… or maybe whales might've been bigger than them."

"Whale?"

"Go to sleep."

Tinsley grumbled. "I can't sleep 'til I know what a whale is. I'm gonna be wondering."

Raven closed her eyes, chuckling softly to herself. "They looked like really big fish but they breathed air. I think the book said some of them could weigh several tons."

"Wow." Tinsley coughed into the pillow. "They must'a lived in big rivers."

"The biggest." Raven smiled. "They lived in the ocean."

"Did the ocean die, too?"

"Yeah."

"That's sad."

Raven rubbed the girl's back. "Very. Please go to sleep."

A moment passed in silence.

"Where did"—the girl yawned—"the poison come from?"

"The bad guys. Plutions." Raven failed to resist the urge to yawn as well. "Stories say Plutions were everywhere, killing everything."

"I don' like Plutions."

"Me neither."

Tinsley stretched, then snuggled closer. "Are the Plutions still out there?"

"I'm not sure. Maybe. The stories say the Plutions smelled really bad, so they can't sneak up on us."

The child murmured something close to 'that's good.'

Hoping the girl had gone to sleep, Raven let herself drift.

A few minutes of silence passed.

"Mommy?"

"Hmm?"

"I won't tell on you."

Raven chuckled.

"Can we go outside again sometime? Like when it's the sun?"

Raven kissed her on the head. "Maybe. Now, go to sleep."

15

DYING AIR

Your mother got mad at me the first time I went to topside. Didn't speak a word to me for a week after. Always said goin' out there would kill me and she didn't want to grow old alone. Damn world's got a sick sense of irony. – Ellis Wilder.

Alarm bells drilled into Raven's skull, pulling her out of a strange dream.

She'd been standing in the doorway of someone's private quarters, unable to go inside. The sense of dread keeping her out didn't frighten her as much as it merely felt 'wrong' to intrude. Not until the clock jolted her awake did she realize it must have been a long-buried memory. Her mother had died after a long illness when Raven had been around five. She didn't remember much about the woman who'd been in the infirmary for over a year, evidently too sick to allow a child that little to visit. The day she finally got the okay to visit her mother, Raven had been standing in a doorway waiting for Dad to call her into the room... but the woman had passed away hours earlier.

Anger at the world pushed aside her fatigue. She cut the alarm and got up, prodding Tinsley to get moving. They both somehow found the energy not to be too sluggish, so had plenty of time to eat breakfast at the cafeteria—more muffins. Today, she made an exception and let Tinsley have a little bit of coffee. As frivolous as it might have been to use up hydroponic tank space on coffee beans, all the admins—and at least forty percent of the adult population—demanded it, and for that, she felt grateful.

Especially that morning.

On the way to her job station, she dropped Tinsley off at the school room. The Arc had an entire hallway section devoted to school space on level five, but it hadn't been used in several generations. Similar to schools before the Great Death, it contained eight rooms for grade levels plus four classrooms intended for high school age students. Years ago, the Arc had enough of a population to use them. Nowadays, the children used one room on level three. No reason to make them walk all the way down into a mostly empty area.

It worried her Tinsley was currently the youngest resident of the Arc. Ariana, at nine, came in second. Cheyenne and Xan, both eleven, came next, with Josh, the eldest at twelve—not including Trenton, who no longer counted as a child at nineteen.

Did they stop asking people to have babies or have they not been able to get pregnant?

She didn't think crummy air quality would have affected fertility, but if people got tired of having kids because Noah asked them to... that didn't bode well. Another potential bad situation would be if they'd run out of safe genetic pairings. Granted, she and Chase could have more kids. Ariana's parents could as well. Raven didn't much care for the idea of having sex with him again, but if the survival of the human species depended on it...

He's not too bad.

Tinsley hugged her and walked to her desk.

Raven waved goodbye, then smiled at Sienna before turning to leave—but stopped when Arianna burst into coughing. She had almost the same skinny build as Tinsley, her low body mass making her the next most vulnerable person in the Arc to bad air. Generations of careful pairing to avoid incest had resulted in most residents being thoroughly mixed in terms of ethnicity. Despite that, some variances occurred. For example, Ariana obviously had her father's Chinese eyes but otherwise looked like a smaller version of her mother, Elena Vasquez.

Cheyenne didn't cough, but seemed half awake, seconds from face-planting over her desk.

Even the normally uncontainable Josh sat still, not making noise, not fidgeting.

The air's getting thin. Low oxygen or elevated CO2 can cause lethargy. Dammit!

She darted off down the hall to the engineering room, not entirely sure what to say, but fully intending to demand Ben do something. She had no proof of low oxygen, high CO2, or chemical toxicity from the hydroponic fluid in the air. The doc said he'd run tests on it but hadn't said a word to her about the results. Regardless, *something* was clearly making the children sick and affecting the smallest ones the most.

Like the bugs. The small stuff dies first. When adults start feeling sick, it'll be too late to do anything.

Her sprinting into the engineering area brought an abrupt stop to a highly animated conversation going on right outside the door to Ben's office involving him, Shaw, and Trenton. What had echoed into the hallway prior to her arrival sounded like more back and forth over the air filters, Trenton mostly doing the 'yeah, what he said' thing whenever Shaw barked at Ben.

Raven ran past Lark, who worked at her table evidently trying to ignore the men arguing, and inserted herself into the circle of men.

"Hey. Welcome to the party," said Shaw, nodding.

"Ben." She came close to grabbing his shirt in both hands, but held herself back. "We have to do something now."

"What's on fire?" He noticed her practically up on tiptoe, and leaned back a little.

Trenton gawked. "There's a fire?"

Shaw closed his eyes, likely asking the Saints for strength inside his mind. "No, boy. She means metaphorical fire."

"The air. Tinsley's been affected by it for a couple wakes. I just took her to school, and now it's other kids, too. Ariana's having trouble breathing and all five of them are lethargic. The CO2 is too high, or the oxygen is too low, or it's from the chemical leak in the hydroponic farm that the filters can't clean. Maybe it's a high concentration of particulates."

"Hold on a moment." Ben rested a hand on her shoulder. "You're saying there's something going on with the air but you don't even know exactly what it is?"

She closed her eyes and bit her lip to keep from screaming. When the urge to do so passed, she exhaled hard and fixed him with an almost glare. "You know all of those things are happening. *One* scrubber should be enough to keep 200 people alive, but we're running all of them and it's still iffy. When you shut them off the other wake, they almost didn't come back on. Next time you power them down, they won't turn back on. Did you see the amount of dust that fell off the filter when Shaw whacked it against his leg?"

Shaw wagged his eyebrows as if to say, 'see, she agrees with me.'

"Okay, okay." Ben rubbed his forehead. "I admit there are several issues going on. The best thing for us to do is address them one at a time as fast and effectively as we can."

"Alarm's going off on the filters," said Trenton. "Started this wake."

"I told you," said Raven. "They're gonna fail. Next time you hit that button, they stay off."

"No not the scrubbers, the filters." Ben looked around the group. "Why don't you three see what you can do for them and I'll check on the scrubbers."

Raven lost her battle with self-control and grabbed Ben by the shirt. "The kids are showing signs of oxygen deprivation or contaminated air. We are *not* going to wait for one of them to drop dead before we take this seriously. You know exactly how this shit goes, and it's the smallest one who dies first."

"Whoa, whoa." Ben grasped her gently by the wrists. "I completely understand where you're coming from. But there's only so much we can do."

"Bullshit. We can do more. You and I both know Noah simply won't."

Ben tilted his head. "Like?"

"Open the primary door and the escape hatch. Vent in outside air. The scrubbers are going to die really soon. The Arc is too old to stay sealed anymore and the air outside is *fine*."

Lark whistled. Shaw clapped a hand over his face, eyes wide. Trenton gave her a look like she'd suggested they all light themselves on fire.

Ben cringed. "That is going to be a difficult option to get past Noah."

She started to throttle him by her grip on his shirt, but Shaw and Trenton pulled her back.

"Easy, girl," said Shaw.

"I'm not a freakin' horse!" snapped Raven.

Shaw laughed, which infuriated her as well as made her feel silly. If she flipped out and lost her cool, it would only make it easier for Noah and any sub-administrator to dismiss her. She took a deep breath, wincing at the obviously metallic flavor.

"Okay." Raven released her grip on Ben's shirt and held her hands up. "I'm calm."

The guys let go of her.

"Humor me and check on the filters. I'm on your side, Raven. Really, I am." Ben smoothed his shirt down. "I don't want anyone to die, especially the kids. You have some good points about the systems, but you're basically talking about trading one kind of death for another. Things would have to be really dire in here for him to even consider that."

Fury welled up. She shouted, "Are you—?"

He raised a hand. "Let me finish. Things would have to be dire in here for him to consider outside air unless we can show him undeniable proof it's our only option."

Raven turned away, arms folded, head down. "Undeniable proof like me carrying Tinsley's body into his office?"

Everyone sucked in a little breath.

"No, Raven. I'm with you. I won't let it go that far. Promise." Ben nudged her arm. "Your mind's full of doomsday scenarios from all those books you read. All I'm asking is we make sure we're looking at one before we act rashly, open the door, and kill everyone."

"We went outside and came back okay," said Lark from her seat.

"Two people taking a quick trip is not even close to the same thing as flooding the entire Arc with potentially toxic vapors." Ben sighed, then rolled his neck around. "Please check the filters, give me a chance to try and up the efficiency on the scrubbers, and let's compare notes in an hour or three."

Shaw and Trenton both nodded, so Raven reluctantly gave in.

Ben led the way into the adjacent room containing the bulk of the ventilation and air purification machinery. The eight CO_2 scrubbers lined up along the far wall like a group of giant, boxy cows at a trough. In theory, one unit had more than enough capacity to re-oxygenate the air for an entire floor level. Eight units working for six levels should have offered plenty of failure tolerance, but after so long... it felt as if the scrubbers barely did anything.

Air coming from the various intake vents throughout the Arc went down a massive conduit to the hydroponic farm, then came back up to this room where it traversed a fourteen-foot-long steel cabinet duct on the right side of the room containing seven banks of filter inserts separated by fans. The main air mover, a huge eight-foot-diameter fan, sat 'behind' the CO_2 scrubbers, sucking air through the primary filter cabinet into the scrubbers, then forcing it into the ducts for distribution out to the Arc again. That giant fan provided most of the suction drawing air in the Arc's various intake ducts.

Ben referred to it as 'Zeus,' since if it became angry, everyone would probably die.

She approached the long primary filter unit, put on her goggles and breathing mask, then lifted a panel to expose a section holding ten inserts, each a forty-by-forty inch square. A stiff breeze erupted from the opening, scattering a wash of pale grey silt on the floor around her. The air blast continued billowing her hair. A thick coating of fuzzy grey dust coated every filter panel, thicker on the right (incoming) side, but it had also accumulated on the left, suggesting air blowing down between filter sections remained saturated with dirt.

"Shit," muttered Raven.

She pulled one square out to examine. Slabs of congealed dust broke off and fell to the floor, bursting apart into starbursts of pale grey. The filter insert had an accordion-fold section of material sandwiched between mesh screens, and it definitely appeared to have been through hell and back. It might have been fiberglass, cotton, or polyester—or some combination of the three. Studying it for a moment convinced her she could most likely hand-build replacements if she had appropriate materials. Unfortunately, that would require waiting for the hydroponic team to grow cotton-plus, the plants to mature, be harvested, and processed into fabric. The production staff could make paper from various vines and stems, which meant a cardboard-like housing might be possible if she couldn't save the existing filter frames.

"I see the way you're looking at that." Shaw gestured at with the demeanor of an old cowboy indicating a dead horse. "Washin' the guts won't work. Tried it yesterday. Damn thing disintegrated into fibrous mush. Been washed too many times."

"All we can do is brush them out dry," said Trenton. "Even being as careful as possible, I broke two of them. The material's just too weak. Softest brush I could find tears the fabric."

She sighed. "Okay, let's take them into a space with minimal air flow, bang them out, and give them a light brushing. Won't be ideal, but it's better than leaving all this crud in the system."

"Good plan." Shaw grabbed four panels out of the section she'd opened. "Trent, you go on and grab the rest of them, bring 'em to the parts room. When you got this whole thing empty, get in there with a brush and clean the duct. If we're still bangin' on filters when you finish, come help us."

"You got it, boss." Trenton began pulling filters out and stacking them.

Raven and Shaw went to the parts closet, a room a little smaller than her quarters full of shelving. It didn't have a vent intake, so none of the dust they knocked loose would be drawn back into the system. She left her goggles and filter mask on, and proceeded to bump the filter squares against the steel shelf, close to the floor.

Shaw did the same.

Armload by armload, Trenton carried filter tiles into the room and left them in stacks. Eventually, he had the whole primary filter unit empty and got to work cleaning the cabinet. Raven tried to find the balance point between gentle enough not to smash the filter but forceful enough to dislodge crud. A few times, she tore holes in the old material from simply handling the inserts.

Air's going to pass through multiple filters. Couple of small holes aren't a big deal.

Two hours later, they agreed no more could be done to resuscitate the filter panels. The fabric inside remained an off-putting shade of dark grey, but it no longer appeared to be growing fur. Trenton's idea of using compressed air sounded good, but the high-pressure blast caused the membrane to disintegrate. Three giant mounds of grey silt had formed on the floor where each of them had been working. Raven volunteered to deal with that while the guys lugged the 'clean' filters back to the machine. She spent a few minutes sweeping up the dust and putting it into an empty plastic drum. The lid would seal it away from going back into circulation. Maybe she could get permission to go dump it outside.

The condition of those filters made one thing obvious: they'd all been breathing contaminated air for a while. She tried not to imagine the same dust coating the inside of her—or Tinsley's—lungs.

It's probably worse in here than outside.

She jogged out of the parts room heading over to Ben, who sat on the floor by the third CO_2 scrubber, using a laptop connected by cable to the machine to run a diagnostic routine. No one had taught her the first thing about it, so all the moving lines, pie graphs, and bar charts meant little. Unfortunately, though a computer, that particular one only had software to run diagnostics for the air scrubbers, not a true operating system.

Raven lifted her goggles up off her eyes. "There's a problem…"

Ben tapped another key, then looked up at her, blinking in surprise. "What happened to you?"

"Happened to me?" She froze, momentarily worried some undetectable toxin from outside made her grow a face tumor or something horrible.

"You've turned grey."

She looked down at herself, her clothes the same color as most of the concrete around them. Her face—except for what the goggles and mask covered had to be the same. "That's exactly the problem I mean. We've been breathing this crap for a long time. You haven't assigned me to the filter unit before. When's the last time someone cleaned those?"

"Fourteen wakes ago," called Shaw from across the room.

"What?" She gawked at him. "This amount of crap built up in just fourteen wakes?"

"Not so surprising." Ben poked a few keys on the pseudo-laptop, causing the display to change to a whole bunch of fluctuating numbers. "Most of the ventilation ductwork running around the Arc has an inch-thick layer of fur lining it."

"Ugh." She cringed. "Why aren't we in there cleaning it out?"

"Because, in order to do so, we would have to shut down the airflow to parts of the Arc in sections. Otherwise, all that crud would go flying down the ducts and end up in these scrubbers. The substrate is… not in the best condition. It's already turned black from the mess getting past the filters."

She banged her fists on her hips. "Dammit. Are you serious? Of course it's getting past the filters because the filters oversaturate in fourteen wakes! We should be cleaning them daily."

The 'you're right. I messed up' look he gave her almost resulted in a fist upside the head. *Lazy son of a… my daughter's sick because you forgot?* She let her frustration leak out on a sigh. *Stay rational. I can't do*

any good if they think I'm crazy. Noah already thinks I'm seeing things from
some unknown poison. Never should have told him about seeing someone on
the other tower.

"Okay, so... it's an emergency. If we all work on it, we can get
through a section pretty quick. Shut off the vents, we go in and scrape
the ducts..."

"Remember what you were saying about the scrubbers' efficiency?
I'm..." He glanced at the screen. "Concerned that shutting down
airflow to any section could rapidly lead to inadequate air quality.
We'd only have twenty minutes or so before the air in whatever part
of the Arc became harmful. In the confines of the vent shaft, you guys
would be the first to pass out."

Despite being terrified and furious, Raven calmly plucked the
computer from his lap, set it on the floor, grabbed his hand, and
dragged him to his feet. Without a word, she hauled him to the door,
across the engineering room, and across the Arc to the admin
corridor and Noah's office.

"You're going to..." Ben looked around nervously. "Seriously?"

"Yep. We will convince him of the need to immediately start
working on a way to ventilate with outside air. There's no reason for
me to mention the filters hadn't been cleaned often enough to prevent
the CO_2 scrubber substrate from becoming ruined, or that the ducts
are years behind on cleaning."

Ben slowed his stride, but didn't pull back against her too hard.
"You're really not afraid of it out there?"

"I'm not afraid of breathing it, no. *Generally* out there, I don't have
enough information to know if I should be afraid or not. But, the air's
fine. Doc took samples from my throat and nose, testing them for bad
shit. He said I'm clean. And I swear to you, I felt better out there. Like
I didn't have a weight on my chest making it harder to breathe."

"I don't feel like that."

She glanced sideways at him. "Neither did I before I went outside.
You don't notice it because it's always there. You notice after it's been
gone a while and you feel it again."

"You know going outside sounds crazy. The entire point of the Arc was to isolate and protect us from the air on the surface."

"I'm aware of that," said Raven, not breaking stride to Noah's door, which she opened. "But it's been centuries. And... in case you haven't been keeping a scorecard of what's breaking down, we are in trouble. I'm not waiting for people to die before demanding we do something."

"So you want to"—Ben glanced to his right, seemingly startled to find himself already in the head administrator's office—"Hi, Noah. Sorry to barge in." He looked back to Raven. "You want to potentially poison everyone because you think we're going to die? What sense does that make?"

She exhaled, shot him a look, and walked up to Noah's desk. "We don't have time to argue about this. The air quality inside the Arc has already deteriorated to a dangerous level. Our CO_2 scrubbers might be completely useless already. The only oxygen we're getting is coming from the plants in the hydro farm. The filters are one giant mass of fur. Hydroponic chemicals are leaking all over the place. Turbines are one stiff breeze away from collapsing. We can't wait for people to start dying before we accept we have a giant problem."

"Slow down..." Noah pushed aside the logbook he'd been occupied with when she burst in. "Explain it to me clearly."

She squeezed her fists tight, but kept a calm face. In as slow and careful detail as possible, she explained everything one at a time, stressing the condition of the turbine towers, signs of oxygen deprivation in the kids, the scrubbers, the filters, the thick layer of muck in the ventilation ducts, and so on. "... which means the only reasonable option we have left is to come up with a way to vent the Arc using outside air."

Noah stared at her for a few seconds before bursting into laughter.

"This is serious." She looked at Ben. "Tell him. I'm not hallucinating."

"I'm... afraid a lot of what she says sounds like what's going on." Ben kept his gaze off to the side, refusing to challenge Noah with eye contact. "Spent a couple hours earlier testing the scrubber units and the monoethanolamine substrate is… well, to put it bluntly, shot. It's supposed to be a clear, viscous liquid, but it's a *black*, viscous liquid."

"Well, synthesize more of it then," said Noah as if he'd suggested something obvious.

"We can't." Ben finally looked at him.

"And why is that?"

Raven screamed 'you should know. You're the administrator!' in her head, but held her tongue.

"We don't have anyone skilled enough at chemistry to do it." Ben fidgeted. "Haven't been able to for several generations now."

"Are there or are there not sufficient educational materials at our disposal to train someone?"

Ben nodded. "Yes, we have the documentation."

"Why has no one been trained?"

"Couple reasons. The coursework requires hands-on experimentation we lack the raw materials for. All the chemicals had been restricted by a previous administrator for 'necessary' projects, not 'playing around in a lab.' Second, most of the electronic components in the chemistry lab no longer work. The machines necessary to assist in the synthesis of chemical compounds haven't been operable in decades. The machines needed to make replacement components for those machines haven't worked in decades. Since we have not had the functional capacity to produce advanced chemicals or electronics in some time, the educational administrator felt it a waste of resources to train people on skills they couldn't possibly use."

"There's an educational administrator?" asked Raven, eyebrow up.

"Not anymore." Ben sighed. "We needed one when they had to manage a staff of twelve teachers. I suppose you could call Sienna the educational administrator in a technical sense now."

Noah's stare could've boiled the skin off a person at ten paces. "Why is this the first I'm learning about this situation?"

"I don't know. You'd have to take that up with Kathryn, my predecessor." Ben's grimace said 'you've been told this multiple times already' but he didn't dare say it out loud.

Sensing Noah about to blame Ben for this entire situation, Raven spoke up in hopes of sparing her boss (and friend) from unjustified retribution. "Does it matter how we've ended up in this situation when there's a way out staring us in the face?"

"Your idea is sheer madness," said Noah, his anger fading. "No one in their right mind would even consider such a thing. We are far better off breathing air with a little dust than air that's deadly."

"Noah..." She leaned forward, resting both fists on his desk. "The air in here is approaching deadly. It's well past dusty. I admit we don't know how much toxicity is possible from the hydroponic growth fluid fumes, but even if you ignore that, did you not just hear Ben tell you the CO_2 scrubbers are probably not even doing anything? There isn't enough oxygen in our air. The turbines might fail at any moment. We lose them, we lose fans. Then everyone dies in their sleep. My daughter is already sick. Ariana is sick. The children are showing symptoms of oxygen deprivation. Daniel is in a coma because of it. He could die."

He pinched the bridge of his nose. "So your solution to us all suffering a sneaky, suffocating death is to poison us all so we die much faster?"

"Dammit!" She pounded the desk. "You know it's not dangerous out there. I went out *twice* and came back fine. My father went out several times."

"Did he tell you how sick he got after the first trip?" Noah raised an eyebrow. "Probably not since you weren't even born yet. He stumbled back in, eyes watering, face puffy, barely able to breathe. It's a damn miracle he recovered. And, if it's so safe out there, where is he?"

Ben whistled. "Not right."

"It's okay." Raven stood straight. "He didn't say it to hurt me. It's a true statement. But... you don't know what killed him. When I went out there, I could've fallen off the turbine tower when it collapsed out from under me. That doesn't mean the air is toxic. Another tower might have fallen and crushed me. Or what if I fell in a hole, broke my neck? There are a thousand ways to die in any environment, but you're assuming one."

Noah shifted his jaw side to side. "I'll have doc run some tests on the air to confirm your worries about the oxygen levels." Noah reached for the phone on the desk.

"Are you going to wait for people to start dying? My daughter can't stop coughing. Now Ariana's started. Daniel might already be dead. What is it going to take?" yelled Raven. "There's so much dust in the air we might as well walk around licking the floor."

Noah paused, his hand on the phone, not lifting it from the cradle. "Perhaps you should visit Preston again and ask him to check you for paranoia or delirium from whatever you suffered exposure to out there."

"Didn't he already talk to you about the tests? He found nothing."

"Tests?" asked Ben.

Raven explained the swabs. "No traces of any identifiable toxin. Everything came back clean."

"Some of the toxins out there are so potent they can have an effect from trace amounts, too little to show up on Preston's equipment." Noah flicked at the corner of his log book.

Raven narrowed her eyes, tempted to throw it in his face she knew about the new Saints. However, she didn't want to get the doc in trouble. "If anyone else went outside, Preston could test them the same way... like Lark. She went out to help me with the tarp."

"What?" Noah blinked. "You took someone out there with you? I authorized one person."

"Umm... the turbine housing had an enormous hole in it. To keep rain out, we covered it with a tarp. That's not a one-person job, even in calm wind. When we went out again, the security team called you to make sure it was okay."

He frowned. "Yes, but they neglected to mention you brought a friend. So there are now two of you who have been exposed?"

"We haven't been exposed to anything but cleaner air than what's down here." She shifted her weight onto her left leg, cocking one eyebrow in a challenging stare. "If you know of anyone else who's been outside recently, have them tested. I bet the doc won't find anything."

"Miss Wilder, I think you need to go take some time and de-stress." Noah shifted his gaze to Ben. "Give her the rest of the wake... and the next one, off."

"I can't just sit around and watch things get worse. I'm not going to let Tinsley die."

Noah again reached for the phone. "If it's too difficult, I can always ask security to help you find a quiet place to calm down."

Ben gasped.

Raven shook with rage. Blowing up on him now would definitely end poorly. Tinsley's life being in danger terrified her enough already. Being separated from her and stuck in jail would be intolerable.

"Fine," she said past clenched teeth.

Fuming, she stormed out.

HAVING NO BETTER IDEA OF WHAT TO DO, RAVEN FOUND HERSELF GOING to the classroom.

So as not to disturb them, she stood in a dark spot, watching the kids interact with Sienna. Every time one of them said something cute, she almost cried. Whenever Tinsley or Ariana coughed, she *did* shed a tear. Her daughter struggling to get math questions right scared the hell out of her. Ariana appeared mildly disoriented, too. Both she and Tinsley kept nodding off. Even though they'd both stayed up past bedtime last wake to sneak outside, her daughter's visible fatigue infuriated her all over again.

He's ignoring evidence just like people did before with the bugs. What is Noah afraid of? Something being true at one point does not mean it will always be true. Okay, so what if Dad had an issue the first time he went out. That's like twenty years ago. Maybe he got a damn cold. He got over it and went back out there. It couldn't have been toxin, or even a Plution attacking him. It didn't sound reasonable free-roaming poisons had been in the air as recently as twenty years ago for there to be as many weeds, grasses, bushes, and flowers as existed now. She blinked in astonishment at a sudden realization. *Pollen... Dad could've had an allergic reaction to plant stuff in the air. None of us had ever been exposed to it before. Noah wouldn't even know what pollen was.*

The soft rustle of someone in a poncho and tread socks approaching made her look to the right.

Ben came around the corner, his clothes rustling. He looked tired, but hopeful… and a little worried.

Guess that means I don't have to worry about the security people.

"Hey."

"He's wrong," muttered Raven.

"It doesn't matter if he's wrong or not. He's in charge. What he thinks, goes."

"Yes, it does matter." She stared down. "His being wrong is going to kill people. Can I tell you something in confidence?"

He nodded. "Sure. Least I can do for you not pulling my pants down in there."

"What?" She blinked at him.

"Figuratively. The vents being a mess are my fault. You didn't bring that up. And you interrupted him before he ripped my head off. So, yeah. In confidence."

She swiped her hair out of her face and stared into his eyes. "If I wasn't worried there's no food topside, I'd have already grabbed my daughter and gone out there to stay."

"Wow." He made a soundless whistle. "You really trust it."

"I trust it more than the mess down here."

"Fair point." He stuffed his hands in his pants pockets somewhere under the poncho. "I have some news you might like."

She smirked. "You didn't convince him to open the door."

"No. Not yet. But I did tell him I don't think you're seeing things or paranoid. Our whole team works on the same systems you do, realizes the same things you do. I talked him into taking the doc's tests seriously, but Noah seems unusually frightened about what's out there."

"So is everyone else. We've all grown up hearing stories." She grimaced, thinking of the Saints she'd seen in their melted suits. "But wounds heal. Why do we assume the planet is going to stay toxic forever?"

Ben scratched at his nose. "Yeah. I'm astounded Lark went out there with you. Figured she'd have been harder to convince than Noah, but... she's right with us in engineering. Noah sits in an office."

"What if we drag him to the HVAC room and show him?" She grinned. "I could even take him on an outside tour."

"I don't think he'd appreciate being 'dragged' anywhere." He chuckled. "Look, just try to keep a low profile for a wake or two."

Raven shifted her weight from leg to leg. "I can't do nothing and just wait for everyone to die."

"That's not what I'm asking you to do. But getting in Noah's face and yelling won't help. Look, give me a couple wakes to look at possible solutions, including if there's a feasible way to draw in enough fresh air and circulate it down here."

She gawked, unsure whether to feel happy he trusted her or worried it meant the systems were much closer to failure than she thought.

"Having something on paper to show him might make it easier to convince him." He looked down, shaking his head. "The filters are shot. Even after cleaning, they're useless. Air can barely pass through them, and they're not pulling much dirt out."

"We don't have time." She grabbed his arm.

He gave a sad chuckle. "I wish I had your trust in the air topside."

"There's an easy way to fix that."

"Uhh... you might have inhaled a slow-acting poison or something. If you're still here a week from now, maybe I'll let you talk me into looking for myself."

"Right..."

He started to walk off, but twisted back to point at her. "Please keep your head down. Give me a chance to work up some schematics."

"I won't scream at Noah again."

Ben's expression said 'you're up to something,' but he didn't press the issue, continuing to walk away. "Enjoy your wake off."

Being given time without responsibility should have felt like a reward or a nice thing, not a chastisement. Raven fidgeted, staring again into the classroom. Tinsley and Ariana lay passed out on their desks. Xan had gotten stuck in a logic loop arguing with Sienna about the word 'address.' He accused her of writing add*ress* on the whiteboard when the definition she tried to get out of him referred to add*ress*—to speak to someone.

He's loopy. How can someone write *the wrong pronunciation?*

Frustrated, and not wanting to disturb the class, she went home. Upon arriving in her quarters, she threw off her poncho and pants, deciding to get comfortable in only her inside clothes and tread socks. Worried and restless, sitting still proved impossible and she wound up pacing—until her gaze fell on Dad's storage trunk. The unassuming olive-drab hard case had originally contained delicate electronic parts, long ago put into use. It came a little too close to making her think of a Tinsley-sized coffin.

Be it from anger at Dad for going away or her unwillingness to stare into the face of her sorrow at losing him, she hadn't opened the trunk since the time she'd moved from the two-bed quarters she grew up in to this one. He'd mostly kept his 'expedition' stuff in it, so while packing up his things, she put a few more notebooks and some gear in it—then pretended it didn't exist.

Part of her always toyed with the idea of disposing of the trunk so she didn't have to look at it and think about him, but now... she practically jumped into a cheer for never following through. All the times he'd gone out there and come back, maybe he found something she could use to convince Noah his fears had no basis in fact.

As nervous as a little girl sneaking into her parents' room to search for birthday presents two days early, she crept up to the trunk, knelt, then sat back on her heels, resting her hands on the lid.

"Okay, Dad. Help us out here."

16

PERMISSION

Hell no, I didn't ask first. After I came back in one piece the first time, they couldn't say it would kill me. – Ellis Wilder.

Dad's trunk gave off a faint sucking sound when Raven pushed the lid up, a watertight seal around the rim separating. A thick layer of dark foam lined the walls, though the contents of mostly notebooks and hiking supplies didn't need so much protection. Air trapped inside still held her father's scent, triggering a lump in her throat. Though it had been four years since he'd vanished, for a moment, it felt as though he disappeared only days ago.

No way topside went from deadly to fine in four years. Dad didn't die to breathing poison. Something else happened to him.

Her hands shaking, she cleared a poncho and two spare filter masks off the top, then grasped the first of many notebooks. Except for varying degrees of damage, they appeared identical—every one of them forest green with 'Arcology 1409' printed on the cover in white letters. Some looked new and unused, others like they'd suffered everything from being dropped in water to turbine gears chewing on them.

For her daughter's sake—and the lives of everyone in the Arc—Raven set aside her emotions and concentrated on searching for anything she could use to prove her case. Her father had filled twenty-four notebooks. Between them and a collection of 'artifacts' he'd brought back from topside, there *had* to be something useful.

A couple hours blurred into oblivion as she went from one notebook to another, pausing every so often to look over an item she almost recognized. Between her technical experience and exposure to the previous world from reading, she guessed at cell phones, a video game on DVD, a heavily rusted handgun, half-melted Rubik cube, and so on. Two-thirds of the items had sustained damage similar to acid corrosion in varying degrees.

Looks like some places out there must have had a little protection. Not everything melted.

While poring over notebook seven, she discovered a journal entry regarding her father going to the remains of a ruined city approximately a two-hour walk 'mostly west' from the Arc. That made her pick up one of the compasses she'd already removed from the trunk, tilting it back and forth. The needle wobbled, definitely interested in pointing only one way. She didn't remember if the white end or the red end pointed north, though. But her inability to remember didn't matter. As soon as she could see the sun, determining direction would be easy.

Rises in the east, sets in the west, said Dad's voice in her memory.

Her father's writing described 'streets lined with hundreds of metal frames of various size,' which had to be cars. Two pages in, he described finding a large interior space that appeared to have been a storage facility of some kind. An enormous building contained shelves and shelves of tools, hardware, building supplies, and all sorts of 'good stuff' he didn't have any room to carry except for the orange-and-black hammer.

"It's mind blowing to think what our ancestors had at their disposal, and their sense of communal survival. To assemble such a vast storage vault of vital supplies anyone could access is truly humbling. I must convince the little bastard to let me bring a group here," said Raven, reading her father's words. "Heh."

'Little bastard' had been his name for Noah, even though Dad was only eight years older than him—forty-nine—at the time of his disappearance-presumed-death. Noah would have been thirty-seven then. He'd only worked as a section admin for a year before running in the election for big boss. Dad didn't think Noah believed he had any chance of winning, but people liked the young, charismatic 'new face.' Her father forever considered him a 'kid.'

Reading Dad's words set off an explosion of hope. How amazing would it be if the ancestors had been so altruistic as to assemble a stockpile of supplies for the community? But... centuries had passed. Could anything out there possibly be useful?

She rummaged the trunk, looking for an 'orange and black hammer.' Removing the next full stack of notebooks revealed an ordinary carpenter's hammer, solid steel, with a black rubberized grip, quite dried up and cracked. Traces of bright orange paint remained on the head, though much of it had worn off even though the tool had no scrapes, dents, or gouges suggesting it had never actually been used to drive a nail. Words stamped into the shaft spelled out: 'Home Depot'

"Amazing..." She tried to imagine a surface city with a parts vault like the Arc had where people went to ask a quartermaster for stuff they needed. That this hammer survived gave her hope she might find other things still in usable condition. Maybe even material she could make new air filters from.

True, she held a solid steel tool, but plastic lasted forever. Thinking about her father exploring ruined cities raised a new hint at what might have caused him to disappear—ancient buildings would be prone to collapse, especially if the Plutions had damaged them.

She couldn't worry about that now. No time for mourning. Reading her father's notes made it sound possible—even probable—one of those old storage vaults might still hold useful materials.

Noah can go to hell. We can't wait. If there is anything there I can use to fix stuff here...

Her mind made up, she went back to the start of that journal entry and read her father's maddeningly brief comments about how to get there. She remembered seeing the tall concrete skeletons of old buildings way off in the distance. Those seemed to line up with the description, but she couldn't remember where the sun had been at the time.

Raven studied the notes, plus a little map he'd drawn. Going miles away from the Arc could lead to her sharing the same fate as her father—disappearing and probably dead. No one would know what the hell happened to her. They'd blame the toxins and keep the Arc shut up tight until everyone died. But if she didn't go, Noah would still keep the Arc sealed until everyone died. She had only one choice: make the trip and come home alive with something useful.

That would prove the outside air is safe.

Well, Dad. I guess I really am your kid.

The door opened.

Wrapped up in her plans to defy Noah, she jumped as if she'd been caught touching herself, expecting to see a security team here to arrest her for 'defiant thought.' At the sight of Tinsley letting herself in, her little face mostly hidden behind a filter mask a bit too big for her, she slouched with relief.

"Mom?" Tinsley's muffled voice broke the quiet. "Is something wrong?"

"Kind of." Raven pressed a hand to her chest, trying to recover from the scare.

"Why are you home early? Are you sick, too?" The girl walked up to her, her posture slouched, eyes half closed like she could crawl into bed and sleep.

I can't leave her here. Dread fear hit her she'd go topside for a few hours and come home to find her daughter suffocated. Overcome, she grabbed the girl in a fierce hug, squeezing a squeak out of her. Tinsley draped over her, coughing.

"Ow."

"Sorry, baby." Raven relaxed her grip. "I'm gonna break the rules again."

Tinsley leaned back to look her in the eye. "You're scared."

"I am, but not of being out there. I'm scared of you being in here."

After a long stare, the child whispered, "Me, too."

"We're gonna go outside, okay?"

Tinsley nodded.

"I need you to do something important first."

"You're not trying to trick me to stay here?" Tinsley narrowed her eyes.

"No. I promise. We're going on a long walk. I need you to go to the cafeteria and take a bunch of muffins without being seen doing it. Then come back here."

The grogginess saturating the child's presence faded noticeably. "How many?"

"At least four, but no more than eight. Enough in case we get stuck out there so long we have to sleep."

"Okay." Tinsley scurried out into the hall, her tread socks squeaking on the smooth concrete.

Raven stared at the notebook. Taking her six-year-old not only topside but two hours away from the Arc sounded reckless and dangerous. But she *couldn't* leave her in an increasingly toxic vault. If she had any way to, she'd bring Ariana, Cheyenne, Xan, and Josh as well.

No way would Sienna go along with that. If I end up detained, we're all screwed. Only choice is getting out there and back before Arianna succumbs. She's the next smallest. Raven bowed her head. *Saints watch over her.* She got up, rushing to put her pants, poncho, and boots on. Even though she trusted the air directly above the Arc, she didn't know what to expect miles away, so she hung the filter mask around her neck.

She ran water into four plastic bottles and packed them in her tool satchel. Carrying it would be far less suspicious inside the Arc than a backpack, plus having the basic tools along could come in handy. Last, she added Dad's spare hunting knife to her belt.

"Always have a knife. Never know when you'll have to cut something, right Dad?"

Tinsley crept back into the room, her arms entirely concealed under her poncho. She nudged the door shut behind her with a foot, then walked over. "You can't see, but I'm smiling."

Raven looked at her. "Did you get anything?"

"Lift my poncho. Can't use my arms right now."

She grabbed the bottom of her daughter's garment, pulling it up to reveal the child beneath. Against her skinny, bare stomach, the girl clutched an armload of muffins. Her tattered red skirt bore so many crumbs, it looked as though she'd used it to clean the cafeteria floor.

"They didn't see you take this much?"

"Nope," chirped Tinsley.

"I'm impressed."

"My powers of sneaky are strong."

Raven swiped a plastic bag from a nearby table and transferred the muffins to it, counting ten. Once she'd dropped the last one in the bag, Tinsley brushed crumbs from her skirt and let her poncho drape down again.

"Ready?"

"Can I pee first? There's nowhere to pee outside."

"Yeah, there is. Anywhere you want." Raven gestured at the door. "Might as well do it now though."

"Eww." Tinsley hurried off to the toilet room.

Naturally, mentioning it made her have to go, too. Afterward, she shouldered her tool satchel and walked out into the hall, child in tow. She acted as if she merely headed to some other part of the Arc on a repair job. Though she passed a few people, no one thought anything of her presence, even when she crawled into the maintenance passage in full view of three residents. She'd been doing it for years so it didn't seem strange. Perhaps bringing Tinsley along might be considered unusual, but they didn't react.

Probably think she wants to watch Mommy work.

At the hour, a chance existed they'd bump into Shaw, Lark, or Trenton in the maintenance tunnels. All of them would likely know she'd been given the rest of the wake off, so they would question her.

I'll tell them I couldn't just sit around. Just checking on fan motors.

Whenever voices echoed into the passage from the hallway outside, she tensed up, but no one crawled in to catch her, nor did anyone seem to be talking about anything interesting, alarming, or worth eavesdropping on. Tinsley, remembering the instructions from last time, kept quiet, dutifully following her through the network of access conduits. The girl didn't look the least bit worried or disoriented, which made Raven suspect she'd broken the rules and gone in the tunnels before.

What child could resist playing in a maze of secret tunnels?

At least she trusted Tinsley's intelligence. Of all the kids, she'd be the least likely to touch pipes, wires, valves, or anything dangerous. Maybe she hadn't gone exploring the tunnels with her friends and simply appeared blasé due to the bad air sapping her energy.

Two turns away from where she wanted to go, Shaw and Trenton's voices came from the left passage out of a four-way intersection. Raven stopped, listened to them grumbling about the idiot who installed an electrical junction box upside down, making it a chore to get at the screws, then risked peeking around the corner.

Shaw lay on his back, feet toward her, arms threaded up under the water and sewer lines, struggling to squeeze a socket wrench into position. Trenton knelt, his back to her, holding a crank light as best he could on the spot. Watching them deal with a hard-to-reach component irritated her in sympathetic frustration. Still, it kept their attention focused.

She crouched in the near dark, staring at the filthy concrete, black pipes, copper tubes, and once-white PVC, waiting for a chance to go past the intersection without being noticed. Opportunity came moments later in the form of the socket slipping off the bolt, falling off the driver, and nailing Shaw right in the head, sending him off on an expletive-laden rant. She scurried across the intersection while his shouting drowned out the clinking of tools in her satchel.

When she reached the passage leading to the escape tunnel behind the locked door, Raven slowed to a veritable crawl, irrationally worried Noah would somehow know she planned to sneak outside again without permission and would have a guard posted. She wondered if he knew about the seemingly pointless maintenance passage with no pipes or wires in it that bypassed the locked door.

Darkness obscured the last fifteen feet around the rightward bend, a good clue the steel plate still blocked off the end. If anyone had been watching the corridor to the way out, some light would have leaked past it. She felt her way down to the end, gripped the plate, and shifted it out of their way.

Against everything that made sense—the reason for her going outside, the risk of bringing Tinsley, not knowing if she'd actually find anything in the ancient's storage place—an undeniable sense of excitement made the jog down the long corridor pass in an instant. Her father had undoubtedly passed to her the part of his psyche responsible for his restlessness and drive to keep going outside.

Too worried about being caught at the last minute, Raven found herself a good way up the ladder before realizing she hadn't tethered her daughter. If the girl fell... She stopped and peered down—at complete darkness.

Tinsley patted her leg while searching blind for the next rung. "Why'd you stop?"

"Forgot the rope."

"It's okay. I won't fall. Can we not stand still on the ladder?"

After a brief internal argument, she decided the less risky thing to do would be to get off the ladder as soon as possible—so she climbed onward, perhaps a little too fast for being unable to see. The echo of her rattling tools announced the approach of the ceiling before she smacked her head into the hatch. She eased up the last few rungs while reaching out above her head until she found the wheel.

Tinsley patted her right foot, again likely searching for the next rung up and realizing she'd stopped.

"We're at the top. Be ready. It's going to be bright out there this time."

"Okay," whispered Tinsley.

Raven spun the wheel to open the mechanism, then gave it a shove, allowing sunlight to flood the elevator shaft. She caught sight of a clear blue sky for only a few seconds before her eyes protested and closed automatically. Unexpected warmth fell on her, as though she'd stuck her face right under the sunlamps in the hydroponic room.

Gah. Ow.

Worried a security officer might see such intense sunlight under the locked door, she hurried blind into the surface world, then turned around to reach into the hole. Peering down away from the sky didn't hurt *too* much.

Tinsley, eyes closed, grabbed the edge of the opening. Raven clamped a hand around the girl's broom handle-sized wrist and hauled her up out of the shaft with one arm while pulling the hatch down using the other hand. Mild coughing interrupted the child's laughter, but she kept giggling.

"It's warm," whispered Tinsley. "Like the farm without the poop smell." She attempted to look around, but cringed at the light. "It's bright!"

Raven still squinted too much to see anything other than the intense glow of the sun, but held her hands out, mystified at the warmth coming from so far away. The grow lamps in the hydroponic farm gave off a similar amount of heat, but only if she got close to them.

"The sun must have a lot of windmills." Tinsley cupped both hands around her eyes as a visor, attempting to look at their surroundings. Upon noticing the vastness of the sky overhead, she let out a soft, "Whooooah. There's no ceiling?"

"Nope. That's what makes it 'outside.'" Raven blinked, wishing her eyes would hurry up and get used to daylight.

She took a breath of air laden with humidity and the taste of plant life, adoring the absence of the rubbery-chemical flavor she'd grown so accustomed to she never even consciously noticed until returning to the Arc after her first time outside. Amid the rustle of leaves in the wind came an odd susurrus like someone making a 'wswsws' sound over a PA system. Despite her eyes still objecting to the glaring light, she still tried to search for the source. Listening gave her a general sense of direction, but nothing other than the crumbling skeletons of old houses and trees stood there.

Must be something plastic in the wind.

Tinsley sat and pulled her tread socks off.

"What are you doing?" asked Raven.

"I don't wanna get them dirty." She prodded the soil with her toes.

Actual shoes or boots had become a rare commodity in the Arc. The machines to manufacture artificial rubber and plastic items had broken down before her father's birth. Some people, like her, still had boots or sneakers, though she had to be the ninth or tenth person to use this particular pair. Without the miracle of duct tape—itself a rarity these days—they'd have completely disintegrated. Kids of generations past had apparently been quite rough on their clothes, as no kid-sized shoes remained.

People in the Arc never expected to go outside and face terrain harsher than smooth concrete. Underground, they needed warmth more than protection from stepping on dangerous things, so the tread socks—much easier to make than shoes—had become pervasive. The child had a good point, however. Wet, muddy socks would not only be miserable to wear, it would ruin them. She almost chided her for going barefoot outside as it seemed risky, but socks wouldn't exactly protect her if she stepped on something sharp.

Hell, her boots probably wouldn't offer much protection either.

"Be careful where you step. There could be metal on the ground, or glass."

Tinsley nodded while stuffing her socks in the tool satchel, then watched the windmills spin.

If she's going to get into the habit of following me outside, I need to make her something tougher than socks. She considered a sandal of sorts, a tough sole held on by wire or something ought to be doable—but she didn't want to go back inside right away and risk getting caught sneaking out again.

"Wow," whispered Tinsley, gazing around at the trees, bushes, weeds, and flowers.

A veritable wall of dense foliage surrounded the open dirt field containing the hatch and the windmill farm. Rising over the greenery, the ruins of old buildings stretched into the hazy sky off to her right.

She fished the compass out, then peered up at the sky for as long as her eyes could withstand. The sun, fortunately, had migrated far enough off directly overhead to give a sense of orientation. Considering school ended for the day, it would most likely be closer to nightfall than morning. That meant the sun would be in the west. The distant ruins also lay in the same direction the sun appeared to be headed.

Raven checked the compass in her hand. The red end of the needle pointed a little bit off from the windmill farm in front of her.

Okay. Red is north. West is to my left... sun and ruins in the same place. That has to be where Dad went.

"The plants escaped," whispered Tinsley.

"What?" Raven chuckled.

"They got out of their tanks." The child spun around, pointing. "And look at those. They're *so* big. Are they gonna hurt us?"

Raven patted her shoulder. "No. They're trees."

"How do you know that?" Tinsley tilted her head.

"Pictures in books. And some of them have trees on the cover. When a bunch of trees are all in the same place, it's called a forest."

Tinsley's suspicion evaporated once again to curiosity. She took her poncho off, standing there in only a skirt and filter mask.

"What are you doing?"

"I like having the warm on my skin." She smiled at the sky. "It feels nice. I'm always cold inside."

Raven nudged her. "We don't know enough about it out here yet. There could be stuff that can hurt us if we're not careful."

"Okay." Tinsley put the poncho back on and fluffed her hair out from under it.

"Ready, kiddo?"

"Yeah." Tinsley adjusted her filter mask. "I don't even care if we get in trouble when we come back. This is awesome."

Raven took her daughter's hand, hesitated for only a moment, then walked westward.

Every step I take is the farthest from home I've ever been.

IN GHOSTLY FOOTSTEPS

Expect anything; regret nothing. – Ellis Wilder.

Dead dirt gave way to softer, darker soil covered in small vines and the shade of trees.

The compass proved handy due to thick foliage overhead blocking off her view of the distant ruins. For the most part, Tinsley kept quiet, too busy taking in the visual splendor of the outside world to speak. She followed the path of least resistance into the forest that took over what had once been a suburban area. A patch of dark paving peeked out from a gap in the dirt up ahead, revealing she most likely followed the path of an ancient road. Centuries of weather left it buried under enough soil to support weeds. A few small trees fought the old pavement, though most grew to either side.

Raven tried not to waste time sightseeing too much, but couldn't help herself. Witnessing the remains of the ancestors' world, most of it so thoroughly disintegrated as to be unrecognizable, stirred curiosity she never acknowledged having before. It had been a few years since she learned about history in school, but some of it came back to her. She assumed the twisted metal forms here and there to be former cars. Large lumps of metal, likely the engines, sat embedded in the ground, corroded down to almost smooth blocks of steel slag. Little remained of body panels or the fabric inside. Some plastic parts peeked out from the soil. Her former teacher had given them some basics on chemistry, but they had never done any practical experiments. Though she understood acid as a concept, she'd never witnessed it in action. However, all these cars, the houses, even fragments of street lamps or traffic lights hidden beneath soil and bushes, all of it fit her assumption of how an object would look after an acid bath.

I really hope that stuff is out of the atmosphere by now.

She took some comfort from the old cars not having disappeared entirely. The remains meant whatever corrosive substance ate them hadn't been around too long, or had been relatively weak and did its damage over a long time.

Everyone thinks the Saints melted where they stood. But what if they died from breathing poison and melted gradually?

She shivered, becoming hyper-aware of her skin. Nothing itched, tingled, or burned, so she set aside her worry the air might still be acidic. Tinsley walked cautiously, sometimes touching leaves they passed near, but avoided getting too close to any wreckage. She flapped her poncho to cool off, as calm as if they walked from their quarters to the cafeteria. Raven found it amusing to see her little daughter acting braver than the entire population of the Arc. Though Lark had gone outside with her, the woman had been on edge the whole time. If Raven had sneezed unexpectedly, Lark probably would've screamed.

Maybe it's just not knowing any better rather than courage. She gazed up at the branches. *Same could be said for me.*

After an hour—by her best guess—signs of suburbia faded entirely to dense vegetation. She suspected they followed the path her father referred to as a highway in his notes, but identified it only by the relatively straight band of much thinner growth, a veritable tunnel made of greenery. Wherever the occasional tree cropped up in front of her, it had pushed chunks of old paving up to make way. They, too, had become overgrown with moss.

Despite knowing civilization had been here, looking at it now, she couldn't even imagine how this land could have been anything other than untamed and wild. She half expected to see orcs or elves spring out at any moment.

I spent way too much time living in daydreams.

Tinsley gasped and clung to her side, staring intently off to her right.

"What's wrong?" whispered Raven, putting an arm around her.

"I saw a monster watching us. When I looked at it, it ran away."

"A monster?" She suppressed the urge to chuckle. *Probably a big leaf swaying.*

"Yes," whispered Tinsley. "It looked like Chewie."

"Huh? Chewie?" Raven lowered herself to one knee.

Tinsley refused to take her eyes off the forest. "You read me the book. He helps Ham Solo in the spaceship. *Star Wars.*"

"Ahh." Raven chuckled. "Han…" She did remember reading a *Star Wars* novel or two to her somewhat recently. "So a tall man-shaped thing covered in hair?"

"Yeah," whispered Tinsley.

"Are you sure you didn't imagine it?"

"Yeah." The girl clung tighter. "He didn't look nice like Chewie."

Raven scanned the woods for any signs of motion. She assumed some insects had to have made a comeback considering all the plants, but anything bigger than that sounded like a child's imagination. The weird 'wswsws' noise came from all over the forest. She now suspected it might be an insect of some kind, as a random bit of plastic making noise in the wind couldn't explain it occurring so many times from different places. Everyone knew the Arc contained the only remnants of humanity, but what if a creature like bears miraculously survived the Great Death? Nature could do weird things. A bear standing up on two legs could look like Chewie to a kid, especially from far away. Maybe new animals had evolved to withstand the poisons. Three or four centuries—her best guess at how long it had been—seemed far too little time for any evolutionary process to produce such a drastic mutation. Any animal adapted to a toxic environment most likely would have become dependent on the toxins, so probably died out in places no toxins existed.

But it couldn't be a person.

Unless... the people who fake died could be living on the surface. She'd seen something move on a distant tower she swore had been a person. The new Saints might have seen her leave the Arc and followed her. If so, they'd have no reason to be hostile—but they could report her to Noah. Not a big deal. If she found something to show him, she'd report herself to Noah.

Bears, however, were a problem—if they existed. The greenish-brown ponchos Raven and Tinsley wore did more or less blend in with the foliage, but they didn't help at all to conceal their scent. She didn't really believe large animals could have survived topside, anyway. While Tinsley did have a strong imagination, she'd never been prone to making up stories that sounded legitimately frightening. She most likely saw something move, but didn't get a good look and her mind filled in Chewie.

"I don't think he wants to bother us, but let me know if you see him again."

"Okay." Tinsley twisted side to side to peer around in a 360. "He's gone."

Raven kept a firm hold of her daughter's hand and resumed walking.

The forest-shrouded highway eventually led them to a breathtaking edifice of decaying concrete covered in leaves, moss, and creeping vines. Raven stopped at the edge of the woods where trees brushed up against the walls of ruined high-rise towers. On her right beyond a line of ruined metal guardrail, treetops reached only a few feet higher than her eye level, the sunken pit in which they grew suggesting she and Tinsley stood on an overpass.

Momentarily stunned at the scenery around her, she turned in place. It struck her as odd for the terrain to shift so abruptly from dense forest to high-rises. The prior civilization didn't build these towers in the middle of nowhere. Whatever smaller structures once surrounded them on the eastern side of the city had vanished without a trace into the foliage.

Ahead, visible roadway ran into the heart of the old city. Chunks of concrete littered everywhere, likely fallen from the towers years ago, around hundreds of ruined cars eaten down to their frames to the point they resembled dead metal spiders curled up on their backs. An utter lack of human remains anywhere in sight got her wondering what happened to all the people who couldn't get into the Arc. Is that why the underground shelter had such a thick main door? To keep out tens of thousands of angry, desperate people trying to force their way in?

She'd never seen any written accounts of what went on outside during the Great Death. People who'd made it into the Arc wouldn't have had any way to observe the outside world, and amid the chaos of the planet becoming increasingly more and more toxic to life, she doubted anyone took the time to write things down, take pictures, or even care about telling their story.

It would've been mass panic. Violence. Probably lots of people dying everywhere. Bodies left to rot, disease.

Raven let out a somber sigh. Thinking about that would do no one any good and only make her depressed. She squeezed Tinsley's hand, grateful to have her. Even though the pregnancy came from a sense of duty rather than a true relationship with a man, she loved her daughter as much or more than her mother loved her. Dad and Mom had been matched by the usual process and asked to have some babies, but they'd actually fallen in love.

Her father always had thought it ironic how she always got on him for taking stupid risks going outside, but she ended up dead to a mystery illness before outside toxins got him. Grief welled up.

"Not now," whispered Raven.

"Hmm?" Tinsley glanced up at her, squinting at the sun in her face.

"Talking to myself. Thinking about sad stuff and this isn't a good time. I've got a mission."

"What for?"

Raven advanced into the city, peering up at the buildings on either side of the street. "Finding stuff we can use to fix the filters. Or something useful enough that I can convince Noah it's not going to kill us to go outside."

"I can tell Noah he's a chicken. I'm six and not scared."

While impressive, the giant buildings gave off intermittent creaks or clatters in time with the wind, unsettling her. If any one of them decided to pick that moment to collapse, their sheer size would virtually guarantee she and her daughter would be crushed.

They've stayed up for centuries. They can last another two hours.

Despite almost every window in sight being broken, not much glass gathered in the streets and sidewalks. Glimmering dust close to the walls warned of sharp ground, but wind and rain had cleared out the open areas. A bent lamp post that looked like a curled finger matched a landmark her father referred to in his notes. She turned left at the corner opposite the twisted post, walking past broken cars, ruined buildings, and enough plastic trash to build a second Arc. If not for the toxic fumes it would produce, collecting it all for processing would've been tempting. The people who worked in the fabrication group could use this raw plastic to make so many different things—but not unless her team could resurrect the air scrubbers and fix the ventilation system.

Unless, of course, she somehow managed to talk Noah into allowing an exhaust vent to be dug out to the surface. That also felt like a bad idea. If they released poisonous plastic fumes into the air, maybe it would attract Plutions. Venting harmful vapors certainly sounded like something those creatures would do.

Nah. Outside air had enough toxic stuff already. Making more is like slapping someone on where they got stitches.

She waded amid the bottles and jugs, so deep they reminded her of a plastic ball pit described in a book. Of course, the story involved a mother losing track of her little boy at a place with amusements. The last she saw him, he'd gone into the ball pit. She didn't finish that one, too worried about it having a sad ending.

Three blocks from where she turned, they reached a huge

intersection, more of a square. A stone structure at the center consisted of a three-tiered arrangement of increasingly smaller bowls atop which stood a blob-shaped obelisk that had probably once been a statue of a person. It gave the suggestion of a human with wings.

Dad said turn right at the angel.

"What were these?" Tinsley poked one finger into a mangled metal spar sticking up into the air from a pile of scrap, then crouched to pick up a rusted coil spring. "They're all over."

"Careful." Raven eased the scrap out of her daughter's hand. "It's dangerous to play with metal that's become rusty."

"Sorry." Tinsley stood and wiped her hand on her poncho.

"The round thing there is a wheel—or was. All these metal lumps used to be cars."

"So many." The child looked around at the courtyard.

It occurred to Raven almost two hours had passed since they snuck out of the Arc. *About time to eat.* She walked up to the fountain and took a seat on the knee-high wall surrounding the lowest basin, a ground-level pool that probably once held a foot or two of water. It still had water in it, brackish green and only a few inches deep beneath an island of plastic trash and empty metal cans. A darker green scum coated the concrete for a few inches above the water line, suggesting it hadn't been too long ago the rain had collected there.

I hope it's not green when it falls from the sky. She peered up, involuntarily squinting due to the sun. The effect of daylight had thankfully lessened from painful to annoying. An astoundingly blue sky stretched overhead, only a few clouds in sight. Two appeared puffy and white, one greyish. *It must have rained the day I went out to the turbine. So grey overhead... the sky looked like poison.*

Tinsley reached into the basin and nudged a plastic bottle, sending it floating across the 'pond' like a tiny boat. Aluminum cans clinked against each other as the bottle bumped them out of its way. Raven fished out two muffins, handing one to Tinsley who sat beside her and pulled her filter mask down to hang in front of her chest. They ate at the center of the abandoned square, surrounded by crumbling high-rise buildings shrouded in green leaves. The occasional noise from windblown debris falling made her jump to look in that direction, still not fully trusting 'Chewie' hadn't been both real and a potential threat. Not real in the sense of being the *Star Wars* character, but a bear—or perhaps one of those mutants her father claimed to have seen. She couldn't think of any reason why a Saint would follow her all the way here, yet had an inexplicable sense something in possession of human intelligence watched them.

I've read too many ghost stories.

Between nibbles, Tinsley pointed at things and asked what they were. Raven explained street lamps, signs, traffic lights, and the general idea of a fountain. She had no explanation for the unmarked metal cabinet on a street corner, but assumed it either held electronics of some kind—probably for the traffic lights—or maybe served as some kind of storage.

A sudden fluttering noise startled a gasp from Tinsley.

Raven peeled her gaze off the large steel box across the square and swiveled toward her daughter, who sat cross-legged atop the fountain wall, staring at a greyish-white bird. The child's eyes couldn't possibly get any wider. Though her body language conveyed fear, her facial expression held mostly curiosity.

"Mommy," whispered Tinsley. "It's looking at me."

"Hold still," whispered Raven.

"Is it gonna eat me if I move?"

Raven resisted the urge to laugh. "No. You'll scare it away. It's a pigeon. Holy crap. A bird."

After a minute or two of silent staring, Tinsley reached out to pet the pigeon. It scurried off flapping its wings, but didn't take flight. The eruption of feathers startled a squeak out of the girl. Emitting an odd warbling noise, the bird pulled a 180 and came scooting back toward her. Tinsley raised one knee almost to her chin in a defensive posture, but the pigeon stopped a few inches away.

"Birds..." Raven, reasonably certain the creature posed no threat to her kid, gazed up at the broken skyscrapers, wondering where it might have made a nest—or how many others could be here.

Tinsley broke a small piece of her muffin off and tossed it to the pigeon.

The bird went for it without hesitation, gobbling up every last crumb in a series of rapid pecks. Three more pigeons glided in to land by the first.

"Uh oh, now you've done it," said Raven.

Tinsley spun to look at her, horrified.

"I'm teasing. I remember reading something about these birds. If you feed one, a whole bunch of them come looking for food."

"Oh." Raven broke off two more pieces from her muffin, each about the size of a kidney bean, and threw them to the birds.

All three pigeons began fighting over the food, grabbing it and darting off, crashing into each other, stealing the muffin bit, and so on. It didn't get vicious, but the birds all seemed to be quite greedy.

Tinsley ate the last of her food before the pigeons came back looking for more. One brave bird swooped in and landed on her lap, going for crumbs that had fallen into the folds of her poncho. The child held still until the bird cleaned up all the crumbs. As soon as she again tried to pet it, the pigeon leapt into the air in a flailing mass of frantic flapping.

"They're wrong," said Tinsley.

"Who's wrong?"

"Whoever said that *all* the animals died." Tinsley reached into the tool satchel for a water bottle. "If they all died, there wouldn't be any left. So some had to live."

Raven leaned over and plucked a pigeon feather from the fountain wall, holding it up to examine it. Tiny filaments of light and dark grey fluttered in the breeze as she rotated it between thumb and forefinger. "That's true. Birds can fly long distances. I wonder if they migrated to the Arctic back then."

"Huh?" Tinsley opened the bottle and gulped down a few mouthfuls.

"You know how the world became hot right before the Great Death?"

"Kinda. Sienna hasn't really taught me much history yet." She gestured around. "It's warm now."

Raven smiled. "They said it was much worse here. So hot that people couldn't survive. Back then, if we went outside, we would've fainted from heat stroke in minutes."

"Wow."

"The Arctic was like the coldest place on the planet. Maybe it didn't get hot enough to kill everything there." Raven took a small metal case from her tool satchel, one she used to hold bits for her modular screwdriver, and put the feather in it. *Proof.*

Tinsley picked up a few feathers as well. Since she had no satchel or pockets, she stuck them decoratively into her filter mask, which still dangled at her chest.

"C'mon. Let's get going. I'd like to be home before dark."

"You want to go back inside?" Tinsley's nose scrunched.

"Yes and no..." Raven leaned back, gripping the stone behind her, and gazed up at the broken buildings. "Mostly because I don't want to leave everyone else down there to get sick in the bad air. Also, we don't have any food. It will take us time to grow food plants outside."

Tinsley shifted around, draping herself on her stomach over the wall so she could reach down into the basin and play boats with bottles. "Yeah. I would miss my friends if we stayed outside."

"Me too. C'mon." Raven stood and tugged on the girl's poncho.

"Okay." Tinsley pushed herself upright.

Raven took her hand, heading across the square to the right, following the description given in her father's notes. Dozens of pigeons littered the area, seemingly appearing from thin air. They couldn't really have come out of nowhere, and it bugged her not to have noticed them earlier. *Maybe they heard us coming and stayed out of sight until they smelled food.*

They circled around the mangled frame of a bus flipped on its side. Most of the seats and some other plastic parts survived. Another look around at the ruins confirmed that, by and large, metal, plastic, and concrete withstood whatever the Plutions threw at the planet. Fabric, rubber, wood, and other materials all disintegrated. At least they didn't stumble across dead people.

Did bones dissolve too or had everyone fled this place?

Five blocks down the street away from the fountain square, she reached the end of the high rises. Here, the buildings only stood four or five stories tall, a few only having one. Many lay in heaps of collapsed ruins, only hints of walls around an open area. A tall strip of bright orange ran across the front face of a huge, relatively intact one-story building on the left. Most of the damage the building sustained appeared focused on the windows and doors, likely from people in the time of the Great Death breaking their way inside. The bright stripe looked like the same shade of orange as on the hammer in Dad's trunk.

"The ground is shiny." Tinsley pointed.

Flecks of broken glass glimmered on the blacktop between her and the building.

Tread socks won't help. "That's glass."

Tinsley curled her toes. "I don't wanna step on that. Am I gonna wait here?"

Sure, and the bear that's been following us would pick right now to show up. "Nah. I need you to stay with me." She didn't know whether to laugh or cry at the idea she trusted her daughter standing here on the sidewalk alone more than leaving her in the Arc.

"But, glass…"

"I didn't say you had to walk." Raven grinned, then crouched so the girl could climb on her back.

Tinsley hopped up and wrapped her arms and legs around her mother. Raven grasped the child's legs behind the knee, supporting some of her minuscule weight, and jogged across the parking lot.

Windblown dirt had collected against the face of the building, half-burying rows of metal push carts. Beyond them, the broken remains of a pair of sliding doors lay under the wreckage of a large motor vehicle someone long ago used to smash their way inside. She scooted between the frame and the brick doorjamb, entering a dim, cavernous space. Hundreds of dead light fixtures dangled from thick steel beams supporting a two-story-tall ceiling. To her left, several rows of conveyor platform stations stood in a line.

Curious, she approached, looking around. The nearest one had a plastic sign on a pole next to it reading '8 items or less.' Each station had a computer screen and keyboard, everything coated in a layer of crusty sediment.

"This must be where the quartermasters worked, keeping track of who took what."

Nothing in sight appeared close to useful, so she walked deeper into the building toward aisles between massive shelves. Junk lay strewn all over the floor, suggesting people had gone crazy, throwing stuff around. Though a good portion of it had suffered irreparable damage from the passage of time, a surprising amount of it appeared potentially useful. At first, it didn't make sense why no one took the tools, pipes, tile, and so on... until she considered they would have been hungry, thirsty, and panicked—not looking for things they could use to repair a living space.

Any food, water, and clothing that might have been stored here would be long gone.

Granted, she had no interest in centuries-old food.

With the exception of an area containing light fixtures, the interior of the storage building appeared free of broken glass, so she let Tinsley walk. The next section she reached contained hundreds of metal cans stacked on shelves. She picked one up, surprised at the weight until brushing at the side revealed a label underneath a layer of grime. Latex paint. Whoever had ransacked the place didn't even bother throwing the cans off their shelves.

I'm no chemist, but this stuff is going to be useless after so long.

She set the can back and kept going.

A few aisles of 'possibly useful but not amazing' stuff later, she found a stack of thick plastic mats. It looked as though someone made small throw rugs out of clear plastic. Tiny spikes studded one side, the other smooth. That baffled her, but gave her an idea: sandals. The plastic appeared dense enough to stop broken glass and possibly sharp metal, especially with only a child's weight on it.

Cloth strips and some hot glue will be perfect.

Alas, she had neither of those here. Still, she noted the location of the strange plastic sheets for later, intending to grab one before returning to the Arc. Those little spikes would be perfect for walking on dirt. Inside the Arc, they'd probably be slippery.

The shelves right next to the weird plastic rugs contained wheeled office chairs. They appeared usable—albeit filthy—but the Arc didn't need chairs. She kept going. Four aisles past that, she about screamed from unexpected excitement.

An entire aisle contained air filter inserts in various sizes. A handful of loose ones in each size sat atop plastic-wrapped bundles containing twenty or thirty. They ranged from eight-inch squares up to rectangles twice the size of the inserts the primary filter duct used.

"Wow..." Raven gingerly picked up a square labeled as 38x38. The ancient filters looked unbelievably clean for their age, but would no doubt be brittle. Then again, if the fabric inside had been made from synthetic materials, perhaps not. "These are almost perfect. And there's so many. The big ones we can cut in half."

Tinsley looked up at her, confused. "You're too happy over tiles."

"This isn't tile, Tins... these are air filters."

The child blinked. "Are they gonna fix the air?"

A scenario of the windmills collapsing, the power going out for good, and the CO_2 scrubbers/fans shutting down played on fast forward in her imagination. "A little. These will get most of the dust out of the air. But, they're not a permanent fix. Mostly, they'll only keep it from getting worse. They'll give us time."

Tinsley grabbed one and lifted it, staggering backward when it flew up unexpectedly fast. "Eep! They're light!"

"Yeah. It's mostly open space and synthetic fabric. Keep that one to bring back." She picked up a twenty-pack, then hurried to the stack of weird plastic mats, grabbing one and rolling it up into a tube to make it easier to lug.

"What's that for?" Tinsley held up her filter panel. "And I think we're going to need more than one."

"This"—Raven patted the plastic—"is going to become sandals.

And you're right. We do need more than one. A lot more. Way too many for the two of us to carry. We're going to take one back as proof."

Tinsley glanced down at the filter in her hands. "If he doesn't believe you, can I bonk him over the head with this?"

"Hah!" Raven grinned. "Tempting, but I don't think it will help. Besides, his skull is so thick it would destroy the filter... and we need it. C'mon. Time to go."

"Aww. Okay."

With the rolled up plastic under one arm, a twenty-pack of filters under the other, Raven gave one last look around the facility, awestruck at its sheer size. *So much stuff just sitting here waiting for people to need it.* She wondered how a society that stockpiled resources like this could have been foolish enough to ignore the warning signs leading up to the Great Death. Could the Plutions have been so advanced humanity didn't have any chance?

Hmm. Maybe they weren't as obvious to them as it is to me reading it.

Shrugging, she made her way out of the building, laughing to herself at the notion of smashing the filter over Noah's head. Tinsley clung to her back until they made it past the patches of shattered glass, dropping to her feet once they reached safe ground.

The sun hid behind the ruins further west, its heat and daylight noticeably weaker, a sign of night approaching. If she could avoid doing so, she'd prefer not to be outside after dark. At least, not until she had a better understanding of what sorts of animals might be out here.

18

BY THE BOOK

We'd be a lot better off without so many damn rules. Someone ought'a make a rule prohibiting there being too many rules. – Ellis Wilder.

R aven didn't know what to expect under the hatch, or even if it would open.

During the roughly two-hour walk back to the Arc, several 'Chewie' sightings—rather hearings—kept her jumpy. Neither she nor Tinsley ever saw anything, but grunts, thumps, and the crackle of small branches breaking came from behind and to their left, as though something followed them.

Tinsley, who'd been utterly fearless in regard to the danger of toxic air, became clingy at having a 'monster' close by. Though Raven thought at least some of the grunting noises sounded awfully human to be a bear, she dismissed it as her overactive imagination. Even if everything she knew about the world was wrong and humans might have survived in places other than the Arc, another person would have tried to talk to her—or attacked.

She kept her hand on Dad's old military knife for most of the walk,

Tinsley's arm threaded through hers. Trying to beat sundown, she didn't dawdle to gawk at ruins, trees, or the occasional scrap of civilization peeking out of the foliage.

Whatever creature followed them didn't reveal itself at the edge of the forest when they reached the large area of open dirt spanning from the Arc's back entrance to the windmill farm. She stopped about halfway between the tree line and the metal square on the ground, peering back into the greenery. Alas, the sun's position below the treetop level made the woods behind her an impenetrable mass of shadows. 'Chewie' could've been hiding behind the nearest tree and she wouldn't have seen him.

I really have read too many scary books.

Somewhat confident no giant furry beast would appear out of nowhere barreling toward them, she walked the last forty yards or so to the hatch. Tinsley twisted to watch the windmills spin against a backdrop of a sky fading rapidly from blue to orange, the horizon beyond the turbines black.

Moment of truth. Are we in trouble?

She grasped the hatch and pulled.

It opened without protest, and no one appeared to be waiting at the bottom. At least, no flashlights turned on.

"Whew… Not sure what I'm freaking about. I'm going to basically admit to it anyway." She exhaled out her nose.

Tinsley rummaged her tread socks out of the tool satchel and put them on after brushing dirt off her soles. Raven took cord from the satchel and tied the filter panel onto the girl's back, then rigged a harness for the twenty-pack of filters and the much heavier plastic mat, hanging them over her shoulder to free both hands for the long ladder climb.

She let Tinsley go first, closing the hatch behind them and turning the wheel.

"It's really dark. I can't see anything," whispered Tinsley.

"Yeah. It's going to be this dark outside soon, too."

"Not really. There's stars up there. It smells bad inside."

Five-ish hours of being outside truly did make the Arc smell like an old sneaker that had stepped in poop.

A few minutes of repetitive climbing later, Tinsley whispered, "I'm on the bottom."

Raven took the last three rungs slow, reaching out a tentative foot until she found concrete, then fumbled around in the dark to find her daughter's hand, then hurried along using one hand on the wall for navigation. At this hour, a strip of glow shone in from under the locked door, giving her enough light to see the steel plate beside the maintenance passage.

No one had moved it back into position, a good sign no one noticed her leave. That would have been a miracle if she didn't plan on going straight to Noah's office and throwing the single filter at him.

That's going to piss him off. Maybe I should talk it over with Ben first.

She slipped into the 'secret' maintenance passage, pulled the plate in place, and hurried through the crawlways to an exit fairly close to the engineering room. Two women she recognized as being on the water team went by as she emerged into the corridor. Neither paid any special attention to her crawling out of the hole. No one would think it unusual for a tech to be in those passages.

"Hope Ben's still 'in the office.'"

She hurried down the hall and swung a left into her work area— finding it empty of people.

Being back in the Arc with no one the wiser about her mission caused an adrenaline crash. She'd been worried the security people would grab her at the bottom of the ladder and throw her right in jail, preventing her from doing anything about the situation. Fair bet if she had been discovered, that would have happened. In the absence of her fear, the exertion of the long overland hike and rummaging caught up to her.

"Yeah... figured they all went home for the wake. Hell with it. Tomorrow." She unrolled the plastic mat on her work table, weighing it down under several fan motors to keep it flat. "These"—she snagged the filter from Tinsley and set it on top of the pack—"are coming with us. Don't want them to disappear on me."

The girl smiled.

They walked home, had a shower to rid themselves of dirt and dust, then changed into their night clothes before eating two more muffins for dinner. Though her dial clock showed the time at 1-0-1-7, almost three hours earlier than she usually went to bed, she didn't bother trying to stay awake.

RAVEN AWOKE SIXTEEN MINUTES BEFORE THE ALARM WENT OFF, AWARE of an odd feeling.

Getting an adequate—perhaps even excessive—amount of sleep resulted in none of the usual post-alarm sluggishness that had become her norm each wake. It should have left her energized and ready to tackle any project, but her head hurt, a faint burn lingered in her sinuses, and her muscles didn't really want to cooperate.

For a few seconds, she freaked out in her mind over walking into an invisible toxin and exposing her child to the same. Had the 'Chewie' following them been a hallucination brought on by some unknown chemical, just like Noah said?

Tinsley stirred, coughed a bit, and groaned.

"Morning, kiddo."

"Mmmn. My head hurts."

"Mine, too." Raven pulled the slight girl upright, into her lap. "Do you feel sick?"

Tinsley yawned. "No. It's the same all the time."

It's not the outside... it's the air in here. Crap! If I'm starting to feel it, the other kids are in big trouble. And elders.

She jumped out of bed. Tinsley raced to the toilet room before Raven could get there, so she hovered by the door waiting. Once the girl emerged and began to get dressed, Raven used the toilet, then rushed changing into her wake clothes. To save time and not waste food, they ate muffins from their remaining stash for breakfast.

Dropping Tinsley off at the classroom on the way to the engineering area presented two problems. One, if her plan worked as she hoped it would, a group would be following her to the ruins today to help collect filters and she didn't want to leave Tinsley down here in the bad air if she could avoid it. Two, showing up at the classroom would almost certainly set off a conversation with Sienna about where they'd been yesterday, missing dinner. While she didn't mind having that conversation, she didn't want the hour long delay it would cause right now. Raven grabbed the new filters and hurried out the door.

Tinsley followed her at a brisk walk straight to the engineering room, not even questioning why they'd gone right past the school.

The room remained empty, but she figured the others simply hadn't arrived yet. She'd gotten out of bed early and skipped the usual twenty minutes at the cafeteria. Having some time to burn, she had Tinsley stand on the clear plastic so she could trace the outline of her feet. Enlarging the cutouts a bit would add a year to their useful lifespan before the child outgrew them.

A small electric saw made cutting the plastic easy. In the midst of doing that, inspiration hit her. She cut out three of each side, stacking lefts on lefts and rights on rights. Rather than hot glue a cloth strip to the top to serve as an ankle tie and toe loop, she sandwiched three layers of plastic together with hot glue, putting the 'sandal straps' she made out of fabric between them, cemented in place. The result: half-inch thick tough-as-armor sandals with spiked bottoms.

Within seconds of Tinsley putting them on to test, Ben walked in.

His casual wave on the way to his office proved he had no idea she'd gone outside yesterday. The man did *not* have any ability to conceal the kind of emotion he'd feel if he knew she'd gotten in big trouble.

"Hey, Ben?" asked Raven.

He stopped, whirling around to look at her. "Oh, that's right. You should be off this wake. I'm not gonna say anything if you want to help out, but keep your head down."

"Actually, I did the exact opposite from keeping my head down. Can we talk? I need your opinion."

Tinsley examined the sandals, took a few steps around in a circle, and gave a thumbs-up. "They're a"—she coughed. "Ugh. They wanna slide on the smooth floor, but they feel good."

"Opposite?" Ben rubbed his forehead. "Don't tell me something in Noah's office is going to catch fire."

She laughed. "No. You know how I feel about topside, right?"

"Yeah." He folded his arms. "What did you do?"

Raven pulled the single filter panel out from under her worktable and held it out to him. "Oh, nothing much. Look at this."

"That's..." He took it from her as if handling the most valuable commodity in the world. "It looks like it's never been used. Where the hell did you get this from? Wait..." He stared at her. "Did you go searching around on level one? Find a storage room we forgot about?"

"No. I'm actually more afraid of level one than outside. I went to the ruins of a city." She started explaining about her father's notes, but paused as Lark, Shaw, and Trenton walked in together, likely from the cafeteria—as evidenced by Trenton carrying a few pieces of toast he munched on. "Hey, guys. Look at this."

They wandered over.

Raven plucked the filter from Ben's grasp and showed it off to them before restarting the explanation of the notes as well as her trip out to get the filter. "There are *hundreds* of filters there. Some are a bit small, but I saw at least 200 giant rectangular ones. We could cut them in half and get two squares the right size for each one."

"That's a little difficult to believe." Shaw shifted his jaw side to side, making his white mustache twitch.

"I saw it, too," said Tinsley.

Lark's jaw hung open. "You brought your kid outside?"

Raven tossed the filter to Ben and folded her arms. "Damn right I did. The air in here is dangerous. Look at her."

Tinsley coughed.

"She took her mask off to eat when we got to the ruins, and forgot to put it back on. She didn't cough at all out there."

"Mom..." Tinsley pulled on her arm. "I didn't forget. I didn't wanna wear it."

"Wow." Ben pinched the bridge of his nose. "Took the kid outside…"

"I was worried if I didn't, I'd come back to find her on the floor." Raven picked Tinsley up and squeezed her. "I don't even like having her inside this place now. Maybe replacing all the filters can help a little, but you all damn well know how much trouble we're in."

The others exchanged conflicted glances.

"Hang on. There's more." Raven pulled the tin of screwdriver bits out of her satchel, opened it, and held up the pigeon feather. "Check *this* out."

"The heck is that?" asked Lark. "Plastic?"

"No. It's a feather. From a pigeon. We saw live birds." She jabbed the feather at Ben's face. "*Live* birds. There is no way you will convince me birds are surviving in air bad enough to harm us. In this novel I read, coal miners carried a canary with them because if they found toxic gas, the little bird would die first and warn them."

"Tweet," said Tinsley.

Everyone looked at her.

"I'm the littlest." She shrugged. "If the air goes bad, I'm gonna warn everyone."

Raven swept her up into a hug, fighting back tears. "No, baby. I'm gonna take you outside before it gets that bad."

"You said this old storage place had hundreds of filters?" Shaw raised an eyebrow. "You found birds, and you spent half a day out there with a six-year-old, and she's fine."

"Yeah," rasped Raven, too choked up for her voice to fit out her throat.

"And you went topside." Shaw glanced at Lark.

"Seriously? She's like the most worried about the toxic air." Trenton chomped a bite out of his toast.

Lark playfully shoved him. "I was. But, yeah. I went out there. Feel fine. Those wind turbines are in *rough* shape. Rusty. Full of holes. The towers' rivets are loose. That little girl there could probably kick one over. It might not be too late to save them, but the only way we'd ever be able to do that is a lot of work outside."

Shaw took the pigeon feather. "This thing's real all right. Getting those filters is the only thing that's gonna keep us all breathing. Even if it's as bad as they say it is up there, it ain't gonna matter real soon. Not so great in here anymore. I'm in. Let's go get them."

"Wait. Wait." Ben raised a hand in a 'stop' gesture. "You can't just *go outside*. We need to get approval first."

Trenton scoffed. "If there's a fire, you don't gotta ask Noah's okay to put it out."

Ben started to face him, but Lark raised her voice. "Yeah. The longer we wait, the more damage is done. We shouldn't sit around for days waiting for him to make up his mind."

"Hang on, everyone." Ben waved his hands back and forth over his head. "You won't even be able to leave the Arc without official approval."

"How'd she get out?" Shaw gestured at Raven.

"Trade secret. Kidding. I can show you guys, but if Noah realizes it's there, he might want to close it off. Oh, look over there." Raven pointed out the plastic-wrapped twenty-pack she'd set on an unused worktable against the wall. "The place had stacks of those."

Everyone stared.

"We need to do this the right way. Noah is not unreasonable... he's just cautious." Ben looked down at the filter in his hand, then back at Raven. "It's our job to make sure he understands the situation enough to make a decision. And the decision is: we have no choice but to get these filters."

"Before something else breaks." Trenton tossed his last bit of toast into his mouth and gave a thumbs up.

Everyone looked at each other in silence. Mutual agreement spread among them, except for Ben who appeared nervous. Raven locked eyes with him, then gestured at the door in an 'after you' manner.

He sighed, glanced over his shoulder at the HVAC room where the CO_2 scrubbers chugged away, probably doing nothing of any use, and sighed again. He nodded at her, then led the team to Noah's office.

The big boss looked up from his logbook in response to the office door swinging inward. He started to open his mouth, but at the sight of the whole tech team walking in, hesitated as if words rushing to get out tripped over his teeth and got stuck on his lips. The single LED bulb close by on his desk accented the grey parts of his salt-and-pepper hair. Her father had been almost a decade older than him, but hadn't sported any grey yet.

Noah's mood cycled from annoyance at an interruption to acceptance at Ben, then worry—until Tinsley's presence added a note of confusion. He waited for everyone to gather in front of his desk, then leaned back in his chair. "This is either incredibly serious or you've misplaced my birthday."

"Serious." Ben dropped the filter on the desk.

Noah picked it up. "What's this?"

"An air filter."

"Why is it on my desk instead of in the ventilation system?" Noah turned it over in his grasp, examining it. "This filter doesn't seem unusual."

"Because you haven't seen the ones we've been using." Lark showed off a dark stain on her poncho. "That one's new. Unused. The ones we have are so saturated with crud they're not filtering anymore."

Noah studied the panel more closely. "Are you saying you've found a way to manufacture new ones? What's the catch?"

"Catch?" asked Trenton.

"Well…" Noah tossed the filter on the desk and leaned back in his chair. "There must be a catch or you wouldn't be in here about to ask me for something you all expect me to decline."

The others looked at Raven expectantly. None of them appeared willing to rat her out.

Here goes. I'm either going to change his mind or end up in jail tonight. Hopefully, he won't call security here with my whole team behind me.

"We didn't make that filter. I found it," said Raven. "Topside. A couple miles away in the ruins of a city. My father had notes. Notes you knew about. He told you about a stockpile of useful things five years ago and you ignored him."

Noah's eyebrows flared in response to the word 'topside,' but not from fear. He appeared annoyed at being disregarded. However, rather than snap at her, he sat in mute discontent. The same look from Dad years ago would've ended with her over his knee or sitting in the corner.

"The situation is bad," said Ben. "The ventilation ducts are encrusted with at least an inch-thick layer of dirt and sediment. Our air-purification tech is so brittle we cannot afford to shut down flow to subsections long enough to clean the ducts out for risk of suffocation. We can't clean the vents with the fans on, or it's just going to blast all that shit into the Arc. The chemical scrubbers are saturated to the point where I don't think they're having any effect beyond mechanically pulling particulate matter out of the airflow because it's a liquid. We've probably been reliant on the hydroponic farm for oxygen conversion for at least a few years now."

Shaw leaned forward. "Those filters ain't gonna be a magic fix, but we're dealing with a multi-layered shit sandwich right now. Dirty air, low oxygen, crudded-up ductwork. New filters will ease one bit of that and maybe buy us time for some other more permanent fix."

"So you are here for what?" asked Noah.

"My team wants to go out to the ruins and recover as many filters as possible from the storage site." Ben nudged Raven. "Show him the feather."

For a few seconds, the loudest sound in the room came from the electric sizzle of the lamp on the desk.

Raven took the feather out and handed it to Noah. He studied it while she explained the pigeons in the city square. "Topside air is good enough for birds to live."

"We don't know they haven't evolved to tolerate compounds and vapors that could be harmful to us. You can't just blithely go from a sterile environment and expect to be impervious to everything potentially out there." Noah placed the feather against a pen holder, as if considering it a new permanent decoration for his desk. "I'm sure you are well aware we've been isolated down here for over 300 years. Any organisms that may or may not exist out there have done so in a tainted environment. Chemical toxins aside, we have been away from germs, viruses, and other things for many generations. None of us have developed an immune response to pathogens living on the surface."

"The first people in the Arc didn't all come in wearing clean suits, Noah." Desperation lent an unusually authoritative tone to Raven's voice. "The people who came in here brought crud with them. People here get sick all the time. It's gotta be worse than being outside since we have a closed environment. One person gets a cold, within days, everyone in the Arc has it. There's nowhere to go to escape breathing air a sick person has breathed."

"Kid's got a point," said Shaw.

"I didn't say anything," whispered Tinsley.

Everyone except Noah and Ben chuckled.

Noah tapped his fingers at the edge of the fat logbook on the desk, thinking. "I have a feeling you intend to risk going out there whether I approve it or not."

"I'm not saying this to be alarmist, but realistic." Ben set his hands on his hips. "Between the crumbling turbines, the scrubbers, the filters, and the sheer age of everything down here... after seeing Raven and Tinsley spend half a day outside and come back perfectly fine, it's clear we are in a bad situation. This is an opportunity we simply cannot ignore. To do so would put the lives of everyone in the Arc at risk."

"So would going outside. What if you bring back a super bug that wipes us out?" Noah frowned off to the side.

"If it was going to happen, I'd have already done it. And so would my father, years ago." Raven cringed a little inside, admittedly never having thought of undocumented diseases as a risk before. Maybe that's why he kept the new Saints isolated. "Doc's tests didn't find anything. We're all going to die a slow miserable death if we stay down here without doing anything. This is at least a chance. You're the administrator... did you get an instruction book for the Arc? What was the expected lifespan of this shelter? Did the designers intend for us to live down here forever?"

Noah stood, pointing at her. "I'd appreciate it if you stopped implying I am trying to kill everyone." He held his arms out to either side. "My primary concern is making decisions that offer the best chance of preserving the lives of everyone here."

"I'm not accusing you of wanting to kill anyone." Raven caught herself near to shouting and calmed her voice. "I'm saying you are making those decisions using information that's a century or two out of date and ignoring physical evidence. You won't even consider letting us put a system together to vent the Arc with outside air, which I *know* will fix most of our problems—until the turbines die. At least let us fix the filtration system. It's beyond moronic to let vital supplies sit out there."

"It's bad in here," said Tinsley. "My head hurts. My chest hurts. I'm kinda dizzy all the time. Outside, I didn't feel bad. I don' wanna die."

Noah couldn't look at the child. He stared into his desk, hands on his hips. "Anyone who goes topside should be prepared for quarantine when you come back."

"Bit late for that," said Raven. "Besides. How the heck would you quarantine anyone down here? Remember, we have a closed ventilation system? You'd have to shut us up in an airtight vault, which would kill us. Also, Dad went out and came back at least eight times, and you never isolated him. Any sort of germs out there would be all over the Arc by now."

"You're forgetting something," said Shaw, his abnormally deep voice resonating in her chest. "Outside crap's been leaking into the Arc for years. Gasket seal on the hatch is gone."

Noah shifted his weight. "Yes, I'm aware."

"So, you're basically just saying that quarantine shit to scare us." Trenton pointed a thumb over his shoulder at the door. "Let's stop wasting time and get some filters."

Despite there being no clear reason for it, Noah still hesitated. The worry in his expression appeared genuine rather than the angst of a shallow despot facing an erosion of his authority. Eventually, he sank into his chair. "All right. I'll let the security team know you have approval to go on a scavenging expedition. Just... be careful out there."

His strange demeanor made Raven suspect he knew—or at least believed—something he didn't want to tell them. She couldn't help but think about the noises following them back to the Arc. If Doc's story about new Saints had been true, and it certainly seemed so, what information about topside had they brought back that Noah kept secret? He'd already consented to them going out there. Pressing an argument could make him reverse his decision.

If it was that bad, he would have mentioned it already. Whatever he's thinking about can't be a big problem.

"You made the right call," said Shaw before facing Raven. "What are we going to need for this trip?"

She peeled her stare off Noah. "A couple bottles of water and decent shoes. We'll need to work out a way to transport a lot of bulky filters back here, but I remember seeing some flatbed carts in the storage place."

Trenton and Lark peered down at their tread socks. Shaw wore actual boots like Raven's, in about the same state of disintegration.

"You only need shoes at the door where there's broken glass," said Tinsley. "But Mommy can't carry all of you past it."

Everyone chuckled.

Raven smiled, thinking of the plastic mat. "I've got a workaround. Won't take too long."

19

FIRST BREATHS

They all thought I was crazy opening that hatch, but all great discoveries require a little bit of insanity. – Ellis Wilder.

Raven cut forms from the plastic mat to make sandals for Lark and Trenton while explaining the route and what they'd seen on the way. She didn't mention her intent to bring Tinsley along with them, nor did anyone ask about it. The girl remaining at her side rather than heading off to the classroom likely implied she would accompany them. Or perhaps they thought she wanted to be with her mother for as long as possible before they left.

She debated whether or not to mention something bigger than a bird might have been in the woods. *They might think I'm nuts or maybe decide not to go. But... if something really is out there, I need to be honest.*

Hot glue didn't take long to set. By the time Shaw finished collecting water bottles for everyone, Lark and Trenton both had sandals like she'd made for Tinsley. She cautioned them that wearing these 'shoes' inside on concrete floors would be slippery as well as grind the little spikes down flat. The little stubs would likely disappear eventually anyway, but they could provide a little extra traction on dirt for now.

The others assembled in front of her, clearly ready to get underway. Ben, of course, would be staying behind. No one pressed him on it even though the looks they gave him all made fun of his 'bravery.' Granted, having most of the people with technical knowledge all go out at the same time didn't count as wise either.

"Lead on," said Shaw.

"Guys, there's something else I need to tell you about." Raven exhaled. "Last wake, when we walked back to the Arc from the ruins, something bigger than a bird seemed to be following us. We never saw it, but it made noise almost like footsteps and grunting."

"I saw it," said Tinsley. "But real quick. Tall and hairy all over. Like Chewie."

Shaw furrowed his brow. Lark appeared confused.

"Whoa, like from *Star Wars*?" asked Trenton.

"Uh huh." Tinsley nodded. "Mommy thinks it's a bear."

"Ack," said Lark. "What if it's a Plution?"

"Didn't stink." Tinsley waved dismissively. "Plutions smell like butt."

Raven started backing up toward the door. "I know it sounds crazy, but I had to say something just in case I didn't imagine it. Whatever we heard left us alone, so it might not even be a problem. If it didn't want to mess with just me and Tins, it's probably not going to want anything to do with all of us together."

Shaw crossed the room to his workstation and picked up a heavy wrench, which he hung about his waist on a utility belt.

"There's no pipes," said Tinsley.

He chuckled. "I'm not bringing it to adjust fittings. It's in case I have to adjust a skull."

Lark and Trenton both scrambled to find the largest knives they could. Once everyone except Tinsley had armed themselves, the group followed Raven out into the hall, through the central core, and down the corridor to the 'official' way out at the end of the admin wing.

Jose the security officer already waited by the door, likely expecting them due to a call from Noah. He shook his head at them as if they'd all lost their minds. Raven got an extra intense look when Tinsley walked past the doorway.

"You're seriously taking your kid outside?" He whistled. "I'm not sure I should allow that."

Tinsley inhaled sharply as if about to yell something, but lapsed into coughing.

"It's safer out there for her," said Raven, the stern coldness of her voice stalling Jose's retort.

"Not really a point to locking this, ya know." Shaw patted Jose on the shoulder. "Gasket's been shot for years. No vents in this extra hallway. You're breathing outside air right now."

"You know about the gasket?" Raven raised an eyebrow at him, finally asking what she didn't want to bring up in front of Noah.

Shaw nodded.

Jose hastily shut the door behind them after everyone entered the escape corridor.

"That was mean." Lark elbowed Shaw. "Jose turned as pale as Noah."

"But accurate." He smiled at Raven. "Noah asked me to check on it a couple months ago. Someone smelled something funny. Traced it back to the hatch."

"Funny smell?" asked Raven.

"Thought it was a dangerous chemical. Didn't stay long, just enough to hear air hissing past the hatch at the top of the shaft."

Tinsley smiled up at him. "You probably smelled the outside."

"Good air smells weird when you've never breathed it before," said Raven, barely over a whisper.

The group made their way down the corridor, Trenton and Lark eyeing the ominous graffiti warning of certain death to anyone who kept going. Even though the woman had already been outside, she appeared on edge. The indifferent confidence borne of teenage immortality also faded from Trenton.

Raven entered the elevator shaft at the end of the passage first, aware of a faint hissing echoing in the distance above. She peered up at a hairline square of sunlight far overhead. Light hadn't been able to leak in before, but material did crumble and fall all over her the first time she opened it. *Yeah, that seal's toast.*

Trenton walked in behind her, peered up the shaft, and whistled, the sound echoing off the bare concrete. "Why do we have to climb this? Isn't there a big door somewhere?"

"Yeah." Raven plucked Tinsley off her feet and set her on the ladder in front of her. "On level one. But the whole floor is off-limits. Something really bad happened up there years ago."

Tinsley started to ascend, her plastic sandals clattering at her side, dangling by their cloth strips. Raven stepped on the first rung. A brief duct tape rip came from her boot, but she couldn't find it. *I should make sandals for myself, but... not now. These will survive one more walk.*

"Must have been *really* bad if they closed it off." Trenton exhaled hard.

"I don't remember that," said Lark.

"I think it happened years ago, before any of us were born." Raven hauled herself up the ladder.

"Shaw was here when people first moved in," said Trenton.

"Hang on, we gotta go back for a sec." Shaw tugged at the younger man's arm. "Trent forgot his diapers."

Raven climbed close behind Tinsley, using her body as a human safety net in case the child slipped. "Level one happened a really long time ago. Not even Shaw was around then. And the big door is so old, the hydraulic pumps we need to open it are probably dead. Nothing sits for centuries without ever being turned on and still works."

"Not exactly true. Look at my wife's mother," muttered Shaw.

Lark and Trenton laughed. Raven shook her head.

Conversation petered out for a while as everyone focused on the climb. At the top, Tinsley flattened herself against the ladder so Raven could reach past her to the wheel. She got her fingers on the mechanism, but paused before turning it, looking at the sunlight leaking in where the gasket no longer sealed.

"I should probably warn you about the daylight. It's going to hurt your eyes at first. You've all been to the hydro farm, so it shouldn't be *too* bad. Out there is like sticking your face in front of those lamps."

"Wow," said Trenton. "Uhh, why did they make such a big tunnel for a little door?"

"This is an elevator shaft. Dunno if they never built the cab or scavenged it for parts." Raven twisted the wheel to unbar the hatch.

"Escape tunnel." Shaw's deep voice filled the shaft below. "There are mounting brackets for explosive charges that would've blasted the top off so the emergency elevator could get out... but they never installed them."

"... or someone took the explosives," said Lark.

"That, too." Shaw chuckled.

Raven shook her head, not even wanting to think about what someone would've stolen bombs for. "Get ready. Here comes the sun." She shoved the hatch upward.

Intense warmth and daylight fell on her face.

Trenton started to emit a cry of fear, probably expecting the horribly toxic mess from all the stories to melt the flesh off his bones, but the noise coming out of him morphed into a startled yelp of pain at the light.

"Well, damn." Shaw sneezed. "That's kinda bright."

Lark grunted. "Worse than last time."

Tinsley scrambled up off the ladder.

"Bad weather then. Rainy." Unable to see much other than glowing radiance, Raven exited the shaft by feel. "This is probably close to as bright as it possibly gets."

The others emerged one by one, both men cursing the glare. Lark, having experienced it once already, merely shielded her eyes and waited. Everyone sat still for a little while, waiting for their eyes to acclimate.

Tinsley pulled her tread socks off and tied the plastic sandals on. "You guys shouldn't wear socks out here. They're too fuzzy and nice to ruin. Outside, they'll get all muddy and dirty and nasty and blech."

Lark and Trenton murmured in agreement.

"Son of a bitch, look at that," said Shaw.

Raven glanced at him, then around, not noticing anything unexpected. "What?"

"The damn turbines are covered in rust. Them two towers are sagging bad."

"Oh. Yeah. I already told you guys." Raven forced herself to keep her eyes open to look at the windmills. Eighteen huge white fans spun lazily in a calm breeze that rustled leaves, tossed her hair about, and made the blue tarp they'd put over number fourteen flap. "Next thing we need to talk to Ben about is doing a survey on those towers and trying to shore up as many as we can with everything we've got before they collapse. One of those things dies, it won't be long before the rest of them overload."

"If Ben's right about the scrubbers not doing anything, we should bypass them and save the electrical drain." Lark tried to look around and gasped at the sunlight. "Wow, it's so bright."

Shaw walked up to stand beside Raven, using his hand as a sun visor. "Might be something we can do to prop them towers up, yeah. Lark's got a point. Shuttin' them useless things down would take a bunch of stress off the system."

"They need to double or triple the amount of active growth beds in the farm," said Lark.

"Plants won't grow fast enough to help." Raven glanced at the hatch, decided to leave it up, and started off to the west.

"Same weird smell I remember the day I checked the hatch." Shaw adjusted his filter mask.

"You're smelling trees," said Tinsley.

"Been to the farm often enough to know the smell of plants," said Shaw. "This ain't it."

"Fresh air." Raven took in a deep breath.

"That's still smelling trees." Tinsley grinned up at her. "Sienna says they used to make the air nice."

"It's like the pictures." Trenton spun in a circle as he walked, looking around. "How is there so much green stuff out here?"

Raven shrugged. "Not sure how it happened. But it happened."

"How about that." Shaw chuckled. "I expected it would be… scarier out here."

"Scarier?" asked Tinsley.

"Yeah. Clouds of green smoke rolling across the ground, black sky, puddles of bubbling acid… you know. Stuff like in the stories."

Lark shuddered. "Maybe a hundred years ago."

"Or two," said Raven. "Or three. We've been underground a long damn time. No one really even knows for sure when the Great Death happened."

"I hope the Plutions went away." Tinsley squeezed her mother's hand.

Raven eyed the woods, on high alert for large, furry monsters. "Me too, kiddo. Me too."

20

THE LOST

The best way to find something you misplaced is to get a new one. –
Ellis Wilder.

No sign of 'Chewie' appeared during over an hour of walking.

Even though she'd only made the trek once before, Raven found it easy to retrace her steps. The trees mostly looked alike, but fragments of the prior civilization peeking out from under the foliage made for good landmarks. Half a wall here, a road sign there, familiar wreckage of a car after that. Also, given the least troublesome route into the woods followed the path of a buried highway made it somewhat difficult to go the wrong direction.

When they reached the edge of the high-rise ruins, her three co-workers all stopped short, gawking. The Arc consisted of six levels. Most of the crumbling structures in front of them had thirty or more. Of course, the Arc also spread out far wider horizontally than any of the skyscrapers, filling out about three-quarters of a square mile. Still, the sheer size of the buildings likely made everyone try to figure out how, exactly, people who lived before the Great Death ever managed to build them.

"What is this place?" asked Trenton in a half-whisper.

"Uhh, I think it used to be called Atlanta." Shaw pulled his filter mask down only long enough to spit to the side.

Lark approached the decomposing wreck of a car, crouching to look at an engine block worn smooth on the outside as though it had been in a sandblast tunnel. "I thought these ruins are Charlotte."

"Charlotte's a girl's name, not the name of a city," said Trenton. "Cities don't have people names like people don't have city names."

"Sienna said it used to be called Virginny here." Tinsley scraped her foot at the dirt, unearthing a small metal object. "An' we're near a place called Rich Man."

"Virginny, huh?" Trenton scratched his head. "Did they make people leave after they had sex?"

Shaw sputtered into laughter.

Raven put her hands over Tinsley's ears. "According to my father's notebook, this place used to be called Phil."

"What'd they fill it with?" asked Trenton, snickering.

She rolled her eyes. "Phil, not fill. With a P. Phil Delphi or something like that."

"Weird name." Shaw approached the nearest building and fussed at the vines covering it. "Doesn't really matter what they called it. It ain't what it was."

Tinsley flapped her poncho to cool off. Like the previous wake, the sun made it quite warm outside. Apparently, her daughter had fully expected to end up outside again from the moment they woke up, and didn't bother wearing anything under the poncho beyond her inside pants. Raven contemplated scolding her, but felt a little jealous her kid could do it and not be embarrassed. Inside pants belonged under outer clothing unless one stayed in their quarters. Then again, the poncho did basically serve as a dress, hanging almost to the ground. Like any other wake, Raven put on an inside shirt under her poncho plus baggy pants. Being outside while covered head to toe made the heat close to unbearable.

She's not coughing at all. A mixture of guilt and joy convinced her not to make an issue of her kid's wardrobe decisions.

"This place is massive." Lark took a few steps past her, gazing up at the buildings.

Raven advanced into the ruins, taking the same path she did the previous trip. Everyone still in the Arc depended on them to keep the air breathable. There would be time for exploration later. Now, she had a job to finish as fast as possible.

Three blocks from the start of the ruins, Tinsley yelled, "Look, people!" and darted off to the right. Raven whirled to grab for her, but missed by inches. The loud clap of plastic sandals filled the concrete-walled canyon between buildings from the child sprinting down the center of an old street.

"Stop!" yelled Raven, breaking into a run after her. "Don't wander off."

Tinsley skidded to a halt, waving her arms for balance, then twisted back with an apologetic—but still excited—expression. As soon as Raven caught up and took hold of her arm, the child pointed. Not far from where they stood, five skeletons lay on the ground surrounded by a circle of wreckage and rubble, almost like they'd built a fortification around their position. Whatever clothing they may have owned disintegrated completely, either due to the sheer passage of time or the former toxicity of the environment. Only a few scraps remained, too small and grey to even identify the type of fabric it had once been.

Shaw, Trenton, and Lark approached.

The position of the bodies, no two in the same orientation and scattered around, hinted they had died a violent death and been left where killed. A sunlight glint near the most distant body caught her eye. Curious, Raven climbed over the mangled frame of a car to the interior of the barricade and approached a skeleton seated on the ground, its back against a mound of concrete rubble. Raven imagined him standing inside it as a defender, being shot in the forehead, then slumping to the ground. A hole as thick as her index finger pierced the bone above the left eye. The majority of the skull's rear portion had vanished, leaving a cavernous opening.

It reminded her of some descriptions of gunshots she'd read in fiction novels. If this person died to a bullet, it would have happened quite a long time ago. Given the total lack of flesh on the bodies and how the skeletons had mostly fallen apart, that made sense.

She shifted her gaze to the relatively shiny strip in the dirt beside the corpse. Curious, she crouched and dug around it, clearing away a layer of hardened silt more like rock than soil. Her curiosity bottomed out at the discovery of a simple pipe, probably a primitive weapon the dead person had been carrying. For no particular reason beyond having already started excavating, she kept pawing at the crusty sediment. Perhaps a part of her father lived on in her, wanting to understand the past by studying their weapons. This person had carried the object, so it must have some significance.

"What are you doing?" called Shaw. "Is that the way to the filters?"

"Aww, leave them. Too far gone to help," said Trenton.

"Stay back, honey." Lark kept a hand on Tinsley. "You're too little to go looking at bones."

"They won't hurt me. They're already dead."

Raven looked back at the others, all waiting for her some twenty feet away beyond the circle of junk. "Just a minute. Checking something."

Further digging revealed a rotted leather strap. What she thought to be a pipe had an unusually oval shape. A few patches of black paint remained not eroded away to plain grey steel. Upon unearthing a spot with a three-inch disc jutting out around the strange object, the overall shape triggered a memory. A book titled *Shogun* in the library, one of about a dozen that still had a cover, depicted a man holding a similar object.

It's a sword!

She grabbed it and yanked it the rest of the way out of the cemented crud. Sure enough, she'd found a *Shogun*-style sword in a scabbard. The cloth parts around the handgrip had vanished, as had most of the decoration on the outside of the sheath. She didn't expect much from the blade, but emitted a faint gasp of shock when she pulled it a few inches out. The sword's blade still appeared serviceable. Curious, she drew it entirely and held it up. The old sword fell far short of gleaming in the sun due to a coating of dirt. It had a couple of rust spots, but astoundingly remained solid given the length of time it had no doubt been there.

"Wow. Mommy found a big knife!" yelled Tinsley.

Raven slid the blade back into the scabbard and stood, gazing down at the skeleton. *Makes sense why someone used a bullet on him. But... why would they leave the sword behind? It must have been total chaos.* She backed away from the dead person. *So much for there being no human remains here. We just got lucky before. Didn't go the right—or wrong—way.*

She vaulted the rubble fortification and jogged back to the others.

"Easy, kid." Shaw smiled. "Didn't think we had time for treasure hunting."

"Sorry. We really don't." Raven held the sword up. "Didn't see any human remains last time. Wanted to check it out to see what might've killed them. Looks like someone shot that guy."

"Guns rule out bears." Shaw chuckled.

"Chewie?" whispered Tinsley.

Raven resumed walking, shaking her head. "No. Those people died a long time ago. Whoever shot them is definitely dead purely from age. I think whatever happened there went on during the Great Death."

She took some cord from her tool satchel, making a sling to hang the katana across her back. Though she didn't know the first thing about how to use a sword, she carried a knife despite having no real idea how to fight with one of those either. The sword, at least, offered a longer reach. Also, she doubted any bears or whatever 'Chewie' turned out to be would be trained in sword fighting.

That creature might not even be real.

A few blocks later, pigeons scattered into the air ahead of their arrival at the fountain square. Lark let out a brief scream of surprise. Trenton dove to the ground. Shaw didn't show any outward reaction, but his lack of teasing the younger man for his display of fear gave away he'd been startled, too.

"Birds." Lark ceased cringing and watched the pigeons racing off. "They're real."

Smiling to herself at the others' childlike awe, Raven headed toward the flipped bus at the corner. "We're almost there. A couple blocks down this way."

Shaw, Trenton, and Lark trailed after her, still enamored with the birds. They wondered aloud at the significance of finding animals alive, and if it meant larger ones might be present as well. Raven brought up her 'warm Arctic' theory about the birds surviving only because they had the ability to migrate northward to escape the killing heat.

Their debate about the effect a theoretical complete polar ice melt would have had on the world stalled when they reached the storage facility.

Shaw whistled. "Damn that's one big building."

The largest single chamber in the Arc, the hydroponic farm, might have been about half the size of this place.

"Lot easier to build big rooms out here than dig them out underground," said Lark. "This really isn't *that* impressive. All they had to do was build walls, not move thousands of tons of dirt and rock."

Tinsley crunched over the glass at the door, sticking her tongue out at them before informing the fragments they weren't allowed to cut her because of her new shoes.

"Here..." Raven walked to a spot near the quartermaster stations, gesturing at a collection of large flatbed pushcarts. "We can use these to transport the filters."

Everyone except Tinsley took hold of a cart and followed Raven deeper into the building. She went straight to the aisle containing the air filters.

"There's so much stuff here." Lark looked around at the shelves. "It's amazing it hasn't been taken already."

"By who?" asked Trenton. "Everyone else died."

"What looter would take lamps and air filters?" Shaw chuckled. "Anyone who would have ransacked this place had bigger problems back then."

Raven led them to the stash of air filters. "Here we are."

"Shit," muttered Shaw. "That's a ton of filters."

Trenton let out a whoop.

They split up and proceeded to load the carts, grabbing the filters closest in size to the ones the Arc needed first, then larger ones. Tinsley helped as well. Though she only stood a few inches taller than the bundle packs, they didn't weigh much. Near the end of the aisle, Raven stooped to pick up a shrink-wrapped stack of giant filters—and froze still upon spotting a man's bare footprint in the dirt next to the shelf.

The plastic sandals didn't do too well inside the building on the smooth tile floor. Tinsley, Lark, and Trenton skated around as much as walked, and occasionally slipped. She looked from the print to Trenton, wondering if he'd taken them off, but he hadn't. Also, his feet were a little smaller than the track. It clearly hadn't come from Tinsley, who had been in here barefoot hours ago. In fact, the print couldn't have been here during their last visit or she would have noticed it.

What the hell? We're the only humans left alive. How is this even possible? The too-human grunts and grumbles that stalked her and Tinsley earlier took on an entirely new meaning in her head. Could 'Chewie' have been some manner of mutated creature like Noah believed existed? Was *that* the reason he looked at them like people asking for permission to kill themselves when he agreed to let them go get these filters?

Fear set her hands trembling. She stood there unable to decide how to process the footprint while the others merrily continued stacking filters up on the carts.

"Pile it high. They're light. We can tie it all down," said Shaw.

"Uhh, hey... guys?" whispered Raven. "The Arc has the only surviving humans, right?"

"Of course," said Trenton. "That's kind of a stupid question, isn't it?"

"Yeah." Lark nodded.

Shaw walked up to her. "She wouldn't ask if she didn't have a good reason. What's up?"

Raven pointed at the footprint. "Trent, did you take the sandals off?"

"Nope. Whoa. Oh, duh. It's a footprint. Probably came from someone years ago." Trenton shook his head and resumed stacking filters.

"Except this is loose dirt. A breeze would erase the footprint. And I'm sure it wasn't here yesterday."

Tinsley gasped. "Chewie!"

Raven whirled, reaching for the katana handle—but her daughter's excited exclamation hadn't come from seeing any creature again. She'd merely made the same mental connection her mother had.

"That's kinda freaky." Lark squatted next to the print. "Yeah, definitely a man. Bigger than my foot."

"What if the Arc isn't the only place humans survived?" asked Raven. "Isn't it kinda silly to assume? If we made it, maybe other groups did."

The others all stared at her in varying degrees of alarm, dismissal, or contemplation.

"The sign we walked by on the way out," said Raven, "you guys remember it said Arcology 1409, right?"

They nodded.

"If the designers only made one Arc, why would they call it 1409? Wouldn't it be just 'The Arcology'?"

"Whoa…" Lark went wide-eyed. "That's like… wow."

"Never thought about it that way." Lark offered a blasé shrug. "Makes sense they wouldn't have trusted one shelter with a couple thousand people to preserve us as a species."

Trenton rolled his eyes. "Come on. Everyone knows there aren't any other people."

"Everyone also 'knows' topside is a toxic mess," said Shaw.

Raven decided she'd much rather have this discussion back at the Arc and stooped to pick up the filter bundle.

A tall, blurry-brown figure dashed by the opening at the far end of the aisle, growling.

"Shit!" shouted Raven.

Lark and Trenton both jumped in shock—and wiped out as their sandals shot out from under them.

Too startled to think, Raven stood there staring at the end of the aisle, dreading the monster would return at any second.

21

CRITTER

There is a perfectly logical explanation for everything. However, it's impossible to have a rational conversation with a child who's screaming in terror. – Ellis Wilder.

Shaw raised the giant pipe wrench in a two-handed grip, moving to put himself between the unknown creature and everyone else. Trenton screamed and scrambled through the empty shelves where the filters had been into the next aisle before sprinting away. Lark also shrieked and ran, heading to the nearer end of the aisle toward the back of the building.

Tinsley yelled, "Monster!" and bolted in the same direction as Lark —who crashed into something out of sight to the left.

As soon as Lark rounded the corner past the shelf row, she stopped short, screamed again, and backtracked to the left.

The child dashed past the end of the aisle, jumped away from something to her right, flailing her arms as she tried to avoid wiping out. Her plastic sandals slipped out from under her, dumping her to the ground flat on her side. Still screaming in panic, the tiny child slid into a display of plastic tubing and crawled into the narrow space under the shelf.

"Tins!" shouted Raven. Any fear she might've had about a creature died, crushed under the need to protect her daughter.

Raven ran after her. The instant she left the aisle, a huge, furry dark shape on her right let out a growl and lunged at her. Caught off guard, Raven screamed. She ducked a furry limb swinging at her face, then darted around the creature, hoping to lead the mutant away from her child. The fleeting second didn't give her much of a look at it, so her mind filled in a bear-human hybrid more than a head taller than her. Bile rose in the back of her throat as she passed within inches of the hairy monstrosity. Not until she'd taken five or six steps into a run did she realize she gagged on a stink similar to broken sewer lines.

The creature took the bait, chasing her rather than trying to drag Tinsley out from her hiding place. Huffing and growling rushed up behind her. She rapidly approached corner of cinder block walls, but the thing would be on her before she could make it to the turn. Desperation mutated into confidence.

Shouting a war cry, Raven grabbed the katana handle and yanked the blade from its sheath. Two steps later, she spun into a swing—and sunk the blade into a plastic bag of dirt. She stood stock-still, breathing hard, staring at the empty corridor behind her. Dribbles of dark brown earth fell from a gash in the side of the plastic bag that had absorbed the front third of the sword.

Faint grunting and the clap of large bare feet distanced down a nearby aisle.

"What the shit was that?" whispered Raven.

The storage building had fallen under an eerie silence, making her fast, raspy breaths seem loud. Everyone else had stopped screaming. No one ran. After a moment, she extracted the sword from the bag, swatting the flat of the blade against her boot to knock dirt off it. Despite having a monster chase her seconds ago, the bizarre sight of dirt in bags left her speechless. Why would the ancestors, who lived above ground, feel the need to stockpile dirt in a storage facility?

Oh, I guess maybe they were saving clean dirt when stuff outside started to be more contaminated than not.

"Mommy?" whispered Tinsley.

She fast-walked down the corridor behind the aisles, passing shelves of flower pots and planter boxes on her way to the display of plastic tubes. "I'm here."

"Chewie almost got me," said a small voice from beneath a shelf.

Raven crouched and peered in at Tinsley, flat on her chest, crammed as far back against the wall as possible. "Are you okay?"

"I hit my knee on the floor."

"C'mon outta there."

"Is he gone?"

Raven stood, looking left and right. The storage building remained silent, no trace of anything moving. It worried her the creature appeared to be smart enough to understand the concept of a sword, breaking off the chase as soon as she pulled it out. "Think so."

Two small hands reached out from under the shelf. Raven set the katana on the floor, and dragged the girl out on her belly. Tinsley rolled over to sit up, pulling her poncho off her legs to examine her knee. She had a minor bruise, which she rubbed while making an annoyed face.

"These shoes aren't good to run in."

"Not on tile, no. Fine outside. We have boxes of old useless sneakers. I'll make some soles for them." Raven took her sword in one hand, the girl's arm in the other, and stood, listening to silence for a little while before returning to the line of half-loaded carts.

Shaw twisted to look at her as she entered the aisle, still in the same spot he'd been standing in when the monster appeared. "You okay?"

"Yeah. Thing took off as soon as I pulled the sword."

"The hell was it?" Trenton appeared at the opposite end of the aisle, visibly trembling, clutching a crowbar in both hands.

"Damn fine question." Shaw rested the big wrench across his shoulder.

Lark crept around the corner and hurried up behind Raven. "Huge. Furry."

"Ghost?" asked Trenton.

"Don't be silly." Lark threw a small filter at him. "Ghosts aren't real and that thing was definitely solid."

"Except when it vanished." Trenton wagged his eyebrows.

"It didn't vanish." Raven attempted rather awkwardly to put the katana away with the sheath still on her back. "It ran down an aisle before I spun around to swing at it."

"Plution?" asked Tinsley.

Raven snarled in frustration, took the sheath off her back, and slid the sword into it. "I don't think so... that thing smelled bad, but not as bad as the Plutions are supposed to. Whatever chased me stank like an overflowing toilet."

"Eww." Tinsley pinched her nose. "Plutions smell worse than toilet?"

"According to the old stories." Lark shrugged. "Never seen one up close so I can't say for sure, but they supposedly smell so bad your throat burns and your eyes water. Can't see or breathe if you're too close."

"Is it gonna come after us again?" Tinsley clung to her mother's side.

Everyone exchanged looks, no one having much of an answer.

Shaw nodded to the side in a 'come on' manner. He led the group around the building, peering down aisle after aisle, then checking an area full of rotted lumber and a half-outdoor section full of plants run wild. That room had plenty of hiding places, so they took their time searching, everyone holding their weapons at the ready.

Lark's abrupt sneeze caused Trenton to scream and flail his crowbar wildly about, smashing a large clay flowerpot to ruin. Upon realizing he'd killed a bit of ceramic, he stood there with a sheepish expression.

"Pretty sure the critter's gone." Shaw hung the wrench on his belt. "Why don't we finish grabbing the filters and get the hell out of here."

"I'm sorry." Raven looked down. "I thought it was safe."

"You did warn us of the critter." Shaw smacked his lips under the filter mask. He pulled it down, took a water bottle out, and drank most of it.

Watching him made Raven thirsty. She gave Tinsley a bottle and drank from another. Lark and Trenton also removed their filter masks to drink.

"You're not wearing a mask?" Lark gestured her bottle in Raven's direction.

"It didn't seem necessary. The air out here is fine." She put a hand on Tinsley's shoulder and pulled the girl close against her side. "You guys notice she's not trying to spit up her lungs anymore?"

Trenton stopped drinking to come up for air. "So that's a bear, huh?"

"An animal wouldn't have recognized a sword." Shaw tapped his boot into the floor.

"That's impossible. They all died." The younger man paced. "Why would they teach us in school how no other people survived if it's not true?"

"Why tell us it's ridiculously toxic out here?" Raven brushed her hand over Tinsley's hair. "Because they don't know any better."

Shaw shrugged and resumed loading filters. "It's been a really long time since the Great Death. Maybe humans *did* die out except for us. Those pigeons came back. Why not people?"

"Because we can't fly to the Arctic to escape fatal heat." Raven tossed her water bottle back in the satchel and grabbed another filter bundle.

"Umm, hey…" Lark paused in the middle of tying filters down on a cart. "I just had a really weird thought."

Shaw chuckled. "Things are pretty weird already, but what'cha got?"

"You know how the Arc is way, way bigger than we actually need and we think there used to be thousands of people living there?"

"Yeah. Some real bad disease killed off lots of people a couple generations ago," said Trenton.

Oh, shit… Raven gawked. "You think they went outside?"

"Well…" Lark smiled weakly. "An event that killed eighty percent of 2,000 people ought to be remembered, right? No one knows what even happened. There's no giant pile of dead bodies anywhere. No records about large numbers of people dropping dead. Don't you think it's strange for the Arc population to drop so drastically yet none of us know what happened?"

Shaw whistled. "Damn. Thanks for that. Now I'm not going to sleep ever again."

"Whoa." Trenton blinked.

"Level one," whispered Raven. "They put all the bodies up there. That's why it's off limits."

"That is one potential explanation, but I have to disagree." Shaw set a pack of filters on his cart. "That many bodies couldn't be stored anywhere in the Arc without the entire place smelling so bad no one can breathe."

Raven folded her arms. "Unless they burned them. Level one could be full of bones and ash." She caught herself and let her arms drop. "No… cremating so many would have permanently filled the halls with smoke."

"Yeah." Shaw patted the filters. "Almost done."

"Is that what all the gunk in the vent ducts is from? Maybe they *did* burn them all. It happened decades ago. Crap would've settled by now." Trenton shuddered. "Have we been crawling around in dead person?"

"Eww," whispered Tinsley.

Raven hurriedly loaded filters onto her cart. "We are assuming the population dropped suddenly. I mean, it looks like it did, but history is only as accurate as the people writing it down. It could've been longer than we thought. Four, five, six centuries since the Great Death. The population might have dwindled gradually… or not. If that happened, we wouldn't have forgotten so much advanced technical stuff. It's like all the chemists, doctors, and electrical engineers died at once, so they couldn't teach the next generation."

"Or…" Lark held a finger up. "Picture this. You went outside and realized it's not a deadly hellscape."

"Yeah… so? What does that have to do with like 1,700 people dying?"

"Imagine like eighty years ago, someone else did that. Wanted to go outside. Some people—like Noah—remained convinced the outside world would kill them. The Arc population divided into two groups: one wanted to go outside, another too scared to try. What if the 'leave' group happened to be seventy-five percent of the people and also contained all the smart scientists and technical staff?"

Raven stared at Lark in stunned silence—as did everyone else except Tinsley, who busied herself playing with a plastic tube she swung around like a sword.

"It is kinda odd to think about some decades-ago plague which somehow managed to kill all the smart people specifically." Trenton laughed. "Brain eating rot?"

"That's… it fits. There's no records of an epidemic and no evidence a large number of corpses had to be dealt with at once." Raven slouched. "So we're the descendants of the idiots who stayed behind."

Shaw looked up from tying down the filters on his cart. "I don't remember seeing a thriving town out here. If what Lark is suggesting really happened, the people who left decades ago might have gone extinct. Staying inside could've been the smarter option."

"Or they went crazy, mutated, or something like that." Trenton pointed down the aisle. "Maybe we just met one of 'em."

"People aren't that furry." Tinsley shook her head.

Trenton faced Raven. "You get a look at it?"

"Not a good one, no. It had an arm. Yeah, furry. Dark. Shaw's height. I guess it could've been like a bigfoot or something."

"A what?" asked Lark.

"Read a book about a supposed monster some people thought was real before the Great Death. Basically, a big furry humanoid with limited intelligence." Raven pulled out cord to secure her filters.

"You just described Shaw," said Trenton.

Shaw frowned and stalked after him. "Come here, boy."

Trenton ran away, circling the carts, though the older man didn't appear to be seriously trying to catch him.

"That's a wild theory." Raven thought it over while tying down her filters. *The escape corridor isn't on any of the schematics and building it doesn't make any sense. Why make an elevator to a deadly toxic surface? But that sign... unless someone put it there to confuse people into thinking the corridor had always been there. What if the 'stay' group included the Arc administrator who wouldn't let them open the big door? The plan might have been to use the Arc as the heart of an above-ground city, which would have required easy access back and forth, so elevator.*

She growled at having way more questions than answers. And she still couldn't explain what might've happened on level one. The idea it might be a huge morgue creeped her out, but Shaw was right. All those dead bodies would have saturated the Arc with the smell of death. *In a closed system, someone farts in the water plant on level six, we smell it upstairs.*

Clinging to the idea the Arc contained the only humans left on the whole planet also didn't make sense. Why did she want to believe it so much when easily dismissing the stories of an intensely toxic outside world?

Chase...

The only reason she'd agreed to get pregnant at sixteen had been her belief the very existence of humanity required it. If it turned out other people lived elsewhere, she might regret having sex with a guy she didn't even like. Maybe she feared it would change her feelings about Tinsley.

No. No way. I do not regret having my daughter.

She walked over and hugged Tinsley, who happily returned it.

Except for the filters less than half the size of the ones they needed, the rest had all been loaded, perhaps enough to replace everything in the system two or three times. A start, but only a way to buy some time.

Hopefully, it would buy them enough to convince Noah he was an idiot.

"Ready?" asked Raven. "About time we went back."

"Yeah." Shaw set his hands on his hips and looked over the carts. "Trent, head over a couple aisles and grab four shovels. Couple spots on the way back, the dirt's a bit deep for these wheeled carts. Used to be a road. We're probably going to need to clear a path."

"Sure." Trenton jogged off.

"And keep your eyes open for Chewie," whispered Tinsley. "He's gonna follow us again."

FALLEN SAINTS

People do stuff for all kinds of reasons, not all of 'em make sense. Don't waste time being upset over why you did something. Figure out how you're gonna deal with the consequences. – Ellis Wilder.

Dragging four large flatbed carts back to the Arc turned out to be a lot of work.

Inside the ruined city, they had to plow aside centuries of accumulated trash, debris, dirt, and whatever old furniture fell out of the high rises. Some stretches of road offered clear going, but more often than not, the carts sat still while the team cleared obstructions or shoveled sediment out of the way. The wheels bogged down in anything deeper than four inches.

Areas where the dirt hardened didn't require shoveling, fortunately true for most of the distance outside the ruins. They still hit a few wetter spots that required digging out of. Also, having to keep alert for the possible return of 'Chewie' added another complication slowing them down even more. Tinsley mostly helped out watching for any creatures trying to approach, but she also tried to clear away dirt with her hands.

The expedition arrived at the hatch much later than she planned on, likely only an hour or so of daylight remaining. What she'd expected to be a two-hour there, two-hour back trip had consumed the entire day. No one brought food since they'd expected to be back for a late lunch but missed it as well as dinner. Fortunately, the cafeteria always kept some food available given people's scheduled wake hours had no relation to the motion of the sun.

"Elevator would've come in real handy for crap like this," said a winded Shaw once they'd come to a stop by the hatch.

Raven, too tired to speak, merely nodded.

"Can't just chuck 'em down the hole. Too far. They'll burst apart." Lark started untying the cord on her cart.

"Where's the tunnel to the big door? Can probably roll the carts straight in there," said Trenton.

"Hah. Noah won't let us open it. And it probably doesn't work." Shaw pulled at the cord on his cart. "And these carts aren't going to go down stairs any better than they would a ladder."

"There's a backup, but it's kind of a one-use-only situation involving counterweights." Raven finished off her last water bottle, drinking it all in one go.

Lark tugged her filter mask down. "Damn. Can't breathe in this thing. Another problem going in the big door is no one's allowed on level one."

"Anyone know why?" asked Raven.

The others all shrugged.

"Let's go eat first. Then we can figure out how to get the filters inside." Trenton patted his stomach.

"What if it starts raining?" Raven yanked the tie down cord off her cart. "Or the furry monster comes by and eats them."

"Left them alone long enough in that place we found them." Shaw spat to the side.

"Might not have known about it. It followed us there." Raven eyed the cord. "These are light. Tie a couple packs together and we can lower them down. Someone stays at the bottom to untie the bundles so we can pull the rope back up. We've got well more than 120 feet of rope here."

"Sounds good." Shaw nodded.

They spent the next hour or so lowering filters into the shaft three and four bundles at a time. Tinsley ran inside to get food for everyone, but came back with Sienna—carrying a big tray of cooked vegetables—and the other kids. Raven kept her head down, accepting her 'sister's' anger at scaring the hell out of her. It didn't even occur to either of them that Sienna had gone to the surface to yell at her without the slightest hesitation. When she finally realized she stood under the open sky, Sienna went speechless and gawked at the orange-indigo sunset above the ruins.

The other kids didn't go up the ladder. They helped move filters around in the corridor, carrying them off to the engineering room. Raven wondered how they got past the security team. Maybe Shaw telling Jose earlier in the day about how outside air had been leaking into the corridor for years spooked them enough to stay away.

Eventually, all the filters made it into the Arc. The flatbed carts could neither fit through the hatch nor did anyone feel the need to suffer the grueling task of trying to lower such heavy things by a thin cord. They'd sit outside until or unless needed again for some other purpose.

The great scavenging expedition done, the team went inside, Raven last. She lingered half out of the hatch for a moment, gazing at the last traces of sunlight disappearing in the west. The idea they'd been relying on the farm for oxygen already and the CO_2 scrubbers basically did nothing paradoxically eased her nerves. Maybe with clean filters, conditions inside would improve somewhat. She doubted Ben had the balls to turn the scrubbers off to ease the stress on the power system. But, if the two sagging turbine towers gave out, they'd have no choice.

Raven heaved a resigned sigh and climbed down. She almost left the hatch open for air, but out of concern 'Chewie' might find it and be dangerous, she sealed the entrance and went inside. Sienna took the kids back to her quarters while Raven and the other techs rushed to replace all the filter inserts in the main unit as fast as possible. The off-the-shelf filters closest in size ended up being a little too small, but the team had plenty of scrap foam to fill in the gaps to force air through the membranes.

Once they finished installing the filters, Raven spent a few hours at Sienna's quarters explaining everything while the kids played a board game on the rug in front of the couch. Josh, Cheyenne, Xan, and Ariana couldn't believe Tinsley had been brave enough to go outside. That they'd come back alive shocked them even more.

Sienna cycled from periods of crying out of sheer frustrated worry to clinging to yelling to laughing. As soon as Raven brought up the pigeons, her best friend turned back into the thirteen-year-old who used to annoy the entire class by asking so many questions. The girl who adored learning had become the woman doing the teaching.

Eventually, she and Tinsley returned to their room, showered off the grime from a full day working outside, and went to sleep.

THE NEXT WAKE STARTED AS NORMAL AS MOST OTHERS WITH ONE crucial difference: hope.

Raven took Tinsley to the cafeteria and ate breakfast with Sienna and the other kids. Once they finished eating, the children followed Sienna to the classroom while Raven headed to the engineering room. Everyone pretty much expected the first bank of filters would need to be changed within twenty-four hours as they soaked up the brunt of the crud floating around the system. Raven thought it odd to have so many filters in a line like that, but figured the original design used different types of filters, starting with screens to trap big pieces of debris, progressing down to finer and finer ones. Somewhere along the line, the techs started cramming the same filter panels in every slot.

Probably after all the real engineers died—or left.

The team assembled in the work room for a meeting with Ben to toss around ideas for how best to clean the vents without setting off dust-mageddon and flooding the Arc with contamination. Raven kept offering 'vent in outside air' as a solution for their inability to shut down airflow to different areas long enough to scrape out the ductwork.

Once Lark seconded the idea, Ben went off on a ramble about how Noah would never agree. In the midst of his yelling—far more frustrated at the situation than angry at his team—a floor-shaking *boom* came from the adjacent chamber, followed by a startlingly loud warning buzzer.

Shit, the scrubbers exploded! Raven leapt off her worktable where she'd been sitting and ran with the others to the doorway.

Sparks and smoke rose from the enormous Zeus fan enclosure. After a few seconds of shocked staring, Raven realized the machine made the scariest sound she'd ever heard: total silence. The heart of air flow in the Arc had stopped beating. Small distributed fans all throughout the ventilation system still operated, but they wouldn't be enough to keep people alive, only extend the amount of time it took for everyone to suffocate. The enormous fan could not be allowed to die.

"Shit," said Ben. "That's a problem."

Without another word—or even picking on the boss for saying something so stupid—the team all pounced on the machinery. Ben ran to get the rest of the team, who normally worked during the other wake while Raven slept. Raj, Peter, and Neal—all a bit groggy from being dragged out of bed—scrambled in to help with the crisis. In short order, the team identified the problem as a failure of the drive chain brought on by an excessive buildup of gunk on the enormous fan. As soon as the drive chain snapped, the motor's RPMs redlined due to having no load, blowing it out in mere seconds. The governor that should have cut power under a runaway situation didn't even have a chance to kick in before the ancient motor cooked itself.

Trenton worked with Lark to repair the drive chain. Raven, Peter, and Shaw rebuilt the guts of the massive electric motor, one of a few things in the Arc they still had legit spare parts for. Raj and Neal checked melted wiring. Ben took the opportunity of a shutdown to clean crud off the big fan.

Once everyone felt they'd done as much as possible, the team crowded around Ben, holding their breath as he reached for the big yellow button.

Twenty-six minutes after it exploded, Zeus returned to life.

The team collapsed to sit on the floor, sharing a moment of silent thanks. The off-hours crew dragged themselves out, heading back to bed.

Trenton chugged water, then gasped. "We knocked a whole bunch of shit loose cleaning the filters a couple wakes ago. Most of it probably stuck to the big fan."

"Damn, I could really use a hit of vodka," muttered Shaw.

"Didn't we run out of that?" Ben looked over at him.

"We did. Shaw drank it all." Trenton smiled.

Shaw overacted a frown. "Damn bureaucrats. They figure we need potatoes for eating more than booze."

Lark chuckled. "The nerve."

"Wow. Too close." Ben patted the Zeus cabinet. "Sorry big guy. I know we really ought to shut you down for maintenance once a month, but the air's so thin we can't afford it."

"We can't afford Zeus blowing up either." Raven stood, thrusting her arm out at the big fan. "If we don't do the routine maintenance, it's going to blow up again. Do you realize what you just said? Things are so bad we can't risk turning it off even for an hour? That is *not* normal. It's going to fail again, then what?"

Ben, and the others, stared at her.

"We could rip ductwork out of level six and fabricate an air intake leading from the surface," said Lark. "Need to figure out an exhaust path, too."

"Break away the ceiling in the shaft. Make it wide enough for two separate duct paths." Raven traced a 'drawing' in midair. "Unless we get the okay to open the main door, then we can use the entire escape shaft as a duct."

Groaning, Ben face-palmed. "He's never going to let us do it."

Raven seethed, furious at the group who decided to pick up and leave, taking with them all the scientists and experts. Even if that hadn't really happened, she pretended it did so she could be furious at them for abandoning the rest to die in a decaying tomb. The mere fact anyone remained alive in here after so long should have impressed her, but it ended up making her angrier. Maybe she should be furious at the people who decided to stay instead. Having seen no sign of a settlement on the surface, it remained unclear if, in fact, most of the Arc's population left years ago. If they had, a total lack of their presence topside suggested things hadn't gone as they'd hoped.

Unless they feared attack and went far away. Or, that's just a bad theory and something killed everyone. Something on level one? Maybe all the scientists and stuff died because they tried to do an experiment of some kind and it went very wrong.

"Screw it." Raven jumped to her feet and stormed toward the door.

"What sort of trouble are you about to cause?" called Ben.

"I'm going to drag Noah to the surface."

"Oh, shit," muttered Shaw. "She's serious, too."

Ben scrambled after her, jogging to catch up in the hallway. "Can you try something less violent first?"

"We'll see how it goes," said Raven, not slowing her stride.

Once again, she barged into Noah's office. He nearly jumped out of his chair at the sudden *bang* of the door hitting the wall. Preston, seated in front of the desk with his back to her, yelped and grabbed his chest. She rushed up to them, pointed at Noah, and said, "Zeus died."

What little color the big boss had in his cheeks faded.

"Momentarily died." Ben ran up behind her, grasping her shoulders as if to collect a runaway toddler. "We repaired it. Amazing team. Clockwork."

Noah slouched, hand to his forehead, almost glaring at Raven for scaring him.

"Good. That shocked you." She folded her arms. "What's going to happen the next time Zeus decides to blow up and we don't have the right parts to fix it? And before you say anything, it *will* blow up again.

Look at the facts right in front of you. Everything in here is at least 300 years old, probably older. All of our machinery has been repaired and rebuilt so many times none of it looks anything like the design schematics anymore. Even our damn toilets are jury rigged. The scrubbers are worthless, every fan motor in the vent system is on its last legs, and one fat pigeon landing in the wrong place is going to topple a tower and destroy our electrical power generation."

"To be technically accurate, the scrubbers are not *worthless*." Ben managed a cheesy smile. "They're operating at four percent efficiency."

Preston muffled a snicker. "Clearly you're drawing a fine line between functionally worthless and literally worthless."

Noah glanced at Preston, at the giant book in front of him which appeared to be a medical textbook, then up at Raven. "Do you have any good news, or did you come here to inform me we are doomed?"

"There are two things we can do to stop everyone in the Arc from dying. 183 people do not deserve to die because you're convinced old stories are true."

"182," said Preston in a somber tone. "Daniel passed away several hours ago."

"Aww, damn." Raven bowed her head. "He was such a nice guy."

"I've got him in a cooler for now. If you want to say your respects, you can." Preston gave Noah side eye. "We are concerned about cremating him due to the effects it would have on the air. My testing suggests levels of certain toxins are accumulating, and CO_2 is approaching danger levels."

Raven snapped her head up, fixing Noah with a steely glare. "Do you believe it coming from the doc?"

"What are your two ideas?" asked Noah, his voice as calm as if they discussed what to have for lunch.

"Either we slap together a series of ducts and fans to ventilate the Arc with outside air, or we… leave."

Preston gasped. Ben did a double take at her. Noah raised both eyebrows.

"Did you just say 'leave' the Arc?" whispered Ben, eyelids

fluttering.

"Yes." She smirked at him. "I've been outside multiple times now for long periods. It's so obvious how much better I feel breathing up there compared to in here. It's like I'm suffocating in slow motion."

"That's rather drastic." Noah gave a weak chuckle. "We cannot simply go outside with no destination."

Raven gestured at the ceiling. "Yeah, we can. We don't have to *go* anywhere but outside. Build a settlement right above us. We already have the turbines for electricity, the wells down on level six for water. We've got food from the hydroponics farm until those guys get a new farm growing outside in natural soil. I'm not saying we go trekking across the Earth, just out into fresh air."

"Umm…" Preston held up a 'wait a moment' finger. "Before we could eat anything grown out there, I'd like to test the soil for contamination."

"Plants are all over the place." She nodded at the door. "C'mon. I'll show you."

"Existing plants don't prove they're not drawing contamination from the ground," said Preston. "They might *look* fine, but they could be toxic. Plants do have a habit of drawing contamination up into themselves."

"All right. That's true. But we still have the farm here. The ventilation system, especially if we pump outside air down here, would be enough to keep the workers safe if everyone else lived outside." Raven paced. "This entire Arc is falling apart. Zeus blew up today. It's going to blow up again, and I don't think we should be down here when it does."

Noah shifted in his seat. "Miss Wilder, there are things going on you're unaware of."

"No kidding." She shifted her weight onto her right leg, hands on her hips. "Wanna fill me in then?"

"You aren't leaving me much choice." He tapped on his desk, evidently still debating with himself if he should speak more.

"I appreciate you not being a despot and just tossing me in jail."

He smiled. "You're too valuable as a tech. All right. Listen to me carefully and know that what I'm about to tell you is not intended as public knowledge."

Too valuable as a tech... is that why he let Dad slide? Raven raised an eyebrow.

"I am aware there is a group of ferals living in the area on the surface. Up until quite recently, we had a small team of technicians who worked primarily on the surface. We have lost contact with the volunteers."

"The Saints," said Raven.

Noah twitched, then eyed Preston.

"That's why you let me go out there to fix the turbine." She looked at Ben, who appeared genuinely shocked to see Noah admit to the existence of people outside, even if they had come from the Arc. "Did they live on level one?"

"No, they did not. And yes, the Saints. They lived on the surface." Noah frowned off to the side. "A jammed windmill would normally have been fixed by them in minutes."

Ben exhaled hard, lips fluttering. "Dammit. I'd been seeing windmills go offline and come back on their own so long I started to wonder if the voltage sensors were faulty."

"I believe these ferals the Saints observed are far from harmless."

Raven rubbed her forehead. "Why the secrecy about them? Why the fake death?"

"It is still deadly out there and we decided it best if the residents did not mistakenly believe it possible to live on the surface without consequence. Also, I am concerned regarding exposure to unknown pathogens. I couldn't have them bringing diseases down here we have no resistance to. We are humanity's last hope."

"Yet you let me, us, go outside and come back..."

Noah rested his chin in his hand, two fingers against his temple. "As you have so exhaustively pointed out, our systems are failing and we did not have the time to do things the right way. All four Saints disappeared without a word, I presume at the hand of the ferals. They have been harassing the windmills for some time, likely mistaking them for beasts they can kill and eat."

"If the Saints aren't on level one, why is it banned?" Raven looked back and forth between the doc and Noah. "Is it a giant morgue because like 1,700 people dropped dead of some mysterious reason a hundred years ago?"

Preston blinked. "Where the heck did you get that idea from?"

"No." Noah bowed his head. "Since I am bringing you into the loop on the most secure information in the Arc, you may as well have the entire story before you do something that will kill people. Level one is off limits due to contamination from radioactive cesium."

Raven tilted her head. "Are you serious? I didn't think we had a nuclear power plant."

"We don't. The cesium in question was used in a medical diagnostic machine. There is no information remaining regarding *how* the machine sustained damage or the capsule ruptured, but we do know highly deadly cesium dust is loose in at least one room up there. To avoid people tracking it into the entire Arc and killing us all, the administrator from multiple generations ago declared level one permanently off limits."

"It's not as if a person would die the instant they went up the stairs," said Preston. "Based on my calculations, the old infirmary is located at the southwestern corner. That's the most dangerous spot, where the cesium is. Most of our walls are made of solid rock and dirt. The radiation falls off fairly rapidly the farther from the infirmary one goes, with little detectable penetration down to level two, even directly below the infirmary section."

"Those areas are generally deserted anyway." Noah picked up and squeezed a stress ball. "They have been for a long time. No one wants a fifteen minute walk from their quarters to the cafeteria."

Preston nodded. "Lucky circumstances. The danger in level one is of people being exposed to the dust and tracking it all over the place on their socks and clothes. Even a small amount can linger in an area and cause fatalities due to prolonged radiation exposure."

"Would it be dangerous to go up the stairs and straight down the main hall to the front door?" asked Raven.

Noah laughed.

"No." Preston shook his head. "We don't really understand how much if any cesium powder ended up being tracked around up there, but even if some found its way into the central corridor, walking directly to the exit and not spending a significant time on level one wouldn't be a problem. Most likely, the exposure would be comparable to receiving an x-ray scan at the infirmary. The issue would be if any dust happened to be in the hallway, it would follow people out on their shoes."

"Does it wash off?" Raven fidgeted.

Preston nodded.

"Why are you asking so many questions about level one?" Noah stared at her. "Have you broken that rule, too?"

She shook her head to the negative. "I haven't. Some of our older residents aren't going to be able to climb the ladder to the hatch."

"So, hang on." Ben paused in thought. "The main reason you're concerned about the surface is these feral things? What exactly are they?"

Raven smiled at Ben. *Is he finally growing a backbone?*

"What I got from the Saints before they vanished described some manner of furry humanoid quasi-ape. They can be aggressive, but every time the Saints caught them throwing rocks at the windmills, the beasts would run off. Almost as if they were terrified of being seen."

Wow. That really does sound like Bigfoot, but if I start talking about my cryptozoology book, Noah's going to think I'm crazy.

Noah mushed the stress ball between his hand and the desk. "They killed the Saints. If we move everyone up to the surface, assuming any potential toxins don't kill us, the ferals will more than likely wipe us out. We don't have weapons aside from a couple batons in the security team. None of us are trained how to fight. Those beasts are taller and stronger than humans and likely outnumber us. We need the protection of the Arc. Simply going outside is not feasible."

Raven grabbed two fistfuls of her hair, but managed not to scream in frustration. "Staying down here isn't feasible either. The Arc isn't protecting us anymore. It's trying to kill us."

"I'm not trying to be deliberately unreasonable. I understand we are in a desperate situation. But down here, we have a chance—even if it's a small one—of figuring out a way to survive. We'd need to have somewhere safe to go in order to abandon the Arc. You can't simply expect 182 people to climb a ladder to an empty field and make it into a home overnight."

Raven paced, her mind scrambling to come up with the best possible response. He'd offered something of an olive branch. Saying the right thing could save everyone in the Arc. Saying the wrong thing and getting on his bad side would make him dig in his heels. That creature they ran into at the storage place had to be one of those ferals. She hadn't gotten the best look at it, but felt pretty sure it didn't stand too much taller than her. No bigger than Shaw. The footprint had been man sized—and man shaped. Nothing like an ape, and definitely not a bigfoot.

What did I see on the other tower? The flash... like the lenses on binoculars. The Saints wouldn't have been so far away, and ferals wouldn't use binoculars or wear green clothing. Her eyes gradually widened as a hopeful realization washed over her. Could it have been a descendant of the people who fled the Arc? What if she hadn't seen signs of a flourishing settlement because the people who left went in the other direction... east. The tower she'd spotted the flash on didn't look as far away as the ruins had been. She could find her way to it in maybe an hour or less. Considering the person she thought she saw had binoculars or something like them, it might be a lookout station.

Raven stopped pacing and leaned both hands on his desk, staring Noah in the eye. "Will you consider the surface if I can find a safe place for us?"

"Hmm." He appeared to be fighting the urge to chuckle, and kept a mostly serious face while waving her off in a 'you go ahead and do that' sort of way. "Be my guest. But please don't stay out there too long, and please come back alive. The lives of everyone here depend on your technical skills."

She straightened. "Keeping everyone alive is exactly what I'm trying to do."

23

CANARIES

As a species, we've always been terrified of monsters. But there have always been people like me who can't wait to find out what's really under the bed. – Ellis Wilder.

R aven sat cross-legged on Sienna's couch, cradling a steel cup of herbal tea in blanket-covered hands. Several months ago, the hydroponics people made a fair attempt at growing citrus. The rinds, among other ingredients, went into a mulch people brewed with hot water. To get comfortable, she'd swapped her poncho and baggy pants for a blanket. Sienna's quarters felt like home enough she had no awkwardness sitting around in her inside clothes.

The kids arranged themselves in a circle listening to Tinsley tell the story of their filter hunt. Surprisingly, the girl didn't embellish 'Chewie' to sound too much worse than it had been. Then again, from the perspective of a six-year-old, she'd seen a giant hairy monster.

"You're serious," said Sienna after a long pause.

"Yeah." Raven stared into the orange-brown liquid in her cup, wondering how many dangerous chemicals might be in the water. It had been boiled to make the tea, so at least any biological threats would be dead. Given the state of the air filtration system, the water purification had to be in rough shape, too. "We have to do something drastic. The Arc isn't sustainable. Maybe we have a couple months or a couple years, but it's all going to collapse a lot sooner than Noah thinks."

Sienna rested a hand on her arm. "I'm worried about you going out there. The world above kills."

"Not the way everyone down here thinks it does. Did you forget you went outside already? You don't look like a molten puddle of goo."

"Heh. Sometimes I feel like one after a long day." Sienna stretched, letting some air in under her blanket. "So annoying. I go right from being frozen to overheating."

"We better not let Chase see us sitting here together in our inside clothes and blankets," said Raven with an impish smile. His reaction to her not liking him had been to accuse her of preferring women. Even if she did, she couldn't have those kinds of thoughts about Sienna. It would feel too much like incest despite them not being biologically related. At least, not that they knew for certain. Distant cousins if anything.

Sienna laughed, nearly snorting her tea. "We should totally mess with him."

"Let's not." Raven smiled. "Too icky."

"Yeah." Sienna leaned her head on Raven's shoulder. "I'm worried about you."

"I'm worried about me, too. That whole 'not wanting to die' thing is the reason I have to do this."

Sienna sat up and scooted to face her. "What are you expecting to do out there? Just look around for another hole in the ground where someone might have built a brand new Arc?"

"No. I dunno..." Raven took a sip of the overly citrusy brew, trying not to wince. "The first time I went out there, I saw someone. At least, it looked like a person. A flash like the sun glinting off a lens came from another tower a couple miles away."

"How did you see someone from that far?" Sienna prodded her. "You're dreaming."

"I found binoculars on a dead Saint. Something moved and it looked like a person."

Sienna raised an eyebrow. "You sure it wasn't that 'Chewie' thing you saw?"

"Relatively sure, yeah. The figure on the tower didn't have fur. Kinda looked like a green poncho. But…" She sighed. "I only saw them for a second. Could have been a leafy tree branch falling. Still, it's got me curious. I want to go check it out. It feels like Noah's really close to believing me. He's worried about these ferals. He thinks they killed the other team he had living outside. If we start building shelters on the surface, he's convinced the ferals will attack us."

"So, he said if you can find a safe place, he'd consider ordering everyone out of the Arc?"

"Yeah."

Sienna frowned. "He's lying."

"What?" Raven snapped her head around to stare at her.

"He's sending you out there knowing you're not going to find anything. You're gonna run around for a while and come back here with nothing. Then, he'll be all 'see, I told you so.'"

Raven snarled under her breath. The chances of her finding an ideal location did seem remote. Not to mention if ferals existed and had killed off the Saints, they'd probably attack her, too. But… she'd come close to one, and it ran away. Could it have been curious instead of hostile? That wouldn't explain why the Saints disappeared, but as she'd said before, a thousand different things out there could kill, none of them being a toxic atmosphere or ferals. Noah didn't know for a fact ferals had killed the new Saints. Maybe they'd gotten bored and decided to go explore ruins only to have an old high-rise fall on them.

Tinsley grabbed her chest, her breathing raspy and labored. Josh patted her on the back, but it didn't seem to help. Ariana lay on her side, sleeping—not too unusual given the nearness to bedtime. But a kid going to sleep before bedtime when Raven's thoughts swirled in worry about dangerous air quality had an altogether different meaning.

Cheyenne appeared drowsy as well. The normally hyperkinetic Josh looked like he hadn't slept in three wakes.

No. I have to at least try. I am not giving up.

Raven shook her head. "I don't know what I'm going to find out there, but I have to look. The ruins maybe. Or something like it. If I can find surviving buildings with hard walls, we won't be vulnerable to attack before we have shelters built."

"We would need a source of water, too. And if it's too far away, we won't have power." Sienna sipped tea.

"That'll happen soon anyway. The windmills are going to collapse or break down." Raven rambled about trying to convince Noah to simply move everyone to the surface right outside where they'd have access to the electricity, food, and water of the Arc while also having fresh air. "It's beyond possible. It *has* to happen. My father talked all the time about living on the surface."

"Yeah, and, uhh… right." Sienna looked down.

"His wanting to live on the surface didn't kill him. Something out there did."

Sienna picked at the cup in her hand. "If he'd have stayed inside, he wouldn't be dead."

"You don't know that. There's bad stuff in the air here. Daniel is dead and he never took a single breath of outside air. Never once saw the sky."

"Why are you making it sound like a tragic thing? Thousands of people have lived and died in the Arc without ever seeing topside. Did you forget it used to be deadly?"

Raven stared at Tinsley struggling to breathe. She wanted to scream, cry, roar in fury, and punch Noah in his smug, pointy nose all at the same time, but ended up merely glowering at her reflection on the surface of the tea. "It's not tragic when people have to stay underground or they'll die. It's tragic when we *know* topside is beautiful and we still hide down here."

"Maybe it looks beautiful, but it could still be deadly. What happened to your dad?"

"His disappearance doesn't prove it's toxic. He could've fallen in a hole or something. The super tall buildings in the ruins looked way unstable. If he tried exploring one, it might have collapsed on him. Or, heck, maybe he was attacked."

Sienna tilted her head in disbelief. "Attacked? By what? There's nothing left. Even the bugs are dead."

"Nuh uh!" chimed Tinsley. "There's birds!" The girl scrambled to her feet and ran over to show off her filter mask, adorned with several pigeon feathers.

"You had to see all the foliage around when you came outside to yell at me," said Raven with a hint of a smile.

"It was dark. Everything was black. And... I didn't even think about going outside. You had me so freaked out my brain stopped working. Saw Tins asking for food at the cafeteria and just ran up that ladder."

"Well, there's plants everywhere. That couldn't happen without bugs. We've seen pigeons. Nature doesn't quit."

Sienna looked up from her tea. Her eyes brimmed with tears, but she gave off more pride than sorrow. "Neither do you. Please don't do anything stupid."

"I'm not being stupid." Raven let go of her cup and took Sienna's hand. "The ventilation system is dying. Good chance it's probably already becoming dangerous in here. Stagnant air full of particulate contamination, chemical vapors from the hydroponic farm, worrisome levels of CO_2..."

"Shit," whispered Sienna.

The kids all—except for Ariana who remained asleep—chanted, "Oooh!"

Tinsley fell over sideways, curled in a ball and coughing. Raven handed her tea to Sienna, then scooped her daughter up off the floor, cradling her in her lap. The coughing subsided in a minute or so, at which point Tinsley snuggled up under the blanket. Josh and Xan started playing a card game involving magical creatures. Cheyenne busied herself with a Rubik puzzle.

Raven held her daughter close, alarmed at the coldness in her skin. She eyed the filter mask, but didn't think it would help. The increased effort it required in breathing might even worsen the situation.

"This book I read a couple years ago was set in a coal mine," said Raven.

"What's that?" asked Sienna.

"Uhh, kinda like the Arc. People dug tunnels underground looking for coal. Some kinda rock that burns. Anyway, the story took place a *really* long time ago. Even people living right before the Great Death would have thought it old. Whenever they went into the mines, they'd bring a canary in a cage. Poison gases sometimes built up in the tunnels. If the canary dropped dead, it was like an alarm telling the people to run away."

Sienna looked at Tinsley.

"Exactly," whispered Raven. "She's my little canary and I'm not gonna wait for her to warn us."

"She's already warning us." Sienna brushed a hand over the child's head.

"We're going to have to go outside sooner or later. I will find a place for us to go." Raven squeezed Tinsley close.

"The Arc kept us alive for generations." Sienna swirled her tea around her cup. "Can't you guys fix it?"

"Yes, it did keep us alive... but machines don't last forever. It's amazing anything we have still works. Maybe I'm wrong about it being months or a year or two... but before we're old ladies, it's going to become poisonous down here and everyone is just going to die quietly in their sleep."

The kids all gasped, staring at her in frightened shock.

"Oops," whispered Raven. "Said that too loud."

24

A PLACE TO GO

People used to think bugs were insignificant. Look where that got us. Just because you're small doesn't mean you can't end the world. – Ellis Wilder.

No matter how much Raven wanted it to, the ceiling above her bed offered no answers.

The labored whirring of a fan motor echoing out of the ventilation duct in the corner no longer lulled her into a relaxed state as it once did. Every imperfection in the sound, every hesitation or rattle, nearly made her get out of bed and carry Tinsley to the surface.

To a point, she understood she overreacted somewhat. Even her tiny six-year-old most likely wouldn't drop dead from bad air any time within the next few weeks. For that to happen, another major system fault—like the Zeus fan blowing up—would have to occur. Something so severe would not go unnoticed. Hopefully, she'd convinced Ben enough so *when* the next big failure happened, he'd push for evacuation. A month from now, Raven wouldn't be able to set aside her fears of passing away in her sleep.

She had time. A little time, anyway, to throw Noah's dismissiveness back in his face.

Worry she imagined the 'man on the tower' into something far more than it was kept her awake. She wanted the indistinct blur to be a person so badly, she feared her mind tricked her. In her half-conscious state, she dreamed about walking across a field of grass up to her thighs, reaching the tower, and finding a piece of metal hanging on a string where the glint came from.

Raven snapped out of the dream as heartbroken as if it had been real.

Even if it ended in disappointment, she had to go out there. Hanging all her hopes on one thing she maybe didn't even see correctly would be a mistake. There had to be something else. Before the Great Death, civilization built things everywhere. She'd read about vast cities connected by roads, some so far apart people needed flying machines called airplanes to go there.

Dad...

She gingerly slipped out of bed, careful not to wake Tinsley, and sat on the rug by her father's storage chest holding a feebly glowing crank light. His notebooks might have information. Perhaps he could help the Arc from beyond the grave. When she'd read about the ruins to the west, she'd gone over a little more than half of his writing. She took the seven other journals she had not yet touched out of the box and opened the one on top.

Reading by crank light proved challenging. Raven ended up lying on her stomach, holding the small device right up to the page. Her father had apparently also seen 'strange two-legged creatures' out in the forest, but his comments always involved motion in the distance or a sense of being followed.

Two notebooks later, she ran to the toilet, then resumed her search.

A few pages into the fourth one, a big circle shaded with a triangle pattern drawn on the left page stood out as unusual since her father hadn't drawn too many sketches in the journals. The addition of a stick figure and some trees near the bottom gave a sense of scale, suggesting the sphere to be roughly five stories tall.

Raven cranked the flashlight up to full brightness and held it close to the text, still sprawled on the floor on her chest like a kid.

Her father wrote about spotting a giant silver ball poking out of the forest in the distance. Believing it to be a Plution spaceship, he hastily left the area. She backed up a page to read the entry before that, which indicated he had set out from the Arc going east.

"East," whispered Raven.

That other tower was east.

She tapped her foot on air as fear, curiosity, and desperation roiled in her heart. A Plution spaceship might be exactly what she needed to find, provided it had been abandoned. Sure it would be as old as the Great Death, as old as the Arc, but they didn't need any of its systems to work, only a ready-made structure strong enough to hold back ferals. Something resilient enough to survive space travel could surely still be able to stop an angry bigfoot.

That track in the storage place looked just like a man's footprint. The ferals aren't as big as Noah thinks. Probably mutant humans who developed crazy body hair.

The chance a usable structure sat only a few days' travel to the east presented an opportunity she couldn't ignore on the chance Plutions might be there. Breathable air, live plants, birds... none of those seemed possible if the aliens remained. Maybe they'd gone home after thinking they'd destroyed all life on Earth. Or, the planet might have healed, and the Plutions died off, unable to tolerate the change of environment.

I have to look at least. She had binoculars. If Plutions still occupied the starship, using it as a base of sorts, she'd see signs of activity from far enough away she'd have the ability to run away if necessary. Aliens being so close would also explain why Noah had such a fear of going outside. Maybe he knew about them, too.

With a plan—reckless as it was—came hope. She shut off the crank light and returned to bed.

Raven opened her eyes to Tinsley kneeling on her chest.

The scrawny child pushed Raven's head side to side by a hand on each cheek.

"Hey," she rasped, her voice a whispery croak.

"Hi, Mommy." Tinsley stopped jostling her head back and forth and sat back on her heels. Frizzy black hair cascaded down her bare chest over prominent ribs, almost in her lap.

She looks more like me than Chase. Raven reached up and brushed at her child's hair, grinning. The only obvious feature the girl had inherited from her prick of a father had been a lighter skin tone. They sometimes joked that the Arc had a 'person printer,' which started with Xan, then Sienna, then Ariana, Cheyenne, and Raven, then Tinsley, and finally Josh as it gradually ran out of ink. Of course it made no sense considering Xan was eleven, half the age of Sienna or Raven. But it still made them laugh.

"Bells shouted at us already. I turned 'em off." Tinsley crossed her arms behind her head and stretched.

Raven couldn't resist the defenseless belly in front of her face, and tickled it.

Giggling, Tinsley fell off her to the side, curling up on the bed and squealing peals of laughter—at least until she started coughing. Raven stopped tickling her, which made the girl pout.

"Sorry I'm sick."

"You're not sick. The air's bad." Raven sat up. "Ugh. I overslept. C'mon. Time to go."

Tinsley crawled off the bed, heading to the toilet room. Raven got up and changed out of her nightgown.

"Mommy?"

She turned to find a naked Tinsley standing there looking annoyed. "What?"

"All my inside pants are in the dirty bin. I don't got any more."

"Dammit. Forgot to clean…" She looked down at herself, realizing she'd been wearing the same set of inside clothes for the past three wakes. Too much panic and chaos going on for her to remember the laundry. "I'll wash stuff when I get back. Or, ask Sienna to do it while I'm out. Wear the least stinky ones."

Tinsley shrugged, crossed the room to the clothing bins, and proceeded to pull dirty items out and sniff each one before tossing them back over her shoulder to the floor.

Faris is an idiot. Raven grumbled to herself about the resource administrator. Allocating cotton-plus to making child-sized inside clothes had been 'not a priority' given how few children they had in the Arc as well as kids' habit of growing out of things. The woman didn't want to waste material on garments that would eventually be useless, and they didn't want to use up space in the hydroponic tanks on cotton-plus when they could grow more food plants. Tinsley's entire wardrobe, except for her mini-poncho, consisted of garments three or more times her age. Raven had worn the same tattered red skirt as a little girl, and they'd belonged to at least two other girls before her.

Tinsley eventually found a pair of inside pants that didn't smell bad, and hastily dressed. She adored the red skirt, mostly because it once belonged to her mother. Generations ago, people in the Arc wore jumpsuits or shirts and pants, back when producing fabric had been routine and no mothers had to steal bed sheets from empty quarters to make inside clothes for their kids. The cotton-plus ponchos required less material and less skill to make—and lasted longer on growing kids.

She waited for the child to finish pulling on her tread socks, took her hand, and hurried down the hall to the cafeteria. Sienna and the other kids had already left, proof Raven overslept pretty bad. She grabbed a few breakfast muffins from the serving area, handed one to Tinsley, and ate while walking to the classroom.

Tinsley stopped at the doorway, peered up at her, and broke down crying. The child clamp-hugged her like she expected never to see her alive again. Her outburst brought silence to the class, all four kids plus Sienna staring at them in the doorway.

"Shh." Raven took a knee, hugging her back. "I won't be out there long."

"I wanna go, too."

I can't bring her anywhere near Plutions. A brief vision of disgusting aliens shooting beams of green slime at them made her shiver. "Not this time, kiddo. The place I'm going might be a little dangerous."

"Don't go then." Tinsley squeezed her.

She took the binoculars from her tool satchel and explained how they work. "I promise I won't get close to bad guys."

Lip quivering, Tinsley gazed down at the floor. "Okay."

Raven kissed her on the head and sent her into the classroom.

Sienna rushed over to the door. "Everything okay?"

"Yeah. Just... she really wants to go with me. Not sure if it's a good idea to take her into unexplored territory."

"Isn't that what you did before?" Sienna poked her.

"Different this time. Dad thinks he found a Plution spaceship. It's in the east, which is the direction I needed to go anyway to check the tower."

"You still believe in those?"

"You don't?" Raven blinked.

"I dunno. I used to." Sienna kicked her toes at the floor. "As a kid. But... aliens seem kind of far-fetched, don't you think?"

Raven fidgeted. True, she hadn't ever seen any documentation about what the Plutions looked like, wanted, or did. All of it came from stories passed along verbally. What she'd read about various aliens in fiction novels had likely fueled the fires of her imagination into making the Plutions out to be something more like creatures of fantasy.

"Maybe. I'm going to be on edge as it is. Having to worry about keeping her safe out there, too." *She might be safer in clean air.* "Oh, umm... I hate to ask, but things have been so crazy I forgot to do laundry. Any chance you might help out? She ran out of clean stuff."

"After class, sure. If you're not back by bedtime, I'm going to lose my shit." Sienna hugged her.

"Dad mentioned the ship is a couple days off. Probably won't be back here by bedtime."

Sienna stared at her for a long moment.

Damn. She's about to try to talk me into staying.

"Just be careful, okay?" Sienna hugged her again. "That's why Tins is upset. You going away for a few days."

"I can move faster alone. And, Dad wasn't in any hurry. Bet I can get there in a day and a half."

Sienna chuckled. "Whatever, just don't do anything dumb."

"I promise I won't." She released the hug, took a step back, and sighed. "Well, let me get started. Faster I'm out the hatch, faster I'm back."

Her child crying in the classroom and her 'sister' staring at her from the doorway came damn close to ending the mission, but better Tinsley cry than run out of air. Hands clenched into fists, she hurried across the Arc, heading to the escape tunnel—until a random idea diverted her to the infirmary. The doc had to be the smartest person the Arc. While he didn't have the 'official' medical education that doctors of generations past did, he certainly possessed the intelligence for it. He also had a giant library of books with all sorts of information, not one of them a made up story.

She ran in the door, startling Preston, who reclined on a sofa in the back corner, reading a book thick enough to serve as a weapon.

"Raven…" He sat up, closing the book over a finger to hold his place. "What's wrong?"

"Nothing. Well, a lot is wrong, but not with my health. I wanted to ask if you knew anything about the Plutions."

He chuckled. "You've been out there a few times. Kind of odd to ask now."

She explained her father's notes about the spaceship. "I want to know what to expect when I get there."

"Hmm. Interesting." Preston replaced his finger with an actual bookmark and set the tome aside. "I've come to consider the story of 'Plutions' as a personification of a concept. Over multiple generations of us living down here in an isolated society, our store of accurate information about the past eroded. Much of it was never in printed form. When the last of the computers failed, all of the information on them fell out of reach. I've read about ancient societies that existed many centuries before the Great Death. They used to worship the sun as if it were a living, thinking god. Even in our present limited scientific awareness, we know it is a celestial body."

"Right…" She nodded.

"Plutions, the notion of alien invaders, are—in my opinion—the same thing as sun worship. It is a bastardization of the word 'pollution.' Some generations ago in the Arc, talk of pollution destroying the world outside shifted to the idea that some manner of creatures had been responsible for the destruction."

Raven stared at him. "You don't believe in the aliens?"

"No. None of the toxins had extraterrestrial origins. The Great Death came about as the result of something humans did. We destroyed ourselves."

"That's stupid. Who would do that?"

He shrugged. "Unfortunately, that's a question I can't answer. Perhaps it could have been an accident. More likely carelessness."

"Dad always said the bugs died out and no one cared. I thought the Plutions did it and we didn't have time to fight back."

"You're not entirely wrong, but no aliens are involved."

Raven trembled with excess energy. *If he's right, I don't have to be scared of aliens. And that's also not a spaceship… what the heck else could a giant silver sphere be?* "Are you sure?"

"As sure as I can be about anything. Oh… to answer a question I'm sure you have, I did perform swab tests on the Saints. None of them had any detectable levels of toxins in their system either."

"That's incredible…"

"It's premature to become excited. There are likely many places out there on the surface that remain toxic and hazardous to humans. Pollution is not evenly spread across the planet. Alas, we have no way to tell how far away anything dangerous could be. If you see areas with no plants growing, or pools of liquid that don't appear to be water, or places full of awful smells… avoid them. Anywhere with a radiation symbol as well."

"I will. Thanks. I gotta get going." She took a step away, but paused. "Do you think Noah will really agree to leave the Arc?"

Preston drummed his fingers on his knees. "He's a cautious man and he does not like change. However, he's not blind to what's going on. I think he maybe has too much faith in your team's ability to keep everything operational. It's like asking me to fix a dead person back to life."

"Yeah." She bowed her head. "What about the ferals? Do you think they exist?"

"I am not convinced they don't." He chuckled. "I've been trying to get Noah to send someone out to where the Saints lived, but he hasn't. The man still believes going outside is a death sentence due to some slow-acting disease."

She shifted her jaw side to side. "Want me to look around? Where is it?"

"Beyond the windmill field at the north end is all I know. Don't imagine it's too far away."

"Okay. I'll check it out."

Preston saluted her with his giant book.

Most of her fear shifted to eagerness. The lives of everyone in the Arc weighed on her shoulders, depending on what she could find topside. Even if she couldn't convince Noah to change his mind, if she convinced enough other people, it might not matter what Noah thought.

This sounds like Lark's theory happening all over again. Half the people wanting to go outside, half being too scared. Or more like three quarters. Whatever. We don't have the same choice they did. Back then, the Arc would have seemed safe. If we don't leave soon, we're all going to die.

She headed to the cafeteria and collected a supply of bread, muffins, and water that should last her three days if carefully portioned. Noah had given her permission, even if it had been sarcastic, so she didn't try to conceal her trip. She started toward the

244 | THE GIRL WHO FOUND THE SUN

exit, but during a final check of her gear realized she'd left the katana in her room. Grumbling, she rushed back for it in case of ferals.

The door to the escape tunnel remained locked, so she backtracked to the security room.

Ann looked over at her. "Hey, kid. What's up?"

"I'm not a kid. You know I'm twenty-two."

"Compared to me, you're still a kid." The redhead grinned.

Raven gestured at her. "You're what, thirty-six? That's not old."

"Thirty-seven."

"Time to fit her for a cane," said Jose from the next desk.

Ann gave him the finger.

"Going topside. Mind opening the door?"

"Again?" asked Ann and Jose at the same time.

"Yeah. Official scouting mission."

Whether she sounded confident enough to believe, or they assumed she'd been in and out so many times now it didn't matter, no one bothered calling Noah to verify her story. Ann got up, took a key from a peg on the wall, and went with her to open the door.

"Good luck out there." Ann patted her shoulder. "Try not to get dead."

"Not high on my list of things to do." Raven smiled, then hurried into the passageway.

She jogged past all the doomsday graffiti, ignoring it. The doc believed the Plutions were an *it*, not a *they*, poison left over from society past. Pollution, not Plutions. If true, it meant people made the silver sphere and it most likely would not be a space ship.

I can't wait to see it!

25

FATHER'S DAUGHTER

Nothing scares me. I mean that literally. When you know something bad happened somewhere and find nothing, it's time to be concerned. – Ellis Wilder.

R aven eased the hatch down and peered up at a vast expanse of billowy grey clouds.

Studying them for a little while convinced her it didn't seem likely to rain soon despite the overcast sky. A steady breeze came in from the east, driving the windmills faster than she'd yet seen them go. Even the sluggish turbine eight appeared to be keeping up with the rest. Perhaps the stronger air currents broke the crud off the gears. Both turbines on the sagging towers wobbled precariously.

If the wind blows any harder, those two are going down.

She headed across the open dirt, hoping the doc's warning of areas where no plants grew didn't apply here. For at least sixty feet around the hatch and all the way into the windmill farm, the ground consisted of dirt and sparse weeds. Something kept foliage away.

Perhaps the Saints destroyed or moved plants that sprang up for some reason.

Fearful a tower might collapse and crush her, Raven kept her distance from the steel lattice structures, navigating the wind farm at a rapid jog. Fifty some feet past the last row of three turbines, she found a path leading down a hill to a relatively flimsy-looking shack that showed signs of recent human habitation. The lower elevation concealed it from view on the ground, the trees hiding it from her when she'd been up on the tower. Someone had stacked up logs of cut wood on the right, near a grill made from scrap metal.

They cooked food out here? Burning... wood?

Raven picked up one of the split logs, surprised at the weight and texture. Knowing wood existed didn't prepare her for the sensation of actually holding a piece. People could use wood to build things. But they also needed trees to purify the air. Destroying trees to make houses or furniture or even fuel to cook with seemed self-defeating. Every tree removed made the air worse. Then again, considering the number of trees potentially existing in the world, one small village couldn't do significant harm.

We still need to be careful. Not take too much.

Once the curiosity of wood wore off, she dropped it back on the pile and approached the door. The Saints had constructed a dwelling from large sheets of metal, some smooth, some corrugated, as well as spars and scrap they bolted together. A simple one-room cabin contained a table, four chairs, four crude beds, and some storage cabinets. Plastic trunks like the one she used for her father's things contained some articles of clothing, canteens, and a few pairs of boots. Judging by the style of the inside pants, all four of the Saints had been men. A cup on the floor by the table and a knocked-over chair suggested someone had gotten up and run outside in a hurry.

Nothing inside gave any clue of violence or why the men had disappeared.

Raven went back outside and walked around the cabin. A bucket hung on a hook near the roof connected via a clear hose to a shower head above a metal plate that offered cleaner footing than mud. She blushed at the idea of showering outside in full view of anyone. Eager to proceed with her original mission, she hastily looked around the surrounding area. A patch of dirt had boot prints as well as bare footprints.

The shoeless tracks reminded her of the one she'd seen in the storage building. To be certain, she slipped one boot off and held her bare foot over it to compare size. Whoever made the print had noticeably larger feet than hers, at least an inch longer and half an inch wider on each side.

"Definitely a man." She stepped back into her boot. "Not big enough to be a monster, or a bigfoot."

It remained anyone's guess if the Saints—the most likely source of the boot prints—had been chasing or chased by the barefoot man. For all she knew, they might have been walking together as friends. Or the Saints found tracks and followed them, never having seen what made them. That didn't seem too likely or they wouldn't have disappeared for good—or rushed off in a seeming hurry.

She looked up from the ground, out over several hundred yards' worth of grassy meadow to a forest line. "Did they go exploring and get lost?"

Nothing here appeared broken, ransacked, or showed any signs of violence. No blood splashed anywhere. She doubted the Saints would decide to abandon the Arc and simply leave, but the 'evidence' here pointed to them doing exactly that as the most likely scenario.

"Or one feral lured them to chase it into the forest and an ambush happened."

Going into the woods in search of the Saints wouldn't address her immediate concern of finding a safe haven for the people of the Arc. Going too far away from water, food, and electricity didn't sound like a great idea either. If the silver sphere turned out to be something her father imagined, she could always try convincing Noah to trust their safety to the security team learning how to fight the ferals. Assuming, of course, that those beings both existed and represented a threat. Being creepy, following people, and grunting a lot didn't prove they had bad intentions. Nothing she'd seen here backed up Noah's belief that ferals had killed the Saints.

Of course, the lack of evidence didn't prove the contrary either.

Raven sighed and gave up on the mystery for now. She jogged back to the windmill farm and scaled Tower 14 for a high vantage point to get her bearings. Up on the platform, the *whuff-whuff-whuff* of spinning ten-foot fan blades on top of the whine of the generator guts spinning made the already unstable tower even more unnerving. At least the tarp remained as she'd left it, keeping water out of the machinery.

At the platform edge, she fished out the binoculars and tried to spot that other tower. It took her a minute to home in on it, her memory of where it had been a little fuzzy. Upon locating it, she zoomed in, hoping to spot the mysterious figure. Alas, the tower held nothing but dangling scraps of wire from the uppermost reaches. Despite being empty, it still gave her an idea of direction. Before setting out generally 'east' in search of the silver ball her father found, she had to check out the tower.

She would either find evidence she hadn't imagined another person up there—or find the plastic bag she'd mistaken for a human.

Or something. I gotta know.

Raven scrambled down the ladder and hastily left the windmill farm behind. Dirt soon gave way to grass as tall as her waist. She drew the katana and sliced a trail into the meadow, snickering to herself at how the characters in that *Shogun* novel would react to someone using a katana as a gardening tool. *They'd probably have me executed for it.* With each step she took closer to the tower, the greater her anticipation and curiosity became. The potential danger of a long trip away from the Arc didn't weigh much on her mind at all, only the need to discover—and the need to find a way to protect her daughter. Twenty-two years spent underground, and now she had an entire planet to see. If not for worrying about the Arc's systems collapsing at any minute, she would have been tempted to collect her daughter and just keep walking.

Is this how Dad felt whenever he went out here?

26

FERAL

It's normal to accidentally touch a hot wire. Don't trust a fool who keeps touching it on purpose. – Ellis Wilder.

n the other side of the tall grass, Raven entered the forest once again. Here, the underbrush didn't require a blade to get past. She glanced down at the compass every so often to keep herself on course toward the tower, a heading a few degrees south from directly east. Dad's notes about finding the giant silver sphere didn't give specifics about where he'd gone more than 'east.' He hadn't seen something flash from the tower, so would have had no reason to consider it significant, merely another piece of ruins from the society before.

Fortunately, it ended up being on the way, requiring little detouring. If she'd simply followed her father's notes and 'gone east,' she'd have come within sight of it anyway. A structure like that tower, an open lattice of steel struts, didn't offer any shelter, nor did it support a windmill or other useful device.

The only reason anyone would be up there is to look around.

If the 1409 part of the Arc's name truly meant other such shelters had been made, hers couldn't be the only group of survivors. Perhaps she had seen a scout who'd gone exploring. They probably saw the windmills.

If they came from an Arc, they'd know what the wind turbines were. Why didn't they investigate? She smirked. *Maybe they did. Level one is empty. No one would have noticed people knocking.*

Not long after the trees behind her concealed the meadow, she became aware of an unfamiliar rushing sound coming from up ahead on the right. The oddity of it allowed curiosity to distract her off course. Arms high to protect her face from leafy branches, Raven advanced toward the weird sound, which increased in volume as she neared. Soon, a vaguely familiar smell added to the atmosphere of vegetation and wet earth.

Water? She sniffed, thinking about the water filtration works on level six. Take away the metal pipes, dusty cavern, and hydroponic fluid stink, the air here smelled similar to standing beside the underground reservoir. The rushing noise made her think of a large broken pipe gushing.

The expected leak turned out to be a fast-moving flow following a channel in the ground, contained only by the dirt. She stood there aghast at the sight of water crashing over rocks. A hundred feet or so to her left, the surface calmed once the terrain leveled off.

Once the shock wore off enough for her to understand she'd found a stream, like she'd read about hundreds of times, she crouched at the bank, dipping her fingers in the cold water. It looked and smelled clean, but she didn't dare try drinking any. The melted Saints she'd found in the wind farm proved at least some of the stories of a highly dangerous environment had been true. With no idea how long ago conditions had improved, she didn't trust unfiltered water.

Granted, this stream hadn't been consumed, excreted, and filtered thousands of times. The water she'd been drinking in the Arc might actually be worse. However, she'd been consuming it her whole life and hadn't suffered a problem yet, so she'd trust her water bottles for now.

Something rustled in the leaves behind her.

The sudden motion nearly made her fall face first into the water. She saved her balance, springing up out of her crouch while spinning to face a tall figure lurking in the branches. The mental image she'd built up of 'Chewie' filled in thick fur and powerful limbs over the vague hint of a humanoid shape. Heart pounding, she backed up a step. Branches crackled as the creature pushed them apart, advancing toward her into clear view.

Raven's fear of a feral monster stalled at the sight of a clearly human man, quite lacking in clothes. Shaggy brown hair reached past his knees, his beard mostly covering his otherwise bare chest. Despite his body hair being thick, it didn't conceal his manhood, which fortunately hung at ease. The wildness in his brown eyes had nothing to do with lust. She figured him for early thirties. If he lived in the Arc, he'd likely have been as pale as Noah, but out here, his skin had taken on a dark tan that reminded her of Baylee, the white girl who spent most of her wake standing around artificial sunlamps.

The sight of a stark naked man, filthy and hairy, left Raven staring in stunned silence.

He had no possessions other than the mud smeared all over him. No weapons, no clothing, not even a primitive necklace of wood beads. From the look on his face, he didn't know what to make of her either.

Probably the first time he's seen anyone wearing clothes. She swallowed the saliva building up in the back of her mouth. "Hello?"

He grunted, then thrust his head closer in a sudden motion that made her jump back.

Is he... sniffing me?

"Can you speak?"

He tilted his head in the manner of a curious dog and took a step closer.

Raven couldn't help but look at his crotch. Still no sign of arousal. Whatever this guy wanted from her didn't involve sex. That could either be comforting or more terrifying. Unsure if this man experienced the discovery of another human being for the first time in his life—or sized her up for food—she continued backing away.

"Do you understand words?" asked Raven.

"Ngh," grunted the man.

"Guess not." She patted herself on the chest. "Raven."

He tilted his head the other way.

"I'm Raven." She gestured at him, hoping he understood she wanted him to say his name.

The man lunged, grabbed her by the wrist, and shoved her hand into his face, sniffing at it.

"Gah!" She struggled to pull her arm back, but he held on, continuing to smell her. She froze, tentatively hopeful the gesture wasn't hostile. *Maybe this is how they say hello?* "Umm. Hi."

He licked her finger.

"Oh, hell no. This is going into weird territory now. Licking's never a good sign." Raven strained harder to get away from him. "Can I have my hand back, please?"

The man's expression shifted from curious to pleased. He opened his mouth, angling his head as if to bite her fingers off.

"No!" Unable to pull her wrist from his grasp, she hoofed him in the balls.

He went up on tiptoe for a second, releasing her arm to grab himself in both hands. Grunting, he stumbled forward and went down on one knee.

"Not food." She pointed at herself, made a chewing gesture, then shook her head.

"Ngh! Rrm. Bah!" The man leapt at her.

She scrambled to her right, too slow to avoid being tackled. The tools in her satchel clanked in a metallic jangle on impact with the ground. Her katana scabbard didn't make for a comfortable landing pad, ramming into her back. He climbed on top of her, grabbing her shoulders, biting at her like a feral dog. Stink like he'd gone swimming down a sewer pipe choked the air out of her throat.

Screaming, she shoved at his chest, barely holding him off. His teeth came far too close to her face for comfort. Raven tightened her two-fisted grip on his chest hair, wrenching him to the side. He howled in pain and forgot about trying to bite her, instead clutching at her wrists. She threw him to the left, rolled the other way, and scrambled to her feet.

Snarling, the man sprang up to all fours, crawling after her.

"Shit!" Raven yanked the sword out and pointed at him. "Stay the hell away!"

He paused, gazing at the blade in confusion.

"Why am I bothering? You don't understand a word I'm saying." She backed up. "I'm going to leave now. You go that way." She pointed with the sword to the left. "I'll go this way."

He grunted.

"Yeah, well *ngh* you too."

Crying out a *whoop*, he leapt at her, reaching.

Raven jumped back while instinctively swatting at his hand. The katana sliced into the flesh at the base of his thumb, sending a spritz of blood into the air. He gave off a horrible scream, clutched his wounded hand against his beard-covered chest, and loped off into the forest, howling.

She turned in place to watch him flee, shaking from adrenaline. No one had ever been violent with her before. Some of the other kids when she'd been school-aged had gotten into fights with each other. Raven had *seen* fights, but never participated. She had no patience for drama and would rather be alone reading, or hanging with Sienna.

Kids trying to punch each other's lights out is kinda different from a dude trying to eat me, literally. She pulled the sword closer, examining the trace of blood near the tip. Despite being attacked, watching a naked man run off screaming in pain from such a small injury almost made her feel like she picked on a child. Defending herself with a sword against an unarmed man had only one way to end: in blood.

He's lucky I didn't cut his hand completely off like the samurai in the book. She wiped the sword off on the grass and eased it back into the scabbard. *Maybe if I actually knew how to use this thing I could've smacked his arm aside without hurting him. Oh well. At least he learned something.*

Trying to grab me equals pain. He's either going to leave me alone or come back with friends.

"Time to go."

She fast-walked away from the stream, using the compass to get back on course.

A few minutes after the sound of the stream faded into obscurity, snaps and rustling in the forest approached from behind. Expecting the man to have come back with a big stick or pipe, Raven yanked the katana out and spun. The instant she spotted a moving branch, she charged, raising the sword over her head in both hands.

Shouting a war cry, she burst into the foliage toward the motion—and stopped short, staring in confusion at a long-haired woman wearing a poncho and filter mask. It took her a second to recognize Sienna with most of her face covered.

Her 'sister' screamed, crossing her arms in front of her.

"Oh, shit..." Raven lowered the blade. "Sorry!"

Sienna took a step back, hand to her chest. "Dammit, girl. What's got into you?"

"Some crazy wild man tried to bite me." She put the sword away. "What the heck are you doing out here?"

"You know what you've been saying about the air?" Sienna fanned herself. "I started feeling it. Tins and Arianna passed out in class. Even Cheyenne got loopy."

"So... you chased after me to tell me I'm right?"

"Not exactly..."

The children emerged from the forest, stepping around the trees they'd been hiding behind. Except for Tinsley, the others were all barefoot in ponchos and filter masks. The six-year-old's filter mask hung down over her chest. Since her job required standing or sitting in a classroom rather than crawling around maintenance tunnels, Sienna didn't have hard shoes, only tread socks, which hung partially out of the thigh pocket on her pants.

Tinsley ran over and hugged Raven.

She looked around at the kids, then at Sienna. "You're *all* out here? What the hell?"

27

EXPEDITION PLUS SIX

Not everything that looks like a dumb idea turns out bad, and sometimes, it's the smart ideas that get us in the most trouble. – Ellis Wilder.

The other children approached, clustering around Sienna. Four wide-eyed hopeful faces—covered by filter masks—stared up at Raven. Josh wore a backpack big enough for Tinsley to crawl inside, most likely containing food and water.

"Thanks for the obvious trail you cut across the meadow," said Sienna. "Tins found the notebook you left out. Figured you'd go east."

"That still doesn't tell me what you're doing here... with all the kids." Raven squeezed Tinsley close.

Sienna fussed at Ariana's hair. "They were all wheezing and dizzy. None of them could focus on school. I got light-headed, too. Maybe it's my imagination, but I couldn't stop thinking about what you've been saying. Got a little panicky the canaries would start dropping."

"Sorry, Mommy."

Raven peered down at Tinsley. "What did you do?"

The girl ground the tip of her plastic sandal into the dirt while flashing a cheesy smile. "Sienna said we were gonna get sick and had to go outside. So I showed her the secret."

Shocked, Raven gasped and crouched to eye level with her daughter. "You remembered the way in the tunnels?"

"Uh huh." Tinsley nodded. "I couldn't move the metal. Sienna had to do it."

She'd only taken her into the maintenance passage to the exit corridor twice. Her kid remembering the route through the maze impressed as well as worried her. *This kid is smarter than she looks. That's going to get her in trouble.* The irony of her thinking about trouble after she defied the rules to sneak outside made her chuckle. Wondering if her father ever thought the same about her brought a sad sigh.

"We're going with you," said Sienna.

"You could've just said you were worried about me."

"Yeah. Well. I am, but… I'm not making it up about the kids getting woozy. You know I didn't really trust it out here, but after Josh's head hit the desk, what choice did I have? Seriously, look at them."

Raven glanced from child to child. None appeared dazed or groggy. Josh even bounced a little on his toes, evidently annoyed at standing still. She couldn't argue they appeared much more awake and animated than the last time she'd seen them hours ago.

"Why do you have that look on your face?" Sienna glanced off to the side. "You're not gonna tell us to go back, are you?"

Bringing every child in the Arc with them out into topside sounded like a fabulously bad idea. Then again, so did leaving them in a hypoxic atmosphere. Reckless as it might be, she'd rather have Tinsley nearby than trust her to the dying ventilation system.

"I don't think there's an obviously correct answer to that question. Mostly, I'm worrying about the feral guy who attacked me. It's not Chewie. Just a man who has no idea what a haircut or shave is."

"Whoa," said Josh. "Another person?"

"No way…" Cheyenne gawked.

"Are you for real?" Ariana scrunched up her nose.

Xan pointed to the side. "You guys did hear the screaming before, right? That was definitely a dude."

The kids exchanged glances as if they'd witnessed a myth come to life.

"Wow." Sienna pursed her lips. "There's people out here?"

Raven waved for them to follow and resumed walking east, holding Tinsley's hand. "I'm not a hundred percent sure the guy counted as people. Just grunted at me. Doesn't speak. Tried to bite my fingers off then take a chunk out of my face."

"Eww," said Tinsley.

"What the heck did you do to him to make him scream like that?" asked Sienna.

"She hit him in the wiener with her sword," said Josh.

Xan grabbed himself. Ariana and Cheyenne cringed. Tinsley peered up with a 'you did not do that' glower.

"No." Raven chuckled. "He went to grab me, so I tried to knock his arm aside, but cut him a little on the hand."

"Wow. Dude screamed that loud from a small cut?" asked Josh.

"Sensitive spot." Raven pointed at the thin skin at the base of her thumb. "And I doubt he's ever been cut by a knife before."

Josh stuffed his hands under his armpits. "Ouch."

"You saw Chewie?" Tinsley reached up to touch leaves from a branch passing over her head.

"It might have been the same guy. Definitely a human. Hair down to his knees, big beard, lots of body hair. A quick glimpse at a distance, yeah I can see someone mistaking him for a bear or wookie." Raven scanned the forest. "Didn't get a good look at the one in the storage facility. No idea if it's the same guy."

Sienna gasped, stumbling over a rock. "Ow. Uhh, if there's a dude out here, he's definitely not alone. People don't spontaneously pop into existence. There might be a tribe of primitives."

"Or he's an exile from another Arc... no wait." Raven shook her head. "Can't be. If he grew up in an Arc, he'd have understood me trying to talk to him."

"They could have a language, just not one we know."

"Maybe he didn't want to talk to you," said Xan.

"Pretty sure if he knew English, he'd have said some bad words when I cut him." Raven ducked a low-hanging branch. "When I tried talking to him, he didn't show any reaction. Might not have realized I'm a human, too, because he's never seen clothing."

"Oh, ick. He was naked?" asked Sienna.

The kids laughed.

Raven indicated the woods around them. "There's no quartermaster out here. If their group is primitive enough, they might not even understand the concept of clothes."

"That also kinda means it doesn't ever get cold here." Sienna wiped sweat from her forehead. "People would have sought ways to keep warm in the cold seasons."

"Maybe they've got blankets or something they wear only when it's cold out? It's pretty darn warm right now." Raven checked her compass again, adjusting course a hair to the left.

"What would they make clothes from? There's no animals for fur. Can't make much out of pigeon hide. Maybe grass skirts?" Sienna shrugged. "But seriously, do you think he'll come after us?"

"Don't know."

They walked onward, randomly conversing about the idea of civilization advancing from primitivism. The kids initially laughed at the idea of people walking around outside without clothes, until Sienna commented that the ferals had grown up never knowing such things existed so they couldn't be embarrassed about it. The kids came to the conclusion never having to do laundry sounded like an awesome idea.

"Did the crazy man have a mask on?" asked Ariana.

"No." Raven smiled back at her. "He doesn't even know what they are."

"Was he sick?" Cheyenne ran up to walk astride Tinsley. "Why aren't you guys wearing your masks?"

Tinsley frowned. "I don't like it. It makes the air smell like butt. It's nice outside. The mask stinks."

Xan tugged his mask down and sniffed. "Whoa. It does smell kinda weird. What is that?"

"You're smelling the scent of clean air, wet ground, and plants," said Raven. "Basically, you're *not* smelling dirty air filters, hydroponic chemicals, and miles of filthy metal ductwork."

"Is it safe?" asked Cheyenne.

"Around here, yeah it seems that way. There could be bad spots somewhere, but those should be obvious." Raven went over what the doc explained about bad smells, puddles of liquid, and radiation warning signs.

Cheyenne pulled her mask down and took a few tentative sniffs.

Within the hour, all the kids had let their filter masks hang off their faces. Sienna held out the longest, wearing hers until Tinsley pointed out the masks were so old they wouldn't do anything. After a few unobstructed breaths, she relaxed. As soon as Sienna made a comment about the weeds and such tickling her feet, the kids went nuts trying to step on—or in—as many different things as possible. None of them had ever experienced grass, dirt, mud, moss, or knee-deep flowing water before.

Raven watched them darting around, worried the voices of happy children might draw unwanted attention. She didn't want to frighten the kids unnecessarily, and a lone man with no weapons or clothes presented only so much of a threat, especially after having one hand cut open. Thoughts of what happened to him gnawed at her. The guy didn't exactly have an infirmary to give him stitches. If she'd only given him a scratch, it would probably heal up okay. If she'd sliced in to the bone, the man could possibly bleed to death or suffer an infection, assuming, of course, any bacteria survived the toxic period.

The kids' energy level seemed much higher than usual, and Tinsley hadn't coughed once. Raven decided to let them be happy for now, and focused on watching the woods for signs of danger. Eventually, the novelty of walking on a surface other than concrete wore off. The children ceased racing about in search of new things to step in and clustered relatively close. Tinsley appeared to sense her mother's nervousness and kept quiet while the others peppered Sienna with questions about the various plants.

Perhaps two hours after the wild man attacked, Raven spotted a steel superstructure among the trees about a hundred yards off course to the left. She veered toward it, eagerness pulling her up to a fast walk.

She stopped upon reaching the base of the tower. It resembled a giant hollow H supporting a wide crossbar overhanging it at least ten feet on either side, each branch having six dangling assemblies of ceramic discs and wire fragments. Some of the ceramic bits had fallen to the ground, littering the area around the tower. A second, similar, tower stood a few hundred yards off to the northwest, oriented the same way, suggesting the fat wires had once been strung along from tower to tower. A ladder ran up the inside of the left strut, allowing access to a small platform six feet under the top spar. Nothing but bare steel appeared to be up there.

"What's this?" asked Sienna.

"Remember me telling you about seeing a flash? This is the tower." Raven ducked a horizontal spar and grasped the ladder, tugging on it to test solidity. It didn't budge. "Be right back."

The kids proceeded to explore the immediate area, picking up the ceramic discs and trying to use them as Frisbees.

"Don't play with those. The pieces are sharp and will cut you," said Sienna, her voice raised.

Raven climbed up to the four-by-six foot platform, tiny compared to the ones on the windmill towers, and pulled her binoculars out of the satchel. Facing west gave her a reasonably clear view of the windmill farm. The blue tarp made number fourteen obvious. If someone had been here and had binoculars or something similar, they could have seen her easily.

Did they notice me look at them and run away? Or did they happen to be leaving at the exact moment I saw this tower? She pictured someone elated to see another human, scrambling down the tower to run over there as fast as possible. But... she'd been working on the turbine long enough to still be outside when they arrived. By her estimate, it had taken her roughly two hours to get here and they hadn't exactly been sprinting. That meant the person ran *away*. But why?

Maybe I did imagine it. That wild man would eat binoculars before trying to look through them... and the thing I saw was green, not naked.

"Whatever. Okay, so this is a dead end."

She clenched her jaw, trying to ignore the disappointment at not finding a person here, or signs of one like a chair or empty water bottles. When Lark came up with the wild idea most of the Arc's population hadn't died, but *left*, her initial opinion of what she'd seen on this tower changed. At first, she didn't believe her eyes, certain no other humans existed on Earth. Hearing Lark's story picked at her optimism, changing that phantom into a lookout for the descendants of the former Arc dwellers.

This elevated position made it quite clear no above-ground settlements existed anywhere close by. Having someone sit up on this tower as a lookout wouldn't do any good. Maybe it had been someone like her father, an explorer, using high ground for a better view.

It couldn't be...

A lump formed in her throat at the thought it might have been Dad. As much as she wanted him to be okay, if he hadn't died, that meant he willingly stayed apart from her for the past four years... and the notebook Daniel gave her with his apology letter made it clear he would never leave for good of his own choice. Her father wouldn't abandon her any more than she could abandon Tinsley for the sake of wandering. No matter how tempting the lure of discovery, it didn't come close to the love she had for her daughter. As a child, Raven had never shown an interest in going outside. However, she probably would have gone with him if he'd asked her. Tinsley had no fear of the world above the Arc. If ever the urge to wander grew irresistible, she would bring her daughter along. But a child needed a home, not a life growing up never sleeping in the same place twice. A child needed food, not a gamble on catching and cooking pigeons.

The Saints had a grill. What did they eat?

Grumbling, she stepped to the other side of the small platform, facing east.

Before I worry about exploration, I've gotta get everyone out of the Arc.

She raised the binoculars to her eyes, scanning the terrain to the east. Across a vast spread of trees, grassland, and more trees, she spotted a sprawl of ruins. These buildings appeared significantly shorter than the other ruins, but the city covered a much larger area. From here, she could almost make out streets littered with decomposing cars. Nothing appeared to be moving around, but even using the binoculars, a person would have been smaller than a flea. She panned back and forth, frustrated the distance kept her from getting a good sense of if it would be worth it to go so far away from home.

A scrap of silver flashed in the distance, beyond the ruins.

She backtracked, but couldn't find it. Forcing herself to stay calm, Raven crept the binoculars to the right, moving as slow as she could. The silver spot, only as big as a pea to her from here, appeared to rise out of the trees beyond the remains of the city.

That has to be the 'spaceship' Dad found.

His notes made it seem massive, at least five stories tall. It appearing so small in the binoculars told her she had a few days' worth of walking ahead of her. Sighing, she lowered the binoculars and checked the compass heading, a little bit north of due east to the ruins. She stood still, staring out over the wavering treetops at the faint pale blur of the ruins. Without using the binoculars, the old city appeared only as a faint variation in color from its surroundings.

Children's voices came from below, the only sound louder than the rustle of the wind in the branches. No huge windmills, no turbine gears, no ventilation fans.

It's so quiet here.

The peacefulness of her surroundings crashed into the urgency of her task. Sure, the people she cared about most were safe with her, but she couldn't leave the rest of the Arc to die. If not for that, she might have been happy to simply continue walking, enjoying nature's reawakening. Many of the books she'd read described forests, mountains, rivers, and so on, but the words failed to capture the awesome scale and beauty around her. Of course, they'd been written by people who didn't spend their entire life underground. To them, trees had been no big deal. An ordinary sight everyone understood. One didn't need a thousand words to describe every detail of something so common.

But until recently, she had only her imagination and a picture or two.

I never want to go underground again.

THE GARDEN

The best part of topside is that it doesn't have alarm clocks. 'Course, something might wander by and eat me in my sleep, but that's a fair trade. – Ellis Wilder.

The children ran over as soon as Raven climbed down from the tower.

"Find anything?" asked Sienna.

"Ruins of another city out there, and the silver ball."

"Silver ball?" Sienna scrunched up her nose. "What?"

"Dad wrote about finding what he thought was a spaceship. It's not… but I want to figure out what it is. There's *something* out there that's huge, round, and silvery. Also want to check on the buildings, see if any of them might be intact enough to use. Looks like they're a lot shorter than the other ones. Maybe they held up better."

"Robot butt!" yelled Xan.

Everyone looked at him.

"What?" Tinsley scrunched up her nose.

"Something huge, round, and silvery." Xan laughed.

"Did you bring enough food and water for three or four days?"

"Food should last five. Water ought to make it three days at least." Sienna pointed her thumb into the woods. "Can we drink from that stream?"

"I'm not sure. One of the books... I remember reading about running surface water being dangerous due to microorganisms. Best option is well water or a spring. No idea if any microorganisms survived. Heck, the water could be fine. Might even be better than what we've been drinking."

"Josh, what are you doing?" squeaked Cheyenne.

Raven and Sienna turned at the same time.

"What's it look like I'm doing?" asked Josh, his back to the group as he peed on a nearby tree. "Do you see any toilets?"

Ariana and Cheyenne flew into a mild panic, apparently not having even considered the idea the outside world wouldn't have toilet rooms. The two girls ran over to Sienna, asking what they were supposed to do when they had to go.

Tinsley matter-of-factly explained the process as if talking to someone who'd never peed before.

They gawked at her.

Raven suggested everyone water the grass here so they didn't have to stop every fifteen minutes.

Somewhat reluctantly, the girls scurried off into the forest for some privacy.

Once everyone gathered in a group after relieving themselves, Raven led them into the forest. Each time they spotted a trace of the old world such as a bit of road peeking out from under the dirt, a sign, random washing machine, and so on, the kids swarmed it and asked all sorts of questions about their find.

When daylight began to dim, Raven looked around for anywhere that might offer shelter for the night. Unfortunately, every direction appeared to be the same: forest as far as she could see.

Hope it doesn't rain.

"Hey," whisper-shouted Josh, sounding frightened. "Look!"

Raven spun toward him, reaching for the katana over her shoulder.

The boy pointed at the dirt in front of him. She lowered her hand, relieved, and walked over to see what he'd found. Sienna and the other kids gathered close as well. Josh squatted in front of a boot print, pointing from it to a few others leading away in a line. They were too far apart to have come from someone walking. Whoever left these prints had to have been running like hell. Again, Raven compared her foot to the print, leaving her boot on. This track, too, appeared to be from a man, or a giant of a woman.

"Definitely a person. Probably man." Raven looked along the path of the tracks, which headed southeast. "Probably running."

"Should we follow?" asked Josh.

"He's going the wrong way."

"Uhh, I don't think you guys understand." Cheyenne indicated the print with both hands. "Someone else was here, and not a naked savage."

"So?" asked Xan.

"So!?" Cheyenne grabbed the boy by the shoulders, shaking him. "That means there are other people! We're not the last ones." The eleven-year-old teared up, trembling faintly while clutching her stomach.

"Why are you freaking out?" asked Ariana.

"Because... we're the only kids. Only five of us." Cheyenne sniffed, wiping a tear. "I thought people were gonna die off like everything else. Now I don't gotta have a baby as soon as I'm sixteen!"

Sienna hugged her.

"What if they don't like us?" asked Xan.

Raven resumed walking, waving for the others to follow. "I think the chances of another person being dangerous are probably low. It depends on if he's a crazy lone survivor or there's a larger group. The more people there are, the better the chances they'll be friendly."

"We should stay quiet," whispered Josh. "If we make a lot of noise, the guy might find us."

Ariana and Cheyenne gasped, clinging to each other.

"If he's nice, finding us isn't bad," said Tinsley.

They walked in relative silence until the daylight faded too much to see beyond about fifty feet. Raven announced they'd stop to sleep here for the night. After a meal of muffins and bottled water, they reclined on the ground to watch the sky darken, revealing stars. The kids oohed and gasped, utterly captivated at the sight. Sienna went back into teacher mode, explaining about space, other planets, and constellations.

"We forgot our night clothes," said Cheyenne.

"Don't need them out here. It's really warm." Josh yawned. "Take your poncho off and use it like a blanket."

Raven used the lumpy tool satchel for a pillow, stretching out with Tinsley tucked against her side. The Arc might be a death trap, but she *did* miss her bed.

"Should we keep watch?" asked Xan.

Josh sat up. "What's that mean?"

"Means someone stays awake to look out for bad guys. Read it in a book about soldiers."

Ariana yawned. "What's soldiers?"

"People who fight bad guys and protect good guys." Xan reclined, lacing his fingers behind his head.

"Bad guys like Plutions?" asked Tinsley.

"Do you think they're still around here?" Cheyenne shifted, trying to get comfortable on the ground.

Raven smiled. "I might have told you something wrong. Spoke to the doc earlier..." She explained how what the stories described as toxic aliens most likely came from a misunderstanding of *pollution*, bad chemicals and such in places they didn't belong.

Aliens wouldn't be a threat, but someone had been in this area fairly recently with boots. They, too, might not be dangerous, but the wild man or his tribe could be. The idea of keeping a watch sounded like a good one. The two youngest kids likely lacked the discipline or attention span to adequately perform lookout duty. She settled on asking Josh to take first shift, then wake her up, and she'd wake Sienna for the last bit.

Much to Raven's surprise, she didn't end up staring at the stars, worrying for hours. Sleep took her right away.

A FACE FULL OF SUNLIGHT PULLED RAVEN OUT OF A DREAMLESS SLEEP.

She yawned and sat up. Everyone else lay sprawled about unconscious, Josh with his mouth hanging open.

Guess he fell asleep on watch.

Sitting there alone at night would have definitely been boring. No surprise a twelve-year-old passed out. Without a more concrete threat than a whole bunch of maybes, Raven guessed she, too, would have failed to stay up. They also didn't have any way to measure two hours aside from counting seconds… and repetitive counting would *definitely* knock her out.

Raven wandered away from the camp to relieve herself. When she returned and rummaged a muffin from her satchel, the soft clatter of tools woke Tinsley, who sat up with one eye open and looked around making such a 'where am I?' expression, Raven burst out laughing. Sienna woke, as did the other girls.

Josh groaned and rolled onto his front. "Ngh, turn the light off."

"That's the sun," said Sienna. "We can't turn it off."

Xan remained asleep until Cheyenne shook him.

While gnawing on muffins, the kids talked about how topside wasn't as scary as they thought before. Sienna confided in Raven she'd become worried Noah would be furious at her for bringing the kids outside without authorization, and they'd take them away, reassigning them to live with their bio parents. Well, except for Josh whose parents had died.

"He won't." Raven nudged her. "You are their mother. You've raised them all since infancy."

"You helped. And I didn't get Josh full time until he was six. You really don't think Noah will blow up?"

Raven finished chewing a hunk of muffin. "Nope. It's me who should be anxious."

"How do you figure that?"

She sighed, lowering her voice to keep the kids from hearing. "Chase didn't want to get attached to Tins because he expected she wouldn't live long. I'm worried if we get around this issue of the Arc falling apart, he might try to take her or like try to become part of her life. She doesn't even know who he is."

"Selfish bastard. He's more worried about being sad than his kid dying. Forget him. You got a big sword now. He tries anything, slice him in the"—she wagged her eyebrows—"wiener."

Raven collapsed against her, laughing so hard she nearly choked on muffin crumbs.

The kids looked over at them.

"What's funny?" called Xan.

"Boring old person joke." Sienna whacked Raven on the back. "Stop choking."

"I'm glad we don't gotta wear the masks," said Ariana.

Xan lifted his from his chest, making a sour face. "Yeah. It smells like my inside pants."

"Nothing smells *that* bad," said Cheyenne.

He regarded her with an unimpressed glance. "You've smelled my inside pants?"

Tinsley and Ariana giggled.

Cheyenne blushed. "No!"

"Then how can you say they smell worse than anything?"

"It's just a saying!" Cheyenne flailed her arms. "Butthead."

Raven finished her muffin, stood, and pulled the satchel strap over her shoulder. "C'mon. People are running out of air. We should get moving."

The kids scrambled to finish eating and throw their ponchos back on. Tinsley appeared to consider going barefoot like the others for a moment, but decided to wear her sandals. Raven checked the compass, got her bearings, and set off toward the ruins.

Yesterday's complete cloud cover had broken up into long separate strands, as though an enormous clawed creature shredded a cotton blanket. Even under the tree canopy, the day had already become warm, and would likely heat up even more. They walked until the sun appeared to be right overhead and the heat grew burdensome. Raven announced a quick rest break for lunch, guiding everyone to an area of thicker trees.

They sat in the shady spot having a lunch of not-quite-stale bread. The kids removed their ponchos to cool off. The boys wore baggy shorts similar to Raven's long pants, with extra pockets on the legs, garments that would likely fit them for another year or two unless they grew abnormally fast. Tinsley would outgrow her skirt relatively soon if the old thing didn't fall apart first. Cheyenne wore a relatively new pair of cotton-plus pants, the same green-brown color as the ponchos. From the look of it, she'd probably only been the fourth child to inherit them. The hem stopped a fair ways above her ankles. Considering how slender she was, those pants had likely been intended for a younger kid than eleven. Ariana wore a sleeveless dress made from an adult inside shirt, a rare article of child-sized clothing.

Everyone sweating so much made Raven worry about their water supply. If the heat kept up, they'd definitely end up having to drink water from the stream. Risking it maybe being polluted or having microorganisms beat dying of dehydration, but not by much. Perhaps she could find a way to build a fire and boil the water first just to be sure. All the ruined houses provided ample wood that wouldn't require an axe she didn't have to chop down a tree she didn't want to destroy; igniting it would be the challenging part.

During a pause in the kids' conversation about the icky heat, a distinct *thump-thump* came from the woods not far from where they'd paused to rest. Everyone froze still. Raven twisted to her left, reaching for the katana handle above her right shoulder while eyeing the foliage in the direction the rustle came from.

A minute or two passed without anyone making the slightest sound or motion.

Expecting the wild man to have returned with others, Raven listened for people trying to sneak up and surround them.

"Did you hear that?" whispered Cheyenne.

Leaves moved in the same spot from which the thumping arose.

Cheyenne clapped both hands over her mouth.

Crunch.

Raven eased the katana a few inches out of the scabbard, trying to draw it without making noise.

The leaves moved again. Something of substantial weight moved closer.

Ariana emitted a faint gasp of alarm.

A brown furry face popped out of the foliage. Ears stuck out to either side of an elongated—and clearly not human—head, a black nose at the tip. Large black eyes widened as the critter also froze.

Raven let go of the sword. Years ago as a kid in school, she'd looked at pictures of a similar creature, but the shock of seeing a living animal so large caused her to draw a blank on its name. She couldn't remember much about it other than a vague notion it wouldn't try to eat them.

"Is that a deer?" whispered Xan.

The creature's left ear twitched.

"Dunno." Josh scrunched his nose. "Don't they have big horns?"

"It's a girl deer," said Tinsley.

Two other deer, each less than half the size of the first, lifted their heads into view out of the greenery. At the sight of baby deer, all three girls plus Josh squeaked in 'aww.'

The deer bolted, racing away into the trees. They vanished in mere seconds, though the thumping of their hooves remained audible for a moment longer.

All fear gone, the kids erupted in cheers, chattering about seeing a real, living deer. They swarmed Sienna, practically demanding she refresh them on that lesson. Evidently, they'd done a few hours' learning about extinct animals two weeks ago.

When Sienna mentioned some people before the Great Death hunted those animals for sport, all the kids gasped in horror. Sienna explained how other people killed them for food. That stunned the kids and led into her telling them about meat. All of them, including Sienna and Raven, had only ever consumed vegetables, beans, and mushrooms grown in the hydroponic facility.

"... it's been many decades, but the original occupants of the Arc bred live animals for food and other things like milk," said Sienna, to shocked gasps.

"Whoa." Raven stared at her. "They never taught us about killing things for meat."

"You know the thing I mentioned the other day about margin notes saying don't share this information? Yeah..." She frowned into her lap. "Maybe I shouldn't have listened to it. The animal pens are on level one. That's probably why they don't let anyone up there."

Raven put a hand on her friend's arm. "No... well, unless Noah lied to me."

"What?" She blinked.

"He said the original infirmary is up there. Big and fancy like hospitals used to be before the Great Death. A machine broke and released radioactive cesium. People aren't allowed up there because it will make us sick and kill us."

The kids all gasped again, staring at her.

"If level one also had animal pens, they probably died when the cesium leaked." Raven cringed.

"Aww..." Josh looked down.

"Wouldn't a whole bunch of dead animals smell really bad?" Cheyenne tilted her head. "Even if it was like a long time ago, we'd smell it, right?"

"The whole Arc smells like butt." Xan smirked. "The stuff in the hydroponic farm is basically liquid poop."

"And sewer lines leak all the time," muttered Raven. "Oh... wait a minute. I just got an idea."

"Do tell." Sienna ate the last piece of her bread.

Raven shared the theory Lark came up with about the Arc's population going from several thousand to only a few hundred in a short amount of time. "I always thought it was something horrible, like a bad disease killing a lot of people rapidly. How else could we have lost all the doctors, scientists, and really smart people? If there'd been a gradual loss of population, people would have been trained, right?"

"Yeah, that makes sense." Sienna nodded.

"What if they left like Lark thinks, and when they left, they took the animals with them?" Raven gestured at the spot where the deer had been. "Some escaped?"

"I don't think we'd have farmed deer... more like sheep, goats, and chickens. Kinda difficult to raise cows underground. They're a little big."

"What's a cow?" asked Tinsley.

Raven stood. "Let's get going again. She can tell us about cows while we walk."

Xan offered to take the backpack for the remainder of the day to give Josh a break. The kids put their ponchos on and formed into a single file line with Raven up front, Sienna at the back, and Tinsley right behind her mother. Barefoot hiking didn't appear to bother the children anywhere near as much as Sienna, who kept finding painful things to step on.

They walked at a steady pace, as fast as possible to go with a six-year-old along. Raven could have made better time alone, but the peace of mind she gained by not worrying if she'd return to find her child asphyxiated more than balanced out the slowdown. Sienna reprised her role as teacher, relaying as much information as she could recall from memory about cows. Admittedly, the description came out basic, but she promised to go over them in more detail once she had her textbooks again. She moved on to teaching the kids about the various plants, trees, and doing her best to explain the purpose of any random artifact from the past society they encountered.

Other than in schoolbooks, Sienna had never seen any of the foliage in person before either. The fascination and wonder in her voice made the woman sound more like a kid herself.

Around early evening, the forest broke up into clumps separated by swaths of grassy areas surrounding the remains of houses. A few traces of paved road appeared here and there, mostly as loose chunks of blacktop jutting up from the dirt. The majority of the houses had long since collapsed into piles of moldy wood and aluminum siding. With night under an hour away, Raven allowed herself to veer off course in search of a better place to sleep than out in the open. Hints of street signs and mailboxes revealed the layout of a former suburban neighborhood engulfed by unchecked nature. Perhaps this land had been woods long ago before humanity forced its way in.

In one cul-de-sac, they found a house that hadn't fallen in on itself. Long boards and/or pipes braced the walls from the outside, likely chunks of debris scavenged from nearby ruins. Tarps of various colors formed a patchwork over the roof and an overgrown garden wrapped around the left side of the house into the area behind it.

Raven had been down to the hydroponic farm often enough to recognize the majority of the growth as food-bearing plants, though from her current distance, couldn't recognize the exact type. Whoever planted it had clearly been absent for a long time as evidenced by the runaway growth and stink of rotting vegetables.

"Whoa. What is this place?" asked Josh. "What are all these piles of junk here for?"

"They used to be houses." Sienna pointed at the repaired one. "They didn't really look like that either, but before the Great Death, the wealthy lived in places like this."

"Wealthy?" asked Cheyenne, scrunching her nose in confusion. "What does that mean?"

Raven started walking to the garden, the others trailing after her.

"Before the Arc, people had this stuff called credit. They gave it to each other in trade for things like food, clothing, toys, basically everything," said Sienna. "If someone gave away too much credit, they got in trouble and all their stuff was taken away. Wealthy means people had a lot of that credit stuff to use. They used to call those who had these big private living places 'Boomers.'"

"Did they blow stuff up?" asked Xan.

Cheyenne and Ariana giggled.

Sienna made an 'I don't know' face. "The book didn't really say why they called them that. Just how Boomers owned houses and everyone else had to live in apartments."

Raven peered over the fence at the garden, noting tomato plants, carrots, cucumbers, greens that looked like potato plants, and a few others she didn't recognize, but also appeared to be vegetables. A brownish muck covered the ground from at least a full season's worth of rotten vegetables that had fallen, but the garden had enough good-looking veggies to make at least a few meals out of.

"What are 'partments?" asked Tinsley.

"They sounded like giant houses where a lot of people lived in small rooms." Sienna peered over the fence into the garden as well.

Raven glanced at her. "Wealth? Credit? I don't remember learning any of that in school."

"Because they didn't teach us about it. We don't use credit in the Arc. Everyone just gets what they need. The book had handwritten notes in the margins telling me not to teach those parts because someone thought it would lead to a recreation of the greed-based society some former teacher believed caused the Great Death."

"If it's off limits, why tell us about it now?" asked Raven.

Sienna shrugged. "We broke the big rule already and went outside. What's stepping on a few lesser rules?"

"That's stupid," said Tinsley.

Raven and Sienna glanced at her.

"They wanted to stop us from doing the same bad stuff," said Sienna. "Credit is bad."

"No." Tinsley shook her head. "That's not what I meant. It's stupid to just *not* say anything. You should teach about it and explain why it's bad, so we know what *not* to do."

"She's got a point." Cheyenne patted Tinsley on the head. "You tell kids 'don't pee on the floor,' not just hope they figure out what a toilet is on their own."

Everyone laughed.

Sienna leaned past the fence, looking around. "Looks like fresh veggies tonight. I wonder if they'll taste different since they grew out from dirt instead of fluid?"

Raven approached the front door. "Hello? Is anyone here? We don't want to take your stuff."

After a moment of receiving no reply, she pulled the door open.

The interior smelled like a boot that had been rained on and dried out multiple times. Dark splotches marked the walls here and there, likely mold. Someone had built a secondary floor out of mismatched wood scraps. Gaps in the construction let her see the original floor a few inches underneath. Large swaths of it had fallen down into the basement. An archway straight ahead led to a kitchen. A former sliding glass door—now a sliding tarp door—sat open, revealing the garden in the back. Water stains on the naked wood floor suggested it had been left open for months.

She gingerly advanced, each step increasing her confidence the repaired floor would hold her weight. Upon reaching the back door, she peered out at the garden—and a rotting corpse sticking out from under a row of bell peppers. Though well advanced into decomposition, enough flesh remained to identify the body as a man. She couldn't tell the age, somewhere between twenty and sixty. Like the wild man, the corpse's hair and beard had grown to astonishing lengths, though he wore a skirt-like garment of plastic sheeting. The combination of an attempt at clothing plus the repairs on the house made her think he hadn't been anywhere near as primitive as the guy who tried to bite her.

Sienna and the kids stepped into the living room, looking around.

"Guys..." Raven turned to face into the house. "I don't want any of you kids going out the back door here, okay? There's a dead person in the garden. He's kinda gross."

The kids froze in place, staring at her.

"He can't hurt anyone, but it's not something children should see." Raven wiped a hand down her face. "I'd kinda prefer not to have seen him, too."

"Another wild man?" Sienna crept into the kitchen, keeping her gaze on the floor.

"Be careful. This is all scrap wood, and no one has shoes. If you get a splinter in your foot, it's going to make walking a big problem."

"Yeah. That's why I'm looking where I step." Sienna stopped. "Think the body's the guy who lived here?"

Raven nodded. "Almost certainly. I don't think he'll mind if we borrow this place for one night. Keep the kids in the front room. Let me see if I can find some decent food."

"Okay."

While Sienna tiptoed back to the living room, Raven took a big plastic bowl from the table and went out the sliding door into the garden. It seemed wrong to eat vegetables fertilized by a dead guy, so she left the bell peppers alone. Over the next fifteen minutes or so, she collected tomatoes, carrots, some strange long green fuzzy vegetables, some smaller unfamiliar green pods, and some potatoes. Something buzzed by her ear, but when she spun, saw nothing.

Weird.

Once she had the bowl relatively full, Raven went back inside. Sienna and Cheyenne sat on a ratty couch, everyone else on the floor. At least here, the former occupant had arranged a few scraps of carpet over the bare wood. She set the bowl down on a small table in front of the couch, then lowered herself to sit beside Tinsley.

Everyone dug in.

Josh stuffed a tomato in his mouth. Xan grabbed two carrots. Cheyenne helped herself to a tomato in one hand, potato in the other. Tinsley, evidently feeling brave, grabbed one of the fuzzy green vegetables and took a bite, making a 'I think I've had this before but I'm not sure' face. Sienna and Ariana each picked up one of the smallish green pods, biting into them at roughly the same time.

In seconds, Ariana's expression went from 'ooh!' to 'something's not right.'

Sienna coughed.

Ariana's eyes widened. She dropped the vegetable, grabbed her cheeks, and screamed like someone burned her. Sienna clamped a hand over her mouth, rapidly kicking her feet back and forth at the floor.

"What's wrong?" Josh grasped Ariana by the shoulders, but the nine-year-old kept screaming.

Raven jumped to her feet to check on Sienna. Tears streaked down the woman's cheeks, and her eyes had gone puffy. Ariana lurched over sideways and threw up in between screams.

"Water," rasped Sienna. "It's like I bit into fire."

Raven and Josh exchanged a brief stare. The boy leapt up and ran to the backpack while Raven pulled a water bottle from her tool satchel. She took the cap off and handed the bottle to Sienna. Josh helped Ariana drink. Xan, Cheyenne, and Tinsley observed the chaos in relative quiet. After a little while of sipping water, Ariana sat there fanning her open mouth while crying. Sienna gasped, staring up at the ceiling and muttering, 'Holy shit' repeatedly.

"I'm sorry… I had no idea…" Raven picked up another of the small green pod vegetables from the bowl. "We shouldn't eat these."

"Why the hell would they be growing in a garden?" rasped Sienna.

Xan picked up the one Ariana bit the end off and sniffed it. Cheyenne and Tinsley shouted, "No!" at him as he raised it to his mouth, but he nibbled on it anyway. The girls held their breath, staring at him.

A few seconds later, his eyes widened somewhat. "Spicy."

"You're not screaming?" asked Cheyenne, incredulous.

He shrugged. "It's not that bad. Just took a little bite. She bit off a big hunk. This would probably be pretty good to add a little to the baked vegetables. I don't think we're supposed to eat them raw or straight."

Ariana took another few gulps of water, then resumed crying.

"We probably shouldn't eat things we don't recognize." Cheyenne reached to take the larger green vegetable from Tinsley, but the little one evaded.

Tell that to the feral guy. Raven smirked.

"This one's not bad. Try it." Tinsley stuck it out.

"Uhh, no thanks." Cheyenne leaned away.

"That's a zucchini," wheezed Sienna. "We have them sometimes. But you usually see them after they're sliced and cooked."

"See?" Tinsley grinned and chomped another hunk out of it.

Xan nibbled on the spicy vegetable.

"Stop that!" shouted Cheyenne. "I didn't even touch one and watching you eat it is making *my* mouth hurt."

"It's really not too bad." He held it out to Josh. "Wanna try?"

The eldest boy took it, examined it, and bit off a piece about half the size of the tip end Ariana ate. In seconds, his pale face went red and be began drooling.

"It's…" Josh pounded a fist into his chest, coughed, then retched. "Not bad." He coughed again, a tendril of snot dangling out of his nose.

"Wow. You guys are all wimps." Xan laughed.

Josh sucked in a breath, then exhaled hard. "Hey, I'm not crying." He coughed again.

Tinsley reached for the dangerous vegetable.

"Don't," muttered Raven. "It'll hurt you."

"I'm not a wimp." Tinsley crawled over to Josh—who hadn't made a move to give it to her—and swiped it from his hand.

"If you bite it, don't blame anyone else." Raven cringed, a battle of 'protect the child' and 'let her learn by experience' raging in her head.

Tinsley nibbled on the bitten end. Within seconds, her eyes said 'OMG mistake' but she mostly kept a straight face. She handed the pod to Xan, coughed once, and scrambled back to where she'd been sitting, rapidly chomping on the zucchini.

Eventually, Sienna composed herself and picked up the remains of the vegetable she'd bitten to examine.

"Do you know what it is?" asked Raven, prior to taking a bite of potato.

"It kinda looks like a bell pepper that's shrunk and withered." Sienna set it aside. "I can't even guess why anyone would *want* to eat those things, but the dude who planted them must have liked them."

Since both Ariana and Sienna appeared not to have suffered serious damage, Raven chuckled. "Maybe he didn't know what they were, either. Just found seeds."

"I dunno." Xan held up the fiery pepper he'd been nibbling on. "A little bit at a time in the same bite as something else is kinda yummy."

"You can have all of them." Tinsley collected the small peppers and tossed them to Xan.

He laughed. "Uhh, no thanks. My head is already sweating."

Everyone ate their fill of the non-combative vegetables, daylight gradually fading. Josh went off in search of a toilet, but returned in only a few minutes as pale and wide-eyed as if he'd found the corpse out back.

"Don't go in there. I think it's breathing." Josh headed for the front door.

"What's breathing?" asked Xan.

"The furry thing growing in the toilet." Josh shivered, then went outside.

Ariana abruptly started screaming again. "My eyes are burning!"

Raven and Sienna rushed to her. Other than red and wet with tears, her eyes didn't appear to be injured.

"What happened?" Sienna used her poncho to wipe at the girl's face.

In a teary whine, Ariana wailed, "I just wiped my face an' my eyes started burning!"

"The pepper," said Raven. "Juice from the pepper on her fingers?"

Sienna swiped the nearest water bottle and poured some into the girl's eyes.

It helped a little, but the nine-year-old kept crying. Sienna held her arms so she couldn't keep wiping at her eyes and making it worse. Raven wet a scrap rag and tried to wash Ariana's hands. One by one, the other kids went outside to pee before bedtime. Ariana didn't calm enough to do the same until after full dark.

Sienna went outside with her.

After they came back in, Raven balanced a heavy hunk of wood on the door so it would fall if anyone opened it, and put another one on the sliding door in the kitchen. Reasonably confident they had a safe place to sleep, she tried to make herself comfortable on the floor beside Tinsley and closed her eyes.

TOGETHER

Someday, maybe I'll head far beyond the ruins. There's so much out there that needs to be found, but nothing's worth losing this time we have. Kids are only kids for a little while, not long enough. – Ellis Wilder.

H ours into walking the next day, Raven still hadn't quite gotten over her dream.

During the dream, nothing stood out as terribly significant, scary, or meaningful. She'd merely been wandering around the high-rise ruins west of the Arc alongside her father. He'd been showing her around, talking about the various buildings and objects as if explaining everything to a child. Her point of view looked shorter than that of an adult, but not too much. Despite the calmness of it, she awoke with a heavy sense of melancholy at not having seen him since a little after her eighteenth birthday. She wondered if he'd found the house by the garden. Would the man who lived there have been alive at the time? None of her father's notes mentioned anything about meeting another person.

He certainly would have made a huge deal out of it if he had.

People in the Arc still mostly believed they were the only humans on the entire planet. Clearly, that couldn't be true, even if the feral man didn't possess a language or any sort of education. The dead guy in the garden might have been feral, too. Running around naked and trying to bite people didn't necessarily prove they had no idea how to plant a garden. However, the repairs to the house couldn't have been performed by a complete savage.

Do humans instinctively know how to use tools and do carpentry? She smirked at herself.

That proof, finding evidence of at least two people not from the Arc, increased her hopes what she'd seen on the other tower had been a person. She resigned herself to accept her sorrow over the dream came mostly from never having the chance to go exploring with her father. Being with him while he did the thing he adored the most would have been magical.

They eventually stumbled across a swath of exposed pavement that hadn't been buried by centuries of shifting soil. It appeared to lead in the direction of the ruins she'd seen from the tower, which made sense considering the people who lived before the Great Death used cars to get around. They would have made a road into large cities.

A light rain fell most of the morning into the afternoon. Everyone put their hoods up. Unfortunately, the cotton-plus ponchos intended as simple one-size-fits-all clothing had no more water resistance than a blanket. The normally flowing garments saturated, sticking to everyone and tripling in weight. At least the children adored the rain, though Sienna and Raven had to keep yelling at them not to try catching drops in their mouth. Considering plants thrived, the rain most likely didn't contain toxins, but no sense being careless.

By mid-afternoon, the rain trickled off to overwhelming humidity. Cloud cover kept the day from becoming too warm, but the wetness in the air made it feel hotter. Soaked to the skin, the burdensome humidity changed walking into trudging.

"What are we looking for?" asked Xan.

"There is a large silver structure I'm hoping might be a metal building. Kind of like the Arc, but not underground. If we can find a place we can defend against the ferals, or better yet, hide from them, Noah will let everyone go outside and get away from the bad air." Raven stared down at her sloshing boots. Each time she stepped, a little water squirted out from the various holes between duct tape strands.

"Oh. What happens if it's something stupid?" Xan's tone didn't have any hostility, more worry.

"What's stupid is moving everyone so far away." Cheyenne gathered handfuls of her poncho, wringing out the green-brown fabric a little at a time. "Being underground is the problem. There's no air. But we have electricity, food, and water. Why not make those house things right outside? It's all dirt. We don't even have to move the trees."

"People don't *move* trees," said Josh. "They cut them down. What do you think the houses are made out of?"

"Credit?" Cheyenne squeezed water out of another section of her poncho, splattering on the road around her feet.

Sienna chuckled. "No, credit wasn't a real thing. Just numbers in a computer. Remember when you play the board games and get points?"

All the kids said 'yeah' or something close to it.

"Credits are like points."

Josh gawked. "Wait, like if I had ten points, I could just change my number to eight and Xan would give me his space guy figure?"

"You'd have to give me more than two points for him." Xan folded his arms.

"And that's the entire problem with credit." Sienna held her arms out. "They had no real value. Just numbers. Two points is a lot to Josh, but if Ariana had a thousand points, two is nothing to her."

Josh laughed. "Ari would never get that many. She stinks at games."

"Unlike you"—the nine-year-old jabbed her finger into his shoulder—"I don't care who wins. I just like playing."

Xan jumped into a puddle with both feet, splashing Josh and Cheyenne. Josh shot him a 'really?' sideways stare.

Cheyenne squealed. "I just dried this off!" She flapped her poncho at him. "Now it's dripping again."

"Get real," said Xan. "Nowhere near that much water."

Tinsley darted forward at another puddle in the road. She jumped —and vanished entirely in the muddy water.

"Tins!" shouted Raven, sprinting over.

Two small hands came up out of the opaque puddle, reaching around for the edge of the hole. Raven grabbed them and pulled her daughter up.

"Oops," said Tinsley. "The puddle's kinda deep."

The other kids laughed.

Raven lifted her the rest of the way out of the brown water and set her on her feet beside the hole. Tinsley wiped mud out of her eyes while Raven lifted the girl's poncho to check her for cuts.

Upon finding no injuries, she exhaled in relief. "Please don't do that again."

"Maybe we shouldn't jump in puddles." Sienna pointed at the twisted remains of a guardrail. "They could be deep holes with dangerous stuff in them."

"Eep!" Tinsley gasped.

"It's all right. Just, please be more careful from now on." Raven kissed her atop the head.

"Sorry." Tinsley jabbed her sandal at the road. "I thought it was a puddle, not a lake."

The other kids chuckled.

Raven held her hand and resumed walking, following the road for about an hour before it took on a gentle downhill grade into a sweeping rightward curve. Dense forest walled them in on both sides, so close roots had broken up the edges of the paving. The occasional tree also grew out from holes in the pavement right in the middle of the road.

A long time has passed if trees in *the street are this big.* Raven peered up along the trunk of a roughly two-story-tall tree jutting up from a huge pothole as she passed under its branches. The curve straightened out to a sharper downhill stretch overlooking a long stretch of highway leading to the remains of a city on the floor of a shallow valley. Raven stopped, emitting a gasp of shock. These ruins spanned a much greater amount of land than she'd expected, easily ten times the space taken by the high-rises. The tallest building in sight looked about six stories high. Her gaze went straight to a spherical shadow poking out of the forest beyond the far end of the old city, farther from the ruins than she'd expected, but not so much so it would add significant time to their journey.

Tinsley wandered to the side of the road and assumed the position to empty her bladder. At seeing that, the boys hurried to the opposite edge and watered the bushes. Cheyenne stared straight down, blushing. Ariana went over to join Tinsley.

Dammit. Why does seeing someone else pee make me have to go? Raven grumbled mentally. The Arc might have had toxic air, but it also had toilets in private rooms. Grumbling at the irresistible need, she stepped over to the left side of the road by the girls and reached under her poncho for the button holding her outside pants up.

Tinsley, finished, went to stand—but her plastic sandal slipped off the paving. Flailing, she fell over forward and vanished, flying headfirst into the bushes. Squeaks, shouts, and thumps grew distant as the child tumbled down the slope beside the road. The commotion stopped in about ten seconds, suggesting the fall hadn't been too long or steep.

"Tins!" shouted Raven.

Silence lasted only an instant before a high-pitched scream came out of the woods.

Without a care to what she might step in or how steep the hill could be, Raven rushed forward into the foliage, arms up to protect her face from branches. She stumble-charged down the slope toward the still-shrieking child. Uneven ground and a jutting root nearly took her off her feet, but crashing into a tree let her remain upright at the cost of a bruise. She gripped the trunk, let out a hard *oof* and pushed herself around it.

The steep grade leveled off about thirty feet from the road. A short ways in front of her amid thick underbrush, Tinsley sprawled on all fours, her face within arm's reach of an eviscerated deer carcass. Raven rushed over, skidding to a stop on her knees, and grabbed her daughter.

"Mommy!" Tinsley leapt into a hug, bawling. "The deer popped!"

Raven brushed the girl's hair off her face and checked her over. The child had a bunch of small scratches and scrapes from the roll down the hill, but didn't appear to have suffered any serious injuries. One small cut on her forehead seeped blood, but she'd suffered worse running into a metal shelf last year.

"Is she okay?" called Sienna from behind and above.

"Yeah," shouted Raven. "She's fine."

"Why did she shriek?"

Raven held the sobbing child, rocking her while patting her on the back. "Dead animal."

The deer's throat had been torn out, its belly ripped open. Unlike the other one they'd seen, this one had multi-pronged horns growing from its head. Most of its entrails lay out on the dirt, though the gore didn't seem like enough for what should have been inside the body, as if whoever killed it took most of the insides with them somewhere else. Much to Raven's complete astonishment, flies buzzed around the carcass. She'd assumed there had to be insects out here somewhere if the plants had returned, but to see them proved even more thrilling than watching pigeons. She didn't even mind the cloud of them landing on her face.

"Bugs," whispered Raven. "There's bugs."

"The deer died." Tinsley sniffled. "Did the bugs do that?"

"I really don't think so. These are way too small to hurt an animal as big as a deer."

She stood and carried Tinsley up the hill to the road. The incline became quite steep for the last five feet or so, requiring she grab onto roots and tufts of grass to keep from falling. When she reached the top, Sienna took her hand and pulled them up. She, too, fussed over Tinsley, wiping at the scratches on her cheek and forehead.

"Why'd you scream so bad for a fall down a hill?" asked Josh.

"Not the fall." Tinsley sniffled again. "There's an asploded deer."

"What?" Josh gawked.

Xan grimaced. "What happened to its ass?"

Cheyenne and Ariana chimed, "Eww!" in chorus.

"An exploded deer?" Sienna raised both eyebrows.

"Yeah. Poor critter looked like it ate something that blew up." Raven swallowed bile. Thinking about it now disgusted her more than looking at it since she'd been too worried about Tinsley. "But... flies."

"Deers don't fly," said Ariana.

"No, it was covered in flies." Raven tried to spot the carcass, but too many trees stood in the way for her to see it from the road. "There *are* insects out here."

"What's flies?" asked Cheyenne.

"Small, black bugs that fly around." Raven shrugged. "Probably why they called them flies."

"Deer is one of those words I was teaching you about the other day." Sienna patted Ariana on the shoulder. "It pluralizes without adding an s. One deer, two deer, three deer."

"English doesn't make any sense," droned Josh.

"Why don't people say 'deers'?" asked Ariana.

"'Cause it makes them sound stupid," mumbled Xan.

Sienna brought up the idea of going to take a closer look at the flies, but the kids vehemently protested going to see an 'asploded' deer. Raven did, however, make another trip down the hill to recover the inside pants Tinsley lost while falling. At the spot she found them hanging from a low-lying branch, she paused to stare at the deer carcass.

Did a feral do that? Awful lot of meat left behind. If the ferals kill deer for food, why aren't they wearing clothing made from deer skin? She shrugged. *Can't blame them... they probably don't know how to make leather and I wouldn't want to cover myself in slimy dead deer skin either.* She squirmed, then fanned herself. *Damn, it's hot. Those primitives might have the right idea.* Just as she started to chuckle, motion to her right accompanied a strong feeling something watched her. She glanced in the direction from which the eerie sensation came and caught sight of a shadow lurking in a thick mass of leafy branches.

"Easy, buddy. I know you can't understand me. Not here to steal your food. Don't want a problem. I'm leaving right now."

A deep, resonant growl came from the shadows, in no way a sound any man could've produced.

Two yellow-green eye spots appeared, glinting in the dark.

"Shit!" shouted Raven.

She bolted up the hill as fast as she could run on such an incline, grabbing trees to pull herself forward. In what felt like an instant, she leapt out onto the road, whirled, and drew the katana, pointing it at the trees.

Empty trees, wavering branches from where she'd rushed by.

No monster.

Whatever it was hadn't followed her.

The kids and Sienna all backpedaled.

"Damn, girl, what the hell...?" Sienna pressed a hand over her chest.

"There's a monster down there," whispered Tinsley. "I heard it."

"Umm." Sienna gathered the kids away from the side of the road. "Let's get out of here."

"What kind of monster?" asked Xan.

Raven took a step back. "Not sure. Big shadow with glowing eyes. Yeah. Good idea. Let's go."

She kept her stare on the woods, backing up along the road for a few minutes. Once it didn't seem likely the monster would chase them, she faced forward and picked up speed, dodging pavement-breaking trees and large holes.

Roughly two miles later, the downward sloping highway leveled off near the start of the ruins. She came to a stop at the first street running right and left across the path they'd been following. Buildings of various shapes and sizes stood close together in both directions as well as straight ahead, all fringed in green. Various bushes, weeds, ivy vines, and other flora sprouted from every surface in sight, as if the buildings had put on 'clothes' made of plant life. Some even had trees growing inside them, branches sticking out windows or holes in the walls.

As with the other ruin, mangled metal husks littered the streets wherever cars had been.

Josh whistled. "Holy crap. This place is huge. Are we gonna live here?"

The boy's voice echoed out over the abandoned city and faded back to silence. Everyone stood there listening to the eerie emptiness of a place that once held many thousands of people.

"I can't answer yet. Some of these buildings look like they're made out of concrete or… whatever those little stones are called." Raven crossed the intersection, heading toward a six-story building on the corner to her left. Beige stucco had mostly peeled away from an underlying surface of rectangular blocks fused together by a substance resembling concrete. It appeared to be the tallest building in the immediate vicinity, a decent vantage point. A series of five metal patios joined by ladders hung from the side facing the first cross street, offering a convenient way to the roof.

"What are you doing?" asked Sienna.

"Going up top for a look around"—Raven pointed at the building —"It's going to be dark soon. If there is anything out here to worry about, I'd rather see it before we get too far in."

"Okay. Be careful. That looks pretty busted. Like it's gonna fall right off." Sienna led the kids to the right, heading for the adjacent side of the building facing the street they walked in on, which continued straight into the ruins.

Raven walked under the lowest metal porch, even with the second story floor, looking for a way up. A ladder sat at one end, retracted, though it appeared capable of extending to the ground. She jumped up and grabbed the lowest rung. Her weight hanging on it didn't make the ladder budge. A few tugs didn't break it loose, so she pulled herself up to the wobbling platform. Holding her arms out for balance, she waited for the patio to stop moving. *Yeah, this thing's falling apart. Just like the windmills."* The rivets holding the entire assembly to the wall appeared as likely to pop out as hold.

Despite that, she trusted it would be far safer than any interior stairs.

"Gonna go inside," called Sienna from around the corner.

"Okay."

Raven gingerly walked to the other end of the platform and started up a narrow metal stairway, clutching the railing in a white-knuckled grip. Every time the steel patios wobbled, groaned, or shifted, she expected to go careening down to the pavement. *Maybe this was a bad idea.* For some reason, she kept going. By the time she reached the third story, she'd become equally afraid of walking down as up, so she pressed on. Creaks and grinding noises came from above and below. A loud *clank* from below, as though someone hit the lowest patio with a metal hammer, startled her. She froze. A faint metallic *ping* followed. Since no one stood there holding a hammer, the only possible explanation involved pieces—probably bolts—falling and striking a lower platform before hitting the sidewalk.

"Yeah... I think I've committed an error in judgement."

She waited for the metal framework to stop shaking and tiptoed up the last stairwell. The platform put her even with the windows on the sixth story. She peered in past heavily grimed glass at a huge, wide-open room with dingy white walls. Two of the room's walls consisted of giant mirrors, also smeared and grimy. A handrail spanned the entire width of the room in front of the larger mirror, baffling her at its purpose. She had no idea why anyone would need a mirror *that* big or a railing to hold while using it. Multiple holes big enough for a person to fit through marred the dark hardwood floor.

"Not good." Raven looked at the metal mesh under her. "These patios are going to collapse at any second and they're still probably safer than inside." Having her suspicions confirmed didn't reassure her too much about an eventual trip back to the street.

She scaled the sixth story wall, using ample handholds where some of the little rectangular blocks had fallen out, and pulled herself up to sit on a three-foot-high wall surrounding the roof. The warped and buckled surface bore numerous holes exposing the interior and appeared so water damaged it probably couldn't support a pigeon's weight. *I'd fall right through that... and probably go all the way to the ground floor.* While the opposite corner closer to the far end of the city would give her a better vantage point, she also didn't want to die. Perching on the relatively sturdy stone wall would have to do.

Looking around at the ruins using her binoculars didn't offer much new information. Countless abandoned buildings, ruined cars, leaves growing everywhere out of control, ruined streets, and no signs whatsoever of any other people.

The scout on the tower had to go somewhere. *Dad needed to pass through this ruin to get closer to the silver ball.* She panned around the trees until she spotted the bizarre structure, then zoomed in. At this distance, the giant orb no longer appeared to be solid metal, rather thousands of triangular panels made of either plastic or fabric. The material, a light matte grey, didn't throw off a blinding glare in the sun, more an iridescent shimmer. Something that moved like fabric but had the lustre of metal baffled her as well as intensified her curiosity. If aliens didn't make it, the bizarre building certainly came from before the Great Death when humanity still possessed advanced technology. Even more impressive, the inexplicable structure didn't appear overgrown or in disrepair.

Whatever they made it out of survived the poison.

Unfortunately, being able to see only the upper third of the ball because of trees offered no information about the object's purpose. On the other hand, she could find no traces of ferals or any 'monsters' moving around.

The wild men have to use some form of language to communicate. Maybe the grunts? Do they have legends about these ruins? Ghost stories? Something must be scaring them away from the place. The one- and two-story buildings would still make better homes than whatever anyone could build out of branches and sticks.

She spent a few minutes examining buildings up close. A sufficient quantity seemed intact enough—at least the exterior walls—that she decided to suggest this place to Noah if the silver ball turned out to be a flimsy curiosity and not an armored spaceship hull. Ferals had only fists and teeth, neither of which could knock down these buildings.

The people of the Arc wouldn't be vulnerable for weeks while they raced to construct above-ground shelters strong enough to withstand attack.

However, this ruined city didn't have windmill generators or any apparent water sources. It definitely lacked a hydroponic farm. Though plenty of land offered the promise of growing vegetables in the future, establishing a reliable source of food wouldn't be quick. Someone would need to stay at the Arc to run the farms while other people transported vegetables back and forth on an almost three-day walk.

This is a possibility. However, it's stupid to go this far away. I'm going to insist we get the hell out of the Arc right away and build on the surface even if I have to drag Noah outside by his ear. Power, water, food, right there. We can handle a bunch of unarmed naked idiots. They're less of a scare than whatever killed that deer.

She let out a sigh and put the binoculars in her satchel before lowering herself over the wall. The metal patios gave off grinding, creaking, and rattling noises as she climbed down, refusing to stop wobbling. Intermittent clanks came from above and below, parts of the patios themselves or rivets falling to the ground. Regardless of what fell, she wanted to get the hell off it as fast as possible. She tried not to jostle things too much but perhaps rushed down the stairs a little too fast to be perfectly safe. At the lowest patio, she ignored the ladder entirely and dropped to hang off the edge by her fingertips, then let go, landing a short fall with only a minor stumble.

Raven scooted around the corner to the front door, entering a small room containing an elevator, a hallway deeper into the building, a door labeled 'stairs,' and a large sign of text. The sign listed various items like dental office, law office, accountant, and ballet school, indicating each one next to a number, sorted by floor.

"Guys?" called Raven.

"In here!" Tinsley's shout came from the hallway to the left of the elevator.

Raven headed in that direction.

Tinsley poked her head out of a doorway about three-quarters of the way down. "In here. Is the only place wifout holes inna roof."

Sienna and the other kids sat on the floor in a room with dozens of chairs all around the outer walls. The decayed mush of former print magazines sat on a low table in the middle. To her left, a large desk held three computer workstations and a sign asking patients to sign in. Sienna and the other kids stood around, flapping their ponchos as if trying to dry them. No one appeared to have anything on under them. Inside clothes and outer pants hung draped from the backs of chairs around the room.

"Did you see anything?" asked Sienna.

"The city is empty. That silver ball is something I can't even begin to expl—"

Crash!

The floor and walls shook in time with a tremendous jangle of clattering, screeching steel outside. Numerous thuds followed, no doubt pieces falling from the six stories above them, knocked loose by the impact.

Raven almost fainted.

The kids all covered their ears.

That had to be the patios collapsing. Shaking from such a near death experience, Raven managed a feeble smile. "Guess I'm not climbing up to the roof again."

Sienna muttered something inaudible and ran over to hug her. "Don't do anything so risky again. What if it fell with you on it?"

"Yeah…" She exhaled. "That would have been uncomfortable."

"Just a little." Sienna poked her.

"What's with the laundry?" Raven gestured at all the stuff draped on chairs.

"It's not good to wear wet clothes so long, and really bad to sleep in them. The ponchos are a little damp, but loose so they shouldn't be a problem," said Sienna. "You should really let your inner clothes dry out. We've been sweating in them all day after it rained."

Raven couldn't argue that. She took off the satchel and katana, set them on the floor, then removed her poncho, which she dropped next to her. Her inside shirt went well past being simply 'damp' and stuck to her like a second skin. She peeled it off, held it above a large flowerpot containing a plastic rhododendron and wrung it out before draping it over a chair back. Her boots came perilously close to disintegrating when she took them off, the combination of rain and days of hiking having ruined most of the old duct tape. Raven put her poncho back on before shedding her outer and inside pants in one combined shove. The sopping wet fabric gathered around her feet, clammy and unpleasant.

The poncho's dampness became more apparent against her bare skin, but, being the outer layer exposed to the wind, it had dried a lot more than her inside clothes or even pants. She hung her pants on empty chairs and, like everyone else, stood there flapping the poncho in hopes of drying it out faster.

"It's probably going to be dark in about an hour," said Raven. "Since we're already inside and drying off, we should probably spend the night here."

Sienna crouched by the big backpack and rummaged for food. "My thoughts, too."

They ate the last of the garden vegetables for dinner. Munching on a potato and zucchini gave Raven the idea of stopping at the same house on the way back to the Arc so they could stock up on food for the return trip. They still had some muffins left, but it would be dumb to ignore a ready supply of fresh eats. She considered suggesting that house as a potential starting point for a new settlement on the surface, but its garden couldn't support 182 people.

"Gotta pee. Be right back." Cheyenne stood and walked out.

A moment after she disappeared into the hall, the screech of metal on metal destroyed the silence. Tinsley cringed. Not quite three minutes later, the girl dashed back into the room looking like she'd seen a ghost, her poncho hood half down over her face from a frenetic sprint. Rather than run to Sienna, she stopped short in the doorway.

"Guys! Guys!" The girl stabbed a finger at the hall behind her while swiping her hood back with her other hand. "You gotta see this! Be quiet!"

In only a poncho, Raven felt conspicuously underdressed for going outside, but stood anyway—and grabbed the katana.

Cheyenne jogged down the hall to an aluminum back door, its glass panels miraculously still intact. The slight eleven-year-old had to ram her hip into it twice in order to pop the door free of the frame. She shoved it open, causing a familiar metallic screech. The other kids covered their ears again, groaning. Cheyenne padded outside into what had been a parking lot, heading straight to the back end by the remains of a tall, moldy wooden fence. A line of trees there had quite well overgrown the area they'd likely been intended to occupy, breaking up the pavement closest to the dirt mound abutting the fence.

The girl pointed at the dirt. "I was gonna hide behind the trees to, you know, but I saw that."

Footprints from at least three different adults wearing boots, or some manner of shoe with a treaded sole, crossed the mound from the other side of the smashed fence into the parking lot.

"People," whispered Cheyenne. "Someone's been here."

"Neat," said Josh.

"Whoa." Xan crouched by the tracks. "Day or two old."

"You don't know that," said Ariana. "Stop pretending."

Xan grinned. "This dirt is soft and it rains. Footprints wouldn't last long."

"He's probably right." Raven crouched between him and Cheyenne. "The pattern from the tread wouldn't still be there if more than a few days passed. Maybe there really *are* people at the silver ball."

"It's not the ferals. These people have shoes," said Sienna.

Tinsley folded her arms. "We're not ferals and you guys don't have shoes."

"You don't have shoes either," said Ariana in a mildly snotty tone. "That's just plastic tied to your feet."

"They're sandals." Tinsley held one foot up to show it off. "How many times have *I* stepped on a rock and hurt myself?"

Ariana raspberried her.

"I mean... not having shoes doesn't make someone a feral, but having shoes kinda proves they're not." Sienna playfully swatted at the girl's hair.

Tinsley started to laugh, but clamped her hands over her mouth.

"People is good, right?" asked Josh.

"People is *amazing*." Cheyenne bounced on her toes. "They're not supposed to be any others left alive. What if all the stories are lies? They said the air's gonna kill us. They said there aren't any other humans left, but there are."

Xan stood, scratching both hands back and forth over his mop of frizzy hair. "Finding people doesn't mean they're going to like us. Or even be nice. Remember history? There used to be wars."

Raven shifted her weight from leg to leg. If, as it seemed, other people might actually be at the silver sphere, they might assume her one of those ferals and expect her to be hostile—at least until she spoke. Also, as Xan said, she had no way to know what those people would do. They had as much chance of being friendly as disinterested or even aggressive.

"Why don't you guys wait here in this building? It seems safe enough as long as you stay on the ground floor. Tomorrow, when the sun comes up, I'll cross the ruins and try to get a better look at the silver orb."

"What if they see you?" Sienna bit her lip.

"Then I try to make friendly contact—or run like hell."

Sienna grabbed her arm. "What do you do if they won't let you leave?"

"I have a sword." She held it up.

"Girl, if you're going to risk making contact, let's stay together." Sienna stared into her eyes. "I'd rather that, even if we get captured, than sit here wondering when or if you'll be back."

"Yeah." Josh puffed up his chest. "We should stay together."

"Me, too," said Tinsley.

Ariana looked down, fidgeting at her long hair. "I'm scared of both, but less scared staying together."

"Yeah, totally." Xan folded his arms. "Stay together all the way. And if the people *are* bad, it's harder to grab all of us at once than just you."

Tinsley kicked her plastic sandal at the paving, the *click, click, click* echoing into the ruins. "People used to be mean to each other because the Earth had lots and lots of people and not much space. Now, the Earth's got lots and lots of space and not much people." She grinned. "They're probably lonely. I think they're gonna be nice."

Raven stared at her scrawny little daughter, barely able to find words. Bringing her to a place with other people, people who might be anything from crazy ferals to survivors from another Arc, could be incredibly stupid. Leaving her, and the others, here while she went off alone could also be dumb in a different way.

These tracks in the dirt only meant someone had been here within the last few days. It didn't prove they'd come from the silver ball, these ruins, or would even still be nearby. True, they *might* return while she's gone, find the others, and… anything could happen.

Tinsley had a point. Before the Great Death, humans fought with each other over land, resources, and maybe that credit stuff. Now, it didn't seem likely any concept of credit or wealth remained. Vast amounts of land sat unclaimed. Perhaps the worst thing to happen would be the other people driving them away, protecting their food and water source. It sounded far more reasonable to think a small group of surviving humans would welcome two women and a bunch of kids rather than view them as a threat.

We certainly don't look like we're going to invade and take over.

Her father had gone off alone, and never come back. She absolutely couldn't do that to Tinsley.

"Okay. We all go." Raven looked down at her bare feet. "In the morning."

"Yay!" Tinsley jogged across the parking lot to the door, the clapping of her plastic sandals on the crumbling pavement ringing into the ruins around them.

"She adores those," said Sienna. "Didn't want to take them off."

"Not like plastic gets wet." Raven chuckled.

"True. Beats going barefoot out here. Not like being in the Arc. I've found every damn rock, pebble, twig, and nugget of concrete in the world." Sienna winced. "At least it's warm though. My toes aren't numb."

Raven followed her to the building. "I'm going to need to make some for myself when we get back. Those boots are about ready to give up."

"Surprised they haven't fallen apart already." Sienna smiled. "Not sure how you can wear boots that belonged to like ten other people before you."

"Easy." Raven headed past the door to the hall. "Picture wearing tread socks, or nothing, and stepping in stuff leaking out of broken sewer pipe. I'll take the old boots."

Sienna gagged.

Once back in the room with all the chairs, everyone settled in for the night.

Not knowing what to expect when the sun came back up, Raven held her daughter close. They could be walking into a bad situation come sunrise, but the Arc didn't feel safe anymore. Everyone back there might already have suffocated, leaving her, Sienna, and the kids stranded on the surface with no true home. That seemed as likely as the people at the silver ball attacking them, or there being no one there at all. Many questions and worries swirled around in Raven's mind, but one truth kept her from losing it entirely:

No matter what happened, if they survived or if they died, at least she and Tinsley would be together.

WHAT WAS AND WHAT MAY BE

Humanity left behind a vast, empty world. Why shouldn't I go out there and look for stuff we can use? Their crap can't be in any worse shape than our crap. – Ellis Wilder.

Sleep didn't come easy for Raven, and once it did, she found herself in a nightmare.

For hours, she ran through a dark forest away from a growling monster. No matter how fast she went or where she turned, the glowing green eyes remained right behind her. She woke abruptly in a pitch black room, everyone else still sleeping.

Sweating, and out of breath from dream running, Raven lay there in a fog until she passed out.

She awoke again to sunlight leaking in from the doorway. Tinsley's slight weight draped across her, the girl's head under her chin. No one else had yet stirred. Raven attempted to sleep a little longer, but it soon became obvious that wouldn't happen. The weird feeling in her stomach could have been excitement as easily as dread. Reaching the unearthly silver sphere would have a powerful effect on her emotionally no matter what it turned out to be. Crushing disappointment if she found an empty nothing. Elation if it held more people—or terror if those people attacked them.

We've come too far to turn back without risking it. Don't have to charge in like an idiot. Look from a distance, get a feel, then make a decision.

Raven eased Tinsley down to lay on the rug, then sat up and pulled her boots over to check them. So many rips riddled the old, black material, she couldn't identify any new ones, but they definitely felt flimsier than before this recent long hike. She had no idea what the boots had even been made from. Except for the sole, the material appeared to be simultaneously plastic and fabric. They'd been produced prior to the drastic drop in population, when the Arc still had people who knew advanced chemistry, electronics, and how to run the complicated machines on level six. She'd read about leather boots—which these clearly were not—but those required the skin of dead animals, another material the Arc lacked. She figured they had to be a synthetic fabric, perhaps plastic spun into a thread-like weave.

If we stay on the surface, we might end up hunting deer.

She pictured herself wearing the costume of Fiona the Huntress, a 'wood elf' character from one of the books in her room still in possession of a cover. Brown leather pants with cross-cording up the outside of both legs, fringed boots, and... well okay. She didn't really want to wear a skimpy halter top. Whoever painted the elf had clearly been a man.

Regardless, a generation or two from now—assuming people survived that long—they'd all be wearing clothing like the elf or end up like the ferals and abandon clothing entirely. One thing to sit around at home with family, everyone in their inside clothes, but quite another to traipse about totally bare in public. Wearing only her poncho, though it covered everything, still felt as awkward as if she'd gone to the cafeteria in her inside clothes.

She cringed.

"Gotta do what I can to stop us from sliding into primitivism."

Lacking duct tape, she took some cord from her tool satchel and did her best to reinforce the boots. Eventually, the others stirred.

They went outside to relieve themselves and returned to claim their dried inside clothes. Raven dressed, put her boots on, and added another cord or two to keep them in place. The left boot's sole flopped about, nearly separated from the rest of it.

I should turn these into sandals. The bottoms are still intact, and tough.

After a breakfast of stale muffins, they filed down the hall to the front door and went outside. A quick glance at the sky reassured her with the promise of nice weather for the day, if a bit warm again. Raven followed the street to the left, going east. As best she could tell from what she'd seen using the binoculars, a stretch of forest separated the silver orb from the ruins, a distance roughly half that of the city's span. Assuming the road they followed here continued in a straight line across the ruins, she figured they could reach the orb at or slightly after noon. If she didn't like what she saw from a distance, they could make it back here before full dark.

The kids kept talking to a minimum, mostly gazing around in awe at all the overgrown buildings, sidewalk-destroying trees, and wreckage of decomposing cars. Cheyenne zipped across the street to check out a small building where a few mannequins in the broken window wore the rotted remains of clothing made hundreds of years ago. The girl sighed in disappointment when a dress broke apart into dust wherever her fingers made contact.

Most buildings' doors hung wide open and the vast majority of skeletal cars sat askew on the road, mushed into other cars or embedded in walls. Some had flipped on their sides. Raven tried to imagine the chaos and terror that must have gone on here as the people unable to get into an Arc freaked out, knowing they would die soon. Had they attempted to flee the city by car? Where would they go if the entire Earth had become deadly?

People don't think when they panic, they just do stuff.

"Look!" chimed Ariana.

Raven stopped short and spun.

The nine-year-old squatted by the curb on the right, in the shade of an old truck that had decayed to a rusted metal frame and engine block. She picked a small stone up off the road, set it in her left palm, and walked over to everyone. The 'rock' had six legs and large pincers, but appeared docile and tolerated being handled.

"That's huge," whispered Josh, gawking at it. "What is it?"

"A bug…" Xan's eyes widened.

"What kind of bug?" Josh poked it.

"Some kind of beetle," said Sienna.

Raven raised both eyebrows. The beetle made most of her socket wrench drivers seem small. It had to be three inches long and more than an inch around.

"Can it fly?" asked Cheyenne, hiding behind Raven.

"Uhh, I really hope not." Xan leaned back.

Cheyenne shivered. "If that thing sprouts wings, I'm outta here."

"Its teeth look sharp. Put it down before it bites you." Josh nudged Ariana.

"Mandibles." Sienna pointed at the bug. "Those aren't teeth."

"Now you're making up words." Xan rolled his eyes.

"I promise that's a real word. Mandibles stick out of the face." Sienna held her hands up to her cheeks, fingers out to mimic pincers. "Teeth are inside the mouth."

Raven gingerly grasped the girl's wrist to steady her left hand. "We shouldn't touch these bugs. It needs to stay alive. We don't know how many of them survived. Maybe hurting one could cause this entire species to die out again."

"Oh, no!" whispered Ariana. As if trying to carry a soap bubble without bursting it, she crept back to where she'd found the beetle, lowered her hand near the street, and let it crawl off.

Two blocks later, Cheyenne pointed at a small kiosk at the street corner. Inside, under an awning, a metal frame held a large picture of a woman in a coral-hued dress. Though the photograph had faded a great deal, enough color remained that her lips had a distinctly inhuman teal coloration. The girl hurried over, admiring the design of the dress, like nothing any of them had ever seen.

"Why are her lips green?" asked Xan. "Is she sick?"

"Maybe people back then had green lips?" Josh scratched his head.

"She kissed a toad." Tinsley frowned. "That was dumb."

The other kids—and Raven—laughed.

"Who was she?" Josh leaned into the kiosk, which contained only a metal bench. "Why is her picture out here? Was she like the queen or something?"

"The country that used to be here didn't have queens or kings," said Sienna. "They had a leader called a president who changed every few years based on who had the most wealth. But the president didn't control all the power. The government was divided into three different branches. The president, the lobbyists, and the people. The lobbyist branch acted as the voice of corporations while the people's branch mostly tried to do what citizens asked for, but the people belonging to them all basically just tried to make wealth for themselves. Whenever the lobbyists and the people didn't agree, the president declared the winner, but presidents had loyalties to one side or the other and always went with their team rather than the best choice. That's why the Great Death happened."

"What's a corp ration?" asked Ariana.

Sienna twirled a hand randomly. "A large, powerful entity with relentless hunger. They gathered all the wealth they could and usually destroyed anyone or anything that got in their way."

"Entity?" Xan furrowed his eyebrows.

"You know, what women have. Entities," said Josh patting his chest, completely serious.

Raven laughed.

"No, no... that's another word. Entity means, uhh, like a being. Something that exists," said Sierra, sounding less than confident.

Tinsley gasped. "Dragons?"

"I don't think so. Dragons aren't real." Cheyenne shook her head.

"But they're big and powerful and take all the gold and burn people." Tinsley flailed her arms to add emphasis.

Raven glanced over at Sienna. "You don't sound so sure."

"I don't think corporations were like living creatures. More like concepts. It's... I dunno. I read it years ago and don't really remember."

"Oh." Raven shrugged. "Hey, wasn't there a court branch of government, too?"

"I think so, but they weren't part of the government, really. They sat on the side and told the other branches what they could or couldn't do. Usually, they changed the laws whenever the president wanted to do something the law didn't allow so they could do it anyway. Whenever the people's branch had the presidency, they'd change the laws to help the people. When the lobbyists had power, they'd change the laws to make the corporations happy so they didn't eat people. The whole thing kept going in circles."

"Wow. That sounds stupid." Josh whistled.

"Where did you read about this?" Raven scratched her head. "I don't remember any of that from school. Didn't we learn about... something about a congress in a house and a judicial branch the president carried and sometimes whacked people with?"

Sienna chuckled. "It's not a physical branch. But, yeah... that's what Ms. Reed taught us. The store room had all sorts of other books. One explained how the old government used to be made up of slaves."

"What?" Raven blinked.

"Yeah. It said the corporations and rich people owned these people called senators, and forced them to do whatever they wanted."

"Slavery is bad," said Cheyenne.

"Yeah." Xan nodded, as did the others.

"Are you sure those books are accurate? I mean they told us the whole world out here was so poisonous and toxic we'd literally melt into a puddle as soon as we opened the door." Raven gestured back down the street. "There's birds, bugs, and deer."

"And people!" chirped Tinsley.

Sienna slouched. "I, umm... well. I mean, they wrote it down to preserve the information. Why would they save if it if wasn't true?" She sighed. "Sorry. You're right. I'm scared right now and not thinking. Just babbling. Some of those books were written as opinions, not facts. I don't have enough information to tell which ones are which. That's probably why they kept them in the storage room."

"Yeah. Doesn't matter anyway. That world's gone," said Raven.

Cheyenne squealed, pointing and yelling, "Furry!"

Everyone spun to follow the girl's extended arm to the left.

Five or six small creatures darted out from a building and disappeared into a storm drain nearby. They looked about eight inches long, covered in dark grey fur, naked tails the same length as their body dragging after them.

"Rats," said Sienna.

"Yeah. I remember those from school." Raven tugged Tinsley away from the storm drain. "They bite. C'mon."

"What do they eat?" asked Ariana.

"Anything they can find." Josh chuckled.

"Plants, smaller animals, bugs, dead things, trash…" Sienna patted Josh on the head. "He's pretty much right."

"Are there any animals bigger than us?" Ariana balance-beam walked up a fallen lamp post, and jumped off the broken end.

"You're not much bigger than those rats," said Xan.

She raspberried him. "I'm bigger than Tinsley."

"Everyone's bigger than me!" the six-year-old flailed her arms while laughing.

"There used to be big animals, but I don't know if they survived." Raven stepped over the same lamp post. "We've been seeing—well, except for the deer, we've been seeing small creatures that reproduce fast. They'd be the most likely to survive a catastrophe like the Great Death. And don't get ahead of me, please."

Ariana scurried around behind Sienna. "Sorry."

"They said no other people existed, right?" Xan raised both eyebrows. "Maybe there *are* big animals. Or monsters."

Raven shivered imperceptibly, thinking about the glowing green eyes. Whatever she saw in the dark looked bigger than a person and had ripped a deer open. Good chance it could do the same to a person. She mentally kicked herself for not paying much attention in school when they learned about extinct animals. Some had been really cute, so she felt horrible thinking about them all being gone… and tried to distance herself from the subject.

"There's no such thing as monsters." Cheyenne grabbed another streetlamp that still stood upright and swung around it once before continuing. "Monsters are just stuff adults make up to scare kids into behaving."

"We thought the ferals were monsters, but they're people," said Xan.

"What growled at Mommy in the trees?" whispered Tinsley. "It had big green eyes that made light."

Josh drew his leg back to kick a rock, but thought better of it since he had no shoes on. "Proving *one* monster isn't a monster doesn't mean there are no monsters at all."

"You really saw something with glowing eyes?" Sienna fished a water bottle out of her small satchel.

Watching her friend drink made Raven thirsty, so she also pulled out a bottle. "I don't know what it was, only that it was big, dark, and yeah, the eyes kinda glowed in the shadows."

"Reflection maybe?" Sienna took another sip, then handed the bottle to Ariana. "Not sure the Earth got poisoned enough to spawn mutant creatures with literally glowing eyes."

Josh wagged his eyebrows. "We don't know it didn't."

"Stop saying crap like that!" shouted Cheyenne. "You're freaking me out."

"Uhh, guys," said Xan in a quiet voice. "If we're trying to sneak up on those other people so we can look at them and see if they're bad guys, it's a really bad idea to yell."

Clack.

The sharp sound echoed, but mostly came from ahead on the left.

Everyone froze.

"What was that?" whispered Sienna.

"A hunk of concrete falling. Heard it a few times in the other ruin." Raven gazed around at the building façades, everything cracked, crumbling, and engulfed by rampant greenery. "We're going to hear rocks crashing to the ground. Nothing to worry about."

"What pushed it?" whispered Josh.

Cheyenne punched him in the shoulder and gave him a 'stop it!' glower.

He grinned.

"The wind." *I hope.* Raven tightened her jaw and walked a little faster, looking around. *About halfway across the city. Just a little ways more.*

DEN OF BONE

It's important because the last time most people didn't bother reading, the Great Death happened. Now come on, kiddo. You don't want to end the world again, do you? – Ellis Wilder.

Flanked by vine-encrusted broken buildings, Raven walked down a street littered with the husks of cars so decomposed they appeared to be tangles of metal noodles. She couldn't help but imagine herself as a character in one of the novels she'd read. For some reason, people living in the decades leading up to the Great Death wrote lots of books about various imaginary end-of-civilization scenarios. Most involved nuclear weapons, zombies, aliens, or some manner of plague. None of those stories envisioned a reality in which only 2000 humans survived the end of everything, or that the end would come about from greed and ignorance. If doc was right about 'pollution,' it meant humanity destroyed itself.

No external threat like aliens, or dramatic event like war dragged the old society into oblivion. They merely did nothing when the bugs began to die off. Sienna thought corporations, be they giant monsters or something more abstract, caused it. Raven figured the people didn't know enough to care or for some other reason simply didn't. Perhaps it was darkly ironic of her to read novels about fictional end-of-the-world scenarios while living after the actual end of civilization.

At Tinsley's age, Raven hadn't liked learning how to read, finding it tedious and boring.

It took Dad starting to read a story to her at bedtime, but stopping at the halfway point and saying 'here's the book if you want to know what happens.' Her little self never could have imagined how much time teenage Raven would spend in the library. Now, her addiction to escaping the Arc into imaginary worlds somewhat backfired on her.

She'd read so many books about zombies and the world after a nuclear war that she half expected to see undead appearing out of every shaded space between buildings, or have a gang of crazy thugs try to drag her and Sienna off to a harem. Crazed gangs scared her more than zombies, since they stood a far greater chance of possibly happening. The dead didn't get back up, but after seeing evidence of other humans, she knew bad people could be real. One, in fact, tried to bite her face off not long ago.

Her imagination played tricks on her whenever ivy swayed in the breeze or a fragment of building thudded to the ground. She kept jumping, wishing she carried one of those 'guns' the characters in books always had with them. Though she'd never seen so much as a picture of one, she imagined them being similar to the crossbow on the cover of the one fantasy book. Only, instead of a cord flinging an arrow, guns somehow used explosions to throw metal pellets without blowing themselves apart. The weapons sounded fearsome, but given she'd read about them in fiction novels, she didn't quite believe them to be as destructive as portrayed. Still, they sounded far more effective than a sword she had never practiced with.

Upon reaching an intersection where a wider four-lane street crossed the one she'd been following, Raven paused next to the rusted corpse of a traffic light to look around. Two blocks to her left, the road went under an overpass. On her right, the street continued for six blocks before ending at a T-intersection in front of an enormous building. The shock of seeing such a large structure kept her staring for a few seconds, trying to make sense of a place even bigger than the storage building where they'd found the filters. Fragments of lettering above the windows spelled out words like 'supermarket,' 'pizza,' 'liquors,' and a few others that didn't appear to be real words like 'kwik-e-kleen.'

"Is that a boot?" asked Josh.

Raven pulled her gaze off the giant building to look at the boy, who pointed to the left. He appeared to be indicating an object in the road beneath the overpass, which did resemble a boot. She took her binoculars from the satchel and raised them to her eyes.

Indeed, an empty boot stood in the road. Not far from it, motion attracted her attention to a bit of fluttering fabric the same greenish brown as everyone's cotton-plus ponchos. Someone appeared to be lying on the ground in the space beneath the overpass, partially hidden behind the wreckage of a truck and pile of built-up debris.

For a moment, she stared at the fabric, unsure how to process it.

It looked too much like their ponchos to be anything else. She could think of only one person who'd disappeared from the Arc recently enough for the poncho not to have disintegrated. A heavy lump formed in her throat. Even if a crazed feral snuck up behind Sienna, she couldn't have forced any voice out of her mouth to shout a warning.

No... wait. Raven closed her eyes hard. *Arcology 1409. There are others. They'd be growing cotton-plus, too. That could be from anywhere.* She cringed at her next thought, and opened her eyes. *Only if the other Arc had most of their people leave or die and started making ponchos because no one could operate the other machines.*

Dreading what she'd find, but unable to resist looking, Raven put the binoculars back in her satchel and approached the overpass.

"Don't we want to go that way?" Josh gestured to his right, down the road they'd been following.

Raven couldn't speak, so she simply kept going without even trying to explain.

Crumbling walls of once-white concrete on either side of the four-lane road supported the overpass, which carried train tracks. The closer she got, the more certain she became the poncho came from the Arc. She crept along the underside of the flipped truck to the corner, and stopped short in horror.

Hundreds of bones lay scattered around the dirt area between the street and the wall under the overpass. Few skeletons remained anywhere even close to intact. Loose vertebrae, ribs, femurs, and skulls lay everywhere, as if someone had deliberately dragged dead people here to dismember them. More than half of the bones weren't human, likely deer or creatures of similar size.

The familiar poncho fabric wrapped around the torso of a skeleton missing its entire left leg, right leg below the knee, and both arms. A filter mask lay a short distance off, its strap broken. The skull lacked a jawbone and bore numerous deep gouges and one half-inch diameter puncture mark on the side, right into the brain. The back hadn't exploded out, so it couldn't be from a bullet.

Cannibals!

She shivered, thinking of the feral who kept trying to bite her… but people didn't have huge round teeth capable of making a hole like that. It had to be a spear. Rusty metal rods about that size stuck out of concrete hunks everywhere in the ruins.

The patter of bare feet jogging on pavement approached from behind.

"Raven, what's—ack!" Sienna jumped back at the sight of the bones. "Holy shit."

"Whoa," whispered Josh. "Dead people."

Cheyenne stopped midway along the length of the truck, before coming close enough to look past it. "Uhh… I don't wanna see that."

Tinsley, Ariana, and Xan didn't hesitate, but Cheyenne grabbed the girls, holding them back.

Xan walked up to stand beside Sienna. "Bones." He peered back at Cheyenne. "It's just bones. Nothing gross."

"Let go." Tinsley squirmed.

Cheyenne didn't.

"I think this is Dad," whispered Raven.

"You don't know that." Sienna rested a hand on her shoulder. "Can't even tell if we're looking at a woman or a man."

Raven squatted, pinched the poncho, and pulled it back, revealing a satchel about half the size of her tool bag. At the sight of E-W scratched into the metal clasp, a phantom fist punched her in the gut, knocking the wind out of her. She opened the buckle and peered in at a familiar notebook cover. Green. White lettering: Arcology 1409.

"Oh, no." Sienna put a hand over her mouth. "That's an Arc notebook. Maybe it's one of the people who left?"

"It *is* one of the people who left, but not a hundred years ago." Raven tugged the notebook from the satchel and opened it. Tears blurred her vision too much to read, but she recognized the handwriting—she'd been staring at journals written by the same person rather often lately.

Sienna crouched beside her, arm across her back. "Maybe someone found his stuff. Doesn't prove these bones are his."

"I know—" Raven choked up. She clutched the notebook in both hands to her chest, bowed her head, and wept for a moment before collecting herself. "I know you're trying to make me feel better. Thanks. I've thought him dead for a long time already. It's not fair to give me hope, especially when that hope means he chose to go away and never come back."

"Sorry." Sienna rubbed her back comfortingly.

Xan grasped a different skull, holding it up to look into the eye sockets. Josh waved a large femur around in the manner of a sword.

"You shouldn't play with the dead," whispered Sienna.

"I know this is him." Raven exhaled a stuttering breath, trying to force herself not to give in to crying. She could do that later in a safe place. Out here, she had to stay alert. Against the huge tide of grief rising up inside her, she flipped to the end of the notebook, wondering if it might explain what happened to him. A little past the midway point, she found the last words her father wrote, in triple-height letters.

I was wrong! So wrong! Not aliens! Foolish stories. I have to get back to the Arc and tell everyone!

"So many." Josh stopped swinging the femur, but didn't drop it. "What killed all these people? Are they from the Great Death?"

"Monsters," said Tinsley.

Raven couldn't quite chuckle at her daughter's innocence, nor could she bear looking back and making eye contact with her. "What did he want to warn us about?"

"Probably the monsters," said Tinsley.

"Umm…" Sienna shivered, looking around at the hollow space off the side of the road, a veritable 'cave' under the overpass. "Kinda odd there are so many bodies here."

"Monsters did it," said Tinsley.

Raven closed the notebook, silent until the urge to snap at her daughter for joking around at Dad's death subsided and she could speak in a calm voice. "It's not monsters, sweetie. There's no such thing."

"Yeah there are. I'm looking at them right now."

Raven whirled around.

Six large cats stood in the road behind the three girls, nearly as tall as eye-level with Tinsley. Sand-hued fur shimmered in the bright sun. Hints of long claws peeked out between the toes of wide paws. Iridescent green eyes ringed in black stared intently at the children closest to them. Dried blood stained the whitish fur around their mouths. Six thick-furred tails twitched in anticipation.

Tinsley regarded the animals with curiosity. Cheyenne appeared paralyzed in terror. Ariana struggled to get away from her, but couldn't.

"Umm," whispered Josh. "I think I know where all the bones came from."

QUIET

Before she died, your mother always told me going out there would kill me. If you're reading this, guess she was right after all. – Ellis Wilder.

Cheyenne trembled in place, completely frozen in terror, still clutching the ponchos of the two younger girls. Tinsley looked back and forth from the cats to Raven, her expression asking if she needed to be afraid. Ariana finally broke loose from Cheyenne's grasp. She gave off a shrill scream and sprinted toward Sienna.

At her sudden motion, the cats rushed.

Three went after Ariana. One pounced Tinsley to the ground. Another charged at Cheyenne. She saw it coming for her and shrieked. The shrill sound hit the great cat like a physical force; it skidded to a stop, ears back. The last two cats sauntered forward in no great hurry, following the runners chasing Ariana.

Raven shouted, "Get away!" as loud as she could while racing to Tinsley.

Ariana zipped past Raven and leapt into Sienna who'd been running a half-step behind.

The cat attacking Tinsley bit her around the left calf and backpedaled, dragging her off. The child looked up, making an 'uh oh' face. Raven's screaming charge startled the cat cringing back from Cheyenne into running off. The one dragging Tinsley scurried faster, but couldn't outrun her in reverse. Raven barreled in, fully intending to tackle the cat, but skidded to a stop by the child when the animal released her and backed up, roaring.

"Bad kitty," said Tinsley, still sprawled on her front.

Raven scooped her daughter up and walked backward, staring into the cat's eyes. Josh and Xan shouted behind her trying to scare the cats away. Ariana wailed sobs, shouting, "Mommy!" over and over.

The cat that left blood trickling down Tinsley's leg surged toward Raven. She tossed Tinsley to her feet behind her, shouting, "Run!" and pulled the katana out. Snarling, the cat reared up, biting at her face. She ducked and backpedaled, swiping the sword up to put it between the fanged mouth and her head. The bite fell short, but a paw slap to the shoulder shoved her sideways. She landed sitting on the street, the cat standing over her.

"Get outta here!" shouted Raven, waving the sword back and forth at it. "Go find a deer!"

It recoiled, seeming more alarmed at the shouting than the blade, keeping its head low. She rolled over onto all fours then leapt up to run, but fell again when the cat bit her on the foot.

"Oof!" Raven landed on her chest, facing the overpass.

Sienna clung to Ariana. Cheyenne and Xan swung human femurs like baseball bats, keeping the cats surrounding them at bay while Josh shouted and threw whatever he could get his hands on at them including rocks, bones, and skulls.

Tinsley stood alone midway between Raven and the group, looking back and forth between one cat holding her mother's foot in its mouth and five cats surrounding the others. Blood trickled down her left leg, but she didn't appear to have too deep a wound or even realize she'd been hurt.

In Raven's mind, she pictured three of the cats noticing her tiny daughter standing there undefended and all going for her at once. Growling, she grabbed the pavement and yanked herself forward while kicking at the cat chomping on her boot. The instant her foot came free, she scrambled upright and ran to Tinsley.

She slowed to a walk after gathering her daughter up into her arms. The warm, gritty touch of pavement under her foot revealed her left boot no longer had a sole—probably still in the cat's mouth. Raven peered back at the one gnawing on the rubbery slab, then ahead at the other five cats. They alternated between cringing back and trying to get a nibble on one of the other kids or Sienna. Surprisingly, all the children's shouting appeared to be making the animals hesitate from committing to an all-out attack.

Cats chase shit that moves...

If she crept away, she might get Tinsley to safety—but doing so would leave the woman she considered a sister plus four kids to the whim of five hungry cats. Dare she risk Tinsley's life to save them? If she took off running, the other cats might instinctively chase her instead.

She squeezed Tinsley, about to apologize when she spotted a storm drain a little less than a block away. *They'll chase me if I run. Gotta give them a chance.*

"Sienna! Drain!" shouted Raven, then dashed down the road.

The cat dropped the boot sole and came after her, as did three of the others, peeling away from the group of kids plus Sienna. Another started to, but a hurled skull bouncing off its head redirected its attention to Josh.

What remained of her left boot flapped about as she hauled ass for the storm drain, not looking back. The soft thumps of heavy cats closed in behind her; she expected they'd take her down before she made it close enough to dive in—so she launched Tinsley across the street in a slide for the drain opening and tried to run faster in hopes of drawing them away from her.

Salvation came in the form of a wooden pole studded with metal climbing spars. She leapt for it, grabbed on, and climbed. Claws ripped at her poncho but didn't break skin. Faster than she'd ever done anything in her life, she scaled twenty feet, then looked back to check on her kid.

One cat crouched by the storm drain opening, intently interested in something inside. Three stood at the base of the pole, looking up at her. The other two chased Sienna and the rest of the kids. The larger of those two pounced Xan, dragging the boy to the ground. He screamed in pain, but managed to roll over onto his back.

Josh had already committed to chasing the one away from the drain and was too far ahead of the others to get back in time to matter for the other boy. Xan caught the cat's first attempt to bite his throat by wedging the femur sideways in its mouth.

Cheyenne flipped in an instant from terrified to fearless, stopping short and brandishing her femur club at the cat nipping at her heels. Her high-pitched war scream caused the cat to cringe away from her.

"Hah," said Raven, giving the finger to the three peering up at her.

The one in the middle sprang up, gripped the pole, and climbed toward her, giant claws digging into the old wood.

"Shit. Of course you can climb."

Having nowhere else to go, she scrambled down to about twelve feet and let go, falling past the ascending cat too fast for it to get a swipe at her. She landed in a reverse somersault, but fear threw her back to her feet before she even realized she'd tumbled.

Xan shoved something into his mouth while somehow managing to hold the cat back using only a one-handed grip on the femur.

Josh's screaming, club-waving fit startled the cat away from the storm drain. He stomped after it, pushing the animal farther away. Sienna tossed Ariana into the opening, spun around, and dashed toward Xan.

An explosion of saliva and green chunks flew from the boy's mouth, spraying the cat in the face. It promptly leapt back, emitting a startled grunt, shook its head, then pawed at its face while groaning, having lost all interest in Xan.

He dragged himself away from the cat, bleeding from the leg where claws had gotten him.

Cheyenne stood up on tiptoe and shrieked, "Go away!"

Her cat cringed, neither attacking nor fleeing.

The climber jumped down. Raven swung the katana at the three stalking up on her, shouting nonsense as loud as she could while retreating toward the storm drain. Cheyenne, upon noticing Raven, edged backward. Sienna grabbed Xan, hauled him upright, and more or less carried him to the drain opening. She lowered him inside, then picked up a hunk of concrete, which she threw at the cat menacing Cheyenne. As soon as the beast flinched, the girl whirled, throwing herself into a headfirst dive at the narrow opening in the curb.

"Mommy!" shouted Tinsley from beneath the street.

Josh ran toward Raven, waving the femur over his head and yelling gibberish. He appeared to be trying to distract the cats off her so she could dive to safety.

Raven grabbed the back of his poncho and shoved him into the storm drain. "You're still a kid. Get in there."

"Come on!" yelled Sienna while sliding in.

Raven backed up another few steps, the cats all closing in on her—except for the one Xan spit on, which had lost all interest in everyone. The animal rolled around on the road, whimpering and pawing at its face. The remaining five appeared ready to maul her any second. She let out one last horrible shout, whirled, and jumped feet-first into the opening.

A cat snagged her by the right shoulder, getting mostly a mouthful of poncho fabric, though the point of one fang sank into her skin.

Josh stabbed at it with the femur. Raven's left arm blurred into a series of frantic slaps at the beast's nose. Someone grabbed her by the ankles and pulled. Fabric ripped by her right ear.

"Let go!" yelled Josh, ramming the femur up out of the slot.

"Mommy!" shrieked Tinsley.

A cat paw grabbed Raven's left arm at the bicep.

Sienna reached up and seized the animal, peeling its claws away.

At the hollow *bonk* of bone on cat skull, Raven popped out of the animal's mouth and fell into a dark, underground chamber.

She landed on her butt at the bottom of a concrete cistern. Xan lay on his side, cradling his leg. Josh held the femur club in both hands, trembling from adrenaline. Cheyenne, next to him, clutched her femur more like a security blanket. She appeared mostly shell shocked, but didn't shiver. Sienna sank to sit beside her, and exhaled hard. Tinsley leapt into her lap, clinging and crying.

Raven's left bicep and right shoulder burned, but she barely noticed the pain, too worried about her child.

She pulled Tinsley's poncho up off her legs, exposing a cluster of small scratches where the cat's smaller teeth sliced. Seeing such superficial injuries should have been a relief, but she couldn't stop thinking about what would have happened if the cat had gotten away with her.

Unable to speak, Raven wrapped both arms around Tinsley and held on tight.

Claws scraped at the metal opening above and behind her. Soft growls and snarls of discontent hovered nearby. Xan couldn't seem to stop drooling. He coughed, fanned at his mouth, and kept spitting. Josh held Cheyenne, patting her on the back while telling her they were safe. Ariana had gone from scream crying to staring mutely into space.

Sienna crouched by Xan, examining his leg. She ripped his inside shirt off, out from under his poncho, and repurposed it into a bandage around his thigh.

"How is he?" whispered Raven, still clinging to Tinsley.

"Scratches on the back of his leg. Deep enough to need stitches but we don't have supplies for that." Sienna unwound the shirt. "Dammit. I need to rinse this off first. Too rattled to think straight."

"Chey?" asked Raven.

"I'm okay." Cheyenne exhaled hard. "Thanks."

Josh shucked the backpack off and pulled out a water bottle, which he handed to Sienna.

"What did you do to the one that got you?" Cheyenne squatted beside Sienna, trying to help her clean Xan's leg.

"Kept a few of those burning peppers," rasped Xan. "Chewed one up and spat it in the damn thing's eyes. Maybe a mistake. I can't feel my mouth."

"Pretty sure the cat got the worse end of the deal." Sienna kissed him atop the head. "Fast thinking."

"Mommy's got a booboo!" said Tinsley.

"Just a little scratch, like yours." Raven reached for the water bottle. "Let me see that when you're done?"

After rinsing the back of Xan's leg, Sienna handed it over.

Raven washed Tinsley's calf. The tooth marks were shallow; thankfully the cat had been merely trying to carry her rather than eat. Still, she figured they ought to be covered for a couple days. Raven pulled her knife, sliced off a bit of her inside shirt, and tied it around her daughter's injury.

"What were those things?" asked Cheyenne.

"Monsters," said Tinsley.

"No… just cougars." Sienna raked a hand up through her hair. "I've never felt so happy to see something while wanting it to die at the same time."

Josh took another bottle from the backpack. "We have two left. Hope that stream is okay to drink, or we won't have any water for the last day."

"It won't be fun, but one day isn't too bad." Sienna finished bandaging Xan's leg. "Now if you'll give me a minute, I'm going to have a breakdown."

"If you break down, Mommy can fix you." Tinsley smiled.

"Heh." Sienna held her face in both hands and sighed. "Shit… I can't believe we survived."

Cheyenne knelt by Raven and pushed her poncho up off her shoulder. "Mom, need to wash this, too. She's hurt."

"Do cougarses always eat people?" whispered Ariana.

"I really don't know. I'll check the books when we get back, and it's cougars, not cougarses." Sienna checked Raven's shoulder.

Having the puncture wound prodded felt like a hot spike stabbing her in the shoulder. Raven buried her face in Tinsley's shoulder to muffle her grunt of pain.

"That's Mom." Xan gave an exhausted laugh. "We almost got our butts chewed off by giant cats and she's teaching us English."

Sienna dabbed at Raven's shoulder, then cleaned the claw marks on her left arm. "It's like someone stabbed you with a pen. Just the tip of the tooth got in. Guess we're not at the top of the food chain anymore."

"Maybe nature is mad at humans for hurting it?" Ariana wiped her tear-streaked face. "I'm scared."

"Pigeons, wild men, rats, some bugs, and now giant cats." Raven brushed Tinsley's hair in a repetitive, calming motion—though probably soothed herself more than the girl. "Maybe we *should* stay underground."

"You don't mean that." Sienna rigged a cloth strip bandage around Raven's arm. "I can hear it in your voice. You love it out here, and seeing nature coming back is a thrill. But, you're freaking out because the kids got hurt."

"Damn right. Maybe I'm glad the Earth isn't a poisonous mess, but seeing it is not worth shit happening to Tins… or any of the kids. Or you. I'm not my father. I'm not gonna go off and get killed and disappear on Tinsley like…" Raven looked away.

Sienna took her hand. "You can be mad at him. Nothing wrong with that. Don't mean you don't love him."

"I dunno. I saw the thing starting to drag her off and…" Raven squeezed Tinsley.

"Air please," rasped Tinsley.

"Yeah. You got off easy. I had four kids scare the shit out of me. Freakin' three of 'em ran *at* the damn cougars, I damn near died."

Cheyenne looked down, guilt all over her face. "Sorry. I dunno what happened. Went from as scared as Ari to like angry."

"I wasn't scared," whispered Ariana, before crawling over into Sienna's lap. "I was *really* scared."

Sienna clutched the nine-year-old like a big doll.

"There's a lot more animals out there than we thought." Josh gazed up at the hole. "The air is awesome. I don't feel tired all the time."

"Or dizzy." Cheyenne tapped her head. "I always wanted to sleep before. And it's so weird being in a place where not everything smells like boiling poo."

Xan laughed. "I think we could'a left the Arc a long time ago."

"That lady you work with thinks people did leave." Cheyenne picked up the water bottle Josh half drained and opened it.

"Yes. Lark could be right." Raven loosened her grip on Tinsley a little. "So many animals and plants around, the Earth had to have recovered quite a while ago. Maybe we stayed underground for too damn long… but—"

Sienna shook her head. "No guilt. Staying there wouldn't have been any better for your daughter's health than cougar teeth. Not sure what would surprise me more between us finding people at this place you want to go or finding everyone back home still alive when we get there."

"Uhh." Josh pointed at Xan. "His leg's messed up and we're almost out of water. We might not be *able* to go home."

"Why does everyone keep saying scary things?" Cheyenne grabbed two fistfuls of her hair. "I'm already scared."

Josh paced. "Not trying to scare you. Just being honest. We can't turn around and go back now. The place is real close. Even with him limping, we can get there in like two hours."

Raven brushed a hand at her satchel. *What did Dad want to tell everyone about?*

"What if there's nothing there?" Cheyenne hung her head, her face disappearing behind her long, dark brown hair.

"Wrong question. What if there *are* people there, and they're friendly." Josh folded his arms.

Xan raised one arm, pointing straight up. "They could be bad guys."

"There is no such thing as countries or corporations or presidents anymore." Josh shrugged. "If anyone is there, they don't have any reason to be mean to us. But, even if they do want to hold us like prisoners or something, they might have a doctor."

Raven lifted her face from Tinsley's frizzy hair. "And what if they're a bunch of ferals?"

"Living in a giant silver ball like a space ship?" Josh smirked. "That doesn't make sense."

"We don't know what the thing is. Could be something people made before the Great Death." Raven exhaled out her nose. "But it doesn't look like it's falling apart. Dad wrote something down... the last thing he said. Something shocked him so much he didn't even describe it because he wanted to get back to the Arc faster. He had to tell everyone something... but that could mean a warning as easily as good news. It had to be really bad or really good for him not to even write a few words about it. We should at least look from a distance before turning around."

"Bull." Sienna prodded her. "You weren't about to turn around. What you *were* gonna say is we wait here while you go check it out. We already discussed that. If they're going to take prisoners, they get all of us or none of us."

"Yeah." Raven hugged her daughter close.

"Mommy, you're squeezing me so much I gotta pee."

Everyone laughed, though none too loud.

A large concrete pipe led away from the cistern. Raven briefly considered suggesting they go down the pipe and try to put some distance between them and the cats, but didn't want to risk ending up lost underground or caught in a cave-in.

So, they waited.

Eventually, Ariana calmed enough to stop sniveling and shaking.

"Sorry about your dad," whispered Sienna.

"Thanks, but, I kinda knew already. He left a notebook with Daniel, asked him to give it to me if he ever stayed gone for more than two weeks."

Sienna blinked. "Old Daniel? The guy who just died?"

"Yeah." Raven jabbed her fingers at the dirt beside where she sat, sad all over again about the old man's passing. *If that idiot Noah had listened to me, Daniel wouldn't be dead.* Granted, almost no one survived even *to* eighty years of age, much less past it. Everyone had more or less been expecting him to go at any minute already. "That notebook was basically Dad apologizing to me for getting himself killed and saying how sorry he was not to be there for me. He'd never leave and not come back willingly."

"You never told me about the notebook..." Sienna bit her lip, seeming hurt.

"I'm sorry, it's just..." Raven's lip quivered. Tears ran down her face. "The apology letter's only like two pages. The rest of it is him writing stories about stuff I did as a little kid. Way little, before I can remember. I haven't been able to read any of it yet... just makes me miss him too damn much."

Sienna hugged her. "I understand. Some things are too painful to talk about."

After another long period of everyone sitting there staring at each other in silence, Josh stood. He jumped up, grabbed the underside of the hole, and pulled himself up to look outside. "I think the cats are gone."

"They could be hiding. Stick your butt out there and moon them, see if they come running," said Xan.

Josh hauled himself the rest of the way out to the road.

"Do not moon the cougars," said Raven.

"Duh." Josh laughed. "He wasn't being literal... and yeah, they're gone. I don't see them. Should I yell 'here kitty' or stay quiet?"

Everyone said 'stay quiet' at the same time.

"Stand there for a bit and keep looking, in case they smell you," said Xan.

"We are not using Josh as bait." Sienna let out an exasperated sigh.

"I'm not bait. I'm a scout."

"What's the difference?" asked Cheyenne.

"A scout doesn't want to be seen." Four or five minutes later, Josh crouched and peered in. "Pretty sure they're gone."

Raven got up, wincing at a faint jab of pain in her shoulder. "At least now we know what killed that deer. Okay. Let's get out of here before we lose too much more daylight."

SILVER

Half of succeeding is acting like you know what you're doing. – Ellis Wilder.

K atana drawn, Raven led the group away from the storm drain.

The lopsidedness got on her nerves within minutes of leaving the storm drain, resulting in her remaining boot and the scraps of the other one going into the tool satchel. None of the cougars had any interest in the torn-off sole. They'd left it on the road. Perhaps enough tape could fix it, so she nabbed it on the way back to the street that cut clear across the ruins to the eastern side.

Once—*if*—they got back to the Arc, she'd probably make sandals out of the boot soles. For now, she went barefoot like everyone else except Tinsley. Plastic shoes held on by fabric scraps might have been slippery on paved surfaces, but they proved remarkably sturdy. The small rip in her poncho would be easy to fix as well. However, between the boots and the rip, she started to wonder if enough time spent outside would leave her as naked as the wild man.

Nothing existed out here to make new clothing from, except possibly deer skin. Problem being, she had no idea how to turn slimy gore into leather. An imaginary scenario unfolded in her head where the kids outgrew their stuff, hers and Sienna's clothes fell apart in a few years, and they all wound up wild savages with only berry juice smeared on their bodies for clothing.

At least I won't have to worry about growing old and looking all wrinkly... We're probably not going to last out here much past forty.

Somewhere, she'd read people long ago considered forty or fifty years old as elderly, back when they still blamed demons for health problems and primarily rode horses. Though, understanding that biology, not supernatural forces, made people sick didn't much matter when she had no medical supplies or knowledge.

Catching herself assuming the doc and everyone else in the Arc had already died, Raven squeezed the katana handle until her hand hurt. *Dad would want me to stay optimistic. Giving up hope is a sure way to fail.*

She glanced at the sword while stepping around bits of concrete rubble and metal scraps. Taking the weapon had been a spontaneous reaction, like a little kid finding a giant knife they thought looked cool. The same way Xan played with the femur pretending he had a sword, she felt silly.

I couldn't even hit a cat with it.

True, her father used to say no one came out of the womb knowing everything. If the people at this other place—provided they existed at all—turned out to be bad, they wouldn't know she had so little skill using a sword. Of course, they also might not even know what a sword is. Then again, the feral sure seemed to. In the storage place by the filters, he'd run away as soon as she pulled it out.

Her father always seemed to know everything about everything and only rarely showed doubt. She'd caught him being wrong once, and when she asked about it, he explained that people tended to respect confidence more than accuracy. Someone who acted without hesitation could convince people far more than a brain like the doc who appeared nervously unsure even when correct.

She spent a few minutes pretending to be a character from a fantasy book, imagining how they'd carry a sword—never mind that if she got into an actual fight, she'd probably step on a rock within twenty seconds, cut her foot open, and look like a fool.

As if by some wordless mutual knowing, none of the kids or Sienna spoke a word after leaving the storm drain. Xan did occasionally grunt or gasp whenever he put too much weight on his clawed leg. Josh took the backpack without prompting or protest. Cheyenne held Xan's arm across her shoulders. Ariana clung to Sienna, clearly terrified the cougars would come back for them.

The occasional pigeon or darting rat caused a few small gasps, but typically ended in the kids enthralled by watching the animals. At least, until Tinsley said, "Ooh, kitty."

Ariana froze statue still. Pee spread out in a puddle around her feet.

Xan held up the femur, all his weight on one leg, looking ready to bash anything that came near him.

Cheyenne didn't seem to know if she should let go of him or raise her club.

Raven spun to face the direction her daughter pointed... and stared in stunned silence at a relatively large housecat trotting off with a mouse in its teeth. Gradually, everyone realized the nearby cat wasn't any threat to them. Xan sighed at the clouds and bowed his head, muttering something that sounded like words he'd get in trouble for using.

Ariana broke down crying.

Sienna comforted her. None of the other kids picked on her for wetting herself, and all stood around patiently for a moment while Sienna cleaned her up. A minor debate ensued as to whether it would be worth it to use up water washing her stained inside pants, or leave them on the ground.

"We're going to run out no matter what and end up either going two days without drinking or risking the stream." Raven shrugged. "Probably doesn't matter either way."

Head down, face red, Ariana whispered, "We need to drink more than I need inside pants. I'm sorry for messing them."

"It's okay." Sienna brushed a hand over the girl's hair. "I almost ruined mine, too."

Raven picked up a plastic jar from the hundreds scattered around, the only relatively intact trash left. She plucked the stained garment from the road and dropped it into the jar before screwing the lid on. "Here. This will keep it from contaminating anything else. We can wash it in the stream later."

Crisis averted, she resumed walking, a little faster and less careful about where she stepped.

Tinsley brushing off almost becoming cougar dinner worried her. Maybe the girl didn't comprehend what might have happened to her, but as Dad sometimes said, the difference between foolishness and bravery depended on the outcome. Having a fearless child in the outside world scared the heck out of her. Ariana had only been chased by the cougars, not touched, and she'd probably never be able to look at one again without screaming.

What's worse... coping with nightmares or worrying my kid's going to jump headfirst into danger?

Seven blocks from the storm drain, they reached another large intersection where a six-lane road ran sideways across their path. A stone pedestal stood at the center, about as tall as her, surrounded by an island of overgrown grass that split the northbound and southbound lanes apart for about twenty yards. An unrecognizable lump of metal atop the pedestal somewhat resembled a human shape. It looked like a statue of a person left in an acid bath. A plaque on the base had blurry squiggles slightly less brown than the rest of it where raised lettering long ago eroded.

No one paid much attention to the monument as the group filed around it and kept going.

This place is so huge. There had to be ten thousand people or more here.

A thought struck her. The Arc basically amounted to eight people getting on a lifeboat and surviving the sinking of a ship that killed a few thousand. *The giant cruise ship in the book had a bunch of lifeboats, though. Having only one for so many people would be stupid and pointless. There have to be more arcologies.*

The ferals might have come from another arcology with a less capable tech team. Perhaps they experienced a catastrophic failure like the one hers faced years ago and evacuated. If people had been forced to the surface and cut off from their hydroponic farm, water source, and power, they might have devolved over generations into ferals. *No. They'd still have language. Could the ferals have somehow survived on the surface the whole time, mutated by the toxins?*

Within minutes of leaving the intersection, the end of the city came into view. The road they'd been following continued away from the ruins into dense forest after crossing a bridge over a giant trench.

Raven cautiously approached the bridge, eyeing dozens of cracks and small holes in the pavement. The concrete walls on either side, in addition to being engulfed in green leaves, had numerous missing hunks exposing metal rods embedded in the stone. Despite that, the bridge did consist of reinforced concrete and steel. It didn't appear anywhere near as likely as the metal patios to collapse.

Cautiously, she advanced a few feet onto the bridge and approached the edge, peering over it down at a river of opaque brownish-green water. The surface, smooth as glass, appeared calm. No doubt the water flowed, but at a gradual speed. Large grey rocks covered in moss lined the banks, extending several feet from the water's edge. Waist high grass covered the rest of the slope from street level down the hill. It looked too steep to be an easy climb, but not impossible. The sharp-edged head-sized rocks at the bottom made it scarier. Tumbling into those would hurt.

She estimated the river to be about four stories below the bridge, give or take a few feet. A fall directly into the water most likely wouldn't kill, but would probably result in broken bones.

"So..." Sienna walked up next to her. "Do we cross or climb down and swim?"

"Ugh. We just dried off." Josh pointed at the bridge. "I don't wanna get my clothes all soaked again."

"Take them off and hold them over our heads?" asked Cheyenne.

Josh shrugged in a 'sure why not' sort of way. "Yeah, but I'm not strong enough to swim and hold this backpack out of the water."

Sienna crept up to the right side wall and leaned over. "The river looks calm, but that doesn't prove it is. There could be a current we can't see waiting to drag us under. Rivers can be dangerous."

If there are people at the silver ball, and they made the footprints we found, they probably walk across this.

"Okay." Raven started out onto the bridge. "This looks less dangerous than swimming in a river we don't know anything about."

The group stretched out into a single file line, except for Tinsley who still held her mother's left hand. Sienna brought up the rear. Xan occasionally made a pained gasp, but managed to keep a pace close to normal walking.

A loud *crack* came from behind along with Sienna screaming.

Raven whirled, staring in horror at Sienna's poncho flattened out on the road, the center drawn down into a hole.

"Mom!" shouted Ariana.

Cheyenne dashed toward where Sienna went down. Her foot hit a weak spot that collapsed out from under her. In an instant, she vanished entirely, poncho and all. Raven about screamed, but noticed a human femur spanning the hole that ate the girl, one small hand tenaciously clinging to it. For seconds, Cheyenne dangled by one arm from the femur braced sideways across the hole. Her left hand came up and gripped the bone.

"Sienna!" shouted Raven. She wanted to run to her 'sister' with every fiber of her being, but forced herself not to. Stomping too hard on the bridge surface could send her plummeting.

"I'm holding on," yelled Sienna.

"Ow!" whined Cheyenne. "Help!"

"Don't run!" Raven padded toward the hole where Cheyenne dangled.

Josh and Xan hurried past her.

"We got her. Get Mom," said Josh. "She's too heavy for us."

"I heard that!" yelled Sienna.

Xan took a knee by the hole and reached down to grasp Cheyenne's arm. "Don't let go."

"Don't worry, I won't," shouted the girl. "But I'm slipping!"

Josh grabbed her other arm.

Raven jogged to the deflated, empty poncho, draped across the road surface as though someone tried to make a trap out of the hole by covering it. She grabbed the fabric and yanked it aside. Sienna clung to an angled steel girder five feet down and maybe twelve feet away, arms and legs wrapped around it. She'd evidently landed on it and slid downhill toward the start of the bridge. Raven's gut churned. Staring down a hole in the road at the river below made the fall appear much scarier. The slab of pavement beneath her could give out at any second.

"Hey," said Sienna in a breathless attempt to sound casual.

"Are you hurt?"

"Just some scratches. Damn ground fell as soon as I stepped on it."

Small nubs of rusted metal stuck out from the edges of the hole. Evidently, severely corroded reinforcing bars had been the only thing holding the chunk of pavement in place.

"What do you think? Should I go swimming or try to climb back up?" asked Sienna.

Cheyenne grunted.

Raven peered back over her shoulder. The boys hauled the girl up onto the bridge. All three of them rolled onto their backs in a heap, out of breath. "You could break your leg if you fall."

"Yeah. I know. But I could slip if I try to climb and fall anyway. Better if I expect to jump than land at a weird angle."

Raven pulled her tool satchel and katana sheath off, laid them aside, then flattened herself on the road, reaching down. "Don't risk it. C'mon up."

"I dunno." Sienna held still for a moment, appearing to be equally afraid of going up *or* down. She eventually pulled her legs in close and sat up atop the beam. "Feels like this whole thing is going to let go."

"It's not moving. All in your head. Just look up at me and not down. Don't worry about slipping. A fall won't kill you, just be annoying."

"Didn't you say it could break my leg?"

"Don't think about that."

Sienna chuckled. "If you're trying to calm me down, it's not working."

"Could be worse. You could be dangling over a 500-foot drop."

Her 'sister' let go of the beam long enough to give her a middle finger.

Raven grinned, trying to stretch her arm down more.

Small hands gripped her by the ankles and legs.

Sienna pulled her feet up onto the beam, took hold of the structure above her head, and gradually worked her way into a standing position. A few inches at a time, she crept uphill along the I-beam toward the hole. As soon as she got close enough, Raven grabbed her wrist in both hands. Sienna lifted her right foot up to a smaller bracing strut to use as a step. The thinner metal spar went flying to the side as soon as she tried to put weight on it—and the big I-beam she stood on fell straight down.

Screaming, Sienna hung only by Raven's hold of her arm as the ten-foot girder spun end over end on its way into the river. The sudden added weight dragged Raven forward. Josh, Xan, and Cheyenne shouted, scrambling to hold on and keep her from sliding into the hole.

Sienna squirmed. "Let go. I'll take my chances with the river."

"No," growled Raven.

"I'm gonna drag you and the kids with me. Just let go, dammit!"

Pain bloomed in her shoulder from the bite wound. Her hips ground into the edge of the break in the pavement. The failure of the superstructure at that spot left nothing between the hole and the water some thirty feet down. She couldn't let go. She couldn't trust Sienna would hit the water and not break both arms and legs, then slip under to drown in some devil current racing along below the surface.

"Climb!" shouted Raven.

"You're gonna make the kids fall. Let me drop."

"Mom!" barked Cheyenne. "Stop being stupid and climb!"

Though Sienna had not yet had any biological children of her own, she treated them no different. She wouldn't risk their safety to save herself. *She's not gonna climb.* Snarling, Raven strained to lift her best friend upward. The three kids kept her from slipping deeper into the hole, not quite able to pull them both up.

After realizing Raven would never let go of her, Sienna stopped struggling to get out of her grip and tried to climb, grabbing on to her poncho. Raven lay there like a human ladder while the woman dragged herself up. Ariana and Tinsley reached for Sienna, but she didn't take their hands, likely fearful of slipping and pulling them down. They grabbed her anyway, trying to help.

Once Sienna's weight pressed Raven into the road more than tried to drag her forward, Josh and Xan let go of her ankles and lugged Sienna to safety while Cheyenne helped pull Raven's upper half out of the hole.

Sienna lay on her side, gasping for air. "You should've let me drop. What if everyone fell?"

"We didn't." Raven sat up, rubbing her injured shoulder. "And if you think I'm going to let my sister fall to her death, you need psychedelics."

"What?" asked Sienna.

"The people who fix mental problems."

"Psychiatrists," said Sienna. A moment later, she chuckled and sat up into a hug. "Thanks, but that was stupid."

"I wasn't sliding. The kids held on to me. Besides, we couldn't all have fit in the hole." Raven pointed at the poncho on the road. "You lost something."

Sienna examined her left leg and side, wincing at the scratches she'd suffered from her brush against concrete. "Now there's a damn first. Dropped so fast I fell right out of the stupid thing. I didn't even step hard on the piece that broke."

"We probably should've gone down and risked the swim." Raven stood, pulled her satchel and katana back over her shoulders, then looked around at the bridge. "We're past the halfway point. No sense going back now. The sides look more stable than the road. Let's stick to the edges."

Everyone tiptoed onto the sidewalk by the waist-high concrete banister. Numerous cracks riddled the walkway, but it didn't have any holes. Again in a single-file line, they crept forward to the end, at last reaching solid ground.

Ariana flopped flat on her chest and tried to hug the road. Xan leaned on a tree, sweat pouring from his face and arms. The bandage on his leg appeared bloodier than before, but he didn't complain about it hurting.

"I don't like bridges." Cheyenne squatted, head in her hands, and breathed hard. "We should definitely swim on the way back."

Raven sat on a big rock beside the road. "Sounds good."

They rested for a few minutes to recover from almost falling through the bridge. It seemed increasingly likely they wouldn't be checking out the silver ball and getting back to the dentist's office before dark.

There are far too many different ways to die out here. She exhaled hard, staring up at the sky. *Not sure which is worse. Eaten by cougars or drowning in a river. At least suffocating in my sleep would have been peaceful.*

Ariana, Cheyenne, and Tinsley crept into the woods together in search of a spot to relieve themselves. A few minutes after they disappeared from sight, they squealed. The noises sounded far too happy to be worrisome, but still entirely strange for a bio break.

Raven stood to go check on them, but they came running back into view.

"Bunnies!" cheered Ariana. "A whole family of them!"

"So cute!" Tinsley bounced on her toes.

"Adorable." Cheyenne grinned.

"Where? I wanna see." Josh jumped to his feet.

"They ran away." Ariana pouted. "We scared them."

Cheyenne grinned. "But there's bunnies! They're real!"

Tinsley folded her arms. "Bunnies were always real. Extinct doesn't mean the same as imaginary."

"Ooh! You know what I meant!" Cheyenne rolled her eyes.

Seems they're over the bridge in more ways than one. "Okay. C'mon. And, maybe we should stay a little quiet now. We're getting close to the orb and don't know what's there."

The kids nodded.

Raven took her best guess at a heading and walked off the road into the forest. A few rocks and roots reminded her she'd lost her boots. Weeds and low-lying plants brushed at her legs. She slowed to reduce the swishing noise from her baggy pants.

About ten minutes after leaving the bridge behind, she caught a glimpse of glimmering silver in the treetops ahead. At this distance and angle, the material reflected sunlight rather well, giving it the appearance of shiny metal.

Dad didn't have binoculars. He wouldn't have seen this thing until he got close. Like... right here. She looked around at the woods. *Is this where he was when he stopped, afraid of Plutions?* He'd always seemed like he had all the knowledge, knew everything. But, he'd believed in aliens, and the legends about them didn't appear to be true. The doc didn't usually explain things with such certainty in his voice, but he'd been quite convincing that the true culprit for the Great Death had been pollution.

If a couple generations of living wild can turn humans into ferals, it can make people turn pollution into Plution. Oh, shit. Dad said he was wrong... stupid stories. He knew this place didn't have aliens!

Raven pulled the binoculars out of her satchel, advancing in a series of short scurries from tree to tree. Sienna and the kids got the hint and mostly tried to keep themselves out of sight as well. Eventually, she noticed a break in the forest up ahead.

"Wait here a sec." She took off the tool satchel to reduce clattering noise, and set it on the ground by a tree.

Sienna furrowed her eyebrows, but didn't protest. The kids peered at her from behind tree trunks.

Here goes. Raven closed her eyes, asking the Saints to help out a little. Not Noah's team, but the ones who died years and years ago to save everyone else, the ghosts that some people believed still walked the halls of the Arc.

Raven approached the edge of the forest and raised her binoculars at the enormous silver sphere, awestruck at the size and complexity of the bizarre object. It had to be six or seven stories tall, made from a spherical assembly of thin metal tubes supporting triangular swaths of a material she couldn't identify. The dark grey iridescent stuff resembled metal but fluttered like fabric. From the outside, the spherical structure had no apparent purpose. Society before the Great Death had vast technologies no one in the Arc could imagine, much less explain or understand. This had to be one of those things.

If the weird bubble of material simply protected some manner of technology from being rained on, it wouldn't make for a good shelter against ferals—or cougars. Somewhat disappointed, she resigned herself to arguing with Noah until he agreed to move to the surface outside the Arc, and panned her view down to look for a possible way into the sphere...

... and about screamed at the sight before her.

The base of the giant orb sprouted from a reasonably intact metal-walled building—surrounded by over a hundred single-room dwellings. Men, women, and children roamed a settlement easily containing thousands of people. Most adults wore jumpsuits that reminded her of pictures she'd seen in the Arc of important individuals, the sort of clothing her great, great, ancestors once made. Children had shirts and shorts, or dresses. None of the apparel resembled history books' photographs of pre-Great-Death society, being far more simple and utilitarian.

Best—or perhaps worst—of all, everyone seemed content and nonthreatening.

Before the binoculars filled up with tears, she lowered them from her face and sank to her knees. *This is what Dad saw... he knew! Those damn cougars killed him before he could tell anyone. Would Noah have believed him four years ago?*

"How could they have been so stupid...?"

"Who?" whispered Sienna, right behind her.

A heavy blanket of sorrow and anger kept her from jumping at the unexpectedly close voice. "Whatever idiot wanted to stay underground." Raven offered the binoculars. "Look… at the base of the ball."

Sienna took the binoculars and sighted through them. "Shit… are we dreaming?"

Raven reached under her friend's poncho and touched the scrapes on her leg.

"Ow!"

"Nope. Not dreaming." Raven smiled.

"Bitch." Sienna playfully swatted the back of her head. "So, umm…"

Raven stood. "They look friendly enough. Wanna go say hi?"

"Yes. Do you think they have a doctor? Xan needs to be checked out."

"They look more advanced than we are." Raven shook her head and trotted back to grab her tool satchel. "They might even have a real doctor."

THE OASIS

Most people think I'm thrilled to find stuff, but they've got it backward. The worst part about exploration is the actual discovery... takes all the wonder out of it. – Ellis Wilder

R aven inhaled a deep breath, steeled herself, and stepped out from the forest into the grassy meadow surrounding the settlement. Sienna and the kids followed close behind. A moment later, a childish voice shouted something in the distance. A few men and one woman also called out. Without the binoculars, Raven couldn't make out facial expressions, but everyone outside in view stopped in their tracks to watch them approach.

She squeezed Tinsley's hand nervously, unsure what kind of reaction to expect.

As they drew closer across the field, thin pipes became apparent, running overhead across the dwellings, water spritzing from the occasional bad joint. The shouts morphed from indistinct calls to phrases like 'someone's coming' or 'outsiders' or 'there's people in the field.'

A group of men and women emerged from a gap in the buildings wider than any other, giving it the appearance of a 'main entrance' to the village. They didn't go too far, evidently waiting for Raven and the others to come to them. Two of the men seemed distrustful at first, but evidently upon seeing two women and five children, relaxed—mostly. One kept looking at Raven, his gaze flicking to the handle sticking up over her right shoulder.

"Well, they're not running out to grab us," whispered Raven. "That guy seems to know what a sword is."

"Good sign." Sienna gave her side eye. "Should I be nervous?"

"Not sure yet, but at least they speak English."

"What did you expect? We're not that far away from the Arc."

"I dunno. The feral didn't understand me."

Sienna chuckled. "These people don't look like tribal savages."

"Not at all. They look like old photos of Arc residents." Raven bit her lip. "Do you think...?"

"Anything's possible. To them, we are probably the savages."

They kept quiet for the last minute or two it took to walk up to the waiting group.

Right, Dad. Be confident. She compressed her anxiety into a little rock, which she metaphorically hid in one hand behind her back. None of the men and women who'd come out to see them appeared to be obviously in charge or of any greater station compared to the others.

"Hello." Raven raised a hand in greeting. "What is this place?"

"Our home," said a man with brown skin a little darker than Raven's. He looked fortyish, and spoke with the poise of higher education. "It has been so for many generations now. You are clearly not primitives. Where did you come from?"

"The Arc," said Raven. "Arcology 1409."

Murmurs swept over the group.

Noticing their reaction to the word 'arcology,' she took a step closer to the man. "Are you from the Arc, too?"

He smiled, trying not to laugh. "Not directly, I'm afraid. Many of us here are descended from the people you are referring to."

"So it's true?" Raven gawked. "Most of the people in the Arc *did* just get up and leave?"

"Yes, roughly 140 years ago if memory serves."

"Some people wanted to stay," added a blonde woman around the same age as Raven. "They tried to stop the others from leaving and some violence happened. You don't look like you've come here for revenge."

"No, not at all. The Arc is dying. I grew up being told the world outside was so poisonous we'd turn into goo if we opened a door... but my father went outside, and he survived. The others, back at the Arc, might already be dead. Maybe not. The systems are..." Light-headed, Raven swooned into Sienna. Hope hit her so hard she cried. Tinsley would neither suffocate in the Arc nor become lunch for giant cats. "I left to look for a safe place."

The man beckoned her to follow him. "It's possible you have found it. I'm Alexander Grant. Come along. Some of you seem injured."

"Thanks. Yes. I'm Raven. That's Sienna, my daughter Tinsley, Josh, Cheyenne, Xan, and Ariana."

The kids waved and said hello as she introduced them.

"It must be bad there if you're wearing those rags." The blonde picked at Raven's poncho.

Alexander led them into the settlement past small houses assembled from slabs of metal or plastic. A few had been made out of stacked concrete rubble glued together by means of a black cement. Hundreds of people came out of doorways or alleys between the houses to look at the newcomers. This place had more children under twelve than the entire population of the Arc. Tinsley and Josh grinned and waved back at the other kids. Cheyenne and Ariana kept their heads down, overwhelmed by the sheer number of people. Xan, normally rather outgoing, appeared to be so focused on walking and not falling over that he might not have even noticed how many people had come out to see them.

The blonde woman and a few others from the initial greeting party followed behind them like security officers escorting prisoners, but they gave off only curiosity.

"You look rather surprised," said Alexander.

"So many people. There's only 183 in the—I mean 182—in the Arc now."

"That is tragic." Alexander sighed. "Our town is spread out over a few square miles. There's more on the other side of the biodome. We're up to about 6,200 people now."

"Holy shit," muttered Xan.

"Xander Michael!" rasped Sienna. "Language!"

"I can always tell when she's mad at me because she makes up new names." Xan grinned.

Raven looked around at the scenery. The small homes had been built with a clear degree of planning, following the routes of walkpaths and copper water pipes. Electrical wiring also ran overhead, fortunately separate from the water lines, suggesting they had windmills somewhere. Most likely on the other side of the giant ball. The overall technology level of this place exceeded the Arc by a decent amount, probably about even with how it would have been originally.

A few kids too small to reliably use toilets ran around undressed, while some adults of both sexes went topless in the heat. It seemed everyone here who wore less than a full outfit or no shoes did so out of choice, not because their society lacked the resources to make things. No one in this settlement wore ponchos, and unlike Raven, the adults also most likely did not still wear the same clothes they got at age twelve. At least cotton-plus was tough.

Alexander brought them to the large building from which the huge silver ball sprouted. The pale grey windowless structure, wider at the bottom than the top looked like something belonging on the cover of a science fiction novel about aliens and starships.

She expected the front door to open mechanically while giving off a soft hiss, but Alexander pushed it in on a hinge, revealing them to be three inches thick and quite non-futuristic. Inside, a smooth-floored hallway reminded her of the Arc, only tile instead of bare concrete. Six other hallways branched off at various distances in both directions. Numerous doors everywhere led to various rooms. The word 'Oasis' appeared occasionally on the walls next to a strange pinwheel-shaped swirl.

Too awestruck to ask about anything, Raven held Tinsley close and followed Alexander to a door marked 'medical.'

"This is your infirmary?" asked Raven.

"Yes." Alexander went in. "Might as well get you all cleaned up and checked out before you talk to Tess."

"Tess?" asked Sienna.

"She's the one in charge. Used to call that office 'administrator', but it changed to mayor a while ago."

"Ugh." Raven sighed. "I hope she's not like Noah."

Alexander regarded her in confusion for a moment before enlightenment gleamed in his eyes. "Oh. The arcology is still running things the old way I see. I'd like to think Tess is doing a good job."

Four people in white jumpsuits, two women and two men, approached.

Alexander smiled at them. "We had some newcomers wander in out of the forest. They tell me they're from the old arcology."

The medical staff regarded them in shock until one man noticed Xan's bloody bandage, at which point he hurried forward, ushering the boy over to an examination table in an alcove at the back of the room walled off by hanging curtains.

"How many of you are hurt?" asked a black-haired woman as pale as her jumpsuit.

"Mommy got bit by a bad kitty. On her shoulder. An' it bit me, too." Tinsley held up her leg.

"Please, follow me." The woman escorted Raven and Tinsley to another alcove. "I'm Iris. Do you know what a doctor is?"

"Yeah. We're not *that* primitive." Raven chuckled. "I'm Raven, this is my daughter Tinsley."

Iris smiled at them, then grimaced. "I'm sure you're likely unaware of how filthy you are. Not to be insulting, but you both smell like you went swimming in sewers. I'm concerned you are at risk for infection." The woman gingerly poked the poncho. "Would you mind taking those filthy rags off? We'll get you fresh clothes after you've cleaned up."

The doctor pulled the curtains closed, turning the alcove into a private room.

Raven hadn't been naked in front of anyone she didn't consider family since having sex with Chase. She blushed. *If they're the descendants of the smart people who left the Arc, she's gotta be a real doctor.*

Tinsley didn't hesitate at all, flinging off her clothes except for the plastic sandals. As blasé as Raven could force herself to be, she disrobed. Iris looked at the bite mark on her shoulder, the claw wounds on her arm, then the abrasions on Tinsley's leg before deciding the shoulder puncture needed more immediate attention.

"Let me look at this before you hop in the shower."

The doctor dabbed at the spot using alcohol and some other mystery substance that burned like fire. Raven managed not to scream, but she nearly fell off the edge of the exam table. Once satisfied with the condition of the wound, the doctor used another fluid to glue Raven's skin closed. That done, she did the same to the claw marks on Raven's bicep before moving on to Tinsley's leg.

"The lacerations your daughter suffered are fairly shallow. They seem to be healing all right and without infection."

Raven shrugged. "I guess most of the bacteria died, too."

"Perhaps." Iris raised both eyebrows.

"Maybe we're wearing rags and smell bad to you, but I can still read. We still have books and school. Can't make new stuff anymore. The air filtration system is inches from complete shutdown." Raven explained her mission to find a safe place for the remaining people in the Arc to settle, and that she doubted Noah had been serious. "He's probably going to laugh at me when I go back to tell him about this place."

"You're going back?" Tinsley gawked.

"I have to at least try to get them out of there."

"That shouldn't be a problem, but you should talk to Tess about it before doing anything. Bear with me a moment. I'm going to draw a little blood for some tests. Is it all right if I take a sample from your daughter?"

"What do you need our blood for?"

"Testing to see if you've got any parasites, diseases, or other conditions requiring treatment."

"Oh. Okay. Sure. Yeah, I'd kinda like to know, too."

After drawing blood—Tinsley sat there watching the needle with little outward reaction—Iris conducted a quick physical on both of them, then leaned close to whisper in Raven's ear.

"Are you experiencing any unusual discomfort in your reproductive organs? Sexually active?"

"No and no. I haven't been, uhh 'active' in six years… unless my hand counts." Raven chuckled.

Tinsley held up her hands. "I count on my hands sometimes."

Iris and Raven laughed.

"Wow, really… that long? Surprising."

"Thanks." Raven smirked, taking it as a compliment to her looks. "Too worried about genetic issues. There's only 182 people in the Arc." She explained how nine out of ten babies came from people being matched and asked to keep humanity from dying out.

"I'm really lucky because my mommy wanted to keep me." Tinsley looked down, swinging her feet.

"That is… tragic." Iris regarded her with a pitying stare.

Iris gestured at a doorway. "All right. I don't see any external parasites or skin conditions. Physical's pretty much done. Why don't you two go in there and clean up? I'll go get you some clean things to wear."

Walking into unknown doors naked didn't rank too high up on Raven's list of fun things to do—at least not since she'd been three— but she suspected the other room would be empty of people and probably contain a shower. She slid off the table and padded over, peeking past into a small room that indeed held a shower stall and toilet.

Tinsley eagerly followed her into the stall.

This water smelled quite different than back home, lacking any chemical essence. She managed to coax Tinsley into removing the sandals, and proceeded to clean up. The water running into the drain ran almost black for the first few seconds.

Eventually, she realized she continued to shower only because it felt amazing and not because she needed to get cleaner. After drying off with towels she found hanging on a nearby bar, she wrapped herself in one and peeked out at the curtain-walled alcove. Soft voices outside the walls sounded like Sienna and the other kids talking to medical staff. Everyone seemed happy and calm. Iris had gone off somewhere else. Not knowing exactly what to do, Raven sheepishly padded out from the shower room and sat again on the exam table, clutching the towel to her chest.

Tinsley climbed up beside her, carrying her sandals.

When she realized only her tool satchel and katana remained—the poncho and her inside clothes gone—Raven tensed. She didn't like the idea of having to run back to the Arc with only a towel to wear, but she'd do it if it came down to it.

The ferals run around naked. Maybe if I streaked back to the Arc, they'd leave me alone. She laughed nervously at the embarrassing, silly idea. Then bit her lip.

Her panic ebbed a moment later when Iris returned carrying a bundle of fabric. "Here you are. Two sets of undergarments, a dress for your daughter, jumpsuit for you, and some shoes."

Raven eagerly accepted the bundle. "Thank you."

Iris gestured past the curtain. "Once you're dressed, head on out to the corridor. Paul will show you to Tess. Do you have any questions for me?"

"Guess we're in decent health?"

"Surprisingly so, yes."

Raven pulled on the shockingly white inside pants and tank top. "How long has it been since the Great Death?"

"I'll assume you're referring to the period where the Earth became largely inhospitable to mammalian life."

"Yeah, that." Raven stepped into an olive-drab jumpsuit.

"We're not completely certain considering our records of the past have a gap. Based on the information our forbearers brought from the arcology as well as what they found here, I'd say about six centuries. But that's an estimate."

"Wow." Raven plucked the clean inside pants from Tinsley's hand, since the child had been gawking at them, and dressed her. "That arcology? So there *were* others?"

"Oh, yes. We believe many such bunkers were created. Again, information is more rumor than fact, but the first few appear to have been the brainchild of a billionaire who believed the warnings about an unlivable planet. Governments eventually built arcologies as well, but only after people started dying and they couldn't ignore the scientists anymore. Those arcologies suffered from the usual problems inherent with government building anything."

"What does that mean?" Raven pulled the dress on over Tinsley's head.

The girl jumped down and ran in circles, twirling around and giggling.

Iris folded her arms. "Built as fast as possible by the people willing to do it as cheaply as possible."

"Wow. That doesn't sound like a smart way to do things." Raven picked up a set of boots somewhat similar to her old ones... only devoid of duct tape and made from greenish fabric rather than plastic weave. They also didn't appear to have been worn before. She stared at them as if she held spiritual relics. "These... are new?"

"Yes. You'll find we're a bit more capable than the conditions you're used to living in. Oasis is by no means caught up to the technologies prior to the collapse, but I suspect this is about as good as it can get. It's astonishing to me to hear your arcology is still functional at all."

Raven told Iris about being on the technical team and spending the past four years fixing and rebuilding things. Her mentioning that the monoethanolamine substrate in the CO_2 scrubbers had become worthless surprised Iris about as much as if that naked savage had whipped out a chess board and challenged Raven to a match. Indignant, she explained how the ponchos happened because of limited materials demanding they make garments a child wouldn't grow out of and their need to hand-sew everything favored a simplistic design.

After she finished putting on the new clothes, Raven took Tinsley by the hand and followed Iris across the outer medical room to the door. Some old clothing from Sienna and the kids sat on a steel table, radiating an awful smell she hadn't noticed before. Having a shower and an hour or so apart from exposure to the garments made their rancid odor obvious. Though, rather than thinking sewer, she recognized the smell as the hydroponic fluid.

Sienna, also in a greenish jumpsuit, and the kids waited out in the corridor beside a twentysomething man who reminded her somewhat of a younger Donnie Chen, Ariana's bio father. The boys and Cheyenne wore shorts and tank tops, Ariana a white dress similar to Tinsley's.

"Good luck and welcome to Oasis," said Iris.

"Is that why it says 'oasis' everywhere?" asked Raven.

"Sort of. I believe the founders named this place *because* the word was all over already." Iris chuckled. "We don't exactly have the technology to print words like that on walls."

"Oasis, huh?" asked Sienna. "I kinda like the sound of that."

TESS

Whenever you have more than eight people in the same place, someone's going to want to be in charge. That's the one you need to keep an eye on.
– Ellis Wilder.

The young man introduced himself as Paul before leading them down a corridor deeper into the building under the giant silver orb.

"My role here is essentially assisting Tess and keeping track of our people. Mostly, who's related to who, who lives in what dwelling, and so on. Since you are from the arcology nearby, it is quite possible you are potentially related to people here. It would be distant relations, but still best avoided."

"How can you tell who is related to who?" asked Sienna. "I mean, for us? Do you have the machines to test people?"

"Yes. Actually, we do. The group who originally established this place consisted primarily of doctors and scientists."

"The ones who left the Arc," said Raven. "Wow, it's true."

"Oh, I meant..." Paul chuckled. "This facility was originally created as a biodome during the collapse. Similar to the arcologies, only they hoped to survive above ground. The sphere you've no doubt seen already is airtight and allowed for the preservation of a habitable atmosphere during the worst of it. By the time the people who left your arcology found this place, I want to say about three thousand people remained from the original Oasis team. From what I learned in school, many of the newcomers were also scientists."

Sienna frowned. "Yeah. Most of the educated people left."

Her explanation of how the Arc had collapsed to near primitivism continued down the hall into an office where an older white woman with short, wavy dark grey hair sat behind a huge U-shaped desk. She wore a dress similar to the ones they gave Tinsley and Ariana, but also had simple black shoes. The woman's presence gave off such a feeling of authority that Raven found herself feeling like a child walking into a school classroom again, hoping the new teacher liked her.

"Ahh, much better." Tess smiled, stood, and walked out from behind her desk, offering a handshake. "Good to see you all cleaned up. I hope the boy is feeling better?"

Xan glanced at the gauze sticking out from the leg of his shorts. "Still stings but I can walk on it now."

"Good, good. My name is Tess Summerfield. I'm the one who gets stuck making all the difficult decisions. Curious where you came from." She gestured off to her left at a blue sectional.

It appeared to be hundreds of years old, but mostly intact.

Paul politely excused himself and left as everyone else except Tinsley took a seat on the giant couch. The six-year-old found the plastic plants over by the window far too in need of checking out to sit still.

Over the course of the next half hour or so, Raven and Sienna explained everything about the condition of the Arc, what they'd been taught of the outside world, the encounter with the feral, the cougars, and their trip here.

Tess listened, nodding or asking brief questions to clarify some things. After, she explained Oasis had grown from an initial group of people sheltering inside a sealed biodome—which now contained mostly hydroponic farm tanks—to a proper town. They did not order people to have children, but did require people wanting to have kids to go through testing to make sure they weren't related. She appeared to like Raven's experience as a tech as well as Sienna's work as a teacher.

"It's quite different here as you might expect." Tess smiled at Sienna. "We have enough children that they are organized by age into different classes."

"I can't believe how many kids are here." Raven whistled. "The most I've ever seen before was my group growing up, and we had nine. I was the youngest."

"By eight months." Sienna nudged her.

Tess nodded at Raven. "Your experience sounds good. While you've no doubt been working on older machinery, your ability to keep them operational is a testament to your ingenuity. I think you'd be happy performing the same role here. Both of you, and of course your children, are welcome to stay. As far as we know, there aren't any other settlements out there beyond a few scattered feral tribes."

Raven sat up tall. "I'd love to stay here. But... I have to do something first."

"Oh?" Tess tilted her head.

"There are probably at least 175 people left in the Arc, and the air filtration system is dying." She explained the CO_2 scrubbers running on a substrate so saturated with dirt it didn't do anything, the windmills being on the verge of literal collapse, and ventilation ducts riddled with grime to the point the gunk formed inch-thick pads. "I have to go back and lead them here.…. If that's okay. I mean, I have to go back and get them out of there anyway, but I'd rather bring everyone here than insist they try to build a village from scratch outside."

Tess showed little hesitation before nodding. "Of course. I sincerely doubt anyone alive in the Arc now even remembers the conflict. My great grandfather was part of the group that left. There's no reason to be needlessly cruel to the ones who stayed behind. Fear of the unknown is a powerful thing."

"So I can go back and bring them here?" asked Raven.

"Of course, dear." Tess smiled.

She looked at Sienna and the kids. "You guys are all gonna stay here where it's safe. Even if I can't convince Noah to leave, I will be back."

"No." Tinsley ran over and jumped in her lap.

Raven squeezed her. "I brought you with me out here because the Arc is dangerous. More dangerous than being outside. Oasis is safe. I can't possibly take you away from a safe place to risk a three-day walk."

"But the cougars! The ferals!" wailed Tinsley.

"Exactly why I need you to stay here." Raven bowed her head. "Alone, I can outrun them."

"Not the cats," said Xan. "Them things are fast."

"Those," muttered Sienna. "Those things are fast."

The kids chuckled.

Xan looked at Tess, indicating Sienna with a thumb. "Mom's a teacher."

"Ferals?" asked Tess.

Raven explained being attacked by a naked man with a beard down to his knees who kept trying to bite her.

"Hmm. Some of our scouts have reported similar tribes, but they haven't been close to Oasis."

"Not that close. I ran into one guy only a few hours after leaving the Arc. Haven't seen any more since."

Tess looked over at Sienna and the children. "I agree with Raven. The world out there is no place for children or those who aren't prepared for dangerous situations."

"She should stay here, too, then." Sienna patted Raven's hand.

"Raven has the sort of determination in her eyes I usually look for in our scouts. It takes a certain kind of person to reach a place of safety, then go right back out there to help other people. I'm sure she'll be fine. However, I'll send an officer with you."

"You have security officers here, too?" Raven blinked.

"Of course. When you assemble this many people in one place, some of them are bound not to behave themselves." Tess sighed. "It is a regrettable fact of human nature."

"Is that why our security officers are so bored? There aren't enough people for anyone to be bad?" Xan grinned.

Tess smiled. "That could definitely be a factor. All right. I assume given the direness of the situation, you'll be looking to get back there soon. Let me speak with Paul for a moment. He'll figure out where you will be living here. Perhaps, you can set off in the morning. You do look like you need some rest and decent food."

"All right." Raven brushed at Tinsley's hair. *One more night hopefully won't be the reason they all die.*

"Can we live in the same place?" asked Sienna. "Or at least adjacent ones?"

Tess cocked her head. "The two of you are a couple?"

"No, we're basically sisters. Not by blood." Sienna grinned at Raven. "We've been like inseparable since age two."

"Oh, I see. I believe we might have some family-sized huts available. We keep building them as materials allow, planning for growth. However, an influx of over a hundred might require some people tolerate tents for a bit." Tess stood and went to her desk. "Putting you all in one dwelling would definitely be efficient." She picked up a phone and proceeded to explain the request for living space to someone, probably Paul.

Sienna looked over at Raven. "Wow. Other people *do* exist."

"And they're nice."

"Not what I was expecting." Sienna exhaled, blowing her hair off her face. A shower had left it hanging loose and straight.

"Nothing's what I was expecting." Raven patted Tinsley's back. The child hadn't stopped clinging since learning she had to stay here. "But my expectations weren't all good."

"That's good." Sienna wagged her eyebrows.

"All right." Tess set the phone down. "Paul will be here momentarily to show you to the housing pod that will be your home. Lara will be in touch with Sienna within a few days about teaching.

Raven, you can speak to Jordan once you're back from the Arc. He's our head of maintenance."

Raven stood. "Wow. Okay. This is real, right?"

"As real as anything else." Tess walked up to them. "Oh, I should probably explain how food and supplies work…"

ABOVE GROUND

People have a damn bad habit of not realizing what's really important until after they forget where they put it. – Ellis Wilder.

The housing pod sat near the end of a 'street' on the eastern side of the orb building, almost at the edge of the village. None of the streets in this settlement had paving, nor the width to accommodate a car. The pod's windows offered a view of Oasis' windmill field. They used smaller turbines, half the size of the ones at the Arc, but they had longer blades and perched atop poles rather than steel lattice towers. The land in and among the windmills appeared to be a literal farm as well.

Workers assembled more pods not far from the one Paul assigned to them. The simple structures varied in size from small dwellings intended for a single person with about as much space as her old room in the Arc to pods like theirs, almost five times bigger. Except for a small toilet/shower room in the back corner, the place had no interior walls, being one large open area. Two bunk beds against the left wall and one slightly larger one-level bed on the right made for five mattresses. The expectation had likely been for parents to share the big bed, and up to four kids in the bunks. With seven of them in the same pod, sharing would be the norm.

Storage drawers held the various pieces of clothing they'd been given, two extra jumpsuits each for Raven and Sienna, dresses, shorts, and tank tops for the kids, along with an astonishing amount of inside pants, which people here called underwear. Sienna made a joke about not having time to wash Tinsley's laundry, since those rags would surely remain in the Arc indefinitely.

Raven tried to figure out sleeping arrangements, expecting she'd take one of the bunk spots with Tinsley, unless she and Ariana—the two smallest—wanted to split one. The boys already voiced claims on the upper bunks, and she had the feeling Cheyenne wanted to stay close to Sienna. She'd been with her the longest despite being a year younger than Josh. The boy had been six when his father died and he moved to stay with them.

Cheyenne didn't know the true identity of her parents, and hadn't taken learning they didn't want her well at all. On the walk to the pod, she'd muttered to Josh about hoping the cougars ate them on the way here if Raven convinced everyone to come. The boy responded with 'what parents? Sienna's our mom.' Both Sienna and Cheyenne had been teary ever since.

From what Raven had thus far seen of Oasis, it exceeded the Arc handily in terms of technology, but fell short of the world before the collapse. Had the scientists not left the Arc, the gap between her home and this settlement might not have been noticeable. Once she got settled in with their technical team, hopefully, they'd teach her new things and she'd have a better understanding of how the dormant machinery on Arc level six compared. Most of the machines that produced electronic components, medical equipment, and other more advanced items seemed far too large to be moved, but it might be possible to disassemble them. Hauling such heavy things up from six stories underground without elevators might, however, be impossible.

Tinsley's somberness at the idea of her going back to the Arc to get everyone faded somewhat when some other children who lived in nearby pods showed up at the door, curious about the new arrivals. The kids ended up going outside to play in a group of at least twenty. Raven could scarcely believe her eyes at seeing a pack of kids so large. Watching her daughter and the others from the Arc laughing and racing around after a ball across open grass brought tears of happiness to her eyes.

Guilt sat at the pit of her stomach, however. Every minute she spent there felt like she tried to cause the deaths of everyone back at the arc. One of the Oasis security officers would show up in the morning, ready to go with her. Part of her wanted to leave right away, but she also knew her body needed a night of proper rest.

The vastness of Oasis made the idea of a single centralized cafeteria impractical. They divided the town into districts, each arranged around a central area containing a place that served food, a well or water tank hooked up to the narrow pipes going overhead, one or more storage areas for clothing distribution, and a small security station. Oasis did rely on a centralized school, which required some children living near the edges to walk roughly a mile.

In talking with Paul, she'd discovered her father's notion of their location had been reasonably accurate. This area used to be called Pennsylvania, the ruined bits of high-rises to the west of the Arc, a city once known as Philadelphia. According to him, the heat and climate around here came closer to what people living hundreds of miles south would've known before the event she thought of as the Great Death. None of the scientists in Oasis thought mammals existed any further south than about 200 miles from here before the temperatures became too hot. Apparently, the ocean had also once been much farther east from where it started. Some of the scouts reported finding the sea only a week's walk from here, farther east.

A desire to go look at the ocean stirred somewhere inside her, a temptation she blamed on her father. Unlike him, however, she needed a better reason than curiosity to leave her child behind. Finding a safe place to live qualified, as did trying to save the people still in the Arc.

Another surprise Oasis had: working clocks. The food stations began serving the dinner meal at 6:00 p.m., and remained open for two hours. Feeling a bit like she'd fallen asleep and gone into a dream world, she followed Sienna outside to collect the kids and go for food.

The contents of the plastic meal tray left her, Sienna, and all five kids baffled. The main partition held clumps of pale, stringy something covered in a light brownish sauce. Another area had beige goo that smelled like potatoes but looked nothing like them. Green beans, at least, she recognized.

Josh, the least shy of their group with the possible exception of Tinsley, nudged a man sitting next to him. "Umm, what is this?"

"Chicken, mashed potatoes, and beans." The man, who had the darkest skin Raven had ever seen, smiled at him, then looked over at Sienna and her. "Don't recall seeing you before. I figured you moved across from the other side, but if ya don't know what chicken is, maybe not."

Ice broken, Raven allowed herself to fall into a friendly conversation with some of the locals. They appeared astonished to learn she'd come from the Arc and none of them ever ate meat before. The kids adored the taste of chicken, but Tinsley and Ariana flipped out when the man, who introduced himself as Anson, mentioned they sometimes had rabbit for dinner. Deer meat also made a frequent appearance. That elicited sad looks from the kids, but not the same protest as talk of having rabbit. Naturally, Xan randomly made comments wondering what 'bunny sandwiches' tasted like, mostly to mess with the girls.

After dinner, they returned to their pod—following a brief period of being lost among the dwellings—and settled in for the night. Raven ended up yielding the big bed to Sienna. The boys took the top bunks, Raven on the lower left under Xan with Tinsley attached to her side. Cheyenne indeed shared the bed with Sienna, leaving little Ariana a bed to herself beneath Josh.

Even though they'd only been outside for three days, stretching out on an actual mattress felt like paradise—as did not wondering *if* she'd wake up. Even though it lacked the blanket-snuggling coolness of her underground quarters, this pod, with its open windows and outside air, wouldn't suffocate her.

MORNING CAME WITH A FAIR AMOUNT OF SHOUTING OVER BATHROOM access.

The boys and Tinsley wanted to just go outside, but questioned if that would be as wrong as randomly peeing on the floor in the Arc. Raven told them to wait and be civilized, since they'd found an actual town and weren't out in the wilds.

Breakfast consisted of toast and preserves. Their new home had a small hot plate and working electricity. Bread didn't require refrigeration and the preserves came in plastic jars small enough to be entirely used up for one meal. Those, too, didn't need refrigeration until after being opened.

Over the meal, the kids chattered about their excitement at living above the ground. Josh gushed at how beautiful the sky was. The girls went on and on about cute furry creatures. Xan mostly appeared to like having tons of other people around, since it made him feel less like humanity would die out.

"Way to make everything sad." Cheyenne tossed a hunk of toast at him.

"Didn't mean it that way." Xan picked up and ate the piece. "It's nice. Way less lonely."

"Do you have'ta go back?" asked Tinsley.

Cheyenne fidgeted. "Seems kinda silly to find a place like this then leave."

"I'm not *leaving*." Raven exhaled. "It would be really evil of me to stay here and let everyone left in the Arc die. You don't think everyone back there deserves that, do you?"

"No…" chimed the kids in unison.

"Not everyone," whispered Cheyenne.

"You don' deserve to die either," said Tinsley.

Raven did her best to reassure them she'd be careful, but the kids kept quiet after that, eating without looking up from their food.

A knock at the door broke the silence a few minutes later.

Tinsley leapt out of her chair and jumped into Raven's lap.

"I got it." Sienna, who'd put on a dress for the first time in her life, padded across the room to the door.

An athletic man in his mid-twenties with a sharp jawline and a small notch of a scar an inch below his left eye stood outside, his beige jumpsuit mostly covered by a poncho colored in a dappled pattern of greens and browns. He wore a backpack and carried a second one. A thin pipe stuck up over his shoulder next to the pack, held in place by a brown strap across his chest. At the sight of Sienna, the man's pale blue eyes gave off warmth and sincerity. "Morning. Are you Raven?"

"No, I'm Sienna."

"Oh. Hi." He set down the second backpack to free up his right hand, which he held out in greeting. "I'm Kyle. Supposed to go with Raven to the old arcology site?"

"Yeah." Raven stood, holding Tinsley. "That's me. I hope they're not forcing you to go."

"No. Asked for volunteers. Both of my great-grandparents came from there. Kinda curious to see it and well, see something so far outside Oasis. I already packed some provisions for us both."

No guilt since he wanted to go, right? "Give me a moment. My daughter's a little upset."

Kyle stepped inside. "Not a problem. It can be scary out there, but she doesn't need to worry."

"Why not?" whimpered Tinsley. "There's cougars."

He smiled at her. "You guys got here okay and you didn't even know where you were going. The two of us can cover ground a lot faster than you can with little legs, right?"

Tinsley bit her lip.

"I'm also a scout. I've been out into the woods a day or so in every direction. Cougars aren't too much of a problem. They usually aren't interested in people. Make a lot of loud noise and they'll usually run. Best to stay upright. Don't crouch or get low, or the cats can mistake us for deer. Their usual prey isn't as tall us we are, so it confuses them."

"You should bring Chey." Josh grinned. "She can scream so loud their ears will explode."

Cheyenne glowered at him, but didn't say anything despite looking insulted.

"There's ferals, too." Tinsley sniffled.

At seeing confusion in Kyle's eyes, Raven said, "Wild man."

"Oh, them. I can handle two or three. They're not interested in a dangerous opponent." Kyle winked at her. "I'll get your mom back here okay. Promise."

"The trip back might take a while longer since there are some older people... if they're still alive." Raven gave Tinsley a squeeze and handed her off to Sienna. "The longer it takes us to get back, the more people could be hurt."

Xan scrambled out of his chair and speed-limped over to his bunk. He rummaged something out of his satchel before rushing over to Raven. "Here."

She looked down at his hand, a hot pepper in his palm.

"For the cats. Just chew it up and spray it in their eyes." He grinned.

"Maybe you can do that." She gently pushed his hand closed around it. "Eating this thing whole would do more damage to me than the cat."

"Mommy?" asked Tinsley.

"Yes?"

The girl grasped the collar of her jumpsuit and pulled her close. "Please don't do what grandpa did. You gotta come back."

For roughly twenty seconds, the people remaining in the Arc faced certain death. Once Raven's guilt crash subsided, she mentally talked her confidence back into fighting trim and convinced herself she couldn't simply stay here yet.

"Hmm." Sienna glanced back and forth between Raven and Kyle. "You two off alone in the forest together? Don't do anything I wouldn't do."

Raven barked a laugh while simultaneously crying. "Thanks. Needed that." She kissed Tinsley on the head. "Be good and stay here safe, okay? I promise we'll be back before you know it."

The child's huge brown eyes accused her of saying the same thing Dad did, but she merely nodded. "Okay. Please come back."

WEAPONS

Biting doesn't work too well for humans, so we invented stabbing, which soon became stabbing people far away with arrows. Then some genius came up with gunpowder, so we could stab people really far away. Somewhere after that came bombs and pumpkin spice. I'm not sure which one caused more casualties. – Ellis Wilder.

Standing around caught in an endless loop of overthinking would end up killing people.

Raven hurried outside, grabbing the spare backpack on the way out the door. She hadn't yet gotten used to wearing a jumpsuit. Not having a loosely draped poncho getting in the way of her arms all the time threw her off guard and got her wondering why Kyle wore one. The backpack, about half the size of the one the boys carried here, didn't weigh too much, but it also got in the way of the katana. She rearranged the cord harness, tying it around her waist so the scabbard hung on her left side. It didn't drag on the ground like she thought it would, but came pretty close.

"So, how far a walk is this gonna be?" asked Kyle. "They didn't give me much information."

"Took us three days to get here, but I'm sure the two of us can go much faster. Kids don't walk as fast and need breaks more often."

"Right… what made you risk taking the little ones along on a journey like that?" He whistled. "Things must be bad where you came from."

"I wasn't planning to. Set off alone hoping to make good time, but Sienna got spooked. The kids were all woozy and passing out. Looked like oxygen deprivation, so she grabbed them and snuck out."

"Oxygen deprivation…?" He scratched his head.

"Do you know about different gases? CO2, oxygen, that sort of thing?"

"Not really." He swung the pipe off his back, which turned out to look an awful lot like how she imagined a gun. "I can whip up a mean batch of powder though."

Raven stared at the weapon, not sure how to feel about it. Her tech side marveled at the object, which had obviously been hand made from steel tubing machined to size. It appeared to consist of a single, long pipe fitted with a latch at the back end connected to a wooden stock and pistol grip. The only familiarity she had with firearms came from reading novels. This thing didn't have any of the openings or little switches on the side, merely a barrel, grip, and trigger.

The part of her not admiring its engineering wanted to back away before it hurt someone.

"It's a gun."

"Yeah." She shifted her stare from it to his face. "I figured that."

"This is why I'm not worried about cougars or ferals."

"Ever see one before?"

"You're talking about the gun, right?"

He laughed. "Yeah."

Raven turned her head to hide her impish smile. "No. But I'm familiar with the concept. An explosive chemical propellant accelerates a metal projectile fast enough to destroy whatever it hits."

"It uses gunpowder to lob a slug."

She glanced at him. "That's what I just said. Are you playing with me or should I start using smaller words?"

"Kinda playing with you, but I don't really do the science words thing. School and me didn't get along. That's how I ended up as an officer, breaking up fights and roaming around the woods."

"Makes sense."

"What did you mean when you said your friend had to *sneak* out? Did she not have permission to take those kids?"

Raven shook her head rapidly. "No... they're her kids in every sense except biology. She's our only teacher and people in the Arc have babies mostly because Noah tells them to. Except for Josh, their birth parents didn't want them. His died. Tinsley's my actual daughter, but her father's a piece of shit. I said sneak because it's one of our rules that people aren't allowed outside."

"So you both snuck out?"

"Not exactly. I got the okay, but I would've done it anyway." She grinned.

Kyle exhaled. "Damn. Why the heck would it be against the rules to go outside?"

"Because Noah, our version of Tess, still thinks it's deadly out here. He's a bit of a chicken."

"Hah. What's your plan if he refuses to let people come back to Oasis?"

She raised her arms to either side and let them fall against her body. "I'm kinda hoping that seeing you will shatter his little mind. He also believes we're the only humans left alive on the planet."

"Interesting. I've never shattered a mind before, unless you count shooting a deer in the head."

Ick. Food though... She doubted she could kill an animal herself without being at the edge of starvation, but she wouldn't have a problem eating meat. "So, I guess you know how to fight?"

"Yep. They train us and we practice at least once a week. Not sure why. It's almost like Julie expects some other town to have an army and come after us, but I suppose it's better to know how to fight and not use it than get caught off guard."

"Or you could just flail at someone with a sword." She laughed. "Found this thing in some ruins to the west. Never got into a fight before that feral jumped on me."

"Doesn't seem like it would be too complicated." He made a stabbing motion.

They walked among the residence pods, occasionally waving at people going about their day.

"It's a lot more involved than that. I mean, it is if you fight someone else with a sword who knows how to use one. There's all sorts of stuff like parries and ripostes and feints. This type of sword is even harder to use because there are like three different stances and each one has a whole different set of moves and countermoves."

"Whoa. Where'd you get that from?"

"Found it on a body."

"I mean knowing all that stuff."

"Oh. Duh. Books. They're made up stories so I don't *really* know for sure how true any of it is, but they sounded convincing. Some had pirates and noblemen who used thin swords called rapiers. Those fights sounded totally different from this other book set in Japan where they fought using swords like this one."

"What's a Japan?"

"Another place. Far away across the ocean." She gazed up at the sky, squinting at the sun. If nothing else, this new jumpsuit handled the heat better. "Don't know if it's even still there. It was an island. Might have been flooded when the oceans got bigger."

"Ouch."

"So…" She rolled her arms around. "Doesn't that poncho get in the way when you fight?"

"Sometimes. Biggest problem is it gives an opponent something to grab."

"Why wear it then?"

"Camo. Makes me harder to see in the forest."

"Ahh." She looked at the gun again, which had to be four feet long with a barrel almost an inch around. "That looks bigger than I imagined guns from reading about them."

"Maybe it is. We didn't have any to compare to. Just notes. It's basically a breech-loading shotgun. One shell at a time. I use slugs though. Don't have to pick all those little pills outta a deer that way."

Guns in the stories varied from flintlock pistols it took a few minutes to reload to machine guns capable of spitting out hundreds of bullets in seconds. A few stories even had lasers or fancier energy weapons, though she thought those had been all made up. Kyle's rifle didn't look as though it would be as slow as a flintlock musket.

When they reached the bridge outside the ruins, he pointed at the side. "This thing isn't safe. We usually walk on the rail."

Her stomach nearly fell out at watching him leap up to walk on top of the wall. A little too far of a lean to his left and down he'd go.

"Yeah, we found out the hard way. Sienna nearly went swimming." She kept her feet on the sidewalk, as close as possible to the wall.

A little shy of the midway point, she indicated the hole that swallowed Sienna. "Cheyenne, the oldest girl, fell in one, too. She would've hit the water except for her bone."

"Bone?"

Raven explained the femur-turned-club, and how the girl had dangled from it because the bone hadn't fit sideways through the hole.

"Damn, that's one lucky kid."

"Would they have died if they fell?"

He exhaled. "Depends on how they landed. If they hit the water feet first, probably would've been okay. Landing flat or on their face, yeah, bad."

"What about the current? Is the water dangerous?"

"Nah. Not here. It's bad about a mile that way." He pointed south. "Sometimes the kids sneak out here to go swimming."

"Sneak? They're not allowed to?"

"Not without some of us to watch for cougars. The cats usually keep their distance from Oasis, but they show up at the river to drink sometimes. Small enough kid, they'd carry right off."

She cringed. "Yeah..."

They left the bridge behind and entered the ruins at a brisk walk.

She told him about their encounter with the cougars and how Tinsley had nearly been dragged off.

"Best not to run. They're cats. Fast motion makes them want to chase."

"Yeah, I figured that out pretty quick."

"Sorry."

She nudged him. "Nothing of you to apologize over."

Not having children along—and not having to sit underground hiding from cougars—did speed up the pace. They cleared the whole ruin in probably a touch under two hours, though it felt faster since they talked the entire time. She described life in the Arc to him while he spoke of growing up in Oasis. He struggled with math and science stuff in school, but also got into a fair number of fights defending another kid everyone picked on because he acted more like a girl than a boy.

"Always pissed me off how they gave Brian a hard time over that. Who cares if he thinks boys are cute?"

She knew of a few people with similar feelings in the Arc, a pair of older women who loved each other, two of the guys who worked in the water room considered themselves married. Elena Vasquez, Ariana's mother, lived with Melanie like a married couple. It astounded her the woman had agreed to have a baby. But then again, Noah managed to talk Raven into doing it at sixteen using the 'humanity is going to die off unless we do this' guilt. She suspected the doc preferred men, though he'd never been romantically involved with anyone she knew of.

At least no one back home cared. She'd never heard of anyone being teased or harassed over who they wanted to live with... probably due to the grim finality that everyone believed. Thinking only 183 people existed on the planet tended to make life seem valuable.

They left the ruins behind, hurrying into the forest as best Raven could remember the way they'd come—and using her compass to keep them going west. In the waning moments of daylight, she managed to find her way back to the house with the garden.

She gathered a few vegetables, which they ate for dinner along with more of the stuff he called 'trail mix' they'd eaten for lunch while walking. Though she'd only known Kyle for a single day, she didn't feel at all nervous falling asleep near him. Mostly, worry about how Tinsley coped with her being away kept her staring at the ceiling longer than she wanted to.

A FEW HOURS AFTER THEY'D RESUMED WALKING THE NEXT MORNING, rustling came from the woods.

Expecting deer, Raven casually glanced toward the disturbance—and nearly screamed at the sight of four scrawny, naked men charging at them. Kyle swung the shotgun off his shoulder, but didn't have time to get his hand on the trigger before needing to use the weapon like a club.

He walloped one man across the head, knocking him over, senseless. Another feral jumped on him from behind. Two ran at her, one suntanned, the other dark brown. They grunted back and forth as if to say 'you go for her legs, I'll get the arms.'

Raven backpedaled, yanking the katana out while ducking the white guy's attempt to grab her hair and circling to his right to put him between her and the other man. The one Kyle clubbed hit the ground on his front and didn't move to get up. Feral Three wrestled him for control of the shotgun, grappling him from behind.

She grasped the sword in both hands, stepping toward the white dude and slashing high. The attack failed to draw blood, but she slashed four feet of beard off. Both men on her grunted in alarm, staring at the sliced mass of hair as if witnessing literal magic happen. After a second, the black guy pointed at her and barked a word that sounded like 'moog.'

They ran at her simultaneously. She raised the sword, yelling a war cry. When neither slowed nor stopped, she slashed downward, slicing a long but shallow wound across the black man's chest, making him

WEAPONS | 369

stop short. The other guy grabbed her by the shoulders; too close for the sword, she rammed her knee into his groin.

He grabbed himself and collapsed to the ground.

The black guy swiped a hand at the blood running down his chest, stared at it, and let out an enraged howl. Raven pointed the sword at him in a 'don't you dare' gesture, but he came after her anyway.

She swung at his face; the man caught the blade in both hands, snarling. Despite the edge digging into his palms, he refused to let go. Raven set her heels, pulling as hard as she could. Still, the man's grip held solid despite the blood dribbling from his hands. He twisted, attempting to wrench the weapon out of her grasp—and seemed likely to succeed.

Thud.

Raven glanced left. The shotgun lay on the ground. Feral Three perched on Kyle's shoulders like a living backpack. He'd gotten hold of a knife, which he attempted to ram into Kyle's throat. Despite the guy being scrawny, Kyle appeared to be struggling to hold him at bay.

The one she nailed in the balls rocked side to side, emitting a repetitive grunt of pain.

Few things she'd ever seen unnerved her as much as the man grabbing her sword by the blade, cutting himself, and refusing to let go. His bulging eyes promised to make whatever they had in mind for her—likely cannibalism—hurt as much as possible.

Kyle gurgled.

The knife point came within a half inch of his throat.

Raven let go of the katana. The sudden release sent the man holding the blade stumbling backward. She dove for the shotgun, scooped it up, and thrust the front end into Feral Three's cheek like a spear before pulling the trigger.

Boom!

Feral Three's entire head exploded in a shower of red gore. The shotgun hammered into her shoulder, nearly taking her off her feet. Feral Three's body careened over backward and hit the ground behind Kyle, who staggered around in a drunken stupor, both hands clamped over his ears.

A vicious yank on Raven's hair pulled her back into the grip of the man she'd nutted. He wrapped his arms around her, one hand clamped around her left wrist, the other arm clutching her across the chest. The black guy, his entire chest covered in blood, grabbed her right wrist and wrapped his other hand around her throat, staring into her eyes while squeezing.

She thrashed, trying to whack him in the sensitive bits with the gun, but the way the men controlled her wrists made it impossible. She could barely move. Pressure on her neck increased, cutting off her air. She flailed, trying to kick for his balls, unable to tell if she hit thigh or if he simply ignored the pain.

The katana blade flashed up behind the black guy, then swung down into the side of his neck. Blood spurted from the wound, pulsing into the air. His eyes rolled back as he lapsed unconscious in seconds, his crushing grip on her throat falling away. Raven coughed and sucked in a huge breath.

Kyle pointed the katana at the feral still holding her from behind. "Let go of her."

He grunted into her ear.

"They don't understand English," rasped Raven before ramming her head backward into his face.

Moaning in pain, the guy lost his grip on her and stumbled sideways, bleeding from the nose. She whirled, rounding the shotgun pipe in a home run swing. The heavy, wooden butt crashed into his chin, shattering the jaw and knocking him out cold. His sinewy body twirled around and collapsed in a heap.

Raven spun in place, scanning their surroundings. Once confident no more ferals lay in wait, she looked down at the four men. Two unconscious. Two dead. None moving.

It finally hit her how bad they stank. She coughed, eyes watering, and held the shotgun out to Kyle. "This is yours."

Grinning, he offered the sword and yelled, "This is yours."

She cringed, but took the blade. "No need to shout."

He took the rifle. "Sorry. Thing went off right by my ear. Ringing's gonna last all damn day."

"Sorry."

"No… don't be sorry." He pushed on a clasp where the steel barrel met the butt, opening the breech. "For a skinny bastard, the guy had a lot of arm power."

"I thought you knew how to fight."

"I do." He pulled a smoking half plastic, half metal cartridge out of the barrel end. "Took the first guy out right away, didn't I? Fighting isn't pretty to look at. Not like in the stories." He pocketed the spent shell and loaded a new one before snapping the shotgun closed. "First thing I learned about fighting is it doesn't matter how good you are, or how fancy you try to be… most fights are going to end up on the ground, rolling around like a pair of idiots. You did well for someone who doesn't know how to fight."

Raven crouched to wipe the blade off on the grass. "I don't."

"Nice move ramming your skull into his nose. Who taught you that?"

"No one. Thought of doing it a second before I did it. The only thing I could think of to get him off me. My head kinda hurts now."

"Beats dead, right?" He turned in place, surveying the woods. "Looks like that's all of them."

Shit. I killed a guy. Raven doubled over, heaved a couple times, and sank to sit in the grass, shaking.

"You okay?"

"Not really. I just killed someone. A person."

Kyle shot a sideways stare at the headless body. "That's debatable."

"Seriously, even if they're nonverbal and functionally as dumb as gorillas, they're still people."

"What's a gorilla?"

She sat there shivering from nerves. "I'll explain later. There aren't enough of us left to kill each other. Every person who dies is a real chance humanity dies off."

"That's what they taught you growing up?"

"Yeah." She wrapped her arms around her legs, burying her face in her knees.

Kyle sat next to her. "It makes sense when you think there are only

200 people left in the world. There are a lot more than that. They built arcologies all over the planet. For another thing, those guys would have killed both of us. If two people are going to die, I'd much rather it be them than us. That little girl of yours still has a momma."

"Yeah." She exhaled hard. The shaking her in hands lessened a bit.

"Last, if you feel this way about ending a guy trying to murder and eat us… there's 200 more people waiting back in your arcology."

She frowned. "More like 175 but, yeah, I get the point."

He stood and helped her up.

"Stupid question."

"Okay?" He tilted his head.

She checked the compass to get her bearings. "In the stories I read, when people get shot, they just kinda fall over. Why did his whole head burst like that? Is that normal? Are the books wrong?"

"Nah. I don't think so. This is a cannon."

"Don't those belong on ships?"

He chuckled. "No, not a literal cannon. I mean it's huge for a gun."

"Oh. You ever shoot a person before?"

"Once, yeah. Another feral. I was out on a scouting team, exploring the wilds to the north of Oasis…"

She fell in step beside him as he told her of an ambush where ten or so ferals attacked his team of three. The way he described it sounded like she listened to her father reading a story from a book. Her shock at having to kill someone eased enough to set aside for the time being. Mostly, she let his voice lull her into a feeling of security. None of the characters she ever read about felt sick to their stomach like she did after killing people, and they often killed lots of bad guys.

Maybe we will make it back home—to Oasis.

3 8

WANDERER'S SPIRIT

I'm getting old, kiddo. Need to scratch that itch and see as much of topside as I can before standing up the wrong way puts me in the infirmary for two days. – Ellis Wilder.

Moonlight, though captivatingly beautiful, didn't penetrate the forest cover well.

Once it became difficult to see, they decided to stop for the night. While munching on more trail mix and some bread, Kyle absentmindedly talked about how sleeping directly on the ground leeched body heat, a problem they didn't have in the house the previous night. Both backpacks contained blankets, which he arranged as sleeping mats. Not entirely ideal, but better than stretching out on bare ground.

She tried to consider blowing that guy's head off as defending herself against a monster. In a way, the ferals not speaking any discernible language helped distance her from the idea of them being human. The exploding skull would haunt her dreams for years no matter how necessary doing it had been.

"How much do you know about those ferals? Like… what do they want?"

He lowered a water bottle away from his mouth. "Not much. There are a handful of scattered groups. Almost impossible for us to tell the different tribes apart. No idea if they attack each other or just us. If they have a language, it's not one we know. Anyone's guess why they attack, probably territorial."

"I think they're cannibals. The first one I saw kept trying to bite me."

"Hmm." He drank more water, swishing it side to side in his mouth in thought. "Maybe. But, they don't have weapons. Biting could just be a means of attack."

She gnawed on her bread. "Did they come from an arcology?"

"Again, don't know. If I see one again, I'll try to ask but I wouldn't expect an answer."

"Ass." She chuckled.

Kyle failed to conceal a smile. "No one from Oasis has tried to study them. Some of the scientists think the tribals might actually be descended from people who weren't able to shelter in an arcology, but found somewhere to take cover that didn't have a perfect seal. Like, they've suffered damage in the head from whatever toxins floated around back then. One of the doctors said something like 'genetic damage' affected their intelligence."

"Oh. That kinda makes sense. I'm not *too* smart, but I did read about DNA and stuff. I guess it would technically make them mutants. Our stories mention there being dangerous mutants out there, but I grew up thinking the word mutant meant like giant monsters with tentacles instead of arms or furry creatures like werewolves."

"What is a werewolf?" He raised an eyebrow.

"A made-up monster from stories. They're basically normal people most of the time, but depending on which universe you're reading about, they either go crazy during the full moon or they can change whenever they want."

"Change?"

"They turn into beasts. Big, furry, claws, teeth."

"You've seen these?" He stared at her.

"No, dammit." She shoved at his shoulder. "They're made up. Not real. Just stories. My point is, everyone in the Arc thinks there are mutants out here and they're giant scary things... not crazy naked dudes."

He laughed.

They sat in silence for a while.

"Do you want to sleep first or should I?" asked Kyle.

"I'm still kinda wound up from shooting a guy. Not sure I will be able to sleep at all."

"Okay, you take first watch then. Wake me when you're ready to sleep." He wandered off to relieve himself, then stretched out on his blanket.

Raven sat in silence, forearms across her knees, gazing into the darkness. Mostly, she listened for approaching threats. "You know, if we were in a novel, we'd probably be making love now."

"What?" He rolled on his side to face her.

"I mean if this was like the books I read, we'd already be madly in love with each other and doing it right here in the woods."

He chuckled. "Little fast for that, isn't it?"

"Yeah, but characters in books do it all the time. Guy and girl who don't really know anything about each other survive a dangerous situation together and as soon as it's quiet, they're doing it. We almost died and ended up saving each other, so we'd be expected to fall in love. Or at least have sex."

"Okay, I admit I'm entirely confused here. Are you suggesting...?"

She bowed her head, thankful he couldn't see how hard she blushed. "No. I'm just babbling. I had almost nothing to do while growing up except play a couple of board games or read a library full of books. I mean, they're all hundreds of years old, so maybe they don't make any sense to us now. But being in the Arc is sorta like being frozen in time. Anyway, in those books, whenever the main character ends up together with the cute guy, they invariably fall in love. Especially if they fight bad guys side by side and almost die or, like, survive a plane crash and get stranded on an island together."

"So, I'm the cute guy?"

Shit. Her face nearly caught fire from blushing harder. *What is wrong with me!?*

"Umm." She coughed. "I guess there's no graceful recovery from that one. Yeah, okay, you are kinda cute."

"You're kinda cute, too." He rolled onto his back.

"Thanks."

He yawned. "Sometimes, life is more like a book than books are like life."

"Yeah... sometimes."

"Your girl's father dead?"

"No."

"Guess you two don't get along anymore?"

She picked up a twig and spun it around her finger. "We never did. He's totally not the sort of person I like being around."

"Did he force himself on you?"

"Not like that, no. In the Arc, we believed we were the only people left on the planet and it's our duty to do everything we can to keep humanity going. But, with less than 200 people, it's not easy finding someone to have kids with who you aren't related to. They keep track, and turned out Chase and I were about as unrelated as possible and only a year apart in age. So, they asked us to make kids. I was only sixteen then, and too naïve to question anything about saving the human race, even if I thought Chase was an asshole."

"Stopped at one?"

"Yeah. He turned out to be more of an asshole than I thought. He expected our daughter to die before she made it to three years old, so he ignored she existed. Totally wanted nothing to do with her. I couldn't have another kid with a guy who'd just throw them away emotionally, ya know?"

"Wow. That's harsh. I'm glad you got out of there."

"The only reason I tried is to protect my daughter. I might've had her out of obligation, but I love her more than anything." She explained the issue with the air quality and Noah's refusal to consider drawing in outside air, convinced it would kill everyone. While she rambled on about that, her mind wandered to Chase. If the remaining people in the Arc haven't suffocated by now and he survived to reach Oasis, would he change his attitude? Did he really expect Tinsley to die and not want to suffer the grief of losing her after becoming attached? Or had it been bullshit?

Screw him. He made his choice.

"Please tell me that's you growling," said Kyle in a sleepy voice.

"Sorry. Just thinking about the asshole. So, yeah... I'm not involved with anyone. Maybe I could get into a relationship with someone after I got to know them."

"That's the way to do it. Not 'you two, baby, now.'"

She chuckled. "Besides, if we fell in love right now and had sex tonight, one of us would definitely die tomorrow."

"Huh? What?"

"Always happens in books. If they have sex, someone's getting mauled. If they fall in true love, one's gonna die. If they fall in true love and have sex, it's going to be a *gruesome* death and the girl's going to end up pregnant with the dead guy's child."

"You read too much."

"Heh. No such thing. The Arc is so damn confining. I had to escape, even if only in my head." She sighed, tossing the twig into the weeds. "I think my father felt the same way. Only he decided to find adventure out here rather than in his imagination. I'm more like him than I thought. Have you ever seen the ocean?"

"Once. From pretty far off. It's big. The water went all the way out to the horizon and as far to both sides as I could see. It rippled in waves, white at the top before they crashed on the shore. The wind smelled like salt. I remember seeing a giant metal thing sticking up out of the water. Sorta looked like a high-rise building, except one side was smooth. White birds were everywhere."

"Seagulls. They still exist?"

"What's a seagull?"

She brushed her fingers at grass she couldn't see in the dark. "White birds that live near the ocean. Not sure what they look like. I've only read about them."

"Oh. Maybe. You want to see the ocean?"

"Kind of, yeah. But... I don't want to leave my kid alone."

"Sounds like you've got a wanderer's spirit."

She smiled. "Maybe a little. Not as much as my father. He loved going out here more than pretty much anything else. Escaping into imaginary worlds is a lot safer."

"True, but still a wanderer's spirit."

"Got it from Dad, all right."

Kyle yawned. "I do, too. But didn't get it from my father. That's why I volunteered for scouting missions. Staying in Oasis all the time is boring. I like a little taste of adventure and fun, all that stuff."

"We should probably sleep. If we stay up all night talking, we'll be in trouble tomorrow."

"Yeah. Good night."

"Night." She yawned.

Ooh. My hands have stopped shaking.

39

CRUSHED

There are occasions when foul language is warranted, even required. For example, when a heavy object falls on your foot or when losing your place in a thousand-page novel. – Ellis Wilder.

The moment Raven opened her eyes to sunlight filtering down among branches and Kyle nudging her shoulder, she knew two things.

Never again did she want to open her eyes to a blank grey concrete ceiling and have only the numbers on her dial clock to give any sense of time. The few days she'd spent sleeping in the dark and having daylight rather than bells tell her when to get up had forever changed something inside her. Not once since leaving the Arc had she wanted to ignore the sun and continue sleeping the way she begrudged the damn bells.

Second, she knew she'd made a complete fool of herself the previous night talking about sex so casually with a guy she'd only known for a day. Where had it even come from? A need to fill the silence perhaps, but why talk about *that*? She couldn't come up with an explanation beyond the subconscious result of being around a guy her age who struck her as a kindred soul and seemed a reasonably nice person. That, and she knew he couldn't be related to her. The Arc had four men within two years either way of her age, one being Chase. All the rest could have been her cousins or some such thing a generation removed. She knew her parents only had two kids, her and an older brother who didn't even make it to his first birthday. Died in the middle of the night. She now suspected the stale air had caused it, but who knows?

If she extended her tolerance out to plus ten years, it expanded the pool to eighteen men, none of whom really clicked with her—not that she made any advances. Between Sienna and Tinsley, she never felt lonely, so hadn't suffered the pressure to attach herself to anyone out of desperation.

But Kyle... a white guy from Oasis couldn't possibly be closely related to her enough to matter. Sure, a chance existed they might share a small amount of genetic material considering some 1,500 to 1,600 people left the Arc years ago and his great grandparents had been among them.

Perhaps some temptation did exist, elevated from her subconscious in the aftermath of the crazy emotional storm that raged from blowing a guy's head off. Certainly it had been unusual to feel so at ease laying there randomly talking with him instead of sleeping. However, she couldn't seriously consider anything happening between them yet. Certainly not while they rushed back to the Arc having no idea if anyone in it even remained alive.

She couldn't make eye contact and barely said a word to him while they ate a trail mix breakfast.

Sienna made me think about it with her comment about not doing anything she wouldn't.

Her friend had four children and hadn't once so much as seen a man naked. Raven distracted herself from her awkward embarrassment at the previous night's conversation by mentally laughing at the imaginary scenario of Sienna going through comical motions of trying to sneak a man into her quarters for sex without any of the kids being aware of it.

Kyle had an odd little smile, which made it even more difficult to look at him even though he didn't say anything awkward. Except for that hinting smirk, he acted as if she'd never even brought up the topic of them having sex.

They set off again following her compass heading and best memory of where to go.

Perhaps sensing her discomfort, Kyle broke the silence an hour or so into the hike by asking questions about the Arc. How was it laid out, entrances, what sort of systems did it have, and so forth.

Raven fell into 'work mode,' explaining everything she could think of to him she figured could be relevant. It made her feel like a soldier from one of the old novels, working out a plan to infiltrate an enemy bunker. More appropriately, soldiers trying to make entry on one of *their* bunkers that suffered a catastrophe. She hoped Noah's foolishness hadn't already killed everyone. If the situation inside the Arc already deteriorated to that point, she might pass out halfway down the escape corridor and end up dead, too. Not like anyone could see bad air.

New boots that actually fit her made walking feel even faster. Her old ones had been as loose as tread socks, floppy and full of holes. Of course, they didn't let her feet breathe as much, so she took them off to sleep. No cougar would rip one of these off. She couldn't wait to get back to Oasis. Temptation to give up and turn around weighed her stride down under guilt. Worse, she caught herself thinking that if everyone had died, she wouldn't need to waste time arguing with Noah and could go home right away.

I'm not going to waste time arguing with him anyway. He doesn't have unlimited power. Ben's already on my side. We'll just ignore Noah and convince everyone else they should leave.

The forest thinned out around them, yielding ground to a swath of suburban ruins she didn't remember passing before. Most of the homes in sight had collapsed into heaps of timber and acid-eaten aluminum siding, everything covered in weeds. One or two intact façades still stood despite the rest of the buildings behind them having vanished. A cracked and weed-infested stretch of old road ran among the ruined homes, disappearing in places where centuries of windblown dirt had accumulated.

"What?" asked Kyle.

"I didn't say anything."

"That look on your face. Something's wrong."

"Oh." She pulled out her compass again and checked her heading. "We're off course. I don't remember going this way before. But… this *does* look like the ruins close to the Arc. We can't be far away. Maybe we overshot or we're a little too far south. If we can find something to climb to see past the trees, the turbine farm ought to be visible from here."

He pointed down the road. "How about that old transmission tower?"

Raven looked in the direction he indicated. Maybe a quarter mile ahead behind a row of smashed houses, a steel tower similar the one she saw the mysterious figure on poked out of the trees. "It's a tower. Should be a good vantage point. Transmission?"

"Yeah. Those towers used to support electrical power lines run over long distances."

"Oh. Not like radio transmission, just… okay. I get it." Raven turned in place, but didn't spot anything to give her an indication of the Arc's position past the dense forest. Not even the soft *whuff-whuff* of spinning turbine blades broke the stillness. Silence didn't worry her too much into thinking she'd gone way off course since the wind barely moved. She stuck the compass back in the satchel and proceeded ahead down the road. "That looks tall enough. I should be able to see the windmills from up there. We *can't* be too far."

She bit her lip, taken by the sudden worry they could be further off course than expected. They'd been moving pretty fast, walking for at least an hour into darkness each night instead of stopping as soon as the light weakened, and taking few breaks—yet still slept two nights. The trip back should have been much faster without having to adjust pace for children. They should have arrived at the Arc yesterday, which meant they must have wasted some time going in circles or backtracking.

These ruins look like the ones surrounding the Arc on the south.

Kyle walked a few steps behind her, carrying his rifle, but keeping it pointed off to the side. After the feral attack, he hadn't put it back on his shoulder. The few seconds it took to bring it around almost killed them both.

At every gap in the trees, Raven strained to peer out at the sky beyond, hoping to see windmills. Each time she found only empty sky, she became more and more convinced they'd overshot. Even continuing west to the tower for a look felt like wasting time going in the wrong direction.

Raven lurched forward unexpectedly, the road buckling under her. In a fleeting moment of pure chaos, the sky vanished amid a deafening roar. The next thing she knew, she lay flat on her chest gazing at thin trails of sunlight shimmering in the dust in front of her. It took her a moment to recover her senses from the sudden fall enough to realize an avalanche of stone chunks and dirt had fallen on top of her, covering most of her body except for her head and left arm.

The sunlight trails traced upward to small gaps in the debris, enough to see she'd landed at the bottom of a round underground tunnel running parallel to the street above it. Rocky points jabbed into her back and legs, well past 'uncomfortable,' but not agonizing.

"Ky—" She choked and gagged on a mouthful of dust. Every convulsion felt like her body sat in the teeth of some giant beast toying with her, the stone slabs grinding into her back. With great effort, she slid her left arm in front of her face, masking her mouth in her elbow. "Kyle?"

Silence.

She grunted, pawing at the ground—smooth curved concrete—but couldn't budge herself. Attempting to push upward lifted her chest perhaps an inch, but the shifting debris stabbed her in the kidney. She yelped in pain and fell flat again.

Panic came in waves. She flew back and forth from wanting to scream for her father to her brain spinning in circles searching for a way out. Struggling barely got her anywhere before she recoiled from the pain. Unable to see much above and behind her, she imagined half a city of debris on her back, a hopeless situation. Again she grabbed at the floor, hand sliding over the ground, yet too much dirt and pavement pinned her down for her to move at all. Neither her right arm, which lay under her chest, or her legs, could budge.

"Kyle!" shouted Raven.

She listened to the rasp of her breaths in the echoing tunnel. He didn't say anything.

After another few minutes of futile struggling, she let herself go limp, cheek to the grit-covered concrete, staring past dirt at a rounded wall. They'd fallen into a giant pipe.

No one's going to find us. We're off course. Tess won't know anything happened until it's too late. We'll die from dehydration before we starve. The debris is going to kill me first. Too hard to breathe. Weight. Crushing the air out of me. I'm... sorry, Tinsley. Raven closed her eyes.

You were right... I should have stayed home.

40

MOMMY

Used to be, I thought nuclear weapons were the most irresistible force made by humanity. Then I had a daughter. Uncontained fission has nothing on a three-year-old demanding something she's set her mind on.
– Ellis Wilder.

Tears flowed down Raven's cheeks into the dirt beneath her face.

Her imminent death didn't bother her as much as imagining Tinsley's reaction to never seeing her again. Time blurred out of meaning. She lay there buried as much by futility as earth. Every time she thought about her daughter asking her not to go away, she cringed in guilt. Could the girl somehow have known this would happen?

She stared at her hand a few inches in front of her nose, knuckles scratched and seeping blood. What a stupid way to die. One small error in navigation. By chance stepping on the wrong spot of road. The ultimate cruelty would be dying so close to the Arc. Perhaps they'd already died, and whatever force controlled circumstance decided she needed to go with her people. She'd go just like her father—he'd found Oasis, knew the truth, and died before he could tell anyone.

I'm sorry, Tins.

Guilt became heavier than the dirt.

Tinsley wailed in the distance of her imagination. She pictured Sienna having to hold her down so the girl didn't run out into the forest searching for her mommy. A scene like that couldn't happen unless someone found her body and told the girl her mother had died. More likely, Tinsley would sit by the window, staring out into the forest day after day, wondering when her mother would come home, never knowing what happened.

The same thing Raven had done after Dad disappeared.

At least being eaten by cougars didn't take him days to die.

"Mommy!" shouted Tinsley from above before bursting into sobs.

Raven jumped, startled out of a brief moment of unconsciousness. She strained to look up at the edge of the hole. No heartbroken six-year-old staring down at her. Only a dream. Hearing her daughter's anguished cry, even in the haze of her pain-addled imagination, struck Raven across the face like a slap.

"Grr. No. I'm not gonna let her wonder like I did."

She shifted her weight left, attempting to raise her body off her right arm. So what if trying to move hurt like hell. Better she kill herself attempting to escape than lay there accepting death. She'd made a promise to Tinsley and couldn't walk away from it. Pain stabbing into her back and legs intensified to the point she could no longer resist screaming. Still, she pushed. The instant pins and needles erupted in her right arm, she tried to move it. Nothing happened. Shaking from pain and fatigue, she held position, waiting for her arm to stop tingling. Dirt dribbled on her face from the mound above her shifting. A scrape of concrete sliding over concrete came from behind.

"Not gonna"—she gasped—"give up on you"—her protesting muscles shook, demanding she stop fighting the weight pushing her down—"like your asshole father did."

A stony dagger under her left shoulder blade felt as if it would burst out of her breast at any moment. Shuddering, she screamed past a clenched jaw, forcing herself to stay propped up on her elbow until finally, at long last, her right arm listened to her brain and moved. She shoved it straight out in front and let herself down on her chest. Debris shifted above her; the jabbing hunks of pavement eased off their assault—somewhat. Her left arm quivered from holding up so much weight for several minutes.

Rasping for breath, she glared at the swirls of dust in front of her face.

Raven held an image of Tinsley's hopeful stare in her mind, concentrating on her daughter's eyes instead of the pain and crushing weight pinning her down. She braced her hands on the concrete under her shoulders and pushed. Bit by bit, she wriggled sideways, shimmying, gradually expanding the shroud of dirt entombing her. Once she had enough room to shift herself a few inches to either side, she elbow-crawled forward until only her legs below the knees remained buried.

Out of strength, she again collapsed along the bottom of the huge pipe to catch her breath.

Gonna get home, Tins. Gonna get home.

Her body shook from fatigue and pain. She summoned up a second wind from sheer determination, forcing herself to roll over and sit up. Though sore, her limbs appeared to have escaped major damage. Seven spots on her jumpsuit had bloodied, the largest patch only three inches across. She looked up from herself at the debris pile, then at the hole above. Roughly six feet of empty space separated the buried pipe from the broken road surface. Given the surprisingly low amount of dirt that fell in on her, most of it had likely been swept away by underground water, a sinkhole. She and Kyle had walked onto a stretch of blacktop suspended over a cavity.

Oh, shit.

"Kyle!?" she shouted, her voice echoing both ways down the pipe.

Raven scrambled to her feet and rushed forward, grabbing larger slabs of former road and dragging them aside. He hadn't been walking too far behind her. More dirt fell in toward the eastern part of the collapse, enough for no trace of him to remain visible.

"No… that's not right." She kept pawing at the rubble. "Dammit! Not right. I didn't touch him. We're not even in love. He's not supposed to die!" Raven leaned back, sitting on her heels, and wiped sweat from her face. *This is where the character screams don't die, I love you, right? If I do that, he's definitely screwed.* She resumed digging. *And I don't love him. Just met him. Okay, he's cute, but I don't even know him. Chase is a complete asshole, but I don't want him to die either.*

She leaned forward grabbing another hunk of pavement. Pulling it aside revealed the tip of the shotgun barrel.

"Kyle!"

Like a burrowing cat, she feverishly raked at the dirt, digging out around the gun and the hunk of curved concrete laying on top of it. The slab proved too heavy for her to move, so after a moment of futile tugging, she leaned down and tried to look under it.

Kyle lay mostly on his back beneath a tangle of road and pipe chunks. The slab of blacktop across his midsection looked far too massive for one person to move. A dozen small cuts smeared his face in bloody dirt, but he still appeared to be breathing. The earth that fell in on top of him cascaded over the pieces of pavement and pipe, diverted mostly to either side, leaving a hollow around his upper body. Hundreds of pounds of concrete and road fragments would need to be cleared away for him to go anywhere.

"I'm gonna need help," she whispered, then yelled, "Kyle?"

He moaned.

Raven flattened herself out and stretched an arm in under the hunk of concrete, not quite able to get her fingertips in contact with his head. "You're alive."

"What… happened?" He shifted his head side to side, squinting. A hand burst up from the dust much closer to her, so she grabbed it and squeezed.

"The road fell out from under us. There's too much debris on you for me to move."

He tilted his head back, looking at her upside down. "Dammit. Are you okay? You're a bloody mess."

"Back atcha. Yeah, little cuts. I'm fine. Bit dizzy, but no bones broke. What about you? Anything broken?"

"Uhh. Don't think so. Can't move much. Leg hurts. That's a good sign, right? Guess my spine didn't snap."

She cringed.

"Where's your pack?"

Raven blinked, not even noticing her backpack had vanished until he mentioned it. "Uhh... no idea. Gotta be down here somewhere. Gonna find it. You need water. I can run to the Arc for help. If they're already gone, I'll go straight to Oasis without stopping. Sleep is for losers."

He mumbled something incoherent. She scurried back to where she'd been trapped, digging until she unearthed her backpack. The straps had torn out from the right side. A heavy hunk of pavement must have hit it on the way down, shearing it off her. Perhaps the pack saved her life; the slab that speared it probably would have impaled her otherwise. She rummaged all five of her remaining water bottles out and passed them to him, each about twenty ounces, plus the rest of her trail mix. If she had to go back to Oasis without him, she would not be stopping to eat.

He had plenty to survive for a few days.

"Hang on. I'll come back as soon as I can."

"I'll be here... if this pile doesn't shift and crush me."

"Don't say that." She closed her eyes, then stood.

"Heh. I'm gonna be okay. We didn't make love, right?"

Raven bowed her head, too sad to laugh but grinned despite the situation. "Yeah. Something like that."

41

BREAKING THE SEAL

How do we know this water is good if it's the only water we've ever tasted? – Ellis Wilder.

Raven climbed up to stand on the outside of the giant concrete pipe. The collapse exposed a smaller six-inch diameter line about halfway between it and the surface. She grabbed it and hauled herself out of the hole.

Once again in full daylight, she looked down at herself, covered in dirt and blood. Multiple sore spots riddled her body, but none hurt bad enough to be crippling. Somehow, the katana remained dangling from her hip. Her jumpsuit had a few rips, but the new boots took the pummeling in stride, dirty but undamaged.

She moved off the street, running alongside it to the tower at the end, which stood on a patch of gravel surrounded by the remains of a long-ago-destroyed chain link fence. Without a care to its stability, she scrambled up the steel lattice until she could see over the treetops. The windmill farm stood off in the distance, north and east of her. They *had* gone off course, though not as badly as she feared. The tower would serve as a landmark to find Kyle again, as the crumbling road led right to it.

After making her way back to the ground, Raven ran for the windmills, compass in hand to keep her going in the right direction. Eventually, she ran out of steam and slowed to a determined walk, weaving around collapsed houses, old driveways, and one strip mall. The sword proved useful for powering through a stretch of densely overgrown forest rather than going around it.

She hacked her way out of the woods to a bare dirt field in the shadow of a huge artificial hill. A too-perfect shape and sharp angled sides made it obviously the product of human engineering. Two concrete walls flanked a large square opening in the south-facing side right in front of her, leading to a tunnel. The passage followed a downward angle underground.

This is the front door...

Seeing the Arc's primary entrance felt like witnessing a myth come to life. She ran down the tunnel until she reached a massive door some forty feet in from the opening, its metal surface stained green and brown in splotches. Crud gathered around the edges of the numbers 1409 embossed a half-inch deep, and also collected in a vertical seam splitting the gargantuan portal in half. Unfortunately, her hopes for finding a way to open it from the outside fell as dead as the computer terminal screen on the wall to the left. Whatever substance stained the door had melted the keys and display screen. She started to open her tool satchel to grab a screwdriver, but decided against it. Any tinkering would require electrical power that probably no longer worked.

Level one has radiation... but the doc said it's not too dangerous in a brief dose, like running straight from the stairs to the door. Maybe I can get it open from the inside.

Better yet, once she convinced Noah to abandon the Arc, her entire tech team would help find a way to open this door. It wouldn't matter if they activated the emergency backup. So what if the door could never be closed again?

Grumbling, she whirled around and ran out of the tunnel, heading north toward the windmills. It bothered her seeing only a few weeds growing in the dirt above the Arc, but she didn't waste time thinking about the implication the soil here might be toxic. Roughly a mile from the main entrance, she spotted a square slab of metal—the hatch.

Hands balled into fists, she jogged for it.

She'd been gone for six days. What if someone had secured the wheel mechanism? Her father never complained about being locked out. Could the security team be so afraid of the myths of poison they wouldn't even go down the tunnel? Jose almost fainted when he learned the seal failed a long time ago.

Standing there staring at the hatch and worrying what would happen wasted time. Raven grabbed the handle and pulled, shouting in delight when it opened. The blast of foul air hitting her in the face nearly made her throw up. Everything down there from the sad little stuffed bear she'd hugged as a child to clothing stank like chemical poo. Living in it constantly made the smell unnoticeable.

Choking on each breath, she clenched her jaw and forced herself to climb down onto the ladder, not knowing if it would end up being a one-way trip. Lack of oxygen would disorient her too much to escape if she went too far. A plan formed as she rushed down the ladder.

At the bottom, she faced into the impenetrable darkness, cupped her hands around her mouth, and shouted, "Jose? Ann? Is anyone still alive in here?"

Her voice echoed back to her.

After a moment of receiving no response, she repeated the shout.

When she again got no reply, her heart sank. Not only did it suggest everyone had already died, it meant she'd have to marathon back to Oasis without food, water, or rest to find help for Kyle.

Shit. Too late. Raven slouched, head bowed.

Something thudded in the distance, almost like a knee banging into a steel desk.

She popped upright. "Hello? Is anyone here?"

The overhead lights flicked on, revealing the graffiti-lined passage in all its dingy glory. Seconds later, Jose opened the door at the end, shining a puny crank light in.

"Jose!" she yelled, shaking her fists overhead in triumph. *The air hasn't turned lethal!*

"What's all the damn yelling about?"

She ran down the hall toward him.

"Raven?" He blinked at her. "What the hell happened to you? You fall down the ladder? And what are you wearing?"

"Jose..." She grabbed his arms, staring up into his eyes. "I found a village. Thousands of people. I think they're the ones who left the Arc long ago. One of them came back with me to warn everyone here. The ground collapsed, we fell in. He's trapped. Need help."

"You need to see the doc." He reached for her hand.

Raven darted around him and sprinted into the hallway. "Not now!"

"Hey, wait." Jose ran after her.

She raced down the admin corridor, rushing by the security station and straight to Noah's office. As usual, he'd been hunched over his logbook and nearly jumped out of the chair when she booted the door aside. He leaned back as she stormed across the room and planted both hands on his desk, looming over him.

"It's time to stop being stupid. I found them. A whole village. Thousands of people. We have to get out of the Arc before it kills us."

He stared at her for a while, the initial shock of her appearance giving way to a suspicious squint. "That's blood, isn't it? What did you do to your daughter and the others?"

She punched him hard enough to send him flying sideways out of his chair. "How could you even think that, much less ask me if I killed my own child? She is perfectly safe at Oasis." Rapid breathing and likely tainted air already made her feel sick and light-headed.

"Oasis?" rasped Noah, cradling his face. "Do you even realize what you sound like? You took your child to an oasis where everyone is happy?" He pushed himself upright. "Not satisfied, you took the other children, too. Thanks to you, humanity is doomed."

"I didn't take anyone. Sienna watched the kids passing out right in front of her. Acting drunk and delirious. She knew the air in the Arc has become dangerous. They snuck out and followed me."

"To this Oasis…" He frowned. "I hope they didn't suffer."

Raven drew the katana and pointed it at him. "Accuse me of murdering my daughter and the children one more damned time."

"Threatening violence is not a great way to convince me you haven't been violent."

"This is *my* blood. From a damned cave-in. We fell into a hole when the ground gave out below us."

He pushed himself back to his feet.

Jose, Ann, Marco, and James—all security officers—entered the office behind her.

"Whoa." Jose reached for her. "Set the knife down, hon."

She spun a quarter turn left, putting her back to a bookshelf and the blade between her and the security people. "He's not listening. Noah's going to kill all of you. Topside is not full of poison. The Arc is!"

"Calm down, dear." Ann moved closer. "You're clearly upset."

"I'm not crying. My eyes are watering because of the shit in the air." She shot a glare at Noah. "I've been out there for six wakes—no six *days*. To hell with hours in darkness. There is night and day. People do not belong underground."

Noah raised a pausing hand at the security team. "I thought you said you took your daughter to this oasis, now she's buried underground?"

The security team glared at her.

"No. Tinsley is alive. Sienna, Josh, Xan, Cheyenne, and Ariana are all alive. The blood all over me is mine."

Hostility among the security people eased back to confusion.

"You said 'we' fell in a hole." Noah picked up a rag and dabbed at his bleeding nose.

"Oasis is real. It's the name of a village. One of their security officers went with me to come back here. He's trapped under a mound of concrete. I can't get him out on my own. The ventilation system here is going to fail. Our windmills are one storm away from collapsing. No power means no air. The scrubbers are already useless. Do you want to end up all clustered in the hydroponic farm desperate for oxygen as you slowly suffocate?"

Jose and Ann exchanged a glance, doubt etched in their cheeks.

"She's been exposed to something out there that's given her vivid hallucinations." Noah walked around the desk and took two steps toward her. "Note the manic gleam in her eyes? I'm sure she believes she's found a settlement of other people out there. But the sad truth is we are the last people on the planet. Only the Arc is keeping us alive. Our world is no longer suitable for human life. It will never be again. Put the sword down and let us help. Preston has medicine that can make you stop hallucinating."

"I'm not hallucinating. I look messed up because I've had six days of clean air and now I'm back in toxic soup. Did any of you ever wonder why you always feel tired? Constant headaches? Ever feel like the room's swaying from side to side? Ever stop short in the middle of doing something and forget entirely what you're doing or why you started doing it?"

James scratched his head. "Uhh, yeah."

"Oasis is not real, dear." Noah crept closer. "Where are the children?"

She edged back against the bookshelf, the administrator and four security people gradually closing in on her. James seemed to have a little doubt. Anna's eyes radiated pity. Marco hadn't quite stopped looking at her like he believed she'd murdered five children. Jose, the only one who'd noticed her new clothes, reached for her hesitantly while mostly looking at Noah as if seeking approval.

They think I've gone nuts. Her need to save the lives of everyone in the Arc exploded into singular focus on a different goal: escape and return to her daughter. She would not deprive Tinsley of her mother in a doomed effort to save people committed to being idiots.

"Move!" shouted Raven while slashing the air over the security team's heads.

Distracted by watching Noah, Jose mistook the feint for a real attempt to take his head off. He screamed at the sudden motion and stumbled over his feet, falling on his ass. Ann, Marco, and James jumped back, all grabbing for the batons hanging on their belts. Raven didn't wait for any of them to speak. She vaulted over Jose and ran out into the hall.

"Stay here and die if you want," shouted Raven. "I tried. You're not going to keep me away from Tinsley!"

Tyrone and Walter, the two largest men in the Arc—who also happened to be on the security team—formed a human wall in front of the door to the escape tunnel. She couldn't hope to get past them without using the katana, didn't want to hurt them, and also didn't trust her ability *to* hurt them before they pinned her down. Either one of them could throw her around like a child.

James and Marco tried to run at her from Noah's office at the same time, wedging themselves in the door together.

Shit. She stared at two immovable objects blocking her only way out. *Unless...*

"Screw it..."

Jose's reaching fingers swiped at her hair. Raven dashed to the left, away from the escape tunnel and the security team scrambling out into the corridor behind her. Running as hard as if Tinsley's life hung in the balance, she raced out from the admin hall to the central core, weaving around a handful of people who all stopped short to gawk at her. Evidently stunned by her appearance—or the naked blade waving around—none did more than stare as she zoomed past them.

Jose, Ann, Marco, and James rushed out of the hallway, shouting at people to grab her. Francis, an older guy in his late fifties up ahead, widened his stance as if he intended to try catching her. Fortunately, the stairwell entrance was in front of him by far enough he'd have to dive forward for any chance at touching her.

The older guy didn't bother trying to leap at her as she cornered, her boot heel squeaking, and rushed up the stairs. Level two smelled even worse, but she didn't leave the stairwell, not even sparing much of a glance down the abandoned corridor. Spray paint on the wall at the switchback to level one read 'off limits' and 'quarantine – danger!'

She rushed up the first switchback to a landing midway between the floors and found the next set of stairs blocked off by a stack of junk she'd forgotten about in her haste. Filling cabinets, tables, chairs, and a coat rack or two. The sword wouldn't help, so she rammed it into the sheath and started grabbing stuff. The first filing cabinet she threw down the stairs to level two knocked James and Ann down with it. She threw a chair *to* Jose more than at him, hoping he'd catch it. The security people jumped back from the second filing cabinet she sent bouncing down the stairs.

"Raven, what the fuck are you doing?" yelled Ann. "That's off limits! You're going to hurt yourself."

She grabbed another office chair and threw it wildly to the right. It bounced off the wall and tumbled to the landing below. "Maybe it's radioactive, but it's the only way out. It's bullshit! Topside is *not* dangerous."

Jose charged up the stairs.

"No!" shouted Raven. She grabbed the barrier and flung herself headfirst into a gap, landing draped over a table turned sideways.

He grabbed her ankle and pulled; she braced her hands on metal cabinets to either side, roaring in determination while kicking at him.

"Almost got her! Marc, get up here. Need a hand," yelled Jose.

"Stop this ridiculousness at once," called Noah.

"Jose, you're a reasonable guy." Raven grunted, struggling to pull herself forward. "He thinks I've gone nuts. I haven't. I can prove it to you all if you let me."

He continued pulling on her.

"Do you think I pulled this jumpsuit out of my ass?"

Jose stopped pulling, but didn't let go.

"I really don't want to kick you in the face." She growled, pushing against the cabinets. His fingers started to slip. "Right now, you're keeping me away from my daughter. My heel's about to tell your nose why that's a bad idea. Please, Jose. Believe me."

His grip let go, sending her forward, flat on the dustiest floor she'd ever seen. A dimly lit corridor spread out ahead of her, littered with furniture, papers, scraps of trash, and tables upended into barricades. Several skeletal bodies lay about, two hanging over the table-walls, three others sprawled on the floor. Long bullet-riddled windows ran down both sides of the hallway, revealing vast laboratories containing long-forgotten medical and computer equipment.

Tess mentioning 'there had been violence' made her briefly imagine two large groups of people having a shootout in this corridor. Gunfire certainly explained how the medical equipment puked cesium everywhere—a bullet hit it.

Whether Jose let go on purpose or merely lost his grip, she couldn't tell—nor did she care.

Perhaps Ann might be able to squeeze through the gap, but none of the guys could. Raven shoved herself upright and scrambled up to as much of a run as she could manage on the slippery dust. Remembering the doc mentioning radioactive powder, she held her breath while fishing the filter mask out of her satchel and pulling it on. Getting cesium on her skin would be bad, but inhaling it had to be much worse.

Behind her, banging and clattering announced the security team clearing the barrier.

Flailing her arms for balance, she ran-skated a few hundred feet down the big corridor to a four-way intersection on a level she'd never seen before. *Hatch is on the north end, so I had to go south to the admin hall. Went right at the middle, then down a west hall. Big entrance is at the south... gotta go south.* She fished the compass out, trying not to let the crashing of metal freak her out. If they caught her, she'd end up in jail and Tinsley would think her dead when she didn't come home —not to mention Kyle would be screwed.

Her compass needle whipped violently to the left, pointing at a big white machine in one of the labs.

The filter mask made breathing the already thin air intolerable. *Maybe* it would protect her from the cesium dust. Somewhat loopy, she stared at the shaking needle, wondering how it had broken.

Shit! Oh, that thing's gotta have a giant magnet in it. Compass is useless here. Uhh, south, right turn, left turn... I...

She chose left, running down another corridor with almost an inch of powdery dust on the floor. Doors, some open, some closed, some wedged on furniture or skeletal remains zoomed past her on either side. Yellow-and-black stripes on a double door at the end of the corridor gave her hope, as did the biohazard sign.

Raven tried to stop, but ended up skiing forward in the thick dust. She bounced face first off the door and landed on her ass. Ignoring the pain in her tailbone, she leapt up and jammed her fingers into the rubber gasket between the two halves. Like the outer door, this one appeared to open by sliding apart. Alas, it refused to move.

She kicked a maintenance panel out on the left side, exposing the control circuitry as well as hydraulic lines for the door actuators.

"Guess I gotta fix it first."

Raven drew the katana and slashed the hoses. Viscous fluid dribbled out. She speared the sword into the gap between the doors, using it as a pry bar to wedge them apart. A spurt of fluid shot out of the severed hoses in response to her shove. The gap widened. Since the left panel moved more easily, she leaned all her weight against it, shoving it aside to create a space she could wriggle by.

Her tool satchel slipped off her shoulder as she squeezed past the door, but she caught it and dragged it through, emitting a gasp of awe as she spun to face the room. The huge chamber had all sorts of machinery hanging from the ceiling, most of which resembled ventilation ductwork and fans. None of it made a sound.

The designers already built exterior venting! Screw it. Too late.

Forty feet away, the inside of the massive metal door glinted in the feeble light from a handful of operating LED bulbs, the Arc's backup system. Nowhere in the tunnels *should* be pitch black. A metal cabinet to the right of the huge door held the controls: buttons for 'open' 'close' 'stop' as well as an intercom to the outside and a dead monitor screen most likely connected to an exterior camera.

A mural spanned most of the left wall showing happy families in pre-Great-Death clothing standing in a flowering meadow under the words: Arcology 1409 – humanity's hope for the future. If she'd seen the painting two weeks ago, she'd have cynically mocked the overly cheerful faces on the men, women, and children smiling at the painted sun. Now, she knew exactly how they felt.

The first time she looked up at the actual sky, she'd probably made the same stupid face.

Tromping boots echoed out in the hallway. Marco yelled in alarm seconds before a loud *whump* followed.

Careful out there. It's slippery.

Raven sprinted across the cavernous chamber to the control box and mashed the 'Open' button. Even though she didn't expect it to do anything, when nothing happened, she still screamed in disappointed frustration. Out of spite, she mashed it again.

An electric buzz came from the ceiling. The floor shuddered under the weight of a massive electric motor winding up.

"Holy shit!" She kept holding the button down.

"Stop!" shouted Noah in the hallway. "You're going to kill everyone in the Arc. Is that what you want?"

The room vibrated. Dust fell off the ceiling.

"You're wrong!" shouted Raven. "I'm not the one who's lost their grip on reality."

Grunts and thuds rushed up to the busted hydraulic door.

A loud *thud* rocked the floor under Raven's boots seconds before the low, demonic whine of a huge electric motor struggling to turn emanated from overhead. The giant door gave off a creak. Centuries of gunk crumbled out of the seam. Whining, the electric motor increased pitch, clearly overloaded.

She mashed the 'Open' button again.

Jose tried to squeeze into the room, but couldn't fit past the gap in the split door. He backed up, giving Marco room to grab the other side. The men shoved at the panels, forcing them apart.

An ear-shattering screech made everyone cringe, grabbing their ears. Two multi-ton slabs of metal broke apart with a bang like Kyle's shotgun going off, the force of their motion creating a mild earthquake. Raven ran to the gap, staring past the inches-wide opening at the tunnel leading to the surface. She bounced on her toes.

Come on. Come on. Come on. Move.

Marco and Jose stumbled into the outer chamber and ran at her.

An explosion near the middle of the ceiling showered the room in sparks, knocking Raven forward like a hard shove. She kept her balance, frozen in momentary horror at the gap no longer widening. The massive door had stopped moving, all the mechanical noise gone. The motor hadn't simply failed, it had *catastrophically* failed.

Jose screamed.

She peered back. Both men lay on the floor amid a cloud of smoke. Small fires littered the floor around them as well as burned on Jose's left arm. Marco swatted at him, trying to put the flames out. She turned back to the door, staring at a gap not even large enough for her to stick an arm into.

No... dammit! She bonked her head against the ten-ton metal slab.

"Wait... failsafe."

Images of the schematics she had studied for so long danced around in her mind. She rushed past the control box to an access panel at the corner. Behind her, the security people and Noah coughed on the smoke from the burning motor. She couldn't see them, which meant they couldn't see her.

As fast as she could move, she crouched low behind a large machine box and rummaged a screwdriver from her satchel. Fighting her shaking hands, she attacked the access panel.

"Haven't you done enough damage?" asked Noah.

She jumped, looking up and back, but he hadn't come out of the smoke, so she kept removing screws. "Ask yourself that."

Noah emerged from the grey billow, fanning his face while suppressing a mild cough. He noted the two-inch separation between the halves of the great door, and stepped back, covering his mouth. "You've killed us. You destroyed the seal." Trembling, he paused to look around and up. "Maybe it's not too late. Maybe we can patch this."

"I'm not the one who sounds crazy now." She removed screw number six and started on the seventh. "You've been sending people out there, the Saints, for years. You have to know the outside is not deadly."

"The contamination is slow! Two breaths is a death sentence. Just because it takes a few years to kill does not make it any less lethal." He waved at her. "Move away from that. The damn thing exploded. You're not going to fix it."

Raven yanked the last screw and jabbed at the top edge with the screwdriver until the panel popped open. "I'm not trying to fix the motor, Noah."

His eyes widened in horror.

She smiled at him while flicking the safety interlock open and grasping a horizontal handle. "I have a present for you."

Noah cringed.

"It's nothing bad. I promise." Grinning, Raven twisted the handle, disengaging the main door from the motorized drive train. "Noah Hayes, I give you sunlight." She pulled the handle toward herself, unlocking the massive counterweights in the walls.

Again, the whole room shook like an earthquake. Both ten-ton slabs of steel forming the Arc's primary door jerked away from each other, ramming open amid a thunderous crash that sent cracks racing across the concrete around the doorway. An unobstructed twelve-by-twelve foot opening inhaled the smoke from the destroyed motor, clearing the room.

The forty-foot passageway outside didn't let *much* sun reach the Arc's first chamber, but a little patch did manage to fall on Noah's tread socks. He looked down at his toes for a second, then stared at her, mouth agape, his cheeks as white as her new undershirt.

"What have you done?"

42

RUBBLE

When I said 'it's easier to ask for forgiveness than permission' I meant me. Not you. You can't use that philosophy until after you turn eighteen. Got it, young lady? – Ellis Wilder.

The security people ran up to her, Marco and Ann grabbing her arms.

Noah braced a hand to his forehead, shaking as if about to vomit.

"Will you stop being such a drama queen?" Raven struggled, looking back and forth from Jose to Ann. "Seriously, guys. You've known me my entire life. Do you honestly think there's even the slightest chance I could have hurt Tinsley or the other kids? Or Sienna?"

Ann looked down. "No, not really, but you didn't seem like yourself."

"Since you guys are here and just got a face-full of outside air, you have nothing to lose at this point. Come with me and look for yourselves. This door is never going to close again. The air you are breathing right now is safe." Raven tugged at their grip. "Kyle's trapped and is going to die. If I am hallucinating like Noah thinks, no one will be there. Come see for yourself. If there's no one there, I'll accept that you're right and I imagined everything. But if he's there, you have to help me convince Noah he's being a moron."

Ann let go. "She's got a point. If two breaths really are going to kill us, we're all dead."

"If she's so sure, why is she wearing a filter mask?" asked Marco.

"Didn't want to inhale cesium dust on level one." Raven pulled her mask off and pointed at the door back into the Arc.

"Doomed," rasped Noah.

"It's bullshit." Raven tugged her arm away from Jose. "The spot where we fell isn't far. It will take twenty minutes to prove me right or wrong. Unless you don't wanna run, then a little longer. If you guys aren't willing to help him, then I have to run all the way back to Oasis and that means Kyle is going to stay trapped there for days."

Noah let out a manic laugh. "All right. Fine. Since you've basically killed us all anyway…"

Drama queen. Shaking her head, Raven strode up the passageway to the surface.

The security people followed cautiously, all gasping when they reached the top and got a view of the forest south of the Arc. Raven stuffed the filter mask in her tool satchel.

"Shit, I'm blind," muttered Jose.

Ann moaned in pain.

Marco sucked air past his teeth.

"Give it a few minutes." Raven folded her arms. "Your eyes aren't used to daylight."

"Crap it's hot." James fanned himself. "Like crawling under the solar lamps in the hydro farm."

Noah paused at the opening, a hand over his eyes, squinting.

"You might want to take those tread socks off." Raven smiled at him. "You'll only ruin them out here."

He sighed.

"So is that cesium story right or were you just hiding proof a rebellion happened?" Raven tapped her foot.

"A stray bullet hit a diagnostic machine. The cesium release is true." Noah frowned and pulled his socks off, shaking dust out of them. "They sealed off all the ventilation ducts feeding level one to keep it from being sucked downstairs."

"Saints… it's so pretty," said Ann. "Have you ever seen so much green?"

The men wandered away from the tunnel, gazing around at the world.

"Noah?" Raven approached him.

He glanced sideways at her.

"I believe you honestly are convinced you've been exposed to some contamination that will cause you to die in two years. I'd like to prove to you your fears are based on lies or maybe just misunderstanding. If you see a man my age who has spent his entire life outside, will that be good enough to prove you're not going to drop dead in two years? You don't need to be afraid."

"That would be nice," said Noah, "but I'm afraid you're suffering delusions."

"Well, you'll be going crazy soon then, too. Come on." She marched off toward the ruins of the suburban neighborhood. "Don't walk on the roads here."

"What's a road?" asked Marco.

"Flat areas that look like stone. There could be cavities underneath them likely to cave in. I don't have any idea why people put huge concrete pipes under roads, but they're there."

Still gawking at everything around them, the security team—and a reluctant Noah—followed her back to the spot where the road collapsed. About a half hour later, everyone gathered around her at the edge of the hole.

"This is why I'm all scratched up. Noah, you should probably stay up here since you don't have any shoes."

"Where did you get those?" Ann crouched, finally noticing Raven's boots. "They look almost new."

"Oasis." She leaned over the hole. "Kyle?"

No answer.

Noah frowned. "Are you happy now?"

"He's hurt. Probably passed out." Raven crouched next to the hole and shouted, "Kyle!"

A groan rose up from below.

Noah blinked.

"Oh, shit…" Jose lowered himself over the edge. "There's someone down there."

"I told you." Raven climbed into the hole.

Marco, Ann, and James dropped in one after the next. Raven guided them to where Kyle lay pinned. Noah hovered at the top, watching the five of them drag chunks of pavement and concrete pipe aside.

"That was faster than I expected," said Kyle.

"Son of a…" Noah jumped down, pale as a ghost. "There really is a person…"

"Yeah. Like I said. There's a whole village." Raven grabbed another piece of concrete.

For the better part of an hour, they worked to clear debris, until finally, they made it to the giant chunk of road. Noah, Jose, James, and Marco braced the edge and lifted it a few inches while Ann and Raven dragged Kyle out from under it.

He lay on the base of the pipe, looking up at everyone around him. "Hello. You must be those friends Raven told me about."

"He's not feral," whispered Noah.

"No. Ran into a group of them on the way here, though." Kyle grunted and sat up.

"Are you hurt?" Raven squeezed his shoulder.

"Give me a moment. It's a little hard to say right now. Everything below the waist is major pins and needles."

Marco crouched to examine Kyle's legs. "Looks like a bunch of scratches. No breaks. That left foot looks like an odd angle. Maybe a sprain."

"Damn lucky," said Ann.

Kyle winced, then chuckled. "Lucky would have been not falling into a sinkhole."

"Can you stand?" Raven pulled at his arm.

"Sec. Still tingling."

"We should, uhh, get him to the doc." Noah wiped a hand down his face.

"Better to bring the doc to him." Raven stood and looked around at the others. "How's the air out here smell?"

"Odd, actually." Jose sniffed. "Kind of sweet."

"We're all used to breathing air that's been reprocessed millions of times. It's laced with chemicals leaking from the hydro farm. It's going through a monoethanolamine substrate so gunked up with crud it's useless."

Kyle held up a finger. "You just said one of those giant words that goes straight over my head."

"Yeah..." She choked up a little, perhaps too happy he appeared to be okay. *Crap. I'm gonna be stupid, aren't I?* "Umm, yeah so... you're smelling clean air."

"Let's get him out of this pit before it caves in more." Noah crouched to help Kyle up.

He stood with assistance, but found his balance. After picking up the rifle and slinging it over his shoulder, he managed the climb on his own, limping only a little once on the surface. Raven tossed her backpack up to Jose—no sense leaving it in the hole—and made her way out as well.

"So..." Noah looked Kyle up and down. "This oasis I'm hearing about. It exists?"

"He thinks I hallucinated it." Raven smirked.

"Yeah. It's real. I was born there." Kyle explained how a biodome made by scientists weathered the worst of the environmental disaster, eventually expanding into a village once conditions had improved. "Around 140 years ago, a whole bunch of people showed up who we think came from your arcology."

Raven rested a hand on Noah's shoulder. "The dead people and bullet holes on level one... most of the Arc wanted to leave. Some didn't. They fought over lies and panic. The ones who stayed were like you, convinced they'd die out here. But no. That's not true. It's time for the rest of the people in the Arc to leave it behind. Our shelter is old. It's dying. The Earth is ready for us again."

Noah squinted up at the sky. "It's worth thinking—"

"No. Not thinking. Doing. I've already told you how many of our systems are inches away from total collapse. Oasis has food, water, power, and thousands of people. Going there is not completely without risk, but staying here is absolute doom."

"What risk?" asked Ann.

"Mostly ferals and cougars on the way there."

"Do I even want to know what kind of mutant a cougar is?" asked Noah.

She laughed in his face. "Wow. You did go to school right? It's an animal. Big cat basically."

"You can't expect us to just pick up and move everyone in an instant." Noah scratched at the back of his head. "Even if I say I'm completely convinced going to Oasis is the right thing to do, it's going to take some planning."

"No. It really isn't. Everyone packs up their clothes and whatever stuff they can carry. We take all the food from the farm that's edible, and we go. It really *is* simple. The hard part is going to be talking everyone into setting foot outside. But you're a natural leader, Noah. You can do it."

A distant cry of joy echoed from the north.

"What the heck?" Noah twisted to look toward the cheering man.

Raven smiled. "That sounded like Benjamin... he probably came up there to see what made the entire Arc shake. Maybe it won't be too hard to get people outside after all."

43

OUTSIDE HOPE

Some people say 'everything happens for a reason,' but that's a load of crap. Life is a roll of the dice, and they don't always come up on winning numbers. But, sometimes, they let ya break even. – Ellis Wilder.

Raven sat in the grass in front of her housing pod watching kids run around chasing a ball.

The dress she decided to try on that morning felt all kinds of weird. Light, airy, and it exposed her arms, shoulders, and almost as much leg as her inside clothes. However, in the heat, with the wind in her hair and grass in her toes, she found it far more comfortable than the jumpsuit and boots.

Fortunately, by the time she returned to Oasis, she'd had a chance to clean up. Tinsley never saw her face covered in bloody dirt. Sienna got the full story of what happened and made her swear she wouldn't go more than a quarter mile away from the village until after Tinsley turned twenty—unless someone would die otherwise or she brought the whole group with her.

Raven still wanted to see the ocean at least once, but it could wait.

Living outside on the surface already felt like an adventure since almost every day brought new experiences and new faces. Perhaps her father hadn't possessed a wanderlust so much as a need to escape the Arc. She figured he might have been happy here.

The survivors from Arcology 1409 had made the three-day trek to Oasis suffering only minor injuries. They spotted cougars on the way, but the cats didn't dare approach a group so large. If any ferals had been around, they kept an even greater distance. People brought clothes and a few personal items with them, as well as the mature vegetables from the farm and the seed stores—using the push carts they'd taken from the place where she'd found the filters. Raven didn't have much she cared to keep, but did bring Dad's storage trunk full of notebooks plus Tinsley's cache of stuffed animals, old dolls, and all the little decorations her daughter had made. Those, she'd already hung up in their new home.

Chase didn't even try to speak to her or go near Tinsley, continuing to act as though neither of them existed. She decided not to care, ignoring him back. Soon, she'd be meeting with Jordan, the guy in charge of the maintenance people here. Rumor had it Benjamin and the rest of the tech team would still be working together here. Keeping Oasis running would be a challenge, but a challenge she eagerly awaited. Sienna already helped out at the school, for now as an assistant to one of their experienced teachers. Adjusting to separate grade levels by age and a specific lesson plan to follow came as a shock to her method of 'winging it' and teaching whatever seemed important.

She debated suggesting another trip back to the Arc to transfer the contents of the library as well as the doc's medical books, though the medical team here had as good or better information. As far as she knew, Preston would probably end up working there. She hadn't seen Noah since they arrived, nor did she really feel an urge to go find out what he'd end up doing. Her world consisted entirely of Tinsley, Sienna, Josh, Xan, Cheyenne, and Ariana.

And maybe Kyle. He'd stopped by once or twice to check on her. When he'd asked if she could fall in love yet without someone dying, she laughed. That she hadn't blushed might mean something. Sienna certainly seemed to think it did.

The laughing pack of kids ran by the other way, all scrambling to kick an inflated ball around the grassy meadow. Trees at the far end of the field rippled in response to a brief surge in the wind. White fluttering insects glided in drunken spirals over an ocean of green dotted in wildflowers.

Raven's seven-ish days away from Oasis gave Tinsley a serious case of the clings upon her return. No doubt the girl would be surgically attached to her side as soon as the kids finished playing, but seeing her finally back to a state of pure happiness put a huge smile on Raven's face.

A long bug with two pairs of wings and a glinting green carapace swooped in and landed on her knee. Raven held still, not wanting to startle or injure it. Seeing bugs proved the world well into the process of healing. Perhaps the entire planet hadn't completely recovered. It most likely wouldn't for many human lifetimes yet to come.

For the first time in her twenty-two years, Raven Wilder felt excited for the future.

fin

ACKNOWLEDGMENTS

Thank you for reading *The Girl Who Found the Sun!*

The idea for this book came from an article I saw some months ago written by an entomologist regarding alarming rates of insect population decline and what that meant for humanity. Perhaps the real world argument was overstated, perhaps not. Either way, it made for a good inspiration for some science fiction. I wish I could remember the source so I could thank the researcher for the inspiration, but alas.

Additional thanks to Ricky Gunawan for the amazing cover art and interior illustrations. Also, thanks to Lee Sheridan for editing.

ABOUT THE AUTHOR

Originally from South Amboy NJ, Matthew has been creating science fiction and fantasy worlds for most of his reasoning life. Since 1996, he has developed the "Divergent Fates" world, in which *Division Zero, Virtual Immortality, The Awakened Series, The Harmony Paradox, and the Daughter of Mars series* take place. Along with being an editor at Curiosity Quills press, he has worked in IT and technical support.

Matthew is an avid gamer, a recovered WoW addict, Gamemaster for two custom RPG systems, and a fan of anime, British humour, and intellectual science fiction that questions the nature of reality, life, and what happens after it.

He is also fond of cats.

Visit me online at:
    Facebook: https://www.facebook.com/MatthewSCoxAuthor
    Amazon: https://www.amazon.com/author/mscox
    Pinterest: https://www.pinterest.com/matthewcox10420/
    Goodreads: https://www.goodreads.com/author/show/7712730.Matthew_S_Cox
    Email: mcox2112@gmail.com

OTHER BOOKS BY MATTHEW S. COX

Divergent Fates Universe Novels

Division Zero series

- Division Zero
- Lex De Mortuis
- Thrall
- Guardian
- Harbinger

The Awakened series

- Prophet of the Badlands
- Archon's Queen
- Grey Ronin
- Daughter of Ash
- Zero Rogue
- Angel Descended

Daughter of Mars series

- The Hand of Raziel
- Araphel
- Ghost Black

Virtual Immortality series

- Virtual Immortality
- The Harmony Paradox

Prophet of the Badlands Series

- Prophet's Journey

Divergent Fates Anthology

(Fiction Novels - Adult)

The Roadhouse Chronicles Series

- One More Run
- The Redeemed
- Dead Man's Number

Faded Skies series

- Heir Ascendant
- Ascendant Unrest
- Ascendant Revolution

Temporal Armistice Series

- Nascent Shadow
- The Shadow Collector
- The Gate to Oblivion

Vampire Innocent series

- A Nighttime of Forever
- A Beginner's Guide to Fangs
- The Artist of Ruin
- The Last Family Road Trip
- The Phantom Oracle
- How Not to Summon Demons
- Ordinary Problems of a College Vampire
- A Vampire's Guide to Surviving Holidays

Standalones

- Wayfarer: AV494
- Axillon99
- Chiaroscuro: The Mouse and the Candle
- The Spirits of Six Minstrel Run
- Sophie's Light
- The Far Side of Promise anthology
- Operation: Chimera (with Tony Healey)
- The Dysfunctional Conspiracy (with Christopher Veltmann)
- Of Myth and Shadow
- The Girl Who Found the Sun

Winter Solstice series (with J.R. Rain)

- Convergence
- Containment
- Catalyst

Alexis Silver series (with J.R. Rain)

- Silver Light
- Deep Silver
- Silver Quarrel

Samantha Moon Origins series (with J.R. Rain)

- New Moon Rising
- Moon Mourning

Vampire For Hire series (with J.R. Rain)

- Moon Master
- Dead Moon

- Lost Moon

Maddy Wimsey series (with J.R. Rain)

- The Devil's Eye
- The Drifting Gloom
- Dark Mercy

Samantha Moon Case Files series (with J.R. Rain)

- Blood Moon

Immortal Operative series (with J.R. Rain)

- Broken Ice

Young Adult Novels

The Eldritch Heart Series

- The Eldritch Heart
- The Cursed Crown

Evergreen Series

- Evergreen
- The World That Remains
- The Lucky Ones
- Nuclear Summer

Standalones

- Caller 107
- The Summer the World Ended

- Nine Candles of Deepest Black
- The Forest Beyond the Earth
- Out of Sight

Middle Grade Novels

The Adventures of Ubergirl series

- My Dad is a Mad Scientist
- Aliens Ate My Homework
- The End of all Halloweens

Tales of Widowswood series

- Emma and the Banderwigh
- Emma and the Silk Thieves
- Emma and the Silverbell Faeries
- Emma and the Elixir of Madness
- Emma and the Weeping Spirit

Standalones

- Citadel: The Concordant Sequence
- The Cursed Codex
- The Menagerie of Jenkins Bailey

www.ingramcontent.com/pod-product-compliance
Lightning Source LLC
Chambersburg PA
CBHW021124260626
47169CB00005B/1439